THE NEW DARK LORD

BOOK THREE

THE NEW DARK LORD

BOOK THREE

Ian B. Urns & A. C. Erinle

To Jessie,
Because publishing a book was easier than writing back.

All rights reserved. No part of this publication may be reproduced, stored in a retrieval system, or transmitted in any form or by any means electronic, mechanical, photocopying, recording, or otherwise without prior written permission from Podium Publishing.

This is a work of fiction. Names, characters, places, and incidents are either products of the author's imagination or used fictitiously. Any resemblance to actual events, locales, or persons, living, dead, or undead, is entirely coincidental.

Copyright © 2026 by Ian B. Urns and A. C. Erinle

Cover design by Nate Artuz

ISBN: 979-8-89539-358-1

Published in 2026 by Podium Publishing
www.podiumentertainment.com

THE NEW DARK LORD

BOOK THREE

Prologue

Everyone seemed to have gone mad, all at once. Nemo found his head hurting, his guts squirming, his hands trembling. Everything was wrong, and broken, and frenzied. Everything was confusing and delirious. He just wanted to go home, but even he found himself caught up in the sudden madness and locked into place.

It was Collin Baird who began the bulk of the screaming, lungs shaking the air like it was some kind of attack. For such a quiet man, he had a remarkable power to make noise. Almost as remarkable as his power to make noise at a man like King Galukar without flinching.

"You stupid, drooling fucking cock splinter," the Kaltan growled, closing in on Galukar and rearing up to scream into his face. It was almost comical. Like seeing a house cat roar down a lion, yet far from bringing his size and strength to bear, Galukar actually looked rather chastened. Not meeting Baird's eye, wincing at every particularly impactful point. Nodding, even. It did not mollify Baird.

"There was no reason to do that, *none*. You just wanted to kill yourself. Well, congratulations, genius, you got someone else killed instead. You satisfied? Or are you going to keep looking for another suitably dramatic way to die even now?"

"I'm . . ." King Galukar hesitated, seeming to swill the words around in his mouth like they tasted bitter. "I'm sorr—"

"And that's to say nothing of the danger to the rest of us," Lilia the vampire queen added, her voice far less overtly furious than Baird's, infinitely more controlled and regulated, but no less chastising. "Had the Dark Lord succeeded in besting Silenos and you, he may have burst forth to destroy the rest of us. There'd have been little we could do in such a situation, you realize?"

Instantly, King Galukar's features hardened, and whatever apology was developing upon his lips died in its womb.

"I won't be lectured on my behavior by some rotting whore," he snarled, taking a step toward the vampire. What surprised Nemo was not that, but seeing *her* take a step toward him. Instantly, Queen Lilia's rage broke through the surface, and her face was inches from the king's, rage boiling beneath her eyes, lips drawn back, teeth . . . long, pointed, jagged. A killer's teeth. In that single instant, the illusion she'd kept so carefully wreathed about herself fell apart, and the predator beneath was unveiled.

"It seems you won't be lectured on your behavior by anyone," she shot back. "Unfortunate given your total inability to think about it on your own behalf."

Nemo didn't see King Galukar reach for his weapon. One moment his hands were empty; the next they simply weren't. Six feet long, the Godblade was a towering mass of iron more than to scale with its own mountainous wielder, now hefted high and ready to come down upon the vampire. She crouched low, nails turning to talons, pupils widening to consume the entirety of her eyes as an unnaturally long tongue protruded from her mouth.

Both of them were halted only as Princess Felicia stepped forward, hands coming down upon one shoulder and another, body trembling as she placed herself between the warring giants of magic and Vigor.

"Stop," she ordered. It was, Nemo thought, an admirably strong command, given the obvious trembling of her voice and body. Both parties seemed almost to heed it.

"Dear," the vampire began, eyes slowly returning to normal, voice . . . more so. It was unnatural to hear her sultry *human* tone after seeing the mask slip just moments before. What she said made it less natural still. "If I choose to attack your father, I do hope you're not delusional enough to think I would even notice the resistance as I tore through your body to reach him."

Galukar stiffened as if a magus had sent lightning coursing through every inch of him.

The Godblade didn't move, and neither did Lilia. They were just in different places between one moment and the next, as if the world itself had misplaced them. Ancient iron bit down into the hard ground, tearing it open, sending a kinetic ripple to shake Nemo off his feet and filling the air with painfully fast clots of debris. Meanwhile the vampiress deftly landed some ten strides away, just beyond the outstretching rent in the ground. She was smiling again, sweet and warm as ever. It sent a chill down Nemo's spine.

"You do not threaten my daughter," King Galukar snarled, eyes wide and bright like bonfires. "Never."

"Holy shit, stop." Baird already had an arrow nocked and drawn, teeth practically chattering. Beside him, Princess Ado was promptly encasing herself in ice, a shelter no doubt. The necromancer Sphera seemed to have disappeared entirely.

Nemo realized just as they did that a fight between Galukar and Lilia would yield a good deal of collateral damage. He started backing off himself.

The king and the queen remained still, locked in place by the other's gaze. Neither one moved, not even King Galukar. They just waited. A pair of statues, moments from animation and ruin.

Then, all at once, Lilia straightened up. Her talons returned to nails, lips re-covered fangs, smile returned. Nemo felt ever so slightly queasy seeing how perfect her mask of humanity was, even moments after its removal.

"Well, I believe that accounts for all our business together, doesn't it?" She hummed. "Silenos Shaiagrazni was the reason for our alliance. Certainly he was the reason for mine . . ." Her lip curled, eyes tightening for a second. By her standards, it was an impossibly great expression. "With him gone, I do not see that any of us have any further business with one another. Save to wait for his return and maintain what he built in the meantime."

Silence followed that, lasting until the vampire had taken another five strides. It was Princess Ado who broke it.

"You're . . . You're leaving, just like that?" she called back, sounding aghast. "You can't. What about . . ." The woman tapered off. Nemo wondered if she was just now realizing how foundational Shaiagrazni's power had been to everything. He'd seen it right away, perhaps due to his own familiarity with the ease such magics enjoyed in overturning any political system, but there had always been a single bond of power and force keeping the fleshcrafter's coalition together. Now that he was gone, all its constituents were free to break apart as they pleased.

And it seemed that some, at least, pleased.

CHAPTER ONE

Hexeri answered nothing so quickly and urgently as a summons from her sire. How could she behave any differently? Most of her kind were released from the bond between progeny and sire early into their existence, within a few decades of unlife. Hers had remained for centuries, and she would have it no other way. There would never come a time when Hexeri was willing to be separated from Lilia, and she now hurried to answer the vampire queen's call as it graced her cognition.

Miles flew beneath her in minutes, and her jog took her to her creator shortly. Lilia was in her own quarters, and God did it feel *good* to be back in their castle once again. There was something about the air, about the skies themselves where they were seated above it, that soothed her. It was, she supposed, the magic of one's own home, nothing special there. Save that it was *hers*.

Black stone, cool air, a familiar layout, and so very much crimson adorning everything. Lilia was seated upon a great sofa stuffed by feathers. It was, Hexeri thought, perhaps the most comfortable piece of furniture in the region, and surprisingly young. Then again, she was older than most antiques.

"You called me?" Hexeri asked, kneeling down beside her sire. Lilia was smiling, as always, but there was a strain to it. The expression was something of a falsity, and knowing as much left Hexeri more uneasy than simply being scowled at would have.

"I did, dear." Lilia was distracted, and that almost terrified Hexeri in and of itself. It took a great deal to distract a mind that had seen so many centuries. Vampires grew quicker as they matured, their wits sharpening and focus perfecting. Hexeri, after a few hundred years, was already more astute than she could have hoped to train herself into being as a mortal. Her sire . . . She shivered as Lilia continued. "I don't like to ask this of you," she began, slowly, reluctantly, "But I need you to infiltrate the Dark Lord's abode in search of Shaiagrazni."

The air grew heavy around them.

"The Dark Lord," Hexeri echoed. "You told me he was more powerful than . . . your sire."

Lilia met her gaze without wavering.

"He is."

Hexeri had heard stories of her grandsire. She reckoned there wasn't a vampire unalive who hadn't. If her sire spoke true, she was being sent into the lair of a creature able to make mountains shiver and clouds choke.

"I'll do it," she promised, forcing her will into the words, letting her own promise give her strength.

It hadn't taken too long to get Ado out of her cocoon, particularly thanks to Collin's own skill in luring terrified, trauma-addled people out of their own defensive positions. What took longer though was the walk.

Aoakanis and Kaltan were in a similar-ish direction from their current position, or at least the roads headed toward both of them were. So, for now at least, despite the sudden unraveling of Shaiagrazni's coalition, they remained together. Collin found that he didn't mind that quite so much any longer. If nothing else, the princess had stopped being quite so snooty, and it was more than a little bit fun to rub her nose in all the times he'd saved her.

"What happens now?"

It was Ado's question, the first one she'd asked in about an hour of walking. She hadn't complained about the trek, uncharacteristically. Collin had noticed that in the past few weeks she'd generally toughened up, growing leaner and harder from the casual exertions of actually doing things herself. Her voice was the same though. No surprise there. People's vocal cords didn't change no matter how hard they became. It still felt strange somehow.

"Nothing good," he said, realizing he'd been walking in silence for a full ten paces. Shaiagrazni was gone, that singular lodestone about which they'd all been balanced. Lilia had put it more or less perfectly—they had no more business with one another beyond maintaining what they had. And he didn't think that would hold long either.

"What do you think about becoming the king of Aoakanis?" she asked him abruptly. Collin coughed in surprise.

Galukar had once killed twenty thousand men, personally, in a single night. The plan had been to die as a distraction, so that his men—a scattered force of merely one or two hundred—could flee while he held the enemy off. He'd exceeded expectations and won rather than heroically perishing, adding another notch to his, at the time, still-growing legend. Even then, marching forth to die against twenty thousand times his number, he'd not been half so nervous as he was now.

"Felicia." He had meant to greet her with his usual booming confidence. The confidence he'd never even really thought to notice, merely felt the effects of on others. Somehow his throat strangled it out of him, dried his mouth, tightened his chest, weakened his voice. Galukar felt like a young man again, standing before his first wife. Except this wasn't his first wife; it was the child of his fourth. And she meant more to him than any other woman ever had. She was his little girl, his daughter.

She was glaring at him, though not actively swearing or throwing things anymore. That was a small mercy.

"Galukar," Felicia replied. He winced.

"Father, please," he offered. "Call me Father."

"Is that your biggest concern right now, Galukar?"

He hesitated, actually weighed the question, but . . . no. No, it certainly was not.

"It's been years," he continued, deciding to move on to more comfortable topics. He hadn't reunited with his daughter just to argue. "You've grown so, so much."

"You weren't around while I did," she fired back. Galukar winced. Everything seemed to be an argument with her.

"I wasn't," he admitted. "And I'm sorry for that—"

"No you're not," Felicia growled. "You've never been sorry, not for ignoring me, and not for bullying me around into doing whatever you decided was ladylike when you weren't."

Galukar was stunned, but only for a moment.

"I am sorry," he repeated. "I really, truly am." He met her eyes and said nothing more. Let her decide unmoved by anything else he might say.

Felicia didn't say anything for a while, just stared back. Galukar realized she was trembling. With rage, with grief, he couldn't say, but some emotion was seizing her into vibrations with its intensity. Her eyes were wet and angular.

"I believe you," she said at last, the words escaping her as a gasp as if they were reluctant to leave. "But that only goes so far."

"I know." Galukar nodded. Waited for more. Eventually Felicia gave it.

"What do you want from this?" she asked, her demand cutting through the pause in their conversation. He'd forgotten how direct she could be.

"I want you to come *home*," Galukar said at last, deciding that only the truth could even hope to reach her. "With me. Your brothers are . . . They're all dead, joined with your mother. Your sisters are married off and belong to other kingdoms and families now. You're all I have left. Only you and I remain. Come home with me, Felicia."

She looked at him long and hard, considering. But distantly. Coolly. It was a deliberate, careful kind of thought left knowingly removed from the emotions behind it, the process of a woman too used to being hurt to risk extending her heart and guts again.

"Fine," she replied at last, relaxing as she did. It wasn't the relaxation of a woman letting her guard down. More a person finally letting themselves drop a great weight. Her eyes remained hard and warded. "Fine," Felicia repeated. "But I'm not going to stop engineering."

Galukar smiled at that. The thought of even asking her to hadn't occurred to him since they'd started talking. Whatever concerns he'd once had with the fact, it all seemed small now. Thin, insignificant. Felicia was returning home. That much was all that mattered for now. He could go about resolving her other issues at a later date.

Felicia had something in common with her father, despite being removed from his physical prowess by more than an order of magnitude. When she spoke, people listened. Swick really couldn't have begun to say why. She *was* physically imposing, at least, a solid six feet tall and built like... well, like a woman who made money by yanking on levers and beating hot metal with a hammer. But plenty of bigger people failed to match her silent authority.

Perhaps it was just the instinctual knowledge that she was perpetually in an awful mood. Pissed off at something a thousand miles away, and likely to take it out on whatever was right beside her. People never went into a conversation with Felicia entirely fearless. Swick himself found his focus aimed fully at her as she entered now. The Red Finger Crew seemed to agree with him because their chattering died as well.

"Did it go well?" he asked.

"Fuck off," she snapped back, then added, "Need work. What have you found?"

Somewhere along the way, at some point between taking off and garroting the Dark Lord with a one-ton anchor, Felicia had become a member of Swick's crew. This was probably a very large gain in objective terms. She was one of only a few people living who knew how to repair and maintain a skyship. It did, however, mean that he spent a lot more time being yelled at than he was accustomed to.

"Lots of work." Swick shrugged, leaning back and feeling a new energy grow in him. Contract hunting had always been his favorite part. "We have offers from your father obviously, as well as Kaltan, Sphera somehow, and even Lilia of all people."

That last remark earned a few scowls and coughs from the crew. Pirates were nothing if not superstitious—well, save for rapists and murderers—and superstition around vampires was about as super as it got. Half the men in this very room thought Lilia ate babies, and the other half thought she fucked them. Swick himself wasn't entirely sure they were wrong.

"I'm going to be working with my father," Felicia told him with a tone that promised more or less the exact amount of negotiation that was always permitted to someone speaking with one of Galukar's family.

Swick reckoned that about decided his next job, then. It wasn't like he had any other engineers.

Sphera did not panic. Her heart was racing out of *excitement*, her blood pumping from *enthusiasm*, and her hands trembling from *eagerness*. That a person might mistake any one of these signs, let alone all together, for panic simply demonstrated how alien the thoughts of a true caster were to the mundane masses.

Why, after all, would she be panicked? Even with both her masters now gone, and the one she'd betrayed the more likely to return, Sphera had everything under control. Even with her Shaiagraznian education cut short, even—

She paused, pushed her thoughts down, continued heading for Prince Nemo. His quarters were as humble as ever, more library than abode, and sure enough, he was coiled around a book strewn out across a table as she entered. The boy looked up at her, eyes wide and face strangely lax as if he were fearful of what she might say.

And he controls a power to almost rival King Galukar's.

It struck her, suddenly, how unfair that was. She pushed that down too.

"Staliga is weak and vulnerable. Your people need a ruler. I can be that ruler." Sphera didn't bother mincing words; she didn't have the time. "Someone with true power in the dark arts, a Hero. That's me. I studied under Shaiagrazni himself *and* the Dark Lord."

The poor boy looked like he'd start *crying* as he stared back at her, with the expression of a man suddenly asked to hold a burning log in his hand and trying not to ask for permission to drop it. He took his sweet time in replying.

"I don't think that would be a good idea," he said at last.

"Why not?" Sphera was legitimately surprised to be contradicted, and more so when the boy made an argument in favor of his stance.

"Because what we need now is to do without attention. You would draw more in. You're a necromancer, and . . . a woman." He said the last part awkwardly, which he shouldn't have. It was a valid point. Men with power didn't like women with power, not one bit.

But Sphera couldn't afford to let Prince Nemo think he was right.

"And yet you will get attention no matter what. All your neighbors remember you serving the Dark Lord, and serving Shaiagrazni after that . . . Well, that hasn't ingratiated you to anyone else."

He hesitated, eyes wavering. Then a new voice cut through the room, Princess Ado's.

"Which is why he's far better off serving under me."

CHAPTER TWO

Silenos Shaiagrazni, named of House Shaiagrazni and one of the foremost wielders of arts most ancient, was bound in chains. They rattled as he walked but did not chafe. Nor, he suspected, could they have impeded him in a serious effort to escape. They struck him as more of a formality on Adonis's behalf, or perhaps a means of inducing an illusion of control in the soldiers who now marched alongside them.

Living men, not undead. Silenos could understand that decision too—guarding a greater necromancer than oneself with undead simply invited the sort of mayhem that permitted prisoners to be freed.

What Adonis intended to do with him, Silenos couldn't say. His former apprentice had not spoken a single word to him as they walked for the past few days, merely continued forward and kept his eyes ahead. There were of course an abundance of uses for a caster of Silenos's magnitude, though being subjected to any one would be a rather undesirable affair. He had kept his quiet regardless. If nothing else, he may find an easier opportunity to escape later on. And at best he might be subjected to some half-cocked rescue attempt by one of his moronic allies. He had time. There was no cost to using it.

Now, fortunately, a change had come. Or unfortunately, as it were, for the change was that Silenos now saw a fortress looming ahead. Made of inky stone, humming with contained arcane energies, the castle was a thing of many spires and immeasurably ominous aura.

His enhanced hearing caught the sounds of screaming upon the winds, and his arcane sight revealed a rich tapestry of agony shaping the magical energies around its atmosphere. Any exertion of will imprinted upon magic, and one as great as horror and despair left a pointedly clear one. This castle was a greater testament to human pain than a face left tight and screaming by the sensation.

A sudden stab of nostalgia hit Silenos as they approached it, and he found himself smiling. It was such a typical example of Shaiagraznian architecture.

Inside, the fortress was much the same. Adonis had never been so very skilled in necromancy and had not even begun his studies in fleshcrafting before Silenos was betrayed; however, his mastery over the materials produced by inorganic processes had been . . . considerable. Clearly it had grown a great deal more, for Silenos found the interior of the structure lined with alloys and compounds that few among even House Shaiagrazni could make. Two theories formed in his mind about the fact, and he tucked them away for later use. Then they reached the throne room.

A Shaiagrazni's throne was very much a reflection of the Shaiagrazni themselves, and so they were invariably grand, indulgent, and performative monuments to unfettered ego and power—the two highest virtues. Silenos felt a stab of pride as he saw his former apprentice take his seat upon this one. He truly had done an incredible job in training him, just another entry onto the list of reasons all of humanity ought to be prostrating before him.

"Leave us," Adonis called, and all the room's guards evacuated it to isolate the two of them. The heavy doors at the back thudded closed with a boom, and Adonis turned his gaze back to Silenos.

"Make yourself comfortable," he offered. Silenos recognized the challenge for what it was, and promptly altered the musculature of his upper body to triple its strength, then triple it again. The steel shackles around his wrists were inches thick, and even he exerted himself in tearing the metal apart. But he did, and the manacles flew from him as their cohesion surrendered against several dozen tonnes of tensile force.

Adonis nodded shortly while Silenos reshaped his musculature to a less powerful, more practical configuration.

"Why was I chained?" Silenos asked his former apprentice. It was the most relevant question, as its answer would determine what sort of conversation this was to be. Outside of war form, Silenos would die if things became violent. Near instantly. The precious moments he needed to transform would not be afforded to him by one who knew of his power.

But Adonis did not begin an attack, merely questioned him back instead.

"Do you know how old I am?" he asked.

Silenos considered the question, dredging the relevant answer up from his incredible mind.

"Twenty-three years, seven months, and eight days," he replied.

"That was when you were cast out of our world," Adonis corrected. "Which, from my perspective, was a quarter of a millennium ago."

That gave Silenos pause.

"I was displaced in time as well as space?"

"As far as I can tell," Adonis confirmed. "I think the Entity did so to fulfill my own pact—to grow more powerful than you."

Silenos almost smiled. Naturally, the spirit of such a request would have been for Adonis himself to be empowered. But Entities did not care about a request's spirit. By simply sending Silenos ahead in time, it had obeyed the letter of its deal without needing to satisfy Adonis by actually strengthening him. It was one of the things Silenos had always been careful to look out for in his own deals, but then he'd had more time to prepare them than Adonis had for that one.

"And what are you doing here?" Silenos asked. Presumably, if Adonis had come to finish him, he would be dead already. Silenos's former apprentice was now a caster of roughly double his own experience, and he had clearly mastered the combat magics of enhancing his own strength and resilience. Less mass-producible than fleshcrafting, less scalable, but far more immediately potent. He had seen himself how a battle between them both would go.

Silenos was not expecting to be told Adonis had come to kill him, and yet what he heard still surprised him.

"I am here for you, Silenos. To find you and bring you back to House Shaiagrazni."

A second passed in silence, bloated and slow. Then Silenos replied.

"You are the one who left me stranded here." He felt his treacherous neurons fire off at that, rage bleeding into his mind, addling his magnificent intellect with simian violence and primitive hate. He ignored it. Adonis did not seem to have noticed.

"That was a long time ago, for me. I have . . . realized the error of my ways. To do what I did was wasteful of House Shaiagrazni's resources. Yours is a talent we could have used."

Silenos was actually unsure what to say, if only for a second.

"You are aiming to redeem yourself?"

"On command of the elders," Adonis confirmed. That did explain a lot, but Silenos saw his former apprentice was far from finished. "However, now I am not sure if there is any hope left. When I first heard of your rising power here, I was pleased. Watching you overcome your initial difficulties, adapt to direct combat, innovate—it's all been fascinating. The weapons you've developed for personal use here may well become the prototypes that usher House Shaiagrazni's fleshcrafters into a new age of combat. And yet you have behaved . . . erratically. Sparing those whom it benefited you to kill, killing those whom you may have used. I doubt your judgment, Silenos."

Silenos was silent, even as Adonis waited a moment for some answer. His former apprentice continued then.

"Your self-sacrifice to save King Galukar confirmed my suspicions. The man is useful, as a pawn, but you could match his abilities with any three of your finest grotesqueries. That you would risk your own existence for his . . . You have changed."

Silenos wanted to hurl himself at Adonis with fists and fingernails, and caught himself only just before he did. It was a warning of how deep the taint of his new emotional core had taken root.

So why do I not remove it?

The practicality was still there—he still needed to predict others, to understand them. Soon he would be free. Soon he would be himself again.

"You are not wrong," Silenos said, at last. "My behavior has been . . . sub-optimal. But perhaps the arrival of a fellow Shaiagrazni is what was needed to correct that. We are both still of the caster's house, trained by them, studied under them. Both of us believe in Shaiagraznian philosophy. We are the most suited to rule this world, and any other."

Adonis hesitated, studying him long and hard, slowly nodding.

"You are still an asset," he conceded slowly. "In power, if not in mind. At worst . . . your behavior can be corrected by House Shaiagrazni proper should we return."

The thought of being disciplined like some lowly apprentice made Silenos's lip curl.

"Very well," he replied, letting the anger uncoil from within him.

Again, Adonis paused. When he continued speaking, it was slowly and deliberately, almost with hesitance. As if even he wasn't certain what he did next was wise. An unacceptable failing in any Shaiagraznian caster: Doubt was the root of all evil.

"I have been experimenting with a means for House Shaiagrazni to make their way through to this world, permanently," he revealed at last. "A means of breaching the dimensional walls and producing a portal through the very Dream itself."

The thought was . . . perhaps the most ambitious one Silenos had ever heard.

The people of this new world were weak and of limited use, for now. But there were great talents among them that might bolster House Shaiagrazni. Further, there were resources. Minerals, ancient magics. A wealth of knowledge to be studied—already, Silenos himself had bolstered his war form using the Vigor of this world, and begun work on the clone by furthering those studies into a more perfected form. The knowledge that his latest project was still buried in his laboratory, beyond his reach, irked him somewhat. But the time for it to emerge would come. As would the time for House Shaiagrazni to emerge.

Silenos imagined, for a moment, the future Adonis was promising. Entire dimensions combed for magical talent, resources concentrated, secrets unlocked. And more. Silenos's master was a being of incalculable power in no small part due to the many millennia she'd had to grow it, but universes with altered flows of time were not so uncommon. If what Adonis proposed came to pass, House Shaiagrazni might leave a named to study for one century and return to find their power grown by a dozen.

Silenos's master might become the standard of power, not the pinnacle. The thought was almost too grand even for him.

"And you need me?" Silenos frowned. That uncertainty was the one thing that nagged at him, but even as he voiced it, the sheer exaltation of what was being suggested washed over him again and returned a grin to his features.

"There is a vital component involved that I lack the power to utilize," Adonis replied. "An Anomaly."

Silenos understood instantly.

"You need my fleshcrafting," he guessed. "And perhaps my necromancy?"

"Affirmative," his former apprentice confirmed. Silenos could see why.

An Anomaly was a being of potential magic more innate and considerable than any other House Shaiagrazni had ever seen, potentially. Most were thin things, their unnatural powers watered down and manifesting instead as primitive mutations or madness. Some though held a more potent balance in their heritage. For an Anomaly was spawned when an Entity *bred* with a creature of baryonic matter. A rare thing, but a known thing. And every so often, one time in a million, such unions yielded something that actually held a sliver of its parents' esoteric powers.

Yes, such a being as that could certainly hold open a hole between worlds. Silenos found himself rather eager to work on one.

CHAPTER THREE

Kelta had always been nasty, and most of the time he'd gotten away with it. That had changed with the death of Walriq and the betrayal of Falls. Now, he'd gone from third-foremost prodigy of Magira to first. His political influence had waxed, and whatever thin, fraying thread of sanity had remained within his wrinkled head had finally snapped.

He giggled as he burned the poor man before him. Kelta giggled, and Julius, like everyone else in the grand hall, remained silent as the grave. The only noise was the sound of crackling flames, and the screaming man wreathed in them.

Deliberate, of course. Kelta was Julius's master, and while his power had never been *close* to Walriq's, the separation between them had not been more than a fraction. Had he wanted the poor sod dead instantly, he'd be dead instantly. The flames burned colder than their creator's full potential would allow, so that he would feel them.

"Now we all know what happens when a magus of Magira dares lie to its archimage," Kelta called out, a sneering twist to his voice that made Julius feel rather cold, despite the heat, upon hearing it.

Lie to its archimage. The burned man had called wind magic superior to fire, and Walriq more powerful than Kelta. But then, speaking one's mind had become a dangerous affair of late. Walriq always had been the limiting factor on Kelta's magic. Now he was gone.

Now Kelta was the voice of Magira, which meant that a lie was whatever he said it was. Magira had become a tyrannical pyramid.

Granted, that was not actually much different than it'd been before. But Walriq and the previous council, at the very least, had been less *mercurial* in their spasms of violent tyranny, and Kelta took just a little bit too much glee in exerting them. He swept his gaze across the room.

"Anyone who has anything more to say decrying fire magic, you can take it up with me now. Or hold your peace."

A deafening silence hit him, then slowly the magi bowed down onto their knees. Julius was among the first to do so. Of course he was. Kelta was the archimage.

The door's opening was like a crash of thunder, amid such quietude. All eyes reflexively snapped toward the entrance of the great hall, through which a man now strode. He was . . . odd.

Tall, broad at the shoulders, and with a shaved head. His skin was dark, features aboriginal, eyes a cold and hard set of daggers thrust into each and every gaze they met. He wore what seemed to be *travel* attire, and instantly Julius got the impression that this was a man accustomed to using his own body and strength to do things.

Yet the *power* around him was something else entirely, setting the air alight almost. It actually stung Julius's mana sense to examine it, and something about it—its structure or its behavior—obfuscated its true depths from any further study.

He couldn't read this man's abilities, but he was on edge instantly. A similar anxiety shot through the other magi crowded around.

"Yes?" Kelta frowned. "Hello? You are?" He strode up to the man, adding a swagger to his walk that was clearly deliberate, clearly forced, and clearly betrayed that his left hip still played up when he moved. He was older than this stranger, obviously. Where Kelta seemed withered by life in his sixties, the black man couldn't have been a day past middle age. In the prime of his life, as a lion was the year before dying to a younger beast.

"Greetings," the stranger said. "I am Archimage Mafari, and I am returned from my quest for enlightenment in the mountains. I have seen much, learned much, and I have come to Magira in its time of need."

A pause followed. It was the very sort of pause one might expect to answer a claim like that. There wasn't a soul in Magira—save for the *women*—who hadn't heard of Archimage Mafari. And not a one among those souls was ignorant that the man had disappeared more than a century ago.

Oh, he'd been powerful. The greatest archimage in centuries, probably longer. But he was as dead as any dead thing Julius had ever heard of. However gifted he was—and the stories claimed he eclipsed all but Arion Falls in talent—he was a dead thing.

But then, the world has been assailed by a lot of dead things recently, hasn't it?

"I'm the archimage here," Kelta snarled. "And you're an idiot for trying to lie about something so obvious." Everyone winced. This stranger was a charlatan, or a madman, but that didn't mean he deserved to be immolated. He, however, seemed devoid of everyone else's fear.

"No," was all he said.

Kelta scowled.

"No what? No, you're not an idiot? No, you're telling the truth?"

"No," the stranger continued, "you are no archimage. You have taken a position defined by wisdom and knowledge, made it into your whore. Something to be abused for pleasure and pride. You are a child with the power to destroy everything around you. Unworthy of your authority, unworthy of your title, unworthy of your magic. You are thrice decried, Kelta the fire warlock."

Every word was delivered with a terrible, focused calm. And each one left Kelta simmering with yet more rage.

"*Fuck you!*" Kelta's scream was drowned out by the roar of his own flames. Blue now, not orange. Hot enough that the stone of the floor cracked, glowing cherry red before transitioning fully to broiling magma as the heat passed over it. The tongues of fire wrapped around the fool who'd claimed to be Mafari, enveloping him completely and disappearing him from sight.

Julius expected, when the fiery curtains parted, there would be nothing left of him at all. That was how a man looked when Kelta exerted his power into killing him fully. Like nothing at all, body reduced to less than ash. Vapor in the air.

But that was not to be the stranger's fate.

The fire choked out, energies dispersing as its power ran to the limit. Amid the inferno, now standing around glowing-hot air, was the stranger. A shield shimmered around him for a moment, perceptible only because of the atmospheric distortion beside it. His eyes were colder than ever as Kelta stumbled back from him.

"Impossible," the archimage croaked, and the stranger shook his head slightly. He seemed *disappointed.*

"What are you going to do?" Kelta whispered, terror turning his voice into no more than a sliver of noise. "What will happen to me?"

He understood, then, that this man was a force beyond his ability to resist.

"Nothing will be done to you," the stranger replied. "You will simply cease to be." He gestured and lanced the air with more magic than Julius had felt since the New Dark Lord's attack upon the citadel, and there was a soft popping noise as winds suddenly collapsed inward and filled a new vacuum in the room.

He blinked, stared, looked around, and found other magi just as confused as he was. Julius remembered . . . someone. Someone violent and dangerous, a terror standing right there, but . . . for the life of him, he could not recall the man's name, face, or anything else about him. Fire, had he used fire? Perhaps not.

Julius frowned. He was a magus, recently graduated from apprenticeship under his master, but . . . who had his master been? So caught in the sea of his own cognition was he that he didn't notice the stranger approaching until he had already come to within two paces of him. Julius froze.

If this man wanted him dead, he knew he would die. There would not be anything he could do to stop him, maybe not even to impede him. But the stranger didn't attack, merely spoke.

"You are the most magically gifted creature in this room, besides me," he began with the note of a man observing a peculiarity of no great significance. Perhaps a quartermaster taking inventory. "You will be my apprentice from now on."

Julius nodded dully. "Okay. Uh, master." The stranger nodded, then turned to the room at large. A hundred sets of eyes fell upon him, and for the first time in his life, Julius wondered if all the high magi of Magira would be a match for the single creature they gazed upon.

"I have allowed Magira to wither in my absence," the stranger announced. "Watched, from afar, as it grew opulent, corrupt, and feeble. Power-hungry imbeciles are granted sway to waste precious talent by killing or maiming those who defy them, while others are left without the means to even realize their own potential."

Uncomfortable murmurs spread at that as feet shuffled. One brave—or stupid—man asked a question.

"Are you telling us women are to learn magic too?" It was a question that had become more common in the wake of Silenos Shaiagrazni's publicly accepting a female apprentice and taking the princess Ado on as his servant, but the stranger's eyes grew hard.

"No," he sharply replied. "Women are empty-minded creatures only suited to carry out the will of men. They are not made for magic."

That mollified the crowd.

"The world is in turmoil," the stranger continued. "Two Dark Lords emerged and gone in the same span, each of their forces destroyed by the other. Now is the time for Magira to take power. To do what we *should* have done a century ago, and lead humanity into the future. Into a world of magic." That certainly drew approval from the group, and Julius realized the man was speaking with a magnetism he'd never seen in another magus. Ever. Most of their kind were awkward, self-absorbed men. Scientists, not leaders. But here was one who might well drive Magira to the future. He found his mouth drying.

"Are you really Archimage Mafari?"

Julius's new master only nodded once, but it was enough to convince him. After all else he'd done today, it would have been enough to convince anyone. The magi of Magira roared their exaltation and began heading out of the hall, and their new leader followed at a dignified, leisurely pace.

CHAPTER FOUR

Sphera hadn't spoken much with Princess Ado, for one crucial reason. She was a cunt.

A while ago, the girl had approached her, tried to discuss imagined commonality between them as women in a man's space. It'd almost made Sphera laugh. She had nothing in common with a noble, let alone a princess, and the fact that her ally had failed to even realize that was a perfect demonstration of why.

Powerful men were bitter, jealous, oppressive tyrants. Powerful women though were *almost* worse. Powerful men at least did not see nearly so great a threat in Sphera, nor feel inclined to crush her with anything close to as much vigor. For all Princess Ado's claims of solidarity, she'd undercut Sphera in a thousand ways after the fact and carefully drawn all eyes to herself.

Of course she had. The very presence of a proper woman—an aristocratic woman—made other women less womanly by association. Femininity was a thing to be earned, and being in the presence of a wealthy woman made its price all the greater. It was just how the fact was seen.

But Sphera kept all of that from her face. Unlike Princess Ado, she couldn't afford to run around hurling insults at whoever offended her. Tantruming was a rich woman's luxury.

"I understand that you're eager to keep a hold of your new territory," she began, using honey and reason rather than the innate fear most had for a necromancer. "But you must understand I'm suggesting what's best for Staliga. You're simply not a powerful enough caster to guarantee its safety, not alone and certainly not measured against my own abilities. I'm a Hero, and I can call on hordes of the undead as needed."

Indeed, Sphera fancied that in any other era she'd have been the most feared user of magic alive. Not the most *powerful*, not yet, but her talent combined with a necromancer's proclivities was a rare combination. It was just her ill fortune that had seen the only two necromancers to exceed her in half a hundred years emerging just as she did.

"We'll do fine" was all the princess said, a smug, knowing smile on her face. Sphera imagined how the woman might look as a reanimate, mindlessly drooling and shambling ahead to get torn apart fighting her enemies. She imagined that image vividly while pressing her with a question.

"Something on your mind?"

"Staliga will be just fine under my rule." The princess beamed. "I happen to have secured a new king, and his abilities in combat may surprise yo—"

"It's Baird," Sphera guessed. The woman's surprise was utterly pitiable. Had she actually believed other people were missing the looks they'd given each other? If nothing else, the crumbling of Shaiagrazni's empire had released that infernal tension coiling around them.

But then, it had done so much more. Not all of it good. Much of it disastrous. And it would unleash more disaster still no matter how Sphera fought to keep it together. Shaiagrazni's empire was crumbling, and she simply lacked the strength to hold it as one piece.

The princess left in a huff, irritated, but not beaten. Sphera had found no victory today. The world would soon be without her master's legacy.

It had not been so long since Galukar last set foot in Arbite, but it felt like years. Decades, even a century. Time had been stretched out by his journeys with Shaiagrazni, days turned into months by the changes to him and the challenges to his suppositions of life. Galukar felt slivers of his former self returning as he gazed upon the adoring faces of his people, and the smile he answered their venerations with came naturally and easily.

Here, at least, he knew his role, his duty, his work. Protector, ruler. King. As he had been for a hundred years, and as he would remain when the Godblade's life-preserving magics finally exhausted themselves upon his aging form.

The festivities were exhaustive, as they always were upon one of Galukar's returns. This time it felt wrong. Only twice before had he been bested in a quest, not counting the Dark Lord. And this marked the first time his power had been outmatched by a fellow human. The Godblade seemed to hum at his back for a moment, as if feeling his doubts and regrets. Galukar sighed.

It seemed a human's strength had its limits after all, and when he died, they would be that much smaller for however long it took a new wielder of the Godblade to emerge. What would they do with it? He'd never given the question much thought before. The answer had always seemed obvious, but now . . .

There were more nuances to power and its usage than Galukar had known. His latest journey had expanded his mind. Unpleasantly so.

He received word of the guest just as he entered his palace. An empty place, now, cold and lonely. Galukar felt the loss of his sons as he moved through to his throne room. There were no words for the sensation of occupying a world in which one's children were buried. He didn't bother trying to find one.

And soon, he was too distracted to have concentrated on the deed even if he'd been inclined. Within his throne room was a stranger. Tall, muscled like a warrior, and with a bald head exposing black skin. His eyes were small and focused on Galukar like needle points.

"I am Archimage Mafari," the stranger declared. "King Galukar, I have heard much about you."

"I know," Galukar replied. The man seemed surprised for a moment. He elaborated, "I know you're Archimage Mafari. We met when I was a boy, sixteen or seventeen, I believe. It was the year before you disappeared into the mountains."

Recognition dawned in the magus's eyes.

"Ah, yes I recall now. Apologies, King Galukar, it has been so very long."

"None are necessary." A year ago, Galukar might have pondered the man's sudden appearance at least, but there was no doubting he was the real Mafari. Even ignoring that he'd not aged a day, his power was the same. Galukar was just arcane enough to sense the arcane, and it pressed against his wits now like a shadow of the Dark Lord himself.

It was a rare feeling, indeed, for Galukar to stand in a room with only one other man and know himself to not be the most potent being present. Mafari seemed to take no delight in inducing it.

"I will be frank, your grace," he began. "I have looked into your recent actions with some . . . displeasure. Aiding the New Dark Lord, even if to oppose the original, is something I would have considered unthinkable for you."

Perhaps Galukar would have agreed with him. Certainly if Shaiagrazni had not made such concessions early on, he'd have refused to accompany him out of hand. The shame was still there.

How did he explain himself? What he'd seen in the man, the glimmers of humanity? He couldn't. Not when even he himself didn't know what to make of them.

"What I do is no concern of yours, archimage," he replied, keeping himself polite, yet injecting some regal sternness into the words.

"Oh, no, it is." Mafari's voice was a thing of iron as he responded. Any archimage was the equal of most, if not all, kings. This was a known fact. Not officially as much as politically. Kingdoms who offended the ruler of Magira tended to wither as they found the precious magi needed to sustain a modern nation denied them. For Mafari, there was a more primal cause to be wary. The air hummed with his power. "You wield the Godblade, King Galukar. You are, by my estimate, the second most potent human alive after me. What you do with that power is so very much my concern."

Galukar remained silent, resisted his body's urges toward muscular twitching and explosive motion. Mafari was standing close, three paces away. A normal man would not have reacted in the time Galukar took to move even double or triple that distance. But a magus's nerves were quickened by touching the arcane, and Mafari's casting was infamously quick.

"You are to sever all ties with the New Dark Lord," the archimage began. "And you will then dedicate your resources to aiding me in putting him down."

"Why?" Galukar asked. The archimage seemed stunned.

"He is a necromancer, a fleshcrafter—an art almost lost here, yet still very much outlawed—and, if rumors are to be believed, a *demonologist*. He seems to have gone down the list of our most illegal magics and practiced them in ascending order." The archimage spoke with no great passion, only a finality. "His powers are dangerous, and they will drive him mad. Maybe not today, or tomorrow, but eventually. He needs to be killed for the good of all."

Galukar had expected some religious appeal, but he had been a fool to do so. This was a magus, not a paladin. The casters of Magira were beings of practicality and rationality, mostly. Of course he would be lectured on the pragmatics of the deed.

"And you wish me to aid you in killing him on this basis?"

Mafari's eye twitched, irritably.

"If it proves necessary, yes, though I have no doubt I can best some petty hedge caster. Wielder of dark magics or not, he did not train in Magira as I did. This House Shaiagrazni of his is doubtless some petty caster's lineage. Whatever sort of prodigy Shaiagrazni is to be wielding more than one magic, he is no match for a true magus."

Galukar decided not to argue. If Mafari was wrong then he would find out himself.

"No," the archimage pressed, "what I am asking you first is mere . . . indolence. Remain as you are and do not lift a finger while I address the rest of Silenos Shaiagrazni's allies."

His blood boiled quickly, and Galukar affixed the magus with a glare.

"Address them how?"

Mafari shook his head softly. "That is no concern of yours, King Galukar. You have my full respect, but this is a matter of the arcane, and there is none more qualified than the archimage of Magira to reside over it. Rest assured, they will all be given a fair chance to repent and redeem themselves."

Galukar thought to the several among Shaiagrazni's subordinates who would sooner die than do that. He would be lying if he claimed to have any great fondness for most of them—though Princess Ado's loyalty to Shaiagrazni had grown to considerable lengths—but the long months of trekking around and working together had instilled some semblance of . . . familiarity. The thought of seeing them perish gave him upset, left him unnerved.

He dully wondered what was happening to him, even as he growled out an answer.

"If I don't like what you're doing," Galukar replied, slowly, carefully, intensely, "then it will stop."

Mafari's face grew hard at that.

"You have become accustomed to wielding power unmatched among our own kind. I understand. I was once in your place. Do not fail to adjust to your new situation, King Galukar. There are forces in this world beyond either of our comprehension, and I have grazed them with my mind. You are no more now than the boy you were when we first met one hundred years ago. If you push me, I will make you . . . less."

Galukar had never been threatened so softly, and yet felt such fear, in his entire life. For one moment, he wondered how much of the truth was in this man's words. Could he match Shaiagrazni? The Dark Lord? He lacked the magical familiarity to tell.

And by the time he could even consider finding out more, Mafari was already gone.

CHAPTER FIVE

As far as coronations went, Ado had to admit she was far from pleased with the state of her own. But then there were other concerns that might be raised. Indeed, she'd raised them. Money was among the foremost—much of the royal coffers had been emptied in infrastructural development intended to yield greater returns in the long run. The consequence of this was that they had become reliant on Shaiagrazni's empire sustaining them through the *short* term, something that would prove rather more difficult now that the damned thing had stopped existing.

So she had to improvise, find the money to hold her nation together. Somehow.

In a shocking turn of events, Ado found that much of her people's wealth was now held not by the royal family but by the richer of its nobility. The ones who'd had sense enough to move afar and hoard their resources, keeping out of Shaiagrazni's way and below his notice until such a time as the storm, Shaiagrazni, had passed. They were back now, like rats sheltering under a bonfire's ruins as soon as the fire was gone and the rain coming down. Ado, fortunately, had gained long years of experience in hiding her contempt from such people.

Certainly, she was better to speak with them than her new husband. There were limits to the strategy of beheading all of one's political opponents.

Today, Ado was meeting with lords Hemron, Balthasey, and Gibgra. They were each, individually, wealthier than her. That fact stung, but it had not been so far from the truth even a year ago, before Shaiagrazni's attack. All of them were bankers, and collectively, they controlled more than half the wealth of Aoakanis. She greeted them with a smile, knowing full well how men liked it when women did that. Being liked was, unfortunately, once again among her priorities. All overnight. She hid the bitterness that festered upon the thought and pushed past it to speak.

"Good afternoon, my lords." Ado beamed.

One smiled back; the others didn't. Ado continued.

"I'm here to discuss the finances of our great nation, and as I'm sure the three of you are aware, our coffers have been somewhat diminished by recent events."

That earned a derisive snort or two.

"Because of Shaiagrazni pissing royal wealth away onto every passing fancy he thought of," Lord Balthasey cut in. "What was it again? Seventeen thousand silver pieces on schooling, twenty-six thousand on medicine, forty thousand on domestic constructions, just off the top of my head? Surely, even a woman has head enough for figures to understand *why* all your money has disappeared."

Ado did not grind her teeth because doing so would erode the pretty smile that worked so well to get morons like these in her lane.

"Of course." She smiled. "You are astute to have raised the crux of our issue so quickly, and yet, tell me, what do you suppose will happen in ten, twenty years as a result of these projects?"

The lords either snorted or growled at that, as stupid people often did when they were called upon to think. The poor dears just lacked the equipment for it, and Ado almost winced at the sound of unfamiliar exercise straining every fiber of their wits almost to the point of breaking.

Ado was moments away from capitalizing when the pigeon interrupted her. The window rattled as if it were being beaten by a woodpecker, and she whipped around—instincts still active from her dangerous time doing Shaiagrazni's work—to find the gray bird's beak rebounding from glass. She crossed the room, letting the creature inside before it broke anything and quickly seeing the message bound to its leg.

The moment Ado took it off, the pigeon dropped dead. Her breath caught in her throat. Such things were heard of, of course. Pigeons could fly fast and long, covering a half-thousand miles each day, if not more. But sometimes five hundred miles was too little for a message's urgency. Magus healers were able to push bodies beyond their limits, and most kingdoms kept at least one in their court to treat the royals.

So, when a message of particular desperation was sent, its carrier bird might cross two or even three thousand miles in a single day to bring it. But the exhaustion remained. It was an alleviation from fatigue, and the feeling of tiredness, not a change in biology. Seeing the thing drop dead of its own tiredness, Ado was reminded once again why fleshcrafting was sought by so many.

Then she pushed the thought aside and hastily opened the message.

Mafari lives. Magi are coming for Shaiagrazni allies. Be wary.—G

G, and Ado recognised that sigil at the bottom too. She scrunched the paper up and ate it instantly, earning a bark of shock from the bankers present.

"Have you gone mad, woman?!" one cried. Ado just smiled.

"Terribly sorry, my lord, it must be a bout of womanly hysteria." Ado headed for the door at as brisk a pace as was possible without drawing any further delays through the alarm of others. "Please excuse me. I think I need to go and have a good cry to get my overwhelming emotions in check."

The bankers would have to die, she idly knew. There would be little shifting them after this, and she needed their money. But the main priority here was King Galukar's warning. Magi, sent by Mafari . . . Ado was about to be attacked by a legend. That had a remarkable way of galvanizing her thoughts.

"My queen," a man called from beside her. "Where are you going?"

"I need to see my husband," Ado replied curtly. "Where is he?"

"But, my queen, what of the mercer's entourage?"

Ado was a moment away from chastising the man for ignoring her question when a sudden realization hit her, and she froze.

"The . . . foreign mercer's entourage?"

"Yes." The servant frowned. "Why—"

The wall behind him came apart in a blasting spray of ruined stone and mortar, littering the corridor with debris, flooding it with dust. Ado stumbled back, the wits shaken from her. The mercer's entourage had been foreigners all of them, unknown to her and her people and granted entry into the castle.

If there was any group for a pack of magus assassins to impersonate, it would be high-class guests such as those.

And they'd have struck the moment they heard her being addressed.

Ado thrust her arms out and upward, solidifying the air before her into a wall of ice. Something hit it—flames. The structure came apart, steam seared her forearms, and force picked her up to toss her backward like a thrown javelin. She landed hard, tumbled back, head spinning, wits scattered, mouth full of blood, and bearings thrown to the wind. Ado just barely sat up in time to see guards rushing forward, knights all of them. One intercepted another blast of flame at the cost of his own life, armor coming apart into a cloud of bright-orange fragments and mangled corpse dropping hard as the others closed on her attackers.

Magi, true magi of Magira, were potent beings. Ado knew better than to try to aid her men.

She scrambled up, turned, and ran. The knights died screaming behind her, Vigor proving less than half a match for Magiran magic and soon the hall was rumbling again as the magi prepared to destroy her. Even from afar, Ado doubted they'd miss.

Another fireball came streaking for her, and she lanced it with a blast of ice to detonate it prematurely. Felt the sting of heat against her eyes even a dozen paces back, stepped away as more attacks came. A blast of searing acid, which Ado hadn't the time to deflect with ice and could only watch flying forth right beside the darts of stone torn from the remnants of her castle's corridor.

Before any of it hit, a new projectile took to the air and smashed into the volley. Pure white flame.

"Queen Ado," Rochtai roared, striding out into the hall and seeming ten times his usual height. Robes flowing, beard billowing in the unnatural winds conjured by so much magic meeting so much more, his eyes were like miniature suns, face like a thunderstorm. "Get behind me, run. I will delay them!"

Ado could see her attackers clearly now, three of them. Two were aged men, as might be expected, but a third seemed roughly her own age and, surprisingly, was the strongest of them.

"I can help," she snapped, but her master silenced her with a glare. Once a student, always a student, she supposed. Ado scrambled up. "Thank you—"

"*Go!*" Rochtai roared, fending off a blast of flame from the youngest magus and deflecting it into the wall beside him. An entire stretch of stone larger than a peasant's cottage was blown outward, obfuscating the corridor once more with aerial dust and raining fragments. Ado saw no more than that because she was fleeing without another thought.

Out through the window, down through the air. She slowed herself with thin platforms of ice, smashing through each one and exhausting her own momentum in the doing of it. She landed hard and sprinted, glancing back to see the castle's wall blasting outward.

Her guards were still thin in number, exhausted by Shaiagrazni's conquest and the battles with the Dark Lord. Of course these men had managed to permeate her defenses so well, and of course they were past Rochtai. He had been among the twenty greatest magi alive, but each of these men was formidable, and it had been three against one.

Those formidable magi stared down at Ado now, continuing their pursuit as she stumbled into the woods.

Collin hadn't been in Aoakanis for even a day before someone tried to kill him. It was a bloody relief. If he'd had to deal with all the pomp for a single hour more, he'd have either killed himself, or killed several other's selves.

The magi had knocked on his door first, asking for him by name. Collin had given it, then watched as a blast of lightning tore the thing off its hinges, blew into the room, and scattered furniture around its electrical discharge. They forced their way through, tripped the wire, and had just enough time to scream before the hundred or so steel-bound crossbows he'd lined a wall with spit out bolts at more or less equal speed to a ranger's own weapon. Some of the projectiles missed, either smashing fist-sized blocks of stone out of the wall or penetrating the thing entirely. Most, though, found their marks, ripping into squishy human bodies and dropping the magic users like sacks of shit.

Collin came out from his actual desk, which he'd had placed beside a stretch of wooden planking erected and angled to disperse his voice and throw off the aim of anyone who tried to attack him through the door. Sometimes it paid to be prepared.

"How . . ." One of the men, a magus Collin now saw, coughed as he spoke, blood spurting out onto his ruined robes. "How did you know?"

Collin frowned. "Know what?" A tapping at his window drew focus to the pigeon, which looked about halfway to dying as he took its message and read through. King Galukar's warning was brief, and clarifying. "Ah, bugger." He looked at the group, smiling. It really did pay to be prepared sometimes. Now all the people telling him against setting up basic security measures able to kill a fomor could eat their words.

Collin snatched up his bow and quiver, equipped his knives, stepped over the magi while they were busy convulsing and dying, and headed out into the corridor. It was madness, chaos, devastation everywhere as magi swept through the castle and laid it to waste.

Another grin sprouted up on his face. Thank fucking God. He was damned sick of nobby politics.

CHAPTER SIX

Nemo stared at King Galukar's letter for a good long while, as if doing so might change its content. Unsurprisingly, it did not. The warning remained, as did the initials and the seal. The handwriting was just what he recalled King Galukar's being, those few times he'd seen him scribbling orders before they were separated under Shaiagrazni's service, and even the manner of speech, if such a pressing note could be called such, was familiar.

There was no denying the note was really from Galukar and, as far as Nemo could tell, completely sincere. It made his heart race, his vision actually blur with the stress suddenly ensnaring him.

"Meet my man at the border of your city."

The command there was unmistakable, which meant that if Nemo didn't obey, it would be an act of disobedience. That could have consequences. The ire of the world's deadliest warrior for one thing, but also disastrous issues for whatever Galukar was planning on him to do.

As much as he clearly loathed certain members of Shaiagrazni's inner circle, he'd not been actively antagonistic. Or at least not *proactively*. Sabotaging others, let alone outright turning on them, didn't seem like it was likely for the old king. So what was this about then?

Nemo sat down, felt his head spinning. He just wasn't used to this. He missed his home, his library. The loneliness had been hard—agonizing at times—but at least it hadn't been a nest of vipers around him. He felt like he'd puke.

Eventually, though, Nemo was forced to decide, and of course made the only choice he truly could. He headed out for Galukar's subordinate, just as instructed. The note was clutched tight in his hand, Xekanis never more than a whisper from his thoughts, body still trembling with uncertainty. He missed his library so, so much . . .

At the edge of the city, after a good half hour of walking, Nemo found himself rather surprised by who was waiting for him, but perhaps should not have been. Swick the Swift grinned as he saw Nemo approach, standing tall as ever and seeming to maintain his perpetual sprinting-ready slouch.

"Alright, boy!" He grinned, managing to somehow yell the words out without yelling at all. Nemo frowned, blinked. He felt his mind sliding against the sky pirate, thoughts threatening to rebound from his face as if by magic. Just focusing on him was a struggle.

"You'll get used to it." The captain grinned, as if he knew already what Nemo were finding so hard. "Now, here's the situation. Galukar reckons you'd best come with us." As he used the collective, a woman emerged from behind him who was taller even than Swick was and looked half again as heavy with muscle. Nemo found his eyes holding on to her much easier, and quickly recognized King Galukar's daughter.

"Why?" Nemo managed to ask, despite the overwhelming *everything* going on.

"Can't tell you," Swick replied. "But you need to come."

Nemo hesitated, saw the woman—Felicia—roll her eyes, and she was speaking over Swick a moment later.

"Magi are coming for you here," she explained. "They've already hit Queen Ado's city, and we've lost track of her location. She may be dead. You're the one they'll try to come for next. So we need to go fast. Faster than they *think* you'd be capable of."

Hence the skyship. Nemo felt the pieces clicking into place. It would've been soothing, if not for one minor thing . . .

"Why are they trying to kill me?!" He groaned, though already knew the answer.

"Demonology, lad!" Swick laughed. "Too good at it for your own good, you are. Now come the fuck on before some bearded buggers drop in and make our balls explode."

Nemo almost followed, then paused.

"And why are *you* here for me?" he asked, forcing steel into his spine as he eyed them both. People didn't just help one another. That was one crucial lesson he'd learned since being freed. Life wasn't like his books. It was worse.

Swick didn't look fazed at all, but Felicia's face softened.

"Because you're just a kid, and King Galukar doesn't think you deserve to be hurt because of powers you didn't even ask for and can't fully control."

She was, Nemo thought, wrong on both accounts, but considering his safe passage apparently rested on her assuming otherwise, he decided not to correct her.

Now I'm a liar too.

They started onto the skyship. Nemo following after. He saw a surprising bulk of men aboard, most busy with one task or another. One of them, a towering, one-eyed man who seemed taller even than Shaiagrazni—almost as tall as King Galukar—was hauling an anchor as big as a person with his own strength alone.

"What about Sphera?" Nemo asked. "She's still in the area. Is she . . . She's on board right?"

Felicia turned to him again, and this time there wasn't a shred of warmth behind her eyes as she replied.

"Sphera the necromancer sided with the original Dark Lord, the man who killed my brothers." Her voice was tight as a garrote. "She can hang for all I care."

Sphera hadn't made a habit of open combat against magi. One might be able to deduce that fact about her by observing her still being alive past the age of twenty. Prodigy though she was, necromancy was not a brawler's art. Her own master had almost fallen to her through the disadvantage of limited preparation and surprise, and she lacked even his fleshcrafting to compensate.

So she moved quietly, and quickly. And subtly. Heeding the warning her sentries had given her—of robed men shimmering with power making their way to her location—and running with it. Literally running with it, with only the barest coterie of a few particularly potent undead to watch over her.

Ironbane wasn't a familiar city to Sphera, and it was incredibly contrived in its construction. She'd memorized only half its structure. As if knowing the fact, her magi pursuers had forced her into the parts she knew nothing of, and the chase was growing confusing. Perhaps inevitably, she found a dead end blocking her. To melt through with shadestuff would expose her position, but as she turned, she found the way back walled off by two bearded men, eyes beady and glinting as they fell upon her.

One raised his hand to the sky, launching a blast of lightning to crackle and dissipate into it. That alone had given her position away. Sphera winced.

The *other* magus was already gesturing, and at the motion of his arm, Sphera saw stones erupt from the ground and great creeping vines dart toward her. *Not* fleshcrafting, of course, just the manipulation of natural plant matter for their own ends, hypocritical pricks. She roared, splaying her own arms wide and sending a blast of shadestuff out.

Vines withered, eroded, died. Both magi scrambled back, one avoiding the shadestuff entirely as it drizzled down the alley. The other—the one who'd attacked her with vines—was splashed in his torso, just one side. That side disappeared, a stew of organ juice and blood slopping out of it as he dropped like a stone.

More lightning, this time coming for Sphera. She hadn't expected her shadestuff to actually stop it—a stupid thought. Of course it did, decaying electricity and heat as it did all other things. Nothing was beyond death.

Certainly not Sphera. Her mental signal came just in time for the first of her undead custodians to drop down behind the lightning magus, one of her master's newly made fleshcrafted stealth units responsible for taking this very city. Direct combat was far from its design purpose.

But it still boasted greater physical prowess than most knights because Silenos Shaiagrazni did not believe in half measures. A single stroke of its scythe-like talons neatly cut the magus from crown to groin, leaving his two halves to split open and paint the alley red. Sphera was then twisting back to the wall.

She had moments before the rest of the magi were on her, if she was lucky. So Sphera burned away two walls—the one that had initially blocked her and the one leading inside a building. With luck, the minor ambiguity would throw off some of her pursuit.

After that, she was running again.

None of Sphera's undead were *far*, but now she drew them closer in. The fear of attracting a focused assault was gone now that she'd already been located, and there was nothing to gain by avoiding denser numbers. Her force crashed right into the magi's ambush.

Her shadestuff splashed against overlapping energy shields and was blocked. Crisscrosses of arcane death burned apart her bodyguards as the undead desperately flung themselves before her to block the attacks. Sphera cursed.

Magi, unlike her, were mere humans physically. Bereft of fleshcrafting by her master, their lack of Vigor made them fragile things. But the destructive power they wielded was exponentially beyond an equivalent warrior. The entire street around her came apart, boulder-sized fragments of stone sent spinning away; paving erupting to shredded gravel. Her guard lasted moments, Sphera moments more.

Then the flames descended, and the half dozen magi who'd outmaneuvered her were engulfed.

"No, Xekanis, I—uh, well, uh . . . Okay fine, but please just . . . just do it quickly." Sphera turned to the remarkably weak voice calling out and found herself surprised to see Prince Nemo staring at the burning magi.

She looked back and realized why at a glance. They weren't just engulfed in fire, but a *thing* of fire. A grinning, anthropomorphic face glinted in the blaze and seemed to lick up the melting flesh and running blood. She shivered, despite the heat. Demons . . . She would never get used to demons.

"Are you okay?" Prince Nemo asked, frowning at her with boyish concern as he jogged over. "I'm sorry if you're hurt. I came as fast as I could."

"I'm fine," she snapped, more harshly than was necessary. In truth, Sphera was shaken. She wasn't accustomed to being at another's mercy, hadn't been since her capture by Silenos. She hated it. "Thank you."

The prince stood there awkwardly for a moment, something slowly worming its way out of his vocal cords. Sphera saved him the trouble.

"Why are you here?" she demanded.

"Swick and Galukar's daughter Felicia are here to rescue me, but they were going to leave you to the magi. I know everything you've done," he practically whispered. "But I don't think you need to die. Not if . . . Please, can you promise me you can become better?"

Sphera felt herself actually *touched* by his words, a repulsive feeling that nearly left her puking on his shoes.

"I see," she croaked, shoving whatever acidic emotions he was conjuring up down. She could deal with those later, when she had the luxury of focusing enough to kill them. "Thank you," she added, ignoring his request.

King Galukar knew. Swick and Felicia were working with him. Sphera had learned that much before splitting from the coalition. King Galukar had known she would be killed, and he hadn't lifted a finger to stop it. Had there been explicit orders to save her alongside Nemo, she would have been saved. But she wasn't. Her blood boiled.

And she was not thinking of the magi as it did.

CHAPTER SEVEN

"Please—" The magus's pitiable mewling was cut off by the fractional tightening of Lilia's grip. Had she wanted, she could have crushed his throat so thoroughly as to disconnect the head from his shoulders. But she still needed information. For now.

His face pale, eyes bulging, Lilia let his fear grow for a moment, watched it erode his mental defenses. Then she assailed his mind.

It was a surprisingly durable thing, which Lilia took to be the touch of magic upon his cognition. As little as she thought of the magi, she had to say there was a notable level of will and mental potence needed to direct the tides of magic with nothing but one's own intent.

But it was still the mind of a man. It was human, *male*, and forty or fifty times younger than Lilia's own. Her will crushed the magus's like a grape underfoot, and he went lax in her grip.

"Who sent you?" she murmured, coaxing the answer from him gently, soothingly, warmly. It was like seeing a fly dropped into honey. The poor creature never had a chance.

"The archimage." He smiled, tongue practically lolling out as he pathetically volunteered the information. The poor thing wanted nothing more than to please Lilia now, even at the cost of giving her information he knew was all that kept him alive. She didn't see a scrap of hesitation in him either.

"Kelta?" She frowned. Lilia had kept track of Magira's luminaries and knew full well that the pyromaniacal lunatic was their new leader. As far as threats went... he wasn't one.

The magus's head whipped around as if he were trying to drive a carriage with neck strength alone.

"No, the *new* archimage." Lilia sighed. She was getting tired of new contenders emerging to suborn a powerful caster's title.

"And who is that?" she prodded. Once more, the lowly creature vomited out his answer.

"Mafari himself," the magus announced, eyes practically aglow. "He is returned from his journey, ascended and carrying the secrets of the world."

Lilia stiffened, scrutinized the man for any hint of deception. Then crushed his skull like an empty eggshell. She stepped back, not bothering to wipe the gore from her hand, glancing around at the mangled bodies of those arrogant fools who'd somehow thought they could ambush her.

Mafari the archimage. Lilia knew the name well, of course. She'd met the man it belonged to. One hundred years and change it had been, but she remembered every detail of their encounter as if it were mere minutes ago. Her skin throbbed where the burns had run along it. She'd spent months healing from the damage he'd inflicted.

Lilia's heart did not beat, but if it did, it would already be racing to rival a hummingbird's. This was one enemy she could not do battle with. This was one disaster she could not send her aid to.

In the absence of Silenos Shaiagrazni and the original Dark Lord, Archimage Mafari may well find the world his for the taking.

The construction was nearing its completion, and Silenos had to confess a feeling of... relief. Not at approaching the final stages but, rather, at finally having been freed from the crippling mundanity of this new world.

For a century, he had taken for granted that he would have the inexhaustible resources of House Shaiagrazni at his disposal. Their materials and wealth, of course, but more than that, the ability to consult fellow masters of the arcane. His equals, and in some cases even his superiors. Silenos had grown accustomed to working alone—something that was never truly unfamiliar to a proper caster—but being cut off from so great a resource had . . . stifled him.

Adonis was a reminder of what he'd had before, and it was thrilling to use him.

Their labor had been well directed and concentrated upon what now occupied much of Adonis's throne room, the only chamber in his fortress he would trust to house such a valuable artifact. Taking the form of a great circular structure, it was composed largely of Silenos's fleshcrafted materials, prioritizing resilience and structural stability. Runic, humming with power, and practically quivering as the air around it threatened to fold inward at its touch.

It was a tempered schism, among the more advanced inventions any in House Shaiagrazni had ever coined. By himself, with his own skills and knowledge only, it would be well beyond Silenos to create such a masterwork. And this one would, if Adonis spoke true, exceed all others of its kind.

How exactly it differed, Silenos could not have said. There was a level of complexity to the esoterica involved that defied even his knowledge of the art. Adonis was vastly superior in the utilization of Entities—Silenos would admit that without having his ego pricked—and the innovations at play here were beyond him.

Adonis had not shared them either, choosing to keep them secret. Silenos had humored his efforts. He had, after all this time, enjoyed the sensation of unknown magics being worked around him, and had savored it as the breath of Shaiagraznian air that it was.

"I think the time for your secrets is over," Silenos pointedly declared, stepping back from the device and studying it once more. It really was an impressive construction. The air seemed to retreat from its edges, as if matter itself feared the touch of it.

An oddly appropriate reaction for inanimate material, if that were the case. The magics coursing through it were deadly in the way shade-stuff was, or even more so. Drawn from depths of the Depths lower than even Silenos's own necromantic powers. He recognised them well enough. The capiliaries of raw creation feeding the material existences in the Dream. The currents in which Entities swam.

But he did not know *what for*, nor what was different.

Adonis paused a moment before replying, weighing Silenos.

"I suppose you are right," he conceded at last. "I admit, I enjoyed keeping you in the dark for its own sake."

Silenos had guessed as much, having enjoyed it just as much from the other end himself.

"And your explanation?" he prompted.

Adonis provided.

"An ordinary tempered schism is used to breach the space between physical reality and the Depths. You, I trust, are aware of this. But it does so only in a limited capacity. Allowing magical energies to permeate the gap, perhaps even fragmented electromagnetic waves. Very occasionally, it might cut through into another part of the Dream. Other worlds and the Depths beneath them might be seen, felt, but not truly touched. It is of more use for creating sources of power than anything."

Silenos nodded in understanding, biting back his impatience.

"I am half your age," he reminded Adonis, "not a tenth."

His former apprentice seemed to understand his meaning.

"Apologies. This device should allow passage into the higher layers of the Depths, and from there we will seek the means needed for a ritual of encroachment."

Silenos took a moment to process the words.

"You are suggesting we physically enter the Depths."

It was not unheard-of for a Shaiagraznian caster. It was, as far as he knew, unheard-of to survive for ones under the age of one thousand. Silenos was perhaps the greatest prodigy in his house's history, but even he did not wish to test himself against a task known for killing casters more than six times his age. Adonis himself was not nearly so old as the seniors who succeeded.

But he was undaunted by the idea.

"We will be able to bolster each other's strength," he noted. "And either of us is already potent beyond our years, you far more so than me."

Both valid points, and yet . . .

"The risk is still extraordinary," Silenos pressed. "What would you hope to gain?"

Adonis tilted his head. "Passage back to our own lands, Silenos. Within the High Depths, there is a creature of particular note—"

"A creature?" Silenos interjected, voice sharper than he intended. "You misspeak, surely?"

"No," Adonis confirmed. "A creature. In a realm of intangibles, Entities, and mere cognitive imprints, I have found a creature. A being with an Entity in its ancestry, and of relatively stable existence."

Silenos had known they sought a stable hybrid. He had not considered that it would be potent enough to live among *Entities* and survive. Such a thing was close to unprecedented.

"And this is the key to returning us to House Shaiagrazni," he guessed. "Or . . . No, you wish to use a sympathetic link. Us, who have dealt with the Entity responsible for displacing us here, combined with the blood of a being tied to its kind. You intend to call the Entity and truly bind it under our power."

Adonis grinned. "Your pathetic mind has not been enfeebled as much as I would have feared, Silenos. Yes."

Silenos allowed the worm to have his jibe, being far above retaliating against such things. He simply pondered their situation.

The Depths was not a physical space, and within it, only true magic held any real sway. Casters, or those of extraordinary will, could ground it to some extent, bringing pockets of causality and reason around themselves as they entered. Such things, unconscious though they were, always exhausted the one responsible though. A physical being in the Depths of any level would hemorrhage mana simply by sustaining their own existence. Their ability to defend themselves, also, would rely on magical consumption to inflict enough semblance of physical law upon any enemies that they could be harmed by physical offense.

Just as an Entity was shackled by the alien laws of physical existence, so too would Silenos and Adonis be within the Depths. They were, however powerful, still living, baryonic things. And Entities of even a middling power would already threaten them individually.

Yet what choice did they have?

"Master," came a voice at their backs, drawing Silenos's eye to the twisted wretch speaking. "I have returned with the item you requested." Prostrated before Adonis was Number Eight. A loathsome being, was Number Eight. Silenos found himself shimmering with jealousy at the sight of it.

Number Eight was a lycanthrope—the magical kind, not the psychotic. According to Adonis, he had been produced when a village wise woman was raped by an Entity of some power, and after several failed attempts to abort the developing product, she birthed the creature now serving House Shaiagrazni. Number Eight was so named as the eighth of many attempts Adonis had made to find a being of sufficient Entity-related heritage for what he had only just now let Silenos know was the sympathetic-binding ritual.

The reason for their tempered schism was that he had proved too thinly related to the Depths for even that much, and yet there were invariably advantages to being tied by blood to such beings.

Lycanthropy was among the more common results of such a coupling—not including more boring ones such as city-obliterating explosions caused by atomic instability, cancers, insanity, singularities expanding rapidly across the globe or ordinary nonmagical beings with an ontological compulsion to commit acts of sadism and sexual predation.

House Shaiagrazni enjoyed using lycanthropes, and Silenos had always yearned to obtain one for himself. He was not surprised to find they existed in this world—anything related to Entities tended to be ubiquitous across the cosmos—but it was a stroke of annoying fortune on Adonis's part that he'd obtained one. Silenos almost considered killing his former apprentice to steal it, but of course he was far too valuable a Shaiagraznian asset for that.

Adonis snatched the trinket being offered to him by Number Eight, then punched the creature for good measure. It hit the far wall hard, rebounded harder, groaned as it fell down.

"Imbecile," the Shaiagrazni growled. "I ordered you here twenty-nine seconds prior."

Silenos studied the lycnathrope, first with mundane and then arcane senses. It would live, he knew. Adonis had restrained some measure of his strength, and further this being had been enhanced on a magical level—doubtless by its master's supreme knowledge of esoterica. He wondered if he might have done better with fleshcrafting.

Yes, obviously, he was Silenos. And soon he'd have a being of even purer Depth blood than Number Eight to prove it.

CHAPTER EIGHT

As far as places one might want to break into went, the Dark Lord's fortress wasn't one. It wasn't just the air, which Hexeri actually found quite pleasing, or the location, which wasn't any great issue for her preternatural body. It was the damned *security*.

Casters were, as anyone of note knew, rather paranoid people. Hexeri imagined she would be too, were all her supernatural might compressed into a tiny, squishy human body. The Dark Lord had kicked King Galukar around like a loose pebble though, so she didn't see what excuse he could possibly have for the absolute excess of defenses he was forcing her to avoid.

If there was not an undead by a door, there were bound spirits. If not those, then strange runic structures that a quick glance told her would hum with alarm at any intruder's proximity. It was like trying to break into the inside of Collin Baird's mind, but with dark magic added on for good measure.

That was why, despite a solid hour of skirting around the structure in search of a vulnerability, Hexeri had yet to even enter it. She buried her frustration, ignoring the animal urge to vent it and start kicking down walls. First, she didn't even know if she *could* kick down these walls. Whatever they were made of, she didn't recognize it. And she'd seen Shaiagrazni's armor stop far too many death blows to underestimate the powers of a caster's mystery substance.

And second, if she made so much noise, her unlife would be measured in minutes. Hexeri was not the predator, not here. She was a rat in the walls.

She wished Collin were with her.

Eventually, Hexeri's orbiting of the place naturally petered out, only as she found her memory already stuffed with details of its features. There would be no more to glean from the exterior.

So she took in a breath she didn't need, held it for an endless period, and sent herself off to infiltrate the fortress.

Of all the places she might attack, a single balcony was the greatest vulnerability. Still guarded, of course—casters and their ridiculous paranoia—but only by two undead. Dullahan, beings that would have been impressive anywhere else.

Comparison to the Dark Lord himself, let alone Shaiagrazni, had made them wither into nothing before Hexeri's eyes.

She came down on the nearest from above, hands crashing into the top of its head with all the strength and weight she could muster. The ground actually cracked under the dullahan's feet, and she felt its spine crumble. Before it had even finished falling, before its ally had turned, Hexeri twisted around the sluggish corpse and struck the other with a kick.

Dullahan were no smaller than humans, and their armor was impossibly heavy. But Hexeri was a vampire. Her strike sent two hundred pounds of undead and three hundred of black steel flying off the edge of the balcony to drop down out of sight. Below, the cold ground awaited it beneath a thousand feet of air. Hexeri wasn't sure how fast it would be moving exactly, but she doubted even an undead of such power as that would survive impact.

There was no time to dwell upon it, regardless. She made her way into the fortress—hastily bashing down the heavy door barring her path—and began hurrying through its corridors.

A study of outer windows had given Hexeri some idea of probable makeups for the corridors and rooms beside exterior walls. Other than that, she was forced to map the place out as she went. The centuries had expanded her mnemonic powers well beyond most of humanity, and she put them to good use moving through the fort. It was still a dangerous lack of knowledge on her part. But then, desperate times called for dangerous missions.

It helped to be faster than was human and helped more to be lighter-footed than was even feline. Neither helped enough. Hexeri was only a minute into her infiltration when she made her first mistake, a minor error on checking her periphery that saw her caught by the sights of an undead.

The fomor came at her like a thrown axe, and behind it a dozen or more middling reanimates shambled after. She turned, sprinting away and hearing a great shriek run through the fortress, dancing along its walls and doubtless reaching the ears of a hundred or more other enemies.

A vampire elder of Hexeri's age was certainly a match for the fomor, even if those undead had thrown themselves into the affair as well. The fight would have been difficult, but not insurmountable. That had been her second mistake—she should've silenced the foe quickly. Hexeri cursed herself even as she tore down the corridor.

A horse would have taken five times what she did to cross it, but the fomor at least kept pace. Hexeri turned corners, focused on building her map even now. Right up until she saw another fomor rear up ahead of her.

She cursed again, made her decision fast. Picked up speed and went to ram the blocking enemy. If she was very, very lucky, Hexeri might kill it before the other could engage her. Hexeri's impact wasn't like a warhorse—it was like an entire formation of them, barded and manned by heavy knights to boot. The fomor weighed ten times what she did and still found itself driven backward to hit the wall five paces back. Cracks ran along the material—not so much stronger than stone after all—and Hexeri tightened her grip on its torso.

Fingers dug in, compressing undead flesh, hooking hard and deep. She roared, threw it down to the floor, and started punching. No time for magic, no time for anything fancy. She released the control on her instincts, let the animal that lived in any vampire come out to play. Fangs slashed, nails raked, skin tore, and rotting blood hissed out.

And the other enemies grew closer by the stride.

Hexeri's concentration only slipped for a second before an arrow-fast tendril struck her, blasting her back against the wall and forcing her to retreat from more. The blood in her enemies was dead stuff, not even feigning animism like in a vampire, and so she called on the shadows to rake sharpened darkness across the attacking limbs. One was severed entirely, dropping heavy and stiff against the ground as others were opened up and whipped back.

She lunged from the charging fomor right before it arrived to aid its ally, hitting the wall and smashing almost fully through it. Hexeri glimpsed starlight from outside the feet of rock. She didn't stop moving.

If Hexeri let herself be caught, she'd be grabbed, slowed, then beaten past the point of even her superhuman body's ability to reconstitute itself. So she kept her feet active and her wits aware. The lesser undead were arriving now, and she halved their number with a contemptuous flick of shadows that tore through bodies and littered the corridor with isolated limbs. That single moment gave the closest fomor opportunity to attack once more, and this time the one she'd bowled over was rising up to join in as it did.

Hexeri was forced to guard the first strike, feeling strength not so short of her own run deep down into the bone. Her shoulder hit the wall, then a tendril hit her head and floored her. Before she was up again, the fomors were on her.

But not for more than an instant before something smashed into one of them, moving so fast that the impact sounded like a bell tolling. The fomor was launched back, trailing an arc of blood in the air, and Hexeri scrambled back to her feet to stare at the newcomer. Tall, covered in white armor, practically aglow with divine magic. It made her eyes water and skin sting, tasted like acid on her tongue. They didn't return her stare.

The figure moved like a Hero, or close to one. A Hero of physical combat more than magic, clad in plate from head to toe but seeming not to feel its weight at all. Their helmed head was a blur, gauntleted fist even more so. Mace the greatest blur of all. Hexeri's eyes barely caught the weapon's head as it streaked to impact the other fomor, unhinging the undead's jaw, breaking the bone clean in half, and sending it spinning back. Precious moments were bought by the motion. She used them well.

Dead blood was stagnant, less inclined to answer her will, but it was still blood. Hexeri concentrated while the fomors reeled and rounded to fight their attacker, and by the time the first was lunging back at the newcomer, her attack was ready. Hexeri lunged too, planting a palm against the enemy's chest and concentrating on its precious ichor.

The blood heated, boiled, then boiled even past boiling. Bursting capillaries, veins, arteries, bursting the cells themselves. Crimson fountains sprung out at a hundred places as the fomor's body contorted and twisted, growing misshapen as the internal pressure fought to be external.

Stories of vampires bursting a person—literally making them explode—were exaggerated. But not by much. The ruin Hexeri's attack made of the fomor was enough to leave even a reanimate still and crumbling.

Though she could only use it on one at any given time, and in the span she took to do so, a fomor could do much indeed. It was fortunate, then, that she wasn't fighting alone anymore. Long before the other could attack her, the newcomer struck it, once, twice, a half dozen times. Their mace moved like falling meteors, crashing into the hardened body of its target to smash bones and leave jagged shards protruding up through the very skin. The fomor weakened, slowed. Hexeri didn't even waste her time boiling its blood, just sent an arc of shadow into all the open wounds she saw and made them deeper.

It didn't take long for the undead to fall, even with its impossible vitality. When it did, Hexeri turned to the newcomer. Her savior, she was forced to admit.

"Thank you," Hexeri growled, taking a moment to pause, biting back her . . . instincts. She was not a thing to appreciate aid from a newcomer, certainly not to have her vulnerability seen. Every predatory, solitary instinct in her deathly mind urged her to *kill* the newcomer, to hide her shame by tearing them apart with tooth and talon, to crack them open and drink of their vital essence.

But Hexeri was too aged to succumb to such puerile urges, especially when doing so would cost her a crucial ally in perhaps the most dangerous territory she had ever set foot within. The newcomer, a paladin she now realized, didn't say anything until they'd already turned on the remaining lesser undead and mashed their bodies into pulp. Then, at last, they removed their helmet to speak.

It came off to reveal a surprisingly young woman with eyes a good deal older than her face, though not nearly as much so as Hexeri's. Her hair was blonde, features sharp, face stern and . . . weathered. She turned to affix her with a gaze that might have cut steel.

"I know what you are," she declared, and Hexeri prepared herself for an attack. "But . . . clearly, we have more important issues here than each other. What do you say to us . . . cooperating?"

Hexeri actually paused a moment, ashamed to know that her surprise showed.

"Let's do it." She nodded. "My name is . . ." She paused, winced, then revealed herself. "Hexeri." The paladin did not seem surprised by her name, though recognition was clear as day.

"I thought so. An ally of Silenos." She sighed. "I am Ensharia."

CHAPTER NINE

The skyship was slow at the moment, and that was about the only reason Swick was permitting its deck to remain heavily used. Felicia was glad. To face her thoughts in the open air, with winds seeming to snatch them away behind her, was bad enough. Facing them cooped up down under the decks, surrounded by grunting pirates, would've been another thing entirely.

A plank creaked behind her, and she whipped around to find Swick himself—her new captain—leaning against a railing. For all his . . . offness, the man seemed entirely at home on the decks, not seeming to sway in the slightest even as turbulence rocked the entire vessel. The benefits of long experience, she supposed. It made Felicia wonder how the fuck he'd gone and crashed his ship in the first place.

"Coin for your thoughts?" Swick asked, not coming any closer. He had a way of speaking that made him easily heard, despite the wind howling as fast as a man could run between the five or six feet between them. Again, Felicia imagined it was practice. This one was more at home miles in the air than she was on land. Than anyone she'd ever *met* was on land.

"We're coming back without Nemo," she noted, and he nodded. "That's a failure," Felicia added, expecting an argument, a falling face, expecting, at least, that the captain would make something of the fact. He just shrugged.

"Kid made his choice. You made yours first."

Felicia bristled, began to argue. Then paused. He wasn't wrong. She'd insisted on not sending another note to Sphera. She'd been the one to push Swick on it. She still wasn't sure why he'd conceded to her, maybe wouldn't ever find out. But when she'd made that decision, she hadn't meant . . .

What, for anyone to die? Except for Sphera, yes. She'd underestimated Nemo, Felicia realized. Failed to consider that the boy was as kind as he was. Kind enough to throw himself into a city under attack for the sake of one woman, at his own expense. Suddenly, she felt a hundred times worse about herself.

"We can't go back," Swick told her, replying to Felicia's question before it could even be asked.

"We *can*," Felicia replied.

"We shouldn't, then." Swick shrugged. "You made your choice. Nemo made his. Now I'm making mine. This isn't the ship that tore apart that battlefield, not now. We don't know how many magi are there, how powerful. For all we know, Mafari himself is waiting to blast us out of the sky. If you told me to swoop in and rescue the kid while he was guarded by a hundred trebuchets, I'd do it, but I won't do this."

Felicia ground her teeth, fighting futilely for some semblance of calm amid her own thundering thoughts. She needn't have bothered. It was nowhere to be found.

"I don't want the boy to die." She scowled. Swick's eyes softened a fraction.

"He has that demon with him," the captain reminded her. "Most terrifying thing I've ever seen. Or, well, maybe . . . fifth."

Felicia couldn't help cracking a grin at that. "Fifth?"

"Well, there's Silenos, obviously." The captain shrugged. "Then the Dark Lord, then Lilia, then Galukar. Xekanis makes the top five but . . . Damn, it's odd that he's that low."

"I can't believe you have a tiny woman above my father." Felicia giggled. Swick looked suddenly defensive.

"She eats people!" he snapped. "And I've heard stories about that battle. Let me tell you, tens of thousands turned on their own allies at a single word from her, maybe more. Mark my words—"

Whatever words, markworthy or otherwise, Swick would have uttered, Felicia never got to hear. The black man appeared before them before he could finish.

For one moment, the world seemed to slow. Swick's eyes went wide, hands blurred into motion as Felicia opened her mouth to scream. Nothing came out. The air was simply ripped out of her lungs, and she dropped to cough and gasp on her knees as the man deftly stepped back from Swick, who now slashed at him with a face frenzied by unexpected battle.

"*Enemy on the deck!*" he roared, and Felicia had never been so pleased to see the man's optimization for flight in action. His voice cut through the winds like they were still air, carrying well down into the underdecks.

But it would still take an age for mundane or lightly Vigorous men to reach them. She sucked in reluctant breaths, forced herself to rise, and splayed her hands out.

Bombs flew forth from them, miniature things of foreign construction. Sourced by the same people who provided all her knowledge over mechanisms. They flew well, surrounding the black man a moment before detonating and shaking the vessel itself with the force of it.

Felicia winced but didn't stop her motions to keep attacking. From her coat, she pulled out her next device, the double-handed repeater that spit iron bolts out so fast, they almost shattered on impact. They shattered now, that much was certain. Splintering apart against . . .

A shield the black man had wrapped around himself, and perhaps the strongest Felicia had ever seen. Her arrows were a match for ranger bolts, able to penetrate stone walls, and here they were turned aside like nothing at all. The man flicked his wrist, and Felicia shot backward with a cry.

Her power was not just in knowledge, nor in Vigor—though Felicia had both. It was Reason. That strange grounding force so many feared as the antithesis of magic. They were right. Where magic undid the world's natural laws, Reason enforced them. Reduced entropy, weakened random chance, made every design less subject to the million unknowable imperfections that a being without such preternatural connection to the world would be forced to contend with.

No human could fly without magic, and precious few with. Felicia was no exception, yet, but she *could* glide, and glide well. At a single gesture, her false wings emerged, catching the winds and tossing her back onto the ship's deck to tumble and roll.

The fight had already degenerated even then, one mast snapped and great holes punched into the decks where attacks had failed and missed. The black man stood amid twenty others, weapons hurled at him to be deflected without effect, face still and contemptuous. Swick was not furious anymore, merely . . .

Terrified.

That fact terrified Felicia herself, because she'd not seen half so much fear on the pirate's face since they'd fought the Dark Lord. Now he looked as if half his body's weight would leave him as sweat.

Finally, all at once it seemed, the black man appeared to grow tired of letting them fight. He gestured once, and the ship tilted downward, casting men off its decks and sending Felicia to roll along it. Even Swick fell, his intimacy with the skies counting for nothing against such power.

Every tumbling body halted, twisted, shot up, and then smashed back down into the deck. Felicia was among them. She felt the hard wood shatter beneath her, stars danced in her eyes, and when she finally regained her bearings, she was staring up at the black man and finding eyes upon her that were colder than any she'd ever seen. Regarding her as less than a person, a *thing*. When he spoke, his voice bore a contempt to match.

"Your father has moved against me," he said, low, calm, controlled. "He will regret that, and you will be how I make him." Without another word, the man reached out, grabbing Felicia's head before she could repel him. Her limbs were bound by her sides by some invisible energy, keeping her from it even if she tried, and she gasped as *something* wormed its way into her mind.

Felicia didn't realize what had happened at first, not even after he released her to drop down.

"Tell me," the man instructed. "What is fluid pressure?" Felicia frowned. Obviously—

Obviously . . .

Her heart lurched, throat tightened, stomach twisted. She was going to puke. Felicia stared up at him in horror.

"You know nothing about engineering, nothing at all," he said simply. "Less than an ignorant peasant, but I have left your passion for it, and the memory of how skilled you once were. Consider this a warning. Do not cross me again, or I shall do far, far worse the next time."

The black man did not leave. He was simply there one moment and gone the next. Felicia just lay there, even when the pressure around her subsided. She stayed still, trembling, breathing. Thinking. She tried to recall the devices she'd used, her bombs and glider. Tried to recall how she'd made them—and found the physical acts of doing so were clear as ever in her memory.

But she knew *nothing* about why they'd been necessary, had no idea about what they'd achieved. Couldn't even begin to guess at what each step had done, why it had done it, how it might have been done better later, or worse if she attempted it too lazily again.

A sob escaped Felicia. She fought it back, for one moment. Then gave up the next, let her lungs take over and empty themselves with more gasping, retching, blubbering heat as the tears began to well in her eyes and the weakness began to radiate through her pores.

None on the deck said a thing; all just looked at her. Felicia didn't meet their eyes. It wasn't contempt she feared, or apathy, or disgust. There was something worse than any of that aimed at her now, she was certain.

And she couldn't bring herself to meet their looks of pity.

CHAPTER TEN

The tempered schism twisted the world, like cloth held tight in a great fist. Silenos had felt the sensation before. Last time, it had come from the malignant magic of an Entity. This time was no less disconcerting, however much he knew that it was for his own benefit.

Once more, Silenos was reminded how petty his magic truly was as reality caved in around him, melted down, and dissipated. Gravity rescinded its hold on him, light fled from his vicinity, and sound became a distant memory as reason itself was delegated to mere abstraction. He turned, or would have if something so constant as direction remained with any substance, and found Adonis nowhere in sight.

It passed, of course, insofar as anything could be described as passing in such a nothing space. Silenos felt solidity beneath him, grunting as his mind slowly plodded through the tedium of restoring order to chaos. Around him was a realm of pure madness, beyond description. Geometry was a liquid thing, chronology outright gaseous. The air hummed and pulsated like musculature, while the ground seemed to retreat from his feet in fear. Far beyond him lay a crest of mountains that rumbled and ran like melting ice, their shapes changing by the moment.

Silenos scoured the protean landscape for any sign of his former apprentice, and found Adonis soon enough. The man was gathering his own bearings, examining something high above. Silenos followed his gaze.

Only rarely would a named of House Shaiagrazni feel true awe, and Silenos decided he did not care for the novelty. Far above him—cosmically far—were great masses moving in slow arcs across the skies. Behind them was a crimson space, not quite atmosphere, not quite vacuum, and through it the great serpentine shapes coiled and shifted along. Each was of a size more common to features of geography than living things. Perhaps unsurprising, for none was truly living. The Entities had not noticed him. Silenos suspected that was the only reason he still lived.

Silently, he made his way over to Adonis's side and kept his magic ready. He was already in war form, having made sure to change his shape well in advance of the transit.

"We are in the Shallow Depths," Adonis told him without needing to be asked. "I can tell by the density of magic in the air."

It was no great surprise. Silenos had studied the arcane for too long to mistake his surroundings for anything else.

"Then let us hurry," he suggested. "I would be done with this sooner rather than later."

The two of them moved swiftly, Silenos propelled by the great musculature and efficient strands of his war form, Adonis by a more magical empowerment. Kinetics, potent magic that, employed at his level, was similar in effect to the Vigor of the new world, albeit requiring constant focus to remain active.

It was nonetheless difficult to gauge distance in any part of the Depths, even ones as shallow—low in magic and grounded in reality—as these. Silenos found his war form covering a dozen feet per kilogram, crossing terrain so fast that a single minute ought to have carried him kilometers. And yet, examining the trail behind him, he would see only a few dozen meters in his wake. At other times, a mere few steps would seem to take him halfway to the horizon.

Space, as was the case with all things here, could not be relied upon. He had to remind himself of that. When one found oneself in the Depths, rationality was irrational.

The greatest concern was keeping a constant distance between him and Adonis. Any Shaiagrazni was loath to rely upon another, but so too would they do so if the alternative was destruction. Silenos had rebuilt some small fraction of his previous countermeasures against death, and yet he had no guarantee they would function were he to perish here.

Indeed, even if they did, he knew for a fact there were Entities not countable among the greater of their kind that could bypass such things. Far better not to take the risk. And so he and his former apprentice guarded each other, forced to huddle like apes around a shared fire.

Here their magic availed them nothing, save each breath. They were neither of them a Dark Lord, not in the Depths. Mere plankton beneath the waves.

Though they were far from alone in that distinction, most Entities would fall under such a category too. More than once, Silenos and Adonis found themselves impeded by a particularly aggressive being of magic and forced to defend each other. Silenos's newly made cannons spit kinesis and flame, ripping into the enemies more through will than physics. Adonis found similar success with his great mace, fighting with several times Galukar's prowess and reminding Silenos why, even with his new Vigor-enhanced war form, he could not afford to take the caster lightly.

Either of them would have perished in such skirmishes, assailed several times by foes with the numbers to advantage them. With both their powers combined, the Shaiagraznis just barely weathered their challenges.

But not without wounds.

Silenos roared as the Entity reached for him. It was a towering thing, in the way that mountains were. Thin and tentacled almost like one of his own grotesqueries, though every inch of it was, following a cursory examination with his fleshcrafting, composed of semicongealed menstrual blood.

This fact did not impede it in the slightest, and he felt an impossible strength tighten about his body. The limbs of his war form locked, armor plating doing as much to resist the Entity as musculature. Neither was enough, not even together. Creaking and groaning ran through Silenos's magnificent body as it was tested by a pressure to rival planetary cores, and surrendered.

It was then that Adonis freed him.

The mace came down hard, and from it emerged a burst of omnidirectional energy that ran through semisolid blood to blast it apart. Silenos fell, beat broken wings to right himself, and focused on repairing them even as he dropped toward the ground. He aimed, fired, struck the Entity near its midsection, and watched his projectile blast apart.

One advantage to his cannon's ludicrous velocity, closing in on four times the speed of sound, was that at such speeds, its projectiles behaved almost like liquids themselves, dispersing as they passed through the Entity. Silenos focused on that fact, let it carry his will and magic into tearing a hole half the size of his war form in it. By the time he'd stabilized himself in the air, it was already closing up.

Silenos bit back his frustration. Battling Entities was never a specialty of his—those rare few among House Shaiagrazni who were regularly called on to do so were invariably masters of more than his ability and experience. He knew, intellectually, that only magic and will could wound one. That their forms were immaterial to them, mere constructs held together by alien cognition and power.

To see it demonstrated, to find his attack foiled by a simple refusal on its target's behalf to obey the laws of physical matter, was another thing entirely. Silenos Shaiagrazni felt fear for the first time in a long time.

Then he buried it, for he had work to do. And none would deny his glorious will.

He conjured his blasting oil as he let himself glide downward, catching nonexistent air upon his broken wings and using absent gravity to aid in his descent. The Entity attacked with great spurts of clotting blood flung from its own body, and Silenos evaded them as best he could. Two caught him—sizzling as they ate into keratin plate and steamed into the air.

Entities enjoyed acid—he had learned that much from his time in the Shallow Depths—and they enjoyed physical contact even more. Silenos saw its tendrils reaching for another grab just before he propelled his hastily made explosive. It detonated in the center of one great limb, ripping it into a cloud of bloody vapor and earning him another few precious moments. Adonis was not so lucky as that.

Though stronger, faster, and more durable, he lacked Silenos's options of versatility and range. His body was quickly being encased in the Entity's bloody substance, compressed just as Silenos's own was. For one moment, Silenos considered ignoring him, focusing on offense. He banished the thought. Even Adonis could not withstand the crushing grip he'd felt for more than a few moments.

Shadestuff erupted from him, screaming into the air in greater volumes than he had ever produced it before. The not-matter came easier here, in its own home, and rained down onto the Entity's limb to . . . do nothing.

Silenos felt true shock take him, just before another limb struck him from the sky.

He landed hard, blood solidifying around him, pressure resuming. Silenos had moments to think. He forced his thoughts to connect with the Entity, fleshcrafting mastery letting him seep his will into the gory body it had made.

Compared to this thing, Silenos's magic was as a candle before the bonfire. But a candle was still *something*. This was not an Old Power, one of the true deep things lurking in this realm. It was a mindless, dull, pitiable creature near the bottom rung in the ladder of its kind. It lacked true sapience, he thought, and perhaps even sentience at that. Silenos wrestled it for control just long enough to find whatever passed for its will.

Then he attacked *that* instead. If nothing else, the strategy was unexpected. It may well have been impossible had his arcane vision—Entity gifted, ironically—not permitted him to locate the nexus of consciousness conducting this pillar of destruction. Soon Silenos's thoughts were hitting it like a ram, scattering its control. The limb broke apart around him, and he burst out through the slackened liquid before it could reform.

This time, he didn't waste his chance.

Silenos fired, and fired again. The acts of reloading his weapon felt unnecessary, intuitively wasteful, and yet he focused upon them more than anything else. He cast great sheets of burning fluid out to adhere against the Entity's body and char the blood black, shattered planes of carbonized matter with shots from his cannon, dumped blasting oil down like an aerial bomber.

All of it was an assault calculated for utmost efficiency, and through that calculation, Silenos focused every screed of his cognition. He ran the figures through his head, agonized over the logic of it, and maintained the mental link between him and his target. Let it drown as he forced an ocean of physical reason into its throat.

The exhaustion came on him like it never had before, near-endless mana supplies suddenly rendered pitiably finite. And yet the results came quicker still.

Adonis carved his way from the Entity's grip, smashed apart limbs, and Silenos felt his will mingling with the air in almost as pervasive a way as his own. The Entity slowly weakened, grew sluggish, began withdrawing. It had been only four seconds since its attack begun, and between it, Silenos, and Adonis, almost a thousand motions had been exchanged. At that very moment, Silenos's regeneration finished.

Instantly, he swooped down to flee. Adonis did not need calling to follow suit. They had never possessed the means to kill this enemy, not if they both exhausted themselves to death in the effort. It was a humbling reminder of where they were, and what they were dealing with.

As the plankton, Silenos considered himself satisfied to have merely evaded their attacker. Even if it was, in the end, nothing more than a marginally larger microbe. They continued tearing through the Shallow Depths, their search now more pressing than ever before.

But their mana had been exhausted by more than half in only that briefest of periods. Silenos's fear reemerged, just as strong as ever.

CHAPTER ELEVEN

"How did you come into House Shaiagrazni?" Adonis asked abruptly. "I have always wondered."

Silenos found himself stiffening at the question. It was not one he had been asked often—perhaps ten times in his life. Each time it reached his ears, he found himself drifting back to the past. Shivered.

"As most of us do," he replied, slowly, carefully. "I was a simple villager at first. Then, in my childhood, our people conquered my home country. All of us were allotted use by House Shaiagrazni based upon our talents and abilities. In my case, I possessed potent enough magic to be inducted as an apprentice."

Adonis nodded, unsurprised. As Silenos had said, it was a typical story. House Shaiagrazni had a policy of ongoing expansionism. New territories were given to newly ascended named to govern, which they would then sift through for new talents among the recently conquered people. Those talented would be inducted into House Shaiagrazni, have their magical gifts tested, and if they proved intelligent, powerful, and willful enough after several decades, ascended themselves to the position of named, where they would be granted new territory to repeat the process over again.

It was a steady, reliable sort of expansion that left House Shaiagrazni smaller than some of its rival empires but ensured the continued quality of its casters.

"I was born into it," Adonis explained, which surprised Silenos quite a bit.

"You always struck me as soft willed, empathetic. As an apprentice, at least," he admitted. Adonis did not seem offended.

"I was," he agreed. "Fortunately, I was able to overcome my weaker nature. What may surprise you more was my mother, Kammani."

Silenos stared at him, waiting to see some hint of a joke. There was none—Adonis was dead serious.

"You are the biological child of my master?" he pressed, still not able to quite believe it. Adonis shared a rare smile with him.

"It is not often I can see you made speechless," he noted. "Yes. You may have noticed I inherited only a fraction of her talents, of course, and talent was never what made her dangerous in the first place."

That much was true. Silenos's master was unrivaled in *power* among House Shaiagrazni—there was no denying—but at least ten had a superior gift for magic. The source of her mastery was simply her age. Stories already spoke of her as an arcane demigoddess when primitive man was first learning to smelt bronze. Some estimated her age at five thousand, others ten. Others still thought her north of twenty.

Whatever the truth was was impossible to gauge. She had already been an ancient thing when records of time were first coined. The count of her years would forever be a task of historic deduction, not cataloging.

But she still reproduced; all in House Shaiagrazni did. There wasn't a strong correlation between the magical prowess of one's parent and one's self, but it existed and was significant enough that all the talented casters were expected to help create more. Most never learned who their offspring were, and vice versa.

"How did you discover this?" Silenos asked. "And when?"

"A hundred years ago, and quite coincidentally. I was testing a sliver of her genetic material as part of an experiment and stumbled upon the similarity with my own."

"You are not a skilled enough fleshcrafter to fully manipulate DNA," Silenos noted. "Who else knows?"

Adonis smiled. "Dimitar."

Ah, that explained it. Dimitar was among the fleshcrafters whose skill exceeded Silenos's own. For now.

Silenos forced himself to his feet, and Adonis followed. They had rested for only a few minutes, but that was approaching the limits of how long they might safely do so in their current surroundings. It would not do to tempt more violence than they had to from the Depths' inhabitants.

For the future, Silenos noted to himself that he ought to travel in a smaller form. Already he had abandoned his towering war form, finding that he needed to fight far less in its absence. It had seemed strange to him, but perhaps it was the Entities' lack of physicality that made them so drawn toward larger examples of it. Their lack of comprehension, of shared tangibility, made the mass of a larger enemy all the more enticing.

It had been, by Silenos's calculations, somewhere between one hour and three thousand years since he and Adonis had set foot in the Shallow Depths. Granted, he had stopped calculating some time ago, for obvious reasons pertaining to the accuracy of his attempts. Adonis was his only measure of progress, skill in esoterica allowing him to track their quarry by magical sensation.

And always, he claimed they were drawing closer.

Crossing the landscape involved imprinting solidity onto it, not just in its geometry but in its basic space as well. It was tiring, like all things were in the Depths, and Silenos could feel the eerie emptiness of his mana as more and more of it was consumed.

Time. Everything was measured in time; everything was *rationed* in time. It was another novelty, and another that Silenos would rather have done without. The prick of feeling his invincibility stripped away was not so harsh this time as it had been when he'd first found himself in the new world.

But it still stung, as it might have stung any other. He continued on his way, Adonis watching him as he watched Adonis. There was a silent understanding, Silenos knew, between the two of them. If another Entity of significant power engaged them, they would simply retreat back to the schism.

They would have no choice.

Scraping came from ahead, and low, pitiable mewling. Silenos glanced his silent question toward Adonis, who answered it with a nod. It was what they hunted; their task was nearing its completion.

Slowly, the two of them moved up toward the noise. Silenos readied his cannon, though he was uncertain of what use it could be, and Adonis himself flared with preternatural force as kinetic energies infused every strand of his anatomy, shielding from harm and bolstering strength. Ahead, they finally saw what they had come here seeking.

It was . . . repulsive.

Perhaps three meters tall, and standing naked as a newborn. Its skin was dark gray, rough, and uneven. Parts were scaled, others covered in tufts of fur, and everywhere it sprouted welts and blisters, pus oozing from them and cracks opening along the surface with every motion. Its head was bald, hands twice the size that might have been expected from a creature of its height, and fingers tipped with yellow, jagged talons that looked better for ripping than cutting. Its lips seemed nonexistent, and needle-pointed teeth were easily visible through its cracked mouth. Orange eyes gazed back upon Silenos, and when the creature moved, he heard—and saw—the shifting of disjointed vertebrae in its back, each one popping from one position to another.

"You . . . What . . . What do you want?"

Clearly, the creature was not accustomed to speaking in large sentences. Silenos could actually hear the sounds of its vocal cords shifting to accommodate polysyllabic conversation. Entities as a rule did not use speech, nor any other physical modes, among one another. House Shaiagrazni had yet to determine *how* they communicated with their own kind, as even their minds were too alien for conventional telepathy to be efficient.

It was fortunate, then, that this one not only spoke verbally, but seemed affected by the same translation magic woven around Silenos when he was displaced between worlds. It backed off as he and Adonis drew nearer, arrowhead eyes narrowed with suspicion. Oddly astute of the creature, it had to be said.

"Greetings, worm," Adonis began, shocking Silenos with his politeness. Perhaps a career in esoterica had affected his mannerisms as well as his knowledge, when it came to the Entities. "We are of House Shaiagrazni, masters of arts most high and casters with power beyond..."

He had been about to say, "Powers beyond the creature's imagination," but caught himself before accidentally making the claim. Under normal circumstances, it was correct. Among potent casters it was, if flattering, in the right direction of the truth. Speaking to a being fathered by an Entity, it was patently ridiculous. Even now, Silenos could feel the magic humming off the creature, and it demanded every screed of his will not to take a self-preservative backstep.

"Other humans," he finished. The creature shuffled backward, head jerking from side to side as it studied them.

"You're here for me," it croaked. Adonis nodded.

"We are."

The creature spat, and its saliva sizzled into the ground. Acid, potent acid. Entities did enjoy spitting acid.

"Well, leave now and save yourself the pain. You can't have me. I want no part in your plans, machinations, or schemes. You have nothing to offer me, nothing I need, nothing I desire. I want only to be left alone, to be left *in peace*. Let me live my life, as I have let you live yours."

Silenos looked at Adonis, and Adonis looked at him. They did not need words to communicate, nor, really, did they need to communicate at all. Their next course of action was somewhat... obvious.

"No."

Silenos aimed his cannon and fired, blasting the solid shell clean into the creature's neck and perfectly hitting the spot connecting it to the misshapen shoulders below. It tore through, burst apart, ripped head from body, and left the shrieking thing to roll while its separated torso spasmed and kicked meters apart from it. Adonis reached down to pluck the head up off the ground, and without another word, they began moving back for the schism.

Their walk back was actually far shorter and easier than their initial trip. Perhaps they had grown acclimated enough to the Shallow Depths that they could navigate more easily, or perhaps it was mere chance. That they had been fortunate enough to encounter the abomination at the very edge of its deeper home was no small factor. It occurred to Silenos that the Entities' attacks, which now came only once or twice rather than more than a dozen times, may have been partially deterred by the creature's head he now carried.

The head in question was a loud thing, barking and snarling, oscillating between threats, insults, weeping melancholy, and a dozen other states, each more irritating than the last. Silenos focused on tuning it out while he worked.

Within the Depths, or any other highly magic-saturated environment, Silenos knew that anything so strongly tied to an Entity's nature would be able to withstand an infinite variety of physical destruction. Aside from decapitation, he might have dropped the hybrid into a star and still failed to kill it. Just like any other Entity.

Unlike its purebred cousins, however, it was not a being of magic alone. There *was* a physicality to it. Silenos was not sure it could survive in the new world forever, and certainly not that its head could. So he stood ready to perform any hasty alterations that might prove necessary to sustaining its life. If the thing died before they could make use of it, their entire affair would have been for nothing.

He needn't have worried. They reached the schism, the Depths distorted around them, and Silenos felt the increasingly familiar sensation of transdimensional movement take him once more. He clutched the hybrid's head tightly, closed his eyes, waited for it to end. And then his feet came down upon solid ground.

They had only a moment before everything around them exploded into motion and violence.

CHAPTER TWELVE

Hexeri had been surprised to find a paladin so deep inside the Dark Lord's territory, let alone within his own fortress. She should have saved up her shock—because it was far more appropriate upon being introduced to the woman's allies.

All of them wore the enchanted, pale plate armor that signified their order. All carried maces, hammers, or axes—mutilating weapons for slaying lifeless beings whose bodies did not need to circulate blood or power organs. All of them shimmered with that annoying divine energy that always felt like a sunburn had. Before sunburns threatened to reduce Hexeri into ashes outright, that was.

"A vampire?" one of the paladins growled, not *quite* setting a new record for the smallest passing time frame between one of their order recognizing Hexeri and moving to attack her. The first one she'd met, Ensharia, held the man back with an outstretched arm.

"At ease, Gladian," she urged him. "This one's an ally."

The paladin, a man apparently, was practically quivering with rage as he replied.

"An ally? Ensharia, we all studied them as much as one another. There is no alliance with a vampire. It will use us and betray us the moment it sees fit, at best. And at worst, it's one of the Dark Lord's minions."

"Do I get to speak here?" Hexeri asked. She saw several of the paladins bristle as she did. Evidently, she did *not* get to speak.

Except, unfortunately for them, she was a vampire elder, which meant she could do whatever she wanted. "I didn't come here seeking any of you out. I'm here to kill the Dark Lord. My sire is known as Lilia. I know you've all heard of her because over the millennia she's personally killed more paladins than have ever existed at any one time. And she was, until his disappearance, working with Silenos Shaiagrazni."

They weren't mollified, at least not for more than a moment.

"And he's gone now," another paladin noted. "So what guarantee do we have that you're not here as some kind of emissary to swap to the second-best option?"

"Not to mention that Shaiagrazni was a necromancer and flesh-crafter himself anyway," another cut in.

Hexeri took a step back, readied herself for things to turn violent, just as the first paladin, Ensharia, spoke up again.

"I worked with Shaiagrazni myself," she declared, sweeping her gaze across her peers. "If anyone thinks that's a sign of the enemy, you can feel free to say so to my face."

Perhaps unsurprisingly, none did.

Ensharia leveled a gaze at Hexeri. "We don't have time to argue. Work with us and we'll let you go. Betray us and I'll kill you myself. You're here to assassinate the Dark Lord?"

Hexeri hesitated, considering lying. Looked at the woman's mace.

"To free Shaiagrazni," she corrected. Ensharia's face stiffened at that, eyes clouding with . . . something.

"He's here," she croaked. "A prisoner?"

"We think so."

For a moment, the paladin said nothing. Then her eyes seemed to blaze with a redoubled conviction.

"Then if you aid us, we'll do what we can to aid you." Her colleagues protested and were stifled at a gesture. Evidently, this one was the leader of her group. Lucky Hexeri.

"Deal," she replied, gaze flickering over the paladins, examining body language. None were pleased, but only one or two even began moving with violence at the backs of their minds. Gladian and another.

Hexeri committed both to memory, studying their armor to ensure she could identify them through it.

Any deal could fall through, and the more people involved in one, the more likely that was to happen. A ceasefire was only as solid as the stupidest idiot present. Paladins, as far as idiots went, were made of denser stuff than most. Hexeri would gain nothing by taking chances, and possibly lose much.

And she couldn't afford to lose now.

Ado ran, panted, gasped. She slipped on something underfoot, smacked her face against a tree on the way down, and saw stars dancing in her eyes before she landed hard, rolled clumsily, and shambled more than sprang back up to her feet.

Her lungs were burning like she was breathing magma instead of air, but she didn't slow down. Couldn't slow down. She still heard the magi behind her, and heard their men more clearly still.

Whoever her initial pursuers had been, she'd lost them. Now it was just a few middling practitioners giving chase—she might have fended them off alone were her mana not almost exhausted already.

Something roared at her back, and she risked a glance over her shoulder. Dogs. Hunting dogs. *Man*-hunting dogs, which Ado had no doubt would have been bolstered by some healer to make them faster, tireless, angrier. She fucking hated magi.

But she could do nothing about that now, just ran. Ran even as the sounds of pursuit grew closer, clearer, more imminent. Ran even as a fireball streaked past her head to engulf an entire tree in burning death. Ran even as something pounced at her from behind, barely missed a bite, and bowled her over.

Ado stared up into the snarling dog's face. Big thing, horrible. Large teeth, wide maw, eyes full of nothing at all but violence. It lunged down to bite her throat out, and she just froze as it came.

Then its head came apart, just broke to pieces like an apple struck by a hammer. Ado felt gore spray down into her eyes, her open mouth, up her nose. She gasped again, coughed, spit the disgusting mess out, blinked the debris from her vision, and scrambled up to her knees.

By the time she could see again, the pursuit party had already dissolved into chaos.

Her savior had arrived.

He was the wind, then he was the rain. Whipping around, leaping from one tree to another, moving so fast Ado's eyes could barely follow him. He seemed to disappear, at times. Then reemerge from thin air elsewhere, cutting a throat or two and whirling away faster than the enemies could turn on him.

Magic flew everywhere, and arrows too. Spears clumsily followed after the man, but they were thrust slower than he could move his entire body, and soon almost as many men were perishing to their own allies as his violence. In under half a minute, carnage had taken over the field. By then, only a few remained, one magus and several soldiers.

They all seemed to realize as much, turning to flee. Ado's savior simply raised his bow, made by Shaiagrazni himself, drew it back, and fired. Each man the iron arrows hit was simply destroyed, the impacts so excessive as to rip their torsos halfway open rather than merely penetrate.

None survived.

"Alright, princess." Collin Baird grinned, swaggering over to Ado—swaggering, the bastard—as if he'd just cut a hundred blades of grass rather than as many men. "Looks like you're never gonna let me off saving you, eh?"

"Queen," she whispered, standing up slowly, thoughts still addled by the shock. "It's queen."

Baird glanced over his shoulder, in the direction of her burning city as if to say, *It's nothing at the moment, sweetheart.* Thankfully, however, he had the decency not to give his thoughts voice.

"There were a lot of magi back there, and they had a lot of men with them. Too many. Must've hidden them somehow for them to have gotten here so suddenly. The city's fucked. We can't retake it."

Ado vomited and did her best not to give Baird the satisfaction of seeing her glare as he laughed.

"That's it then," she croaked. "Right? You have no plan, do you?"

His laughter tapered off, and he thought about it.

"Thing about Kaltan," Baird noted, "is that they're always ready for a fight. Comes with the territory of being randomly thrown into them year after year for a whole generation. Do you think this Mafari asshole would waste resources on a target that well defended, when he already knew where its leader was and had already sent a force out to assassinate him?"

Ado followed his logic, slowly, finding her distraction a gnawing blockade against thought.

"He wouldn't," she said at last, feeling a stab of . . . something. Hope? "And . . . you're my husband now," She felt some way about that, and forced the emotions aside before they could fester. "Aoakanis is your nation just as much as mine."

Flattering, she had to admit. Ado had remained its primary ruler, despite historic custom. Then again, historic custom would've decried her for marrying a commoner too. Custom was, she had come to decide, idiotic shit, and she would ignore it at her pleasure.

Baird just nodded.

"And it's strategically important," he added, almost reluctantly. "Shaiagrazni had all sorts buried here. I don't want those old bastards getting their grubby hands on his experiments. God knows what they might do."

Ado shuddered at that.

She'd seen barely anything of Silenos's innovations, and did not practice anything related to either fleshcrafting or necromancy. Even as she feared them, she had felt tempted to examine them. Knowing that even a glimmer of understanding gleaned through his work would revolutionize what she knew of magic. And knowing that it would be knowledge well beyond her power, age, and training.

Any magus who lived long learned to fear dangerous knowledge, and any magus who lived famously learned to seek it. Without a doubt, Magira's denizens would tear apart the entirety of Aoakanis in search of Silenos's works. And what they might learn from them could leave them unbeatable.

"We need to stop them," Ado hissed, remembering Rochtai, remembering her palace, remembering her sense of safety and how instantly it had been blasted apart by those repulsive pigs. "We need to fucking kill them all."

Baird got that look in his eye, the one she'd seen a hundred times before. Distant, angular. At once burning with an intense focus and aimed at something so very far away that Ado couldn't imagine what it might be. It was like he wasn't even there, but he spoke with no hint of distraction.

"Yeah, that much I can do." Without another word, he started walking.

Ado followed after, legs still throbbing from the torture of her chase. "You have a plan?" she asked.

"Not as such." He shrugged. Distracted, suddenly. He always did that. Disappeared into himself when there was killing to be done, as if it were a higher calling he alone enjoyed. Men, Ado realized, enjoyed killing far too much.

"We're heading to Kaltan," she realized.

"Right on the money." He grunted, not seeming to notice himself talking even as he did. "That's where I have men, weapons, maybe even some of Shaiagrazni's leftover blasting oil from the siege. If we're going to kill thousands of people, I'm afraid you'll need more than just me. Probably."

"And me." Ado wasn't sure why she said it, thought about taking it back. Didn't. "Aoakanis is my nation. I'm its queen. That means something."

Baird was polite enough not to reply by telling her exactly what *he* thought it meant, but she could see it in the scorn bubbling up behind his eyes.

"Think what you want," she snapped. "But I need to do this, and I can help. You know I can."

Her powers hadn't exactly grown since they'd met, not by more than a percentage point or two, but her skill had, and her experience in using them for combat was exponentially heightened. Ado wasn't a war magus, might never be one, but she had more raw power than nineteen out of every twenty who were. She *knew* she could help even a Hero or near Hero like him.

Baird looked at her long and hard, and after a few moments, it seemed, he knew it too. He nodded, slowly at first. Then more confidently.

"Alright," he said at last. "Okay. But you follow my lead. This isn't politics anymore; it's combat. We're going to kill and keep from being killed. If you break a nail, you move on."

Ado steeled herself.

"Just hurry up. The sooner we can kill these murderous bastards the better."

CHAPTER THIRTEEN

The skyship seemed to wobble in the air, which was Galukar's first sign that something was wrong. He needed only the one for his breath to snag in his lungs.

She's fine. She's fine.

But no matter how much he repeated the sentiment, no matter how much iron he bolted it down in his heart with, it did not change the doubt slowly building. It ate him from within, seeming to drain his strength like those few miserable days where the Godblade had been taken and his Vigor stolen.

She's fine.

Galukar had lied to himself for a hundred years, and for the first time in weeks, he wished he could do so again.

The ship began to drop. For one moment, panic sprung up, and Galukar was about ready to sprint across the city and plant himself, ready to catch the fucking thing as it crashed. It didn't, of course, merely continued to slowly descend, controlled despite the clear battering its aerial dexterity had taken.

And still too damned far for him to glean anything of what was happening aboard.

Galukar watched, and waited, and paced, and cursed. He had to mind his footsteps, finding himself cracking the granite of his balcony by exerting too much strength in each stride. Anger was dangerous in a wielder of the Godblade. A century had taught him that much at least.

The ship landed, perhaps two miles from him. Galukar crossed the distance in under a minute, simply leaping from his tower and trusting in his own resilience to weather the fall. He ended his sprint just as he saw Felicia making her way down the boarding ramp.

She was *alive*. His spirits had never been lifted so fast and so completely by anything, not by the return of the Godblade. Galukar was just moments from snatching her up into an embrace when he saw the look upon her face. It stopped him dead, froze the joy in his heart. Left him hollow and fearful all over again.

"What happened?"

His daughter looked up at him with eyes Galukar remembered well. The ones he'd seen after destroying Arbite's skyship. They'd only been a glimmer, then. A candle. Now he saw the bonfire.

"My . . . My memories. My . . ." Felicia's voice cracked, and she told her father only in slow, sporadic bursts of coherence, regularly strangled off by the treacherous lungs that kept gasping where she meant to speak. He understood anyway. Listened, for perhaps the first time since she'd been born.

The anger came fast.

Galukar turned from Felicia, took three steps away. Beside him was a statue of his ancestor Karugar. It was a large thing but, he had heard, only to scale with the man as he had been in life. A thing of marble, it weighed more than eighty stone. More than some warhorses.

He grabbed it, dug his fingers in, gritted his teeth, and twisted. Galukar's arms flung the statue like it weighed nothing at all, and it soared far from him—disappearing to land near the center of the palace's acres-broad pond. A trebuchet could not have flung it so far, but the rage in Galukar's arms had not been exhausted yet.

A scream came from Galukar that even he didn't recognize, and his foot smashed down into the ground. It shook, shivered. The very earth feared him, dirt blasting apart into a gaping crater, air filling with debris as cracks ran through the bedrock beneath. The thrill of combat was starting to seep into him now, the hunger for blood.

He was *Galukar*, and he'd allowed some pitiful caster to . . . to . . . *hurt* his daughter. It was unforgivable, unacceptable. He rounded, ready to sprint his way to Magira then and there.

But Felicia stopped him. Not by doing anything in particular. She just stared at him. Backing away, hands raised, trembling. Her face, he saw, had been scraped where flying stones had caught it, blood starting to well beneath her superhuman skin.

"Father, *please.*"

Galukar's anger drained in a moment, replaced by another cocktail of emotion. One that hurt far, far more. But one he welcomed. He lowered his hands, calmed himself, dropped his gaze.

"I'm sorry," he whispered. "Felicia, I'm so—" His daughter hugged him before he could say another word. Galukar didn't think there was much to it. Probably she just needed to hug something. He wrapped his arm around her all the same, held her tight and felt her tremble. She didn't cry.

Neither did he, nor did he rage. Galukar had seen too many times what he brought upon himself by doing that, so instead he stood there and stewed in his regrets.

Mafari wanted his cooperation, and the archimage would get it. Galukar would hate him until the day he died, but he had greater priorities than crushing those he hated. Protecting those he loved.

Ado was a failure, a fraud, a wretch. Collin wouldn't have minded any of these things, if the woman hadn't insisted on telling him every other step.

At first he nodded, sympathetically. Not quite listening, mind, not after the first hour, just remaining there, smiling and urging her on, letting her release her acrid thoughts and cleanse them from her system. But the cleansing just didn't stop. The *whinging* just didn't fucking stop.

Collin hadn't spent much time around women—almost none, really, before Shaiagrazni's coalition—but he was fairly sure all of them weren't like this. Probably, it was a feature of royalty. Well, he didn't like it.

"Have you considered that it wasn't entirely your fault?" he tried, after a while. "Shaiagrazni did demolish most of your defenses already, thanks to your father resisting, and then there was the conflict with the Dark Lord. A single grotesquerie might've changed this, but you didn't even have that."

She seemed to think about it, and for one glorious moment, Collin thought she might actually shut up. She didn't, just found another avenue for her complaints and regrets. Discovered new failings to agonize over.

Collin wondered, vaguely, whether an arrow shot high into the air would land with enough force to kill . . . just, for instance, a flesh-crafted ranger of almost-Hero abilities, made to be even more durable than he already was.

His own arrows were iron, of course, and so much of their velocity would remain, at least if Shaiagrazni's advice on wind and ballistics was anything to go by. Would it go through the skull? Maybe not easily. Maybe not easily enough for a clean kill. So it'd need to be a neck shot, and—

"Are you even listening?" Queen Ado asked.

"No," Collin replied. Truthfully, because he was an idiot.

Her glare was quickly sparked, and quickly grown. Like a wild animal staring at him.

"You haven't been this entire time, have you?" she growled.

"That's not true," Collin replied, taking a step back, so intense was her rage. "I listened . . . to the first hour or so."

They'd been walking for the better part of a day, or rather he'd been walking and she'd been sitting in a repeatedly remade icy sledge he was pulling behind him. Sad fact was, Queen Ado wasn't nearly a match for his physical prowess. Collin was stronger than most warriors, and hauling a meager two hundred or so pounds barely even slowed him.

If she was grateful to have been spared the exertive walk, Queen Ado did not make the fact apparent in her features.

"I fucking hate you, you know." Collin froze, then turned to properly look back at her.

Ado had insulted him before, snapped at him. And he'd done it back. But he'd gotten the impression she was warming up to him, at least. However aloof she could be—however sheltered—she seemed, if nothing else, of a decent sort compared to most nobs. Someone able to change her mind when it needed changing, able to see past people's stations if only eventually.

But what he found in her stare now was *hatred*, of a more distilled kind than he could recall seeing anywhere else.

"You always thought you were above it all." She spit, actually *spit*. Collin stared at the foaming drool rolling down her chin. "Better than me. You're *not*. You're *nothing*, understand? Shit. Scum. You should be worshipping me, thanking me just to be allowed in my presence, you dirty-blooded fucking rat."

Collin went cold, but not from her words. He saw a potential enemy the precise moment before she became one in truth, lunging at him with a madwoman's fervor and more strength than Collin would ever have thought her body capable of mustering.

But not nearly enough.

He didn't even exert himself holding her back, just grabbed Ado by one shoulder and held his arm straight. She snarled, clawing at him, eyes wide. Collin shoved, lightly. Not lightly enough. The queen shot back like a trebuchet stone and landed hard, tumbling away from him in the muck.

She was up fast.

This time, it was ice Collin had to contend with. He chose *not* to, leaping aside as the great lances cut through the space he'd just been occupying.

Collin was a more potent fighter than Ado, deadlier in every measure. But she was a caster. In terms of sheer destructive power, even he couldn't match her. And unless he was as willing to kill her as she was him, there wasn't a single advantage to be found in her frail body.

More ice, a volley of it—all conjured by one woman instead of a company of archers. Collin rolled, and dove, and scrambled, and cursed as the icicles flitted by him faster than he reckoned a wooden bow could manage. Some hit trees and sank in deep. Others broke on impact. Either, he reckoned, had no business being in him.

It was inherently a delaying tactic, fleeing from her. Collin went through the basic mathematics of his situation. What would run out first—his luck or Ado's mana?

She'd been exhausted when he found her, but had had time to recover. He wasn't exactly evading her *narrowly*, but she wasn't exactly missing by a yard each time either. The thought of seriously hurting her made him uncomfortable.

But it was feeling increasingly like the only option he could humor.

That changed as Collin caught the movement. A fleeting thing, barely even there. It lasted a tenth of a quarter of a second, less time than a loosed arrow stayed in contact with its driving string. But he saw it, he caught it, and he turned his next dodge into a lunge. Ten yards separated Collin from his target. He crossed them faster than a human could react.

But not faster than whatever he'd seen. It was darting away already, like a sunbeam caught in dust. Not caught by Collin either, his thrown knife missed and beheaded a sapling behind its target. He turned the bladed attack into a physical one.

If it had been a human Collin was lunging toward, they might've done something stupid. Frozen up or kept retreating. But the vampire, which was what he now recognized the enemy as, just planted their feet and met his tackle with all their considerable strength.

Unfortunately for them, he'd had a plan for that. In the time they needed to right their footing, Collin broke his grip and slipped around, grabbed one leg to yank it up, and kicked the other out. They fell slowly, gravity a lazy thing by his standards, and he'd already freed another knife before they were one-quarter of the way to reaching the dirt. Steel came down against pale flesh, and the vampire stiffened.

Collin smiled, but it came out as a snarl.

"Release her or I'll kill you," he growled, drawing the blade across their neck. Slowly enough for them to react, fast enough for Ado not to. They had moments to stop their throat from being cut, their neck sawed open. Collin wondered if he'd get their head off before Ado's magic hit him.

Evidently, the vampire wasn't sure either. They released her.

"You're one of Lilia's bastards," Collin told the thing, recognizing its face as he studied it. "Why are you trying to kill us?"

For a moment, the vampire looked defiant. Then its face fell.

"Mafari—you know he's back by now. My mistress is aiming to . . . curry favor."

"By killing us," Collin finished.

"So you see—" The vampire got halfway into their sentence, then Collin found the answer to his question of decapitating it. The knife bit deep, sawed the rest of its way through, and separated head from body. He stood.

No use leaving an enemy alive, not one who was aiming to preserve its people. They'd need to move fast.

CHAPTER FOURTEEN

The attack was more sprint than battle, just like any good blitzing assault was. Hexeri and the dozen paladins tore off down the corridors with every ounce of their considerably superhuman speeds, mustering a wind ahead of them and practically shaking the walls with the sounds of their footfalls.

Hexeri winced. She was loud enough already, sprinting like this. Any one of the paladins, clad in hard, heavy steel as they were and with all a living body's innate clumsiness, would have been louder still. Twelve of them at once must surely have alerted every enemy within the whole fortress.

And they were numerous and widely spread enough that there was simply no avoiding them, regardless of speed.

Dullahan came by the dozens but perished fast. Hexeri had expected the powers she knew were typical of a paladin. These ones exceeded even that. None save Ensharia was remotely close to her equal—and even she did not hit that mark fully—but the other eleven all fought with a physicality and skill that was rare among their kind. One unit of defenders after another was torn apart, tied into combat by the wider mass of paladins and then cut to pieces as Ensharia or Hexeri turned their own strength to the encounters.

Fomors came and put up more resistance. But fell too. Then, after a while, more concerted efforts to halt them were made. The group smashed into a hastily assembled barricade, tangling with the dullahan manning it just as fomors smashed through the wall at their backs and pincered them from the other side. It was the most vicious fighting yet.

Hexeri rolled beneath a tendril, lashed shadows at the creator, and watched it stumble. A dullahan's axe came for her head, and she caught it by the handle, drove it back to its wielder's face, and thumbed one of the undead's eyes out. It didn't spasm with pain, but when she burst the other, it began swinging wildly. Tireless or not, unfeeling or not, the simple mechanical facts of sight were still a limit. Hexeri switched to more pressing threats.

She smashed another dullahan's helmet in, filled a third with shadow, and watched the necromantic substance writhe and crush it from within. The fighting was dying down, casualties mounting. Ensharia was straddling the neck of a fomor, smashing its skull with mace blows so strong, every impact sounded like rolling thunder. Hexeri ignored her, ignored everything. Just focused on fighting and killing, keeping her back guarded, her body in motion, her magic in flight.

All told, they lost a paladin, and two more were wounded, forced to hang back. The others seemed to do so with heavy hearts. Hexeri just noted that one of the ones she'd been worried about turning on her was among the discarded pair. As they disappeared around the corridor, closer now by far to the center of the Dark Lord's power, a figure emerged ahead.

Small, lithe, sinewy. Its body seemed covered entirely in scar tissue, from head to toe, face bound behind a metal mask.

They all froze. It wasn't a large creature, not well armored. It twitched with life, rather than undeath, moaned as it moved, pain seeming to rack its body with even the slightest motion. Hexeri could make out ridges of bone pressing up at every joint, as if it had shattered its whole body and healed improperly. Her hearing, superior to that of the mortals beside her, could even detect the malformed skeleton creaking and groaning with movement.

But somehow she couldn't bring herself to approach the creature. Couldn't bring herself to even try.

"Stay back," she warned, glancing at the paladins and finding herself surprised to see them obeying. Some instinct, perhaps. An intuition of what they were facing.

Hexeri's thoughts on the matter were interrupted before they could advance much farther. The creature moved.

It gasped, jaw unhinging with the cry of pain that erupted from it. Legs spread wide, fingers splayed, nails gouging into the stone underfoot, it shivered and shook, rattled and rocked. Roared a scream of agony so intense and pure that even Hexeri had never heard its equal. Not in life, not in centuries of unlife. She felt the magic washing from their enemy, then saw the *change*.

Skin split; hair emerged. Thick in some parts, gone in others. Covered by open wounds in others still. Blood streaked down the creature, and sickening cracks filled the air as its every bone snapped, twisted, lengthened, and reknitted back together. She realized what was happening only as its mask split apart and a scarred face fell to the ground beneath.

Where once something human had been, there was now only the simian-canine shape of a wolf head. The werewolf roared and pounced. Stone exploded beneath it like a meteor had struck the floor. Fifty yards separated it from Hexeri, gone in a second. Then it came down upon the nearest paladin like the guillotine blade upon a condemned neck.

Enchanted plate availed him nothing, Vigorous anatomy less. The man just erupted, body caved in, bones pulverized, meat pulped. He exploded like a butcher's sack crushed beneath an elephant's foot, spraying the air with gore, obfuscating the werewolf's position for a single instant.

That instant was time enough for raking claws to open another man's chest spine deep and drop him beside his obliterated ally.

Hexeri backed off, blindly hurled shadow at the lycan, and watched her magic roll off its hide like water on stone. This was bad. This might be the end of them all.

Ensharia, of course, did not hesitate for a moment. Even as her own allies backed away in fear, she closed and swung her mace like always. The werewolf twisted aside, faster than thought, and retaliated with another swipe. The woman's armor wasn't enchanted plate though. Hexeri had recognized the mysterious substance Shaiagrazni called keratin earlier, and saw its strength now as magic claws dug in, penetrated, but failed to do more than draw a few beads of blood from its wearer. The surprised lycan took another mace swing, this one successfully landing under its jaw and sending it back.

But only half a step. Faster than them, stronger than them, tougher than them. Hexeri took a moment to marvel at the stories of the creature—the vampire killer. And marvel at how all of them had managed to fall short.

A hand whipped around, caught Ensharia's helm. Closed fisted, not clawed. She still flew back, body hurtling like she was cast from a sling and smashing into the wall hard. The corridor trembled, and the other paladins attacked with a cry.

Of the five swings coming for the werewolf, fewer than half hit. It was so fast the mere humans, though successfully encircling it, may as well have been moving through liquid. Hexeri watched the assault continue; an axe barely break the skin, a flail bounce off its skull, a war pick dig into its thigh, a hammer rebound from the ribs. Then the werewolf's moves came. Two men opened up like meat on a carving block. It was the chance she'd needed, and her blood magic reached a crescendo as Hexeri lunged, grabbed the lycan, and concentrated.

But the ichor in this enemy was too magical, too potent. It warmed but didn't boil, and the werewolf struck her as it had the others. She flew the full length of the corridor before hitting a wall and being embedded into it.

Hexeri's skull broke like an eggshell. It wasn't easy to render a vampire incapacitated, scarcely more so than killing them. But she'd found the limit. Her body began to shut down, consciousness drifting, anatomical damage simply too intense for her vessel to continue housing whatever cannibalistic imprint still remained of her spirit. Her mind wavered, ran, drizzled away. She would waken, that much she knew. This was not a killing wound.

But this fight was no longer hers. She watched the werewolf tear apart those paladins who still stood to resist it and found her thoughts racked by a final question.

How could I have been so stupid . . . ?

Hexeri awoke, gasped reflexively for air she didn't need, plucked herself from the mangled stone. She heard the ruckus before she saw its product, a wall blasted inward and flying debris filling the room. Then the tide changed.

She'd been gone for a minute, maybe. Long enough that the paladins had all either died or stopped their fighting, cowering back from the werewolf as it circled around them, snarling and twitching. The beast looked up at the explosion, coiling itself back for another pounce as a tall, broad-shouldered bald man strode into the corridor. His skin was black, his eyes considering. Magic an ocean's weight against her senses.

Hexeri recognized Archimage Mafari just before his enemy sprang into motion.

The werewolf struck something that might have been translucent to mortal eyes, but stood out in Hexeri's vision as a great discolored plane in the air. The shield buckled, collapsed just a moment after Mafari's eyes widened and the archimage disappeared. He reemerged from nowhere, twenty yards from the werewolf and raising his hands in a sweeping gesture.

Already, the lycan was turning to smash into him. Too slow this time. The air ruptured, peeling back into a great circle of orange-hot *something*. The stuff sprayed out in a torrent, as if there were some great pipe it was exiting, moving impossibly fast and blasting the lycan off its feet upon impact. The creature screamed, slid back as it was driven down the corridor and buried under glowing, burning, bubbling . . .

Magma. It was *magma*. Conjured through a portal, pressurized somehow, and left to vent itself into the enemy. Mafari stemmed the tide only after a few more seconds had passed. His hands were already moving as the werewolf got to shaky feet.

It was hurt. And Mafari wasn't done. The archimage gestured again, and more light glimmered before him. This time, Hexeri didn't see what emerged, not fully. Just streaks of gray—rock, she thought—before they smashed into the werewolf faster than anything not fired from Shaiagrazni's cannons. The creature flew back, rolling, scraping, blood flecking from it. Another distortion in the air emerged beside it, and another jet of magma thundered into its body while it was down. The werewolf was driven into the corridor's wall. Then through it.

Hexeri watched it just disappear, plummeting down out of the fortress to smash against the stone below. Could it survive that?

She wasn't sure. It was a large creature, heavy and dense. It would fall faster than a man, and land harder even at the same speed for all its mass. It was wounded already.

But it was so, *so* durable. She caught herself hoping against hope that gravity would do what she hadn't managed, then rose, shakily, to her feet.

Other figures were entering the corridors now, magi. Hexeri saw the deferent gazes they shot to Mafari, the awe. She half understood it herself now. But that didn't change the cold fear of having his gaze fall upon her.

"I know what you are," he told her, calmly, flatly. The tone of a man ready and willing to do everything he just had all over again. Unnecessary—the first gout of magma would crush Hexeri by itself.

"Progeny of Lilia," Hexeri confirmed. "At your service." She was loath to defer, but she was much more opposed to death than she was humiliation. The archimage just turned. "Detain her and the paladins. Let us venture farther inward."

It all came as a blur. No more frenzied flight through the fortress, just an orderly march. The resistance was, Hexeri realized, destroyed. The Dark Lord's servitors and guardians either crushed already or driven away. She was impressed, despite herself.

But not half as impressed as when they entered what was surely the Dark Lord's laboratory.

"What *is* that?" One of the magi gasped, staring, Hexeri presumed, at the great ripple in the air and the humming, glowing, *whispering* construct of matter and magic that surrounded it.

"An abomination," another growled. "Archimage, do you want me to destroy it?"

Mafari eyed the man as if he'd just been propositioned and was not remotely flattered.

"Of course not. Doing so could cause whatever dark magics it channels to spiral out of control. Can you not feel their intensity already? This fortress, the land around it, and perhaps the continent would be razed."

Every face present, save those that were too black or bloodless to do so, paled.

"We will guard this area," Mafari continued, heedless of the fear. "I suspect the Dark Lord, perhaps Shaiagrazni too, has disappeared through this gateway. They will return, if so. I will find a way to close this portal and trap them. Failing that . . . I will meet them as they leave it and crush them both."

Without another word, the archimage vanished.

CHAPTER FIFTEEN

The portal—the rift, whatever it was—remained blessedly stagnant at first. Or perhaps not so blessedly. Its relative inactivity gave the present magi nothing more to focus on than Hexeri and the surviving paladins. The men had it easiest. They were . . . men.

Hexeri had, of course, been called a whore. She'd been called a whore often. She was a powerful woman, and powerful women tended to attract that label more than perhaps any others.

What surprised her though, what actually shocked her despite her long inoculation against the word, was being called a whore more times within a single hour than she perhaps had in the totality of her unlife before it.

It was *almost* impressive, but more . . . concerning. The type of thing to actually leave her wondering if something was diagnosably wrong with the magi. They didn't seem to even know any other words. Every other sentence from any of their mouths contained it—they used it like it was her and Ensharia's names.

The paladin, at least, did not seem any more bothered than Hexeri was. Not surprised at all, even. Hexeri wondered whether she'd had close encounters with the magi of Magira before, then tucked the suspicion away for later. She had greater concerns for the time being.

"Bitch," came a voice, high and sort of jittery. Hexeri looked up to see she was being addressed by one of the magi. Well, at least he'd chosen the *second* most popular word instead. "You're being moved. Come this way." Hexeri didn't glare, or anything else that might set him on edge. If she was to make her move, she'd make it when guards were low and tensions thin. The shackles around her wrists were *heavy*, but raw strength wasn't everything. She'd broken out of thicker more than once before.

Ensharia was not being left behind, Hexeri saw as she moved. Rather the paladin was being taken elsewhere—as were the others. Splitting the prisoners up. Not a bad idea, and, given it was being used now, it implied the magi were occupying a considerable area within the fortress. Hexeri wasn't sure how useful that information would be, but it was more information in any case. She committed it to memory as she moved.

Halfway across the room, with her arms still bound and her form still watched too laxly by the arrogant magi surrounding it, Hexeri caught a change in the air. Doubtless, it was the product of her centuries. A moment later, the magi seemed to pick up on it too, tensing and staring. A few seconds after that, even the paladins were turning on the portal.

It was moving but remaining still. Twisting but remaining straight. The most deafeningly loud silence Hexeri had ever heard, the most blindingly bright darkness she'd ever seen. The most terrifying mundanity she'd ever felt. And whatever it was—whatever was happening to cause the sensation running down her dead nerves—it was growing more intense with every moment that passed. Instinct took over, and not just hers.

Magic came flying at it in a great fusillade, fireballs, jets of water, twisting black thorns, and shots of steel. Boulders, sandblasts, magma, lightning, coils of air, acid, poison, pure energy, and psionic beams. Every way there was to kill that was not illegal within the walls of Magira seemed to be unleashed at once. She felt the air contorting, the room threatening to come apart at the sheer intensity of it, and then Hexeri witnessed two figures emerge from the portal and stride out into the maelstrom.

One, the larger, was the Dark Lord. He stepped forth and simply absorbed the attacks with his armor and body. The other, Shaiagrazni, stood behind him and began to transform, body shifting and warping. It seemed to be the exact opposite of how the lycan had done it. There was no inner beast breaking out from beneath; rather his new form was being constructed from the skin level out.

It took him only seconds, Hexeri thought. Difficult to be sure, even for her eyes, through the maelstrom of magic. When he was done, he and the Dark Lord simply lunged at the magi without exchanging even a single word.

To call what followed a massacre would have been to speak too lightly. The Dark Lords moved through the hundred or so magi as if they were helpless children, armor turning away magical blasts like a gentle breeze. Weapons ripping through shields like spiderwebs. Shaiagrazni wielded some great whip, swinging it through the air and bisecting a half dozen men with every crack. His cannon had been replaced by that arcane *flame* weapon, and Hexeri felt the heat of it as great pools of blazing liquid were splashed around the room to consume their victims.

For his part, the Dark Lord, the original Dark Lord, seemed comparably effective. Less overtly destructive perhaps, less able to mount up the casualties, but no more impeded by his enemies. Where his mace went, lives ended. He walked through the hail of magic without even responding to his enemies' attacks, and Hexeri felt somewhat queasy at the sight of bodies simply bursting apart into, as far as she could tell, pure liquid each time they absorbed one of his hits.

All that, and the sheer speed of the casters was like nothing human. In perhaps five seconds, they had both emptied the room of bodies. Living ones, at least. Their remains still littered the place, and the floor seemed to now be colored red.

Hexeri realized then how astonishingly hungry she was, body moving before her mind could direct it. She dropped down to her knees, extended her tongue, and began licking the ichor up. It was honey on her tongue, joy itself. Life in all its infinite nuances and wonders. And it was hers, falling into the depths of her being and fraying apart to become stuff of pure, reanimating magic.

Magus blood was a delicacy she'd had the pleasure of trying before. She gorged on it now, actually clearing out a patch several feet across by the time she'd finally had her fill. Hexeri looked up, lower face spattered with gore, to find several eyes upon her.

Shaiagrazni looked impassive. The Dark Lord, without his helmet now and a surprisingly young-looking man of handsome dignity, was if anything amused. Ensharia looked more disgusted than Hexeri had yet seen her, while the other paladins remained too helmeted to tell.

She didn't feel any sudden flashes of self-consciousness. That was a fledgling's prerogative. Hexeri simply flooded the insides of her shackles with darkness and pulled the substance taut, letting the fragile mechanisms within break and dropping the bonds off of herself. She found the deed easier than usual.

Magus blood. For a while, a few hours, days, or even—given how much she'd drunk—weeks, everything with magic would be easier. There were benefits to stealing the essence of others for life.

"Alright, Silenos." She greeted him with a nod. "I'm here to rescue you."

Shaiagrazni eyed her for a moment, just one. Then tilted his head as he replied.

"Adonis, there are intruders in your fortress. I imagine this means your lycanthrope has been killed."

"Annoying." The Dark Lord—apparently named Adonis—sighed. "It will take centuries to create a new one."

Hexeri felt her guts turn to liquid and started sprinting before a conscious thought on the matter could even form. She was fast, inhumanly fast, but today her legs might as well have carried her at a sloth's pace. The doorway she lunged toward was splashed with burning oil from Shaiagrazni's weapon, barring her way. At a glance back, she saw the other prisoner, Ensharia, immobilized just as efficiently.

The other paladins were not. Those idiots made the mistake of attacking the man called Adonis and were torn apart sooner than an eye could blink.

"*No!*" Ensharia screamed, wrestling against the Dark Lord for a single moment before Silenos Shaiagrazni glided over to take her from him. Her body was encased in . . . a magus. Or what was left of him, organic tissue of his corpse melted down and wrapped around her like some bony cocoon.

"Be still," Shaiagrazni urged her. "You are a most valuable research specimen. It would irk me if you were to damage yourself in any way before I was able to properly study you."

"Bastard!" she snarled, not seeming to hear him. "I was right about you. I knew it then, and I know now. I'm glad I left. I only wish I'd known better than to ever aid you in the first place."

The Dark Lord's head tilted. "Ah, this is the paladin you gained assistance from early on, Silenos?"

"Yes," Shaiagrazni confirmed, looking far from pleased. "I was, as you have probably inferred, desperate at the time."

Ensharia's scream would have woken a sleeping dragon, but it didn't faze either of the men now holding her prisoner. A shrieking baby would have been no less of a threat to them, Hexeri suspected. That was simply the level of power they operated in. Dark Lord and New Dark Lord. It was fitting they shared a name, and would have been even if it weren't for their new cooperation.

But a question still gnawed at her.

"This is odd." She frowned. "Not even . . . just normal-you odd. This is stupid odd. Why are you doing this? Why are you making enemies of Lilia's progeny, of your only envoy into the paladins? I don't get it. You've been playing politics well before now, and suddenly you just abandon it all? What's . . ." Her eyes flicked to the portal. "What are you planning?"

Shaiagrazni eyed her, his gaze like a midwinter's night.

"The only reason I do not cripple you for your insolence is because you showed some deductive prowess in asking that question the way you have," he informed her. "I am Master Shaiagrazni, not Silenos."

She decided not to say more, at that. Hexeri didn't know how much leniency she'd earned herself, or how quick this apparently unmasked Shaiagrazni would be to punish her when it ran out. It was no great shock to see him change so suddenly. Hexeri had known too many men to be surprised by double-faced ones anymore. But it was a concern. He had been their last hope against Mafari. If he was no longer even *interested* in cooperation—

No, back up. Why was he no longer interested in cooperation? He surely still had something to gain from the most powerful active vampire in existence, unless . . .

"I do not need you anymore," Shaiagrazni explained, a note of triumph in his voice. "My days of scraping and bowing to your petty customs, of appeasing your inept leaders, are over. This is the tempered schism." He gestured to his portal, wrist rolling and fingers splaying in a flourish. "You could not even begin to fathom its complexity, but to simplify the matter, it is rending apart the barriers separating worlds. Once it is completed, it will be able to do so permanently and completely."

Hexeri's heart would have stopped then and there, if it hadn't already centuries ago.

"Yes," Shaiagrazni continued, apparently recognizing the dread in her face. "You are right to be afraid. Because soon enough, House Shaiagrazni themselves will emerge to take this world, and then move on to take all others. The cosmos belongs to the strong. And we are the strongest."

CHAPTER SIXTEEN

Silenos felt an overwhelming sense of déjà vu as they began the preparations to summon the very Entity that had displaced him. It was not the pleasant kind, rather the kind that came when one had already been burned and now heard the crackling of flame and smelled the sterility of smoke.

"*They* will not be able to interfere with this, will they?" he asked Adonis, gesturing at their now-bound prisoners. Ensharia still glared at him with undisguised hate, Hexeri with unhidden fear. Both sentiments felt nostalgic to Silenos. It had been so very long since he had enjoyed a proper reception from others.

"They will not," Adonis replied. "I am far beyond your childish understanding of esoterica and have taken steps to ensure the Entity will not be able to communicate with them at all."

Silenos nodded. "Good."

They continued their work in relative silence, neither having much to say to the other. Not compared to the imperative of combining skills and empowering their work. Once more, he was overcome with the satisfaction of using his powers alongside a near equal. Silenos let himself appreciate the sensation while it lasted.

But it did not last long. If there was any downside to the state, it would be that. They needed so little time to accomplish anything with their knowledge combined.

The summoning was completed, and the world became an ocean of magical power.

Silenos would have been impressed at any other time; it was, after all, the strongest Entity he had ever conjured. But his time in the Shallow Depths had spoiled him. Nothing he'd encountered there was a match for this creature, but the magical ambience was more than any one being could fill the mundane world with, however great its presence. He forced himself to look at the broken geometry of its body.

Changed, since the first summoning. That was no great surprise. Entities were loath to remain stagnant. Save for their magic. As always, this one was beyond impressive. Wielding the power to change the world, or break it. The power to do . . .

Anything?

Silenos felt a sense of unease building in the pit of his stomach, a mental conflict too abstract and distant for him to understand.

"Entity, we have conjured you, and now we bind you. Defy us if you dare."

It dared, instantly. Magic thrashed against the walls of its existential cage like storm winds against a mountain, but the binding held strong. With Silenos's and Adonis's power combined, and levered by the hybrid's esoteric nature, they had conjured a shackle even this being could not break.

And yet he *did* feel it strain. A terrifying sensation. Even with two named of House Shaiagrazni amplifying their potence a hundredfold, it was making the binding *strain*. Silenos again felt that feeling.

It can do anything. A thought was brewing in the back of his mind, too great to give voice, too dangerous. Too *wrong. Immoral* and *unforgivable.* He banished it, yet it remained.

"What would you ask of me."

Even now the Entity framed its response as a request. Silenos glanced at Adonis and saw that his fellow Shaiagrazni, of course, had caught the deception.

"Demand, Entity, we demand of you. You will obey us, no matter what." The binding shimmered, constricting the being with a tightening noose of magic that would have beheaded a mountain. Even the Entity shrieked in agony.

"**And what would you demand of me.**" The voice echoed in Silenos's mind, unchanged by the torment inflicted upon its owner.

He remained silent, letting Adonis speak. He was the one who'd mastered esoterica between them. The results of his last attempt still stung, easily avoidable oversight though they had been.

Adonis inhaled, readied to speak. The words came out.

"You are to resurrect the magus known in this world as Arion Falls, freeing his cognitive essence from its necromantic cage and restoring his body."

The silence was deafening.

"**Granted.**" Silenos wondered whether he was imagining the note of amusement or, rather, whether he was imagining it more than he was the Entity's voice as a whole. It was gone before he could ponder the notion more, simply disappearing like a lost memory.

Slowly, Silenos turned to Adonis. The look upon his face was not rage, nor quite disbelief. It was . . . stupefaction. A simple refusal to respond, as if his features had been paralyzed by the shock of what he'd seen.

He must have been more practical in calling upon his magic, for Silenos's cannon caught him directly in the face and merely blasted him back rather than removing the head from his body. Everything exploded into motion at once, after that.

Adonis erupted from the ground only a second into Silenos's transformation. It was a very long period of incapacitation, by the standards of their inhuman reflexes, but not nearly long enough. The wall of flames wrapped around him bought precious milliseconds longer. Silenos used it to continue his transformation, to throw himself into the safety of war form. To unbalance Adonis by drawing his attention to the imminent completion, and thus distract him from the great volume of blasting oil already conjured with his fleshcrafting.

It detonated just as he leaped over it, shaped container of keratin compressing the blast enough to direct a considerable fraction of it upward. It was nothing like the shaped charges Silenos had seen cut clean through heavy metal plating, and Adonis's magically strengthened flesh was nothing like mere steel, but the primary aim had been to blast him from Silenos's sight. Time was what he needed. Every second was a treasure beyond price. He'd just won several more.

Silenos did many things very quickly. He extended a tendril of nervous tissue from his shoulder, wrapping it around the tempered schism and interfacing with its magic via the tactility it provided. As he did, he stormed toward the bound prisoners. Hexeri and Ensharia were the closest. He would have called it fate were he a savage imbecile whose intellect had been tainted by superstition.

The vampire was free already, and the paladin, Silenos saw, had already half snapped her own shackles when he tore them asunder with one swift tug. She glared up at him.

"This changes nothing," Ensharia spit. "You're still—*What the fuck?!*" Silenos interrupted her as the tempered schism split reality once more by reaching out to grab the woman by her head, then hurling her across the expansive room and through the break in reality. Hexeri had barely even reacted when he did the same to her, while the hybrid did not even protest at receiving such treatment. And then it was his turn to lunge for it.

Adonis burst back down from the ceiling, slamming into the floor before him. Silenos's cannon screamed. It was a blank shot, filling the air with more smoke than Adonis would have expected, clouding his vision and confounding him just long enough for the streak of shadestuff to hit home. Silenos saw his former apprentice stumble away, and *then* blasted him with his primary weapon.

He double loaded it, pressing it beyond its structural limits and feeling even his own augmented bones and armor plating shiver at the strain of its own power. But the results spoke for themselves, and they spoke loudly. Adonis shot back as if he'd been the object caught in Silenos's barrel, barging into a stone wall and breaking it beneath his mass. Silenos didn't pause to check the damage. He couldn't afford to grant his enemy even an instant. He'd almost been beaten by Adonis before—had been beaten, and would have perished without interference. This was an enemy who demanded every screed of his focus.

So he fired again, while Adonis was still reeling. The explosive shell engulfed him, and a moment later, another solid slug drove him farther into his den of cratered stone. Silenos let off another shot with every other stride he took toward the schism, tempted to hope that each would prove the last his enemy could survive. Of course, he knew better. His makeshift weaponry had not been made to slay an enemy of high-Shaiagraznian war magic. It would struggle against his own defenses, and Adonis may well have exceeded even those. He cast more shadestuff over him to compensate, fired again, again. Another step to the schism.

Motion exploded outward, seeming to shake the entire room. Silenos's next shot went high as Adonis went low, scraping beneath it and driving his mace upward for Silenos's ribs. His free arm, now shaped into a shield, caught the blow, and Silenos stumbled away. Adonis tried to close, hissed as Silenos's tail whipped out to drive a self-destructive liter of shadestuff against him. The necromantic substance ate away the very limb that had wielded it even as it attacked Silenos's foe. He ignored the pain, shut the relevant nerve endings off, and *fired again.*

Somehow, Adonis twisted aside from his cannon and smashed his mace down against its barrel. Keratin surrendered and collapsed inward, and Silenos was disarmed. Almost. His shield rammed against Adonis's chest and sent him stumbling before he could follow up— Silenos had learned a thing or two about melee, however undignified it was. He used his chance well, reshaping his cannon.

There was no time for a complicated firearm, so he settled for a lance of hardened nacre and restructured his mangled tail tip into a similar barb. Adonis backed away for a moment, cautious. Silenos drove on before his former apprentice could gather his wits and realize that he still had the vast advantage in close quarters experience. A thrust, which would have been parried were it not a feint. Silenos feinted again with the whip of his tail and used Adonis's involuntary flinch well as he cracked the shield down. His limbs were longer by far, owing to his towering height, and the reach was his. Between his long lance and short shield also, he had greater options at any distance.

But the strength was Adonis's. The speed too, and perhaps even the resilience. Silenos's war form was, fundamentally, a compromise. If it could match an equal master of close quarters magic, then no Shaiagrazni would ever choose anything else. If it was unstoppable in the new world, it was only because Silenos himself had such a laughable excess of raw power over its residents.

That was not an advantage he enjoyed here. Close to double Silenos's age, Adonis was his equal in the fields of mana reserves and magical weight. Perhaps, by some small margin, even his superior. Silenos roared.

It was not some animalistic bellow, of course. The indignity of that would kill him as sure as his enemy's mace. No, Silenos *roared* to make use of the carefully reconstructed abdominal musculature he'd devised following his and Adonis's initial bout. They proved effective. As Silenos's ears warded themselves off and barricaded against the sound, Adonis's remained vulnerable. The stone underfoot split apart under the atmospheric pressure of an engine made to generate sound more perfectly than any other. Pneumonic strength, blasting oil, other hydraulic mechanisms that all worked in cohesion.

Blood trickled down Adonis's ears, running out of his helmet. It was, Silenos thought, remarkable. He had not only failed to instantly perish, but was still conscious. An utterly infuriating display of contempt for his will, demanding punishment.

But not now. Silenos's ability to torment Adonis at his will had been left in the past. For the moment, he settled with smashing the caster aside and hurling himself through the schism. He watched, falling back into it, as Adonis righted himself, clambered to his feet, and prepared to give chase.

Then paused and, with a gesture, closed the opening after him. Silenos was given a few moments to wonder which of them had actually gotten the better of the other in that exchange, then the schism sealed itself and rendered his question moot. It was over now, which meant Adonis was no longer a problem.

Not until Silenos had survived whatever he was falling toward . . . Or failed to.

CHAPTER SEVENTEEN

THEN

Silenos didn't like these strangers, not one bit. They were all too . . . smug. Thought more of themselves than they ought to have, and talked funny. It was like being lectured in cursive. They looked like him, at least. Sharing the bronze-brown skin and dark eyes of his village, but that was all they had in common. Especially now. Silenos's village was changing before his eyes, buildings demolished and replaced with new ones, people herded around for "evaluation."

He was one of those people, except the strange outsiders had taken one look at him and barked something about "anomalous brilliance." That sounded about right to him, but it'd led to his being separated from the rest of his people and dragged off somewhere else. Then walking, a lot. Walking through one building to another, shuffling onto strange metal birds that stayed too still and didn't flap their wings to fly, then riding inside the bellies of those birds to be taken somewhere else. Where he'd walk again.

There had only been one other person for company on the journey, meeting Silenos somewhere around the third bird he was ushered onto and staying with him from that point onward. About his age of eleven, the boy was tall but reedy, seemed to quiver with every moment as if expecting the air itself to strike him, and never met anyone's eye.

Silenos didn't like him, found him annoying right off the bat. But he struck up a conversation because the alternative was hours of silence.

"What's your name?" he asked. The boy actually shrank back from him, not meeting his eye as he answered.

"Juragai," he murmured.

"What are you doing?" Silenos demanded. "Why are you acting as if I'm about to bite you? We're just talking."

The boy still didn't meet his eye, nor did he lean forward again. "Sorry," he replied, still not meeting Silenos's gaze. It cast a pulse of fury through him, left his teeth grinding, but Silenos buried the irritation and just moved his eyes ahead.

As the journey progressed, he did get more conversation from the boy at least. He was also from a settlement conquered by this House Shaiagrazni, though his had been a more defended city. Silenos felt a stab of worry as he heard the name Erogyn. It was one of the more martial places in the region, home, he had heard, to at least a hundred thousand warriors sustained by magically grown crops, and the casters to support them.

But the way Juragai told it, they'd fallen in less than a day. Just who were these people they were heading toward, and what did they want with him?

Silenos was to find out before long.

The great metal bird began to descend, and Silenos was granted a look out of its window as it did. He saw an impossibility sprawling out beneath him. A city the size of a country, buildings like mountains, spires caressing the skies themselves. It was all constructed with the most bizarre architecture he'd ever seen. Impossible shapes and structures he couldn't begin to guess at the solidity of towering over the streets, which all measured wide enough that a whale might lie across their breadth.

The boy called Juragai and Silenos were, for once, of a mind as they saw it draw closer. Falling completely silent. This wasn't a group of strangers they were approaching; it was a civilization of . . . of gods.

As the bird finally stopped on the ground, they were ushered out of it and swiftly toward one of the buildings. The building, Silenos realized as he approached, was by far the tallest, measuring what he could only estimate was literally miles high. His mouth dried at the sight, hanging open, eyes wide with disbelief. A glance at Juragai showed the other boy had fallen close to catatonia.

Of course, both of them continued walking. How could they not?

Wide halls surrounded them within the building, displaying an infinity of wonders Silenos had no context to name, let alone understand. Great monsters that seemed frozen in place, artifacts humming and spitting sparks where they clung to walls, works of art, grotesqueries of nightmare—every shade on the spectrum of awe seemed displayed upon the walls.

To his shame, he found himself snaking closer to Juragai as the two of them continued on, guards shepherding them up through the building. The boy reciprocated. When they reached the stairs, a question occurred to Silenos.

"We're not going to the top floor, are we?" He frowned.

"You are," one of their custodians grunted.

"But we can't!" Silenos rejoined. "My legs will give out. It's too high!"

"Just walk." The man's voice was low, hard. He was not making a request. Silenos grimaced and began the ascent.

And yet, it was over in under a minute. Just a few dozen steps took Silenos to a sprawling room with transparent walls that looked out over every angle of the spectacular city and seemed suspended above the streets below by . . .

Miles.

He felt suddenly queasy. These people didn't even need to obey the laws of space itself. No wonder they had faced no resistance.

"We're on the highest floor," he croaked.

"Second highest." Juragai frowned. Silenos glanced at the boy.

"What?"

"S-sorry."

"Just explain it. What do you mean second highest?"

The boy looked at his feet, as if embarrassed. "It just . . . is, you know? I felt the . . . power that was doing whatever needed doing to send us this high so fast, and it wasn't wrapped around the top floor."

Silenos glared at him. "You're telling me you felt that from outside, when you could see the whole building?"

He'd felt something, he admitted, but only now, inside and surrounded by it.

"Time for talk is over," the guard cut in. He was an ugly creature, tall and broad, flesh seemingly encased in biological armor. Silenos shut up promptly as he spoke. "Follow."

Of course, they followed. Silenos had always prided himself on being a strong-willed, rebellious soul. A day in the company of House Shaiagrazni had taught him better than that. Fear, apparently, would teach a person things they never even *wanted* to know about themselves.

The guard took them to the first of their trials, a test of will. They held their hands over flames and retracted them only when given permission. The intent was for most to fail and merely see how long they *could* obey. Silenos passed easily, he learned, more than tripling the average time. Juragai barely succeeded.

Their next test was worse still, much worse.

Control. Silenos was taught the basics of grasping his magic and giving it direction, then he was forced to do so on a scale of millimeters and instants. He was hurt when he failed, and hurt more when he succeeded. Pressed to a point of racking agony so great that every coherent thought was a trial in and of itself. He was closer to Juragai's performance in this regard, able to exceed most of the tested still, but far from easily. If anything, he was surprised to see how well the other boy did. Perhaps his spinelessness was not actually spine deep. Though perhaps it was.

More tests came, then more still. Silenos passed each one by far. Juragai passed most by a hair, failed some, and succeeded at others by a greater margin still. In the end, there was only one left—the examination of magical prowess and intuition.

It felt strange. Casters had always been a distant thing to Silenos, not known to his tiny village. Juragai seemed more comfortable with the prospect, though he himself claimed that he had never even suspected himself to be countable among them. An impoverished child apparently, one without the resources or time needed to hone mana. Now the damage of that deprivation would be seen.

Both of them placed their hands upon a gem of humming, unsettling power and waited. Silenos watched his stone discolor, light green hues bleeding into its glassy transparency. He waited for the entire volume to change, but it didn't. Only a fraction, a fifth, perhaps more or less. He glanced up at the attendant, concern hitting him, but they seemed far from disapproval. Shocked, even.

"Congratulations, prodigy," she croaked. Silenos felt that word echo around in him.

Prodigy.

Apparently one-fifth was more than most managed, a great deal more. He grinned. Prodigy. It was far from unfitting, and it sat with him as he glanced over to Juragai.

And saw the boy's own crystal was still having color oozed into it. Crimson, rather than Silenos's green. One-fifth of it changed, then one-quarter. Then, he thought, close to a third. Silenos looked to the attendant and saw pure disbelief upon her face, a tremble in her body, a blistering awe shining out from behind her eyes.

"I . . . must notify my superiors about this." She gasped, practically *sprinting* away. Silenos scowled at Jurgagai when they were alone.

"Sorry," the boy mumbled.

"For what?" Silenos snapped. "You didn't *do* anything. I'm still special."

Still *almost* as special. Silenos tried to hide his frustration, but it probably slipped out anyway. Fortunately, he wasn't left with it to fester for long. The attendant returned, and several guards returned with her.

"This way, if you please," she began, eyes flitting between Silenos and Juragai, face . . . tight. Posture somehow wary, head dipping slightly as she spoke. If Silenos didn't know better, he'd have assumed it was *reverence* he was getting from this woman. But adults weren't reverent to children. It just wasn't done. Was it?

House Shaiagrazni were a strange lot . . .

They followed the attendant as she led them into a smaller chamber, walls marked with odd sigils, and at a single gesture, it hummed with power. Power Silenos could feel, now that he'd been inducted into at least the very basics of magic. It whipped them away. Upstairs.

The top floor of House Shaiagrazni's tallest tower was not as high as Silenos would have thought. It was higher. Higher by far, peaking well over any of the clouds and struck by wind currents so strong they were actually visible. He shuffled into it absently, staring out at the broad windows, the indulgent decoration, the *power* on display everywhere.

Could I have this one day?

It was a sudden thought that even he couldn't identify the origins of, but irresistible in its promises. Perhaps he could. He'd surprised the attendant, been called a prodigy. That couldn't happen often, right? Whatever the average was to become a Shaiagrazni caster, he had to be above it, right? Quite a bit above it. So . . .

One day, perhaps he could. One day, perhaps, he could be among the most powerful beings . . . anywhere, ever. He wasn't sure how to feel about that, enticement aside. It felt too big. Too dangerous. Keep your head down and know your place—that was what he'd been taught.

But now the people who'd taken control of his village without effort or delay were telling him his place might be very high, indeed.

The thought was interrupted as Silenos and Juragai came to a stop before a tall bronze-skinned woman of wavy black hair and almost incandescent-pink eyes. She was quite literally the most beautiful thing—human or otherwise—he had ever seen, and she smiled.

"Good evening, worms," she said happily. "I am Mistress Kammani, Ancestor of the Shaiagraznian Science, Dominator of Reality, and Progenitor of Arts Most Ancient, Elder of House Shaiagrazni. I will be your master from now on, teaching you both the art of Shaiagraznian magic."

Juragai, surprisingly, spoke first.

"I . . . I don't think I could learn—"

"Do not be humble," she interrupted sternly. "It is immoral. Now, what are your names?"

A pause, then they both, as one, realized how awful an idea it would be to keep her waiting. They gave them.

"Silenos," Kammani echoed. "I like your name. Well, Juragai and Silenos, prepare yourself for your studies. You are inducted aspirants of House Shaiagrazni now."

CHAPTER EIGHTEEN

Silenos landed just a few yards from Ensharia, seemingly having fallen from the sky itself. The ground beside her was springy, bouncy. It shook as he impacted it, waves of force actually running through its substance and rebounding her up a few feet into the air.

She'd forgotten how big he was, in that monstrous form of his. This one was changed somewhat. Armor plating rearranged here or there, limbs tweaked in shape and weaponry different. She recognized him, nonetheless.

"You . . ." Ensharia backed away from him more out of reflex at anything, feeling sick just to be near him. Shaiagrazni's eyes snapped onto her lightning quick, urgency burning bright enough to be easily recognized despite his monstrous visage.

"Do not back any farther away," Shaiagrazni hissed. "It is dangerous enough that you spent entire milliseconds here without me, and fortunate that I had the prescience to select an area of the Shallow Depths with such disparate temporal speed to your world."

Ensharia understood perhaps one word in two from that linguistic volley, but she'd learned that Shaiagrazni didn't speak so hastily or desperately over nothing. She halted, despite herself, looking around.

"Where . . . Where did you take us?"

The vampire, Hexeri, moved in to just behind her, clearly not wanting to chance proximity with Shaiagrazni. His body slowly shrank down as he spoke, abandoning his war form for reasons beyond Ensharia.

"The Shallow Depths."

Ensharia frowned. "That's oxymoronic."

"And you are just moronic," he replied. "Be silent. The world you have seen is not all there is, and that would remain the case even if you had visited each one able to support life. There is more to reality than realms hospitable to our fragile existences."

There it was. Ensharia had missed a few things about her time with the caster—he had, in some ways, been uncommonly good to her. Not caring about her sex, valuing her for ability more than anything. But that abrasive, sneering contempt was never more than a word away. She tried her best to untangle the man's invaluable knowledge from his valueless superiority complex and decode what she was being told.

"So we're somewhere . . . magical? Nonphysical? But . . . Hang on, what do you mean support life? This place is supporting our lives."

"Speak for yourself," the vampire cut in. "I don't need supporting."

"Yes," Shaiagrazni explained impatiently. "You do. You do not eat, drink, or breathe, but were it not for my magic enveloping us all and stabilizing the area around us with causality and logic, your very matter would evaporate and break. The substance of your body still exists around the core tenets of all physical matter. Without them, you would have no body."

Ensharia didn't think a vampire could actually pale, but this one looked like it might.

"Why couldn't you leave me be . . ." came a groaning voice. All eyes moved to the source, a . . .

Oh fuck, a *severed head* dangling from Silenos's side. He glanced down at it, sighing. The thing was repulsive—monstrous, even. Larger than normal, misshapen, looking almost as if someone had decided to beat a normal cranium into pieces and stopped one quarter of the way in.

"Be silent," Shaiagrazni told the head, looking at it with genuine annoyance. "That goes for the rest of you as well. I am thinking." His face twisted with concentration, the very same kind Ensharia had seen infect his features when he was agonizing over one creation or another. The weaponry she'd heard he'd unveiled since her departure was impossible to assess from stories alone. Some claimed he was an upstart hedge wizard, others that he had a personal cannon able to disembowel mountains. The former Ensharia knew for a fact was false. The latter . . .

The latter she found herself *hoping* was. The days of Silenos Shaiagrazni being an ally of good had died with her friends, and now the regret at ever having let him trick her was welling up anew.

Something rushed overhead, dragging Ensharia's gaze upward. Her legs went weak at the sight.

"*Dear God . . .*"

"Yes." Shaiagrazni sighed. "Yes, it's all very terrifying and beyond your comprehension—as I said, be quiet. You do not need to distract me while processing your idiot existential crisis."

Ensharia *was* quiet, but it had nothing to do with his angry insistence. She remained as silent as the mouse catching sight of a gliding hawk, trembling, staring, and wishing with everything she had that it would not take note of her as she had of it.

This time, she was fortunate.

The paladin looked like she may lose consciousness at any moment. Silenos considered the prospect and found himself hoping she would. His thoughts were scattered enough already, cracking at the edges. He felt slivers of molten doubt creep into him. Cognition poisoned, decaying. The foundation of one hundred years' moral conviction turning soft and fragile beneath him. What was wrong with him? What had he been thinking?

He had not been thinking, evidently. He had been *feeling*. And now he had *felt* himself into doing the unforgivable. Even Adonis had not committed so great a wrong as this. He, at least, had betrayed only a single named of House Shaiagrazni, not the name in its entirety.

He at least had had the excuse of being a mere apprentice, not a mature master of the House.

"Please, kill me."

Silenos felt his fury bubbling up as the hybrid interrupted his thoughts yet *again*.

"I will not, but I can hurt you very, very badly if you continue to inconvenience me."

Adonis had turned on him instantly, though there may still have been a chance for him to repeat his ritual. Why had that been? The answer was obvious. He had seen a traitor to House Shaiagrazni and moved to dispose of them without hesitation. As he should have done—as each and every one of his fellow named was taught from the beginning of their induction to do. Traitors were not suffered within the household of casters.

"Kill me," the head continued. "And I can help you get back to where you came from."

Silenos paused, then reached down to raise the severed hybrid up and stare into its face. Not its eyes—never those—but the tip of its nose. As close as he could come without risking the gaze of a being so deeply infused with the touch of an Entity.

"Explain how," he demanded, and found his fury triple as the hybrid grinned.

"No, caster, no, not that easy. Your word first that you'll kill me once it's done."

Of course he wouldn't. Silenos had far too many uses for such a creature to simply destroy it. Even putting aside the fact that he wasn't sure he *could* kill it permanently, he would sooner remove one of his own limbs than dispose of such a resource.

But then, there was nothing to lose here from deception.

"I promise," he replied, and saw the hybrid scrutinizing his features for a moment. Silenos carefully paralyzed his facial muscles as it did. When it seemed satisfied, he continued. "Assuming you can in fact help me escape this place."

"I can!" the hybrid spit. "I surely can."

"What *is* that?" another voice cut in, Ensharia's. It seemed that everybody would be interrupting Silenos's thoughts today.

"The hybrid offspring of a baryonic life-form and an Entity. I do not care what variety of either. It bears a degree of connection leading from one level of reality to the other—partly occuring in both, never entirely in just one. Its very existence makes travel between these levels easier for that reason. Think of it as a conductor in . . . Ah. Think of it as . . . Think of it as a wedge leaving a door partly opened."

She was still entirely lost, he thought. So it was fortunate that Silenos did not care in the slightest.

Unfortunately, she was not finished with her questions.

"So we can get back to the real world?"

"This world *is* real," Silenos snapped. "But, yes. From here we can return to your world, theoretically." Though he had to admit he was not entirely certain how long it would have taken until this very moment. There were an endless number of schisms within the Shallow Depths, and more here now that they were at a higher level than he and Adonis had ventured into. But it was impossible to vet them for any degree of control. Silenos could not actively seek out ones leading back to the new world as he was.

When he had fled from Adonis, his plan had been to retreat into another world altogether and one day perfect his own esoterica enough to make an alternate path to House Shaiagrazni. An investment of centuries, perhaps a millennium, on his part. Why?

So that Arion Falls would live.

His anger threatened to bubble up all over again. *Why?* What was wrong with him? What pathogen had infested his cognition deeply enough to induce *this*?

"Thank you."

Silenos turned to the words, finding the vampire, Hexeri, was eyeing him, face a mix of wariness and . . . gratitude.

"You didn't have to get us out of there," she noted. "It almost got you killed to try, but you did. You could've just grabbed the head and made your own retreat. Instead, you helped us escape too. Thank you for that."

"*Aaaaaaaaaaaaaaaaaaaaaaaaaaaaaaaaaaaaaaaaaaaaaaaaaa aaaaaagh!*"

Silenos's scream took even himself by surprise, and it certainly shocked the two women, who now backed away from him, staring with wide eyes and readied fists. He kicked at the ground, tearing great clots of it free and sending them hurtling into the air, entire body trembling, fists balled and thrashing toward the sky. His discharge of fury lasted no more than a few moments, but drained him as if it had been hours.

Why had he done that? Screamed like some . . . some . . . *animal*. What was wrong with him? What was *wrong* with him?

Silenos saw the confusion in his new travel aids' faces and found himself without the chance to either address or ignore it. A shriek washed over them all, far away, rattling the air and growing closer by the moment. They turned in unison to its source.

A shape, a thousand shapes. All twisting and writhing around one another. The thing had fifty heads, seventeen limbs, skin of bronze, and weeping, pus-frothed sores where metal connected to stony flesh below. Its eyes glowed with the light of stars, teeth protruded as taloned fingers from fungal gums, and its body was a long serpentine thing scaled in shared secrets and armored with treacherous friends.

"Be ready," Silenos growled, already assuming his war form. "An Entity approaches." He examined its magic, careful not to look at the thing dead-on and get an unforgettable glance behind the curtains of reality. Its power was great. Greater than his, to be sure, though a trifling thing beside the magic of certain other specimens he'd encountered here.

With Adonis, it would have been a trivial opponent. Without him, it might well be the death of them.

"How do we fight it?" Hexeri asked, always the more pragmatic.

"Will," Silenos told her. "Concentrate upon it. Use your *intent* to wound. Ground it through anatomy, experience, hatred—whatever focus works best. But ensure that every strike lands with the intent of killing and destroying. And do not, at any point, assume it to be dead."

There was time to say nothing else. The Entity's great wings—rainbows protruding from its backs and rotting at the edges—crested the air, and it swooped down toward them as a coiling arcane missile. He raised his shield, flooded the air with flames, and steeled his mind.

The Entity collided with him in an explosion to fragment stone and rend steel, yet its shock wave perished millimeters in the air and did nothing. They shot back, straining against each other with magic and might.

Perhaps, Silenos mused, he should have simply done battle with Adonis. Perhaps a single enemy of greater power than him would have presented shorter odds than these.

CHAPTER NINETEEN

THEN

It had been five years since Silenos's induction into House Shaiagrazni. After the first, he had learned more about magic than he had known there was to learn. After two, he had learned more than most actual casters. In his fifth year, Silenos would have been considered a master already, by most people's standards. He could have fled the household to make his fortune teaching the art anywhere in the world, more or less. This was not entirely his own talent at work. The simple fact was that House Shaiagrazni's mastery of the arcane was unrivaled.

Save, of course, for the Shungard. Pagan deities: blood-drinking, heart-eating, soul-rending gods of old. House Shaiagrazni's homeland had once been dominated by similar beings. Gestalt coagulations of nascent human will and ambient magic, formed and empowered over long millennia of consciousness and unknowing intent. He hadn't yet seen one, not a true specimen, but he had heard stories. Boulders thrown across horizons, tanks torn fully in half, buildings reaching as high as mountains split from base to head in a single stroke.

His first mission for House Shaiagrazni in the field was *not* to do battle with one of these beings, nor their bastard offspring. It was merely to lay waste to one of their outposts. And, of course, Juragai was joining him.

Fifteen grotesqueries accompanied him, each handmade by one of House Shaiagrazni's esteemed fleshcrafters. Two, smaller, hung at the back. A contingent against unpleasant surprises. The assault began quietly enough. Or as quietly as lumbering tonnes of keratin and meat could manage. The grotesqueries encircled the encampment, opening combat by firing their rotary cannons into it.

Great, screaming, multibarreled death dealers, spitting out thirty-millimeter projectiles by the centisecond. They tore through barricades, makeshift buildings, and, most easily of all, bodies. Drawing the enemy out to foolishly engage them in the open, cutting them apart before any could so much as fight back.

Save for one.

This figure, close to three meters in height and perhaps half the mass of Silenos's grotesqueries, came down upon one of the attackers with a hammer that looked close to half his own mass. It struck magically woven metallic armor, a gift from metallicists to overcome the limits of organic matter's resilience. In this case, they did not overcome them. With a sound like lightning hitting steel, the armor buckled and broke. Ribs drove inward. Meat was pulped. The grotesquerie shot back and fell down. Its rotary cannon continued screaming, then fell silent as the hammer returned again and again. Two more blows crushed its head to mulch. The first had destroyed its hearts.

Savage though they were, the servants of the Shungard had become skilled in killing grotesqueries.

The warrior roared. Silenos estimated he was some champion of the Shungard pantheon, likely bearing a blood connection to their deities. His body shimmered with an innate magic that even House Shaiagrazni could not match outside of temporary concentration. And he moved so fast that Silenos's own eyes could scarcely follow, fleshcrafted though they were.

Within a fraction of a second, he was bringing his hammer to bear against another grotesquerie as the remaining eleven fired. Shells wider than thumbs hammered into his back. They broke the skin, inflicted a thousand minuscule scratches and scrapes. They may as well have been beestings or thrown gravel, for the towering warrior merely ignored the wounds and focused on breaking apart his enemy. He repeated the process for the next, and the next after that. Silenos orchestrated the grotesqueries, spacing them apart and overlapping their fire to ensure the Shungard bastard was never able to shield his body with any of his enemies. Still, he killed.

But still he slowed.

"This won't work," Juragai muttered. "He's going to outlast them. At the very least, he'll dispatch all our grotesqueries before the contingency ends him. Send them in now."

Silenos glared at his partner.

"He's being pelted with thousands of armor-piercing rounds every second, maybe tens of thousands. He'll fall."

Juragai simply shrugged, not meeting Silenos's eye, not challenging him. He'd left him doubtful anyway, the bastard, and as the enemy continued working, Silenos began to see that his partner had been right. Only a few grotesqueries still remained when he finally surrendered to caution and sent in the contingency.

Fleshcrafted by Kammani herself, they moved like whispers on the air.

One caught the enemy champion's arm just as he was about to bring it down upon a grotesquerie. With a tug, it snapped his elbow like dry twigs and left the man's weapon to clatter from loosened fingers. Almost simultaneously, the other skewered him with a great lance built into its forearm.

Silenos winced at the sight. The weapon did not strike a spot of particular vulnerability, not an open wound or thin body part. It simply drove itself fully through the back and exploded out of his front, running his torso through and dumping his blood outward by the liter. The champion spasmed, gurgled as ichor fountained from him.

That was when the first of Kammani's grotesqueries struck, taking his head off with a single swipe and scything through preternatural tissue as if it were no sturdier than mundane flesh. For a few moments, the body remained standing, twitched. Then it collapsed all at once, landing with a meaty thud in the dirt.

Not much of the encampment was finished following that. Much of it having been incidentally destroyed by the massed rotary-cannon fire.

It was no matter. Silenos doubted anything of much worth would be found in such a place regardless. The survivors would be vetted for ability or use and killed if they produced further resistance. He began the doing of it.

Grotesqueries—only a few remaining now—encircled the settlement as people stepped forward and addressed the attendants Silenos and Juragai had been lent. Analysts, trained and equipped to scan a person's biology and arcane signature for traces of hidden potential. To determine what utility, if any, they could provide House Shaiagrazni. Depending on each one's natural abilities, their treatment would vary. Those of innate gifts deserved more than those without them.

It was all tedious. Rarely would an ability of true note be discovered, and Silenos had not sincerely expected he would find the excitement of seeing one here. Still, he had been given his task and had no intentions of deviating from it. If only because House Shaiagrazni treated deviants . . .

Well, he had just seen the very way in which House Shaiagrazni treated deviants.

Minutes passed, an hour. Silenos remained bored. His monotony was alleviated only at a fortuitous glance to the edge of the settlement, where he saw Juragai gesturing at something beyond his field of view. His stomach sank, and Silenos was heading toward the apprentice before he knew what was even happening. Instincts, in this moment, quicker than deliberate cognition.

"What are you doing?" Silenos hissed, trailing off as he saw with his own eyes what the answer would be. A pair of children were just a few meters ahead of Juragai, freezing as they saw him. He'd been gesturing for them to back away. To leave, silently and secretly. The apprentice's eyes went wide.

"I—" Silenos punched him. There wasn't an ounce of magic in his attack. It was a thing of pure physicality and fraying temper. Juragai was, however, a good deal smaller than him. It sent him straight to the ground and drew blood from his crumpled nose.

"You fucking idiot!" he snapped, looming over the smaller boy. The children scattered. Silenos was too distracted to care. "You fucking, fucking *idiot*!" Juragai was slowly dragging himself up, wincing, flinching at every move Silenos made. It just made him angrier. How dare he be so pitiably fearful of something as minor as a punch to the face? Had he no idea what more he might bring onto himself?

"I'm sorry," the smaller boy began, not meeting Silenos's eye. It made him want to throw another punch.

"Was that what you planned on telling Mistress Kammani?" he snapped. "That you're *sorry*? I'm sure she'll understand that much. She has a reputation for forgiveness, right? It's someone else I must be thinking of who's famous for turning people into sentient sex toys."

That hardened Juragai's eyes, which surprised Silenos. Not much could draw ire from the boy, let alone enough for his spine to harden in the face of conflict.

"Why do you think I was being sneaky?" he snapped, looking around even as he said it. "You won't . . . you know."

Tell her. Tell Mistress Kammani. Silenos would not tell the truth to one of the most powerful, cruel beings ever to live. Would he not? He—

Footsteps behind them. Silenos whipped around. Kammani herself was approaching as if the very mention of her had worked as a summons.

What had she heard? How much had she seen? Silenos realized, with a stab of terror, that Juragai's nose was still visibly bleeding from the punch. From *his* punch. In his rage, he'd not thought that to strike an apprentice of House Shaiagrazni was to strike their master's property. They were privileged, above the mere servitor caste, but only insofar as their potential to one day be more.

Neither Silenos or Juragai had met that potential yet, and whatever punishment Kammani deemed suitable would be one he had no choice but to endure. She stopped walking just a pace or two short of them, eyeing Juragai with an arched brow.

"And what happened to you?" she asked. The question was light, idle. She did not seem, particularly, to care. But Silenos knew better than to think that would have any effect on whatever punishment he received. Half the tenets of House Shaiagrazni had been written by the woman before him. She had not done that for a lack of belief in their wisdom.

Just when Silenos was about to confess, Juragai spoke up instead.

"A ricochet, mistress," he volunteered. "We were standing too close when the grotesqueries engaged one of the enemy's supposed demigods. A shot rebounded from their body and, I believe, struck me in the face. It was from quite a distance, so most of its kinetic energy had already been exhausted, but it hit hard enough to do this. I am uninjured."

She studied him for a second, eyes seeming to pass clean through the boy's body. Silenos hated his mistress's stare. Hated how insubstantial he always felt before it. Like his skin was mere fog.

"Idiot," she replied. Juragai screamed as his kneecaps exploded as one, blood bursting from his legs. He dropped to the ground, foaming at the mouth, thrashing in agony, and Kammani watched as his pained spasms slowly weakened with exsanguination. At last, just as it seemed he would die, she healed him with a gesture, then turned and headed away.

Silenos helped his fellow apprentice stand.

"Why did you lie?" he asked, too stunned to even feel anything at the fact.

"The punishment you'd have faced if I hadn't would be . . ." He shivered, hand moving down to the now-repaired flesh between his legs. "Awful."

That was when the anger came, all at once like water through broken floodgates.

"And if you'd been caught in your deception, it would have been a thousand times worse!" he spit. Juragai opened his mouth to respond, eyes hard with defiance, but Silenos cut him off. "No, no excuses, no buts. You need to toughen up, Juragai. Your softness—your kindness—will get you fucking killed It's a weakness here, not a strength." He hadn't noticed his own fatigue as he said that, his own draining exhaustion.

Juragai remained silent, and so Silenos spoke again.

"For your own sake, please, rid yourself of this compassion."

CHAPTER TWENTY

Silenos Shaiagrazni just sort of disappeared as the creature—whatever it was—hit him. Hexeri braced herself for the wind of its impact, but none came. Even the sound barely did. Wrong, distorted, but without quite any *distortion*. It was like the poorly recalled memory of a sound heard decades, even centuries in the past. Something spoken of time and time again, mutated by retellings.

Everything here was like that. Wrong, in a way that made her skin crawl. But the impact, that was realer than any she'd seen before. Shaiagrazni was blasted off his feet, all however-many tons of him, and whipped high into the air.

Neither she nor Ensharia even had the chance to act.

High above, the caster was at least making a nuisance of himself. In moments, the demon—Hexeri guessed—was engulfed in flames, shrieking and thrashing around. Shaiagrazni clung onto it, twisting his grip and bringing himself away from its maw. A useless effort. Another maw just sprouted up right before the spot he was climbing to, locking onto him anyway as tendrils burst from the thing's belly.

No, *entrails*. Its guts had claws and teeth, acid-tipped fangs that sank into Shaiagraznian armor and carved down into the flesh to leave bloody foam oozing out. Silenos Shaiagrazni screamed in pain. Then he and his enemy smashed down into the ground.

The shaking of earth underfoot was like a distant memory too.

Ensharia lunged ahead before Hexeri could, much to her chagrin. The paladin was actually her equal on a physical level, and seemed to have none of the self-preservation that slowed others down in combat. Granted, it also dragged her right into the path of a tendril as it tore off one of her pauldrons and acid scarred the flesh beneath. Her mace smashed the tip off while she stumbled back from yet more attacks.

That was when Hexeri's arc of shadows thudded into the thing's side and dug in deep. It squealed like a stuck pig, a sound that only grew louder as Shaiagrazni brought his shield down hard into its mouth.

The mouth closed around it and took his arm off with a single crunch of armor plating and viscera. Shaiagrazni stared at the stump that had once been his limb. Surprised, Hexeri thought, was the strongest emotion in him, far outstripping pain or agony. Probably he'd not considered that a thing could exceed him of all people by so great a margin.

Her shadows kept splashing down into it as a rain of jagged splinters, digging deep and settling under its flesh. Trailing minute lengths back to her fingers. Hexeri grew them within it, then pulled hard and expanded them all at once.

The demon was tugged back just in time to miss its second bite, and Shaiagrazni helped it on its stumble away from him by aiming his cannon arm at the thing's leg and firing. Hexeri winced, seeing the limb fall apart but . . . not rightly. It was as if the matter of this thing's body simply refused to fully interact with anything else. Fog, almost. Collapsing back in to partially reform even as it was broken apart. Not healing so much as failing to even register its own damage.

Some of it, at least, stuck. Perhaps that was the function of will. Hexeri threw some more into her next fusillade of darkness.

Another tendril came for her, broke as Ensharia's mace smacked it down. Then Silenos was leaping, flying with the beat of sprawling wings, and blasting into the demon's back from above. Again, the damage seemed ephemeral to it, and its focus turned now to the paladin. It was halfway through lunging for her when Shaiagrazni's great bulk came down atop it, his whiplike tail tangling its own tendrils into a knot and his cannon pressing hard against the back of its neck.

If it had interacted with the blast as it should have, Hexeri thought the thing might have been decapitated in truth. As things were, it merely roared and twisted around, body actually reshaping to face Shaiagrazni as its limbs thrust back and dug into him. Blood and pus burst from his body in a dozen places, and he fell back beneath it, mauled like a mundane man beneath the weight of a bear.

Hexeri could do nothing but continue her attack as Ensharia closed to aid him.

Between the two of them chipping away at it, and Shaiagrazni keeping it ensnared within a melee against the only one able to even slightly weather its savagery, the demon actually seemed to slow down. Hexeri wondered at first whether it was her imagination, nerves fraying at the thought. But, no. Its weakness was growing, slowly like a tumor, but growing, nonetheless. They just needed to maintain the pressure.

Snapping filled the air, grotesque and a thousand times more real than any impact shock Hexeri's ears had received. The sounds of Shaiagrazni's body breaking down, she realized. Her efforts redoubled, she threw every ounce of magic she could muster into the demon. One javelin of darkness followed another, ripping chunks from it, slowing it more, weakening it.

But not as fast as it weakened Shaiagrazni. Moments later, she saw the fleshcrafter's arms fall limply to his sides, watched the demon rear up in triumph, and stared helplessly as it brought its countless limbs down into his torso.

For the second time, she heard a sound with perfect clarity. Silenos Shaiagrazni's chest simply caved in, ribs bursting apart. His upper and lower body became separate entities, and the man's gore spurted so high into the air that it would have reached his war form's head even if it were standing upright.

Instead it rained down across all of him at once, painting his broken form while it lay twitching. As the demon stepped back, Hexeri's dread reached a crescendo. Its eyes flitted from her to Ensharia, considering, pausing. Then it turned and flew away.

She stood in disbelief for a moment. At the horror of what she'd seen, at the fortune of her surviving it. Then her concern turned to Shaiagrazni.

Or what was left of him. Putting aside the sizable fraction of his body that had been outright severed, much of it was . . . liquefying. Dissolving and bubbling before her eyes like ice pressed against forge-hot steel. Hexeri found herself heading to his side, hands hovering impotently around him, confusion surely written across her face.

Ensharia was beside her, just as useless. Both stared as Shaiagrazni's eyes began to flutter around. Twisting, darting about. He blinked once. Then, she realized, his concentration hardened as his body started to reconfigure.

"Dear God," Ensharia whispered. "What is he *doing*?"

Silenos watched the gaping morons with some satisfaction as he reconfigured his body. It made sense, he supposed. In all likelihood, this was the first time either of them had ever seen a true wielder of the arcane enter such a state. In fact, given what he knew of the new world's pitiable magic, it was unlikely they had even heard of what he was about to do being hypothesized.

He hoped it was an enlightening experience for them because he certainly did not intend to do it again.

Two primary concerns were before Silenos, and either on its own would have been an issue. Both together may well have killed him. The first was the simple matter of biomass. Silenos, ordinarily, could overcome such a lack. There was an abundance of biological matter around he could draw on—subterranean life-forms or bacteriologic sources, or, failing all else, merely the endlessly inefficient process of conjuring it from raw mana.

Here, there were no organic lifeforms save him and his companions. Compensating for that with raw mana would eat into his already dangerously depleted reserves and shorten the too-slight time he had before the Shallow Depths burst his bubble of rationality and obliterated him.

Secondly, he had to concern himself with the continued sustaining of his own life. With his body in such a mangled state, it was only deliberate magical exertion that kept his mind from passing as well. The former demanded utmost skill and precision from Silenos, the latter a good deal of concentration being diverted elsewhere.

He simply could not reconstitute himself while sustaining his life, nor could he afford to compensate for precision with raw power. So Silenos found another strategy.

Within his body was a genetic code. This was nothing unusual—it was how bodies were formed and sustained. Silenos had long since copied and memorized his own, and he put it to use now. Slowly, he formed embryonic matter in exact accordance with his own biology—making some choice changes to tissue density and nerve conductivity that would shorten the process of fleshcrafting his disgustingly *natural* product into a suitably effective state. As he flooded the embryo, both with mana and matter to fuel its accelerated growth, he was able to sustain his cognition with only a bare exertion of will and magic.

"He's . . . Oh God, he's doing it. He's . . . I think he's healing!" It was Ensharia who said it, Silenos was dimly aware. A distant voice barely piercing the fog of his senses. Thought and sensibility were necessary for him; sensory input, for the time being, he could do without. If any hazards arrived that demanded his attention, they would either ignore him or he would die. He concentrated upon the processes of sustaining himself.

The body grew, undergoing weeks of progress within mere moments. Then years of natural growth in minutes. Far from being *easy*, it still demanded a considerable fraction of his remaining mana. A human body would, with perfect efficiency, consume around forty to fifty megajoules of energy in the process of growing. Silenos's haste made this process a dozen times less efficient. His addled state perhaps halved that remaining efficiency. The exotic nature of his product quartered what was left. After several gigajoules' worth of mana had been removed from him—enough to almost *atomize* a body, let alone assemble one—he was, at last, complete.

Only one final step remained: to transfer his consciousness. Silenos did so easily enough. He unbound his cognition—his essence or soul as others would say—from the meat of his brain, then deposited it into the new vessel. Sensation returned as an instantaneous flood.

"I live," Silenos announced, getting up with a grunt. Ensharia's and Hexeri's eyes were wide, almost disbelieving.

"You . . ." It was Hexeri who had begun speaking. Ensharia seemed quite beyond words. "You . . . You . . ."

Silenos's head tilted. Genuine confusion was the only reaction her stare invoked. It was one of the few things Silenos had encountered that truly baffled.

"What is the matter?"

The vampire took her time in responding, seeming to need a few moments more before she was finally able.

"What . . . Why are you a woman?"

Silenos looked down, tilting his head. His—her, now, Silenos supposed—body had been made for nothing so vitally as speed. She decided honesty was the most appropriate response.

"I cloned myself," Silenos explained, making sure to use small words so the woman would understand. "In order to create a new body for myself as quickly as I could. This involved making a . . ." She did not know what an embryo was, Silenos realized. "The simplest, earliest form of a developing human's body. These start as female until particular conditions emerge that change them to male. I did not wish to waste time or effort inducing those conditions, as I had other concerns, and so my body remained female."

Experiencing the hormonal changes that caused this physical transformation would have wasted yet more mana, and so Silenos had stifled them.

The vampire just stared, and Silenos wondered if she'd heard a word she said.

"Why didn't you make yourself a man?" Ensharia cut in, looking even more confused than the vampire. So much so that she was only just now even asking. Silenos sighed.

"Because I do not care. I believe I have made my view of sex and its relevance toward a magic caster quite clear. Now stop wasting my time with these incessant questions." It did feel strange to hear her own voice now, so high had it become. Silenos mused on that as she began walking.

The women—her fellow women—followed after.

CHAPTER TWENTY-ONE

Ensharia wasn't sure whether the vampire had merely been strangely quick in getting over Silenos's . . . change. Perhaps she herself had just been strangely slow. Perhaps not. He'd changed fucking *sex*. She. Was it she?

She almost asked, but then paused at the thought of entering a conversation with Silenos. He—she, damn it—was busy, Ensharia thought. Hands down on her own body, eyes tightened somewhat, magic humming in the air that already hummed so much of magic. The head was tied to her hip, protruding somewhat more now given that the hip in question was . . . Dear God. Ensharia looked away fast.

It was just too nauseating. Silenos's voice had changed, but she almost thought it might be *easier* to deal with everything if it hadn't. She was still . . . Silenos. Speaking, gesticulating, and enunciating in the exact ways she always had, making the new pitch of her vocal cords all the more jarring. Ensharia caught the vampire grinning at her from the corner of her eye.

"Something funny?" she snapped, which only widened the grin. She still wasn't sure what to make of this one. On the one hand, Ensharia had learned that her own biases—particularly those formed through education by the paladins—could lead her astray. On the other . . .

It was a *vampire*. The stories all converged on a few key details about her kind, and none of them good. Ensharia wouldn't be dropping her guard just because one species had proved themselves better than the rumors. She still felt some way about that, but didn't have time to unwrap it.

"It's just funny seeing a paladin so . . . I don't know." The vampire shrugged. "Normally, your sort go straight to mace-swinging anger. You're more tempered at least. Makes your bafflement cuter to look at." She smiled, not in a particularly endearing way, and Ensharia found that she didn't like being called cute any more by a vampiric woman than she did by living men.

"How long have you been working with Shaiagrazni?" she asked. "A few weeks?"

The vampire actually had to think about it.

"Months, I think," she said after a moment. "Yes, months. Though there's been a lot of work between that—we've not spent much time actually interacting."

"I can tell," Ensharia noted. "You're still with him."

The vampire's brow arched.

"Right, you and he had a falling out didn't you?"

"*A falling out*," Ensharia spit. "He killed thousands for no reason at all—using some weapon that he *could* have changed to spare them but was simply too lazy to. No, he made me think there was more to him than evil, somehow, and I was stupid enough that it took me a long, long time to realize otherwise."

Ensharia wasn't sure when she began panting, nor when her voice raised so high. She caught Silenos from the corner of her eye, worried for a moment the man—woman, fuck—may have heard.

Of course, she hadn't. While enveloped in her work, Silenos wouldn't have noticed a falling star unless it hit her directly.

"What have you heard of him recently?" the vampire asked. Ensharia bristled, raising her guard. Even she wasn't fully sure why.

"Mixed reports. Cruelty, devastation. Conquest." She spit each word like it tasted foul. In fact, they did. The vampire seemed as indifferent to Ensharia's disgust as she was to everything else.

"And nothing else?"

Ensharia hesitated at that. It was, for some reason, tempting to lie. But she found the truth escaping her anyway. Why, she couldn't say.

"I've heard other things: construction done within the regions he conquered to uplift those in poverty. Widespread education and . . . mixed reports regarding the battle with the Dark Lord."

The vampire nodded, as if this was all expected. A remarkably frustrating habit.

"Do you know how Silenos was captured?" she asked.

Ensharia actually didn't. Loath as she was to look stupid by admitting her ignorance, she knew it would be all the worse to guess badly in an effort at concealing it.

"No."

"King Galukar, the idiot, threw himself into a portal the Dark Lord opened to escape—I think with demonology. You need to understand, the Dark Lord was vastly beyond his power. He had no chance at all of besting him alone."

Ensharia went cold. "Galukar?" she croaked. "Really?"

The vampire's gaze didn't waver. "It would've been like a child fighting a man. In fact, it was. And King Galukar would be dead . . ." She nodded toward Silenos. "If Shaiagrazni hadn't leaped in after him to save his life. That is how he—she—was captured."

Ensharia dwelled on that, considering it.

"What I said about her risking her life to free us stands too," the vampire added. "And we both saw the demand she made of the demon, to bring back Arion Falls."

That was what struck Ensharia in the end. Falls had been a misogynistic prick for each day she'd known him, but . . . he'd been so young. And he'd been seeming to grow, at least, in some respect. Hearing of his potential being squandered by an early death had touched her in a way she hadn't known it would. Seeing Silenos resolve that had touched her more deeply still.

"You're trying to make me think he—she—is different now," Ensharia realized, rounding on the vampire. "Because it benefits you if we work together better."

The creature called Hexeri looked at Ensharia with a level, sterile stare. She was not offended, nor defensive, nor, as far as she could tell, hurt. Merely patient.

"I'm trying to help you realize that whatever glimmer of good you've been torturing yourself over getting tricked into seeing might not have been a trick at all," she said softly. "I'm trying to help you realize that your judgment wasn't as bad as you seem to think it was, and . . . maybe introduce Silenos to the best chance she has at becoming less . . ."

Less Silenos. Ensharia didn't need the sentence finished to understand. This one was eerie to speak with. Kind and cold all at once. Speaking with her was like being bound in ribbons of silk.

"Some of the stories about your kind are true after all, aren't they?" she asked without thinking. The vampire smiled. Ensharia considered her next move for a moment, then headed over to Silenos's side.

The woman had grown her height, though not to the same towering scale that had once left her just a few inches shy of Galukar's own. She was lean, still, and was only halfway finished in reapplying the changes that had evidently given her skin such a curious texture before. Ensharia found it disconcerting how much of a likeness she saw in her compared to Silenos's previous body. As if she were her own daughter, perhaps.

Is she a she? The grammar had not, as far as Ensharia knew, been invented. She defaulted to what felt right.

"Silenos," Ensharia began. "Do you mind if I have a word?"

Silenos's head snapped around so fast Ensharia found it seemed almost artificial. Like a thing locked and cocked in place, a crossbow loosed at the trigger pull. She had forgotten how inhumanly the caster gesticulated.

"Yes," Silenos replied. Ensharia waited for something more, some elaboration—perhaps a hint of what she thought about the prospect.

Then Ensharia remembered whom she was talking to, and realized that none would come. She resisted the urge to show her frustration. That, above all else, would probably be pointless. Silenos wouldn't even know what it meant.

The old lessons she'd learned of how to speak with Silenos came rearing back up. Ensharia would be dragging this conversation along by its tail, she knew.

"It's been a while," she noted. Silenos nodded, said nothing. She continued. "I remember we didn't exactly part on the best terms."

Silenos tilted her head. Her hair was longer now, shorter than immediately after she had finished her regeneration—the woman had cut it from its original waist-length along with her unnaturally extended nails—but still longer than before. It waved and rippled as she moved.

"I have come to understand that I . . . offended you," Silenos said at last.

Ensharia felt her temper boiling back up.

"Offended me," she replied, jaw tightening with the effort of biting back a scream.

"Upset," Silenos amended.

"How?" she challenged her.

Silenos eyed Ensharia, seeming somewhat confused.

"How did you upset me?" Ensharia pressed.

Silenos thought about that for quite a while.

"You view the lives of others as having innate worth, beyond simple productivity and capacity for accomplishment. You think sapient life suffering is, itself, immoral. It . . . upsets you. And so what I did upset you."

It was all delivered so *strangely*. Not through the tone of one merely deducing what she said, rather . . . someone introspecting.

"Have you been feeling that?" Ensharia asked. "About . . . Galukar, Falls?"

Silenos's eyes grew cold, and Ensharia changed the topic instantly.

"It has been a long time," she repeated. "And, to be frank, Silenos, I . . . I think I did miss you. Or I missed the person I thought you were. Who I realize was not as far from you as the person I then went to think you were as I left."

Even in her own ears, it sounded a jumbled and messy thing to profess. But then, it was a jumbled and messy set of thoughts. Ensharia almost winced.

Silenos, though, merely shook her head idly.

"I . . . I believe that . . . it is conceivable"—she was speaking slowly, almost exertively—"plausibly true even, that I felt a sliver of loss at your departure as well." Her face twisted up, as if the very admission revolted her. Probably it did. But Ensharia was past caring. Despite the madness of it all, the fact that she was speaking to perhaps one of the more objectively evil creatures she had ever met, Ensharia smiled.

"That means a lot to hear." She beamed.

Silenos snapped instantly.

"It means *weakness*," she hissed. "You understand? A taint upon my glorious cognition, a festering wound in which the pathogen of emotion and sentiment can spread. A feebling of my intellect and collapse of my rationality. This thing you call humanity—this pitiable, mewling, infantile process—it is something I have long since purged myself of. I purged it carefully and deliberately, you understand?" Her throat caught upon itself, eyes suddenly wet. With rage or sadness, Ensharia couldn't tell.

She hadn't backed off. That much was a shock even to her. Was it Silenos's temporarily diminished threat, in the aftermath of their fight and her reconstruction?

Or did Ensharia just find herself confident that the caster would not hurt her?

"What made you choose to be like this?" she asked. A glance over her shoulder showed that the vampire Hexeri had already retreated to, Ensharia thought, the exact limit to how far Silenos had warned both of them she could maintain her "bubble of logic." If anything, Ensharia admired the woman's restraint for not fleeing farther.

Silenos's answer came after a long delay.

"I do not wish to speak of that with you," she replied. "Do not ask me again."

Ensharia thought she detected a hint of pain there. It terrified her more than anything else Shaiagrazni had ever shown beneath her eyes. A caster moved by egocentrism or megalomania could do so much evil, but always of a predictable and rational kind. A person motivated by pain?

They might do anything in the world.

Silence hung between them, but Ensharia couldn't bring herself to move away from Silenos's side. After another few minutes, she was rewarded as Silenos spoke again.

"I am a traitor to my people," she breathed. "I internalized all the right ways of living a life. I learned the true ethics by which all should govern themselves. And I chose to defy them. I have no excuse. The code of the world was laid out before me, and I consciously broke it. Can you imagine that?"

"Yes," Ensharia replied, thinking back to how she hadn't slain Silenos upon seeing her necromancy. How she'd opened up to the orcs. How she'd broken a thousand other tenets of her order, and been vindicated almost every time. "Yes," she repeated. "I can."

CHAPTER TWENTY-TWO

THEN

Seven years since House Shaiagrazni had accepted Silenos. He had seen so very much, felt so very much.

Done so, so very much. His powers had expanded beyond what most masters would even have thought to try for. As much of that was due to his own prodigious nature as the knowledge of his teachers, and yet he was under no illusion of what that meant. With half the cause for his growth, he would now be a potent caster. With all of it, he was among the ten thousand most formidable alive. In another century, he hoped to be a named. Maybe less.

Prodigies always had a comfortable place in House Shaiagrazni, of course. Prodigies among the twenty most gifted in history even more so.

He had graduated now to the point of learning mostly through example and assisting his mistress, rather than studying. Silenos's memory was a potent thing, one of the countless abilities he had been tested for before induction, and he had long since memorized entire tomes of knowledge regarding the arcane.

Nothing in *Entities*. His own people had called them demons—superstitious nonsense he now knew—but . . .

Superstition.

When had his culture become superstition? When had the stories his father used to soothe him to sleep with festered into a source of shame? When had everything in all the world that had once been good suddenly become bad?

More often, these days, Silenos found himself pondering that. And invariably the results of that consideration would leave him... uncomfortable.

What harm did hearing of Old Harriol do? What harm could come of Silenos giggling at the silly man as he got himself into trouble, then tricked himself out of it by begging and bargaining with the gods until they once more made the mistake of showing him mercy?

Apparently, it did all the harm in the world. And Silenos had been considering why that was. Clearly, it was not the meat of the story House Shaiagrazni feared. But he could not for the life of him think what else it may be. There was a piece missing from the picture, a puzzle impossible to assemble. And that bothered him more than anything else.

If only because, among the countless traits that saw him excelling so easily within House Shaiagrazni, perfectionism had manifested more strongly in him than most.

Silenos's quarters, like most everything else Silenos owned, were comfortable things. They would have taken up quite literally one-tenth the land area of his own village, and were made entirely of smooth stones that demanded exhaustive processes to produce.

Anywhere else. In House Shaiagrazni, such structures emerged when a wrist was flicked with intent. Not Silenos's, not yet, but one day he imagined it would be.

His furniture was all comfortable to the point of perfection, refreshments endlessly replenished, entertainment... exotic and beautiful. He had worried when his sexual desires first began that they might be chastised.

It had been a foolish concern. His own mistress had an endless parade of women and men into her quarters and out. She did not, Silenos thought, actually sleep. At least not nearly as much as she spent her time wearing false ears, stripped nude, and behaving like a dog.

The few times he'd found her in the process had been seared into his memory with a permanence he doubted even magic could reverse.

A knock came upon Silenos's door, interrupting his thoughts. That may have been an annoyance, were he thinking about anything else in the world. Today, it tempted him to blindly reward the knocker with their pick of his possessions.

Which would have been redundant because on the other side of the door was among the few people to not only match his luxury, but exceed it.

"Hello, Juragai." He sighed, feeling suddenly, stupidly relieved. Whom had he been expecting, their mistress?

Puberty had not been unkind to Silenos's fellow apprentice, leaving him taller by far, and at least a hair less wiry. He was now less sickly than *lean*, and his eyes had grown more astute as age progressed them. He met Silenos's gaze without backing down.

That had been a recent lesson for him, as their mistress grew tired of seeing her apprentice constantly shy from the glares of others. The lessons had been agony, but blessedly short. Most of Mistress Kammani's were. Juragai did not break eye contact anymore. And he didn't seem, oddly enough, anywhere near so frightened.

"May I come in?" he asked, fidgeting slightly. He did that when his nerves were biting at him. Silenos paused only a moment, then nodded.

"Of course."

Juragai ushered himself into the apartment, looking around. He always did, despite having seen the interior a good fifty times already.

"I do like your sense of decoration," he breathed. "So much less . . . gaudy."

Silenos understood that well enough. Everyone else in House Shaiagrazni seemed desperate to cram as much value per liter into their own quarters as they could, even at the expense of aesthetic, comfort, or anything else. Everything in their world was about power and status.

Their world? My world, surely.

Perhaps, perhaps not. Silenos was an apprentice. True, a growing one. True, one mere decades away from earning his name, if all went well, but there was still a tangible separation between him and the seniors of their house.

"What did you want to discuss?" he asked his friend, seeking sanctuary from his own thoughts.

Juragai hesitated. He took his time in responding, as if he were repeating the words to himself silently and ensuring they held no flaws. A habit Silenos shared. One learned such things quickly under Mistress Kammani's tutelage. Even contractions became a pointless risk, he had found. Even his thoughts were starting to emulate the habit.

"Why do you serve House Shaiagrazni?"

The question took Silenos quite by surprise, though perhaps it should not have. It was a broad one, multifaceted and ambiguous. The sort that could mean so very many things. Half of which were terribly dangerous.

"In what regard?" he asked. "Why am I an apprentice?"

Juragai confirmed with a nod, and Silenos hissed in a wisp of breath without meaning to. This question, above all, felt . . . uncomfortable.

"For knowledge," he said mechanically. "For understanding. To empower my consciousness and elevate my cognition to a higher order of . . ." He trailed off upon seeing the look on Juragai's face. Not judgmental, but merely . . . patient. He was hearing an expected answer, and knew already that it was no good.

Just as Silenos would have. Silenos felt his temper fray.

"Stop looking at me like that," he snapped. "It's all true. House Shaiagrazni know more about magic than anything in this world. They are challenging gods and *winning*. Their success has proved above all doubt that their ideology is supreme. Under their rule—under our rule—the strong flourish and the weak are pressed to strengthen. They are humanity at its most distilled. Intelligent, driven, accomplished. I serve House Shaiagrazni because it is right. Because they deserve my servitude."

It was, perhaps, as perfect a declaration as Silenos himself had ever made, and entirely improvised. Improvised, and hollow.

"I see." Juragai's eyes had a distance behind them now, and he nodded. Polite, not friendly. "Thank you. That was all." The boy made his way out, not bothering to say anything else. Leaving Silenos alone with the strange feeling of discontent welling up in his gut.

NOW

Travel through the Shallow Depths was a great deal safer with the hybrid's head, to an extent even Silenos had not anticipated. It was not a mere factor of directions—for the geometry twisted and warped often enough that such a concept became redundant fast—but rather that it possessed some sort of instinctual grasp of which routes were safer and which more dangerous.

It meant they made better time, expended less mana in battle, and avoided the constant danger of clashing with Entities. Only twice did they encounter violence, both times against Entities less potent than Silenos herself. She'd have made short work of them, had her body not still been in the process of its repairs.

The head had been asked, by Ensharia of course, why it took such measures to preserve them all if it wished to die anyway. Its response had been the height of simplicity—because it knew the Entities would do vastly worse than kill it. Not stupid then.

Travel was made more fleeting through conversation, for all of five minutes—or possibly several aeons—before that turned sour with argument. It was, of course, Ensharia instigating. Latching on to mild perceived slights on Silenos's part and insisting they become a source of conflict.

"What do you mean my idea of good is the root of all evil?!" she snarled, quite unnecessarily, Silenos thought. She tempered her sense of intellect in anticipation and responded.

"There are certain impulses that remain within the human mind and shackle it. Empathy, compassion, altruism—all very tempting, very dangerous sensations. Our function as a species, as any species, is the accumulation of power and ability. To do this as best we can, we must acknowledge it and make it our priority. To be weak is to be *immoral*. Weakness denies one agency; it leaves one unable to right wrongs or resolve conflict. Only the strong may take ethical action, and so only the strong have earned the decency of separation from animals that similarly lack agency. What you believe is an easy, tempting animal instinct that threatens to weaken all who permit it space within their own minds."

Silenos's mind in question quivered as she said it, with guilt, regret, rage. She buried the emotions, as she was becoming dangerously accustomed to doing. There was no time for some tantrum now. And certainly not here.

Ensharia eyed her with more disgust than consideration.

"So power for power's sake. That's what you call moral? Power justifies itself? You need it to be moral, but the only morals worth acting on are a desire for power. Is that about what you're saying?"

She hesitated, then confirmed. "Yes."

Ensharia shook her head, seeming caught between awe and bafflement.

"That's not morality. That's just powerful people justifying why they can do whatever they want. If you want to talk about animal instincts, then respecting strength is up there with any other. It's not *moral* or praiseworthy to value power, Silenos. It's just cowardice with a lot of words to try to justify it. I do what I do because it's right, because a person's inability to defend themselves doesn't mean they deserve whatever happens to them. What do you do if some new magical house comes along with a thousand times House Shaiagazni's strength and tries to conquer you?"

Silenos did not hesitate before replying.

"We would welcome them," she answered. Ensharia shook her head again.

"And I would fight them. Yes, even knowing I would lose. Because my morals come from what is right, not what's easy."

Silenos took a moment to consider that, finding the words striking some chord in her. They angered her more than anything, and that anger turned into yet more. A tangible reminder of how deep her mental corruption had already seeped. It repulsed her.

Cowardice.

The word alone had little weight against her. House Shaiagrazni put little value in courage alone. But to have her people's virtues dismissed as nothing more than a simian deference born of fear and weakness, that stung. Stung so much that it was a struggle not to respond with impulsive fury.

Had that been the intent? No, Ensharia was speaking her thoughts without consideration for anything but that. As always. Silenos's response fell mutely from her lips as the head cut in.

"Sorry to interrupt." It groaned. "But the schism is ahead." Silenos's eyes snapped forward, scrutinous and alert, but she still felt the rift before she saw it. Indeed, she barely saw it at all.

CHAPTER TWENTY-THREE

Lilia had been anticipating many visitors. Some had met that expectation, and others had not. One of the rare few to surprise her *with* an appearance was the necromancer Sphera.

Such a pretty young thing, and clever, Lilia thought, she walked into her quarters looking far more tattered than she once had. And rather quickly. It'd been a week since Staliga had been hit by Lilia's reckoning, not very long at all to travel so far across the continent. She wondered how the girl had done it. One of Shaiagrazni's flesh-crafted transports, or had she improvised with mere necromancy?

The latter. A fleshcrafted mount would have been faster. Not that horses able to sprint without pause were in any way slow.

"It's nice to see you, dear." Lilia smiled, and she meant it too. The girl was a fresh face, a feminine face, against so many others. They hadn't spoken much, which Lilia thought was a shame. But that hadn't kept her from holding an eye on the pretty young thing.

She would have made an exquisite entry to her lineage, Lilia thought.

"Good evening," Sphera replied with a bow that might have been rather humorous in how low it went were the girl's situation not so starkly desperate. Instead it just conjured sympathy. "Thank you for granting me an audience."

"Oh hush." Lilia sighed. "I don't need thanks for a little thing like this."

The necromancer didn't flush. Lilia would have seen it even beneath her dark skin. She seemed entirely immune to manipulation of *that* kind. For the moment at least.

"Nonetheless, thank you," the necromancer replied. "I imagine you know what I'm here to discuss?"

"Explain it as if I don't." Lilia nodded her on.

"Alright. King Galukar warned Prince Nemo of the archimage Mafari's plans to kill him. He didn't warn me. I'd guess that he didn't warn you either."

Lilia made a show of chewing her lip. She'd found such idle gesticulations tended to lull humans into a sense of likeness. They didn't feel at home talking to a still corpse, not even one that talked back.

"He did not," she confirmed. "I know for a fact he sent warnings to Collin Baird and Queen Ado, naturally. It is not lost on me why we were exempt."

She decided to leave out that it was because of what Sphera had *done*, but what she *was*. Doubtless, the girl was imagining some commonality between them in that regard, and Lilia saw no reason to burst her bubble. Not when it could be put to such better use intact.

"As I suspected." Sphera sighed. "Clearly, he is no longer either of our ally. So I say we salvage this burned bridge and make the most of it. I propose we work together to protect ourselves from Galukar, and from Mafari especially."

Elegantly done, Lilia thought. A shade blunt perhaps. Sphera had made a mistake in delaying too long as she entered—that had only made it obvious her plan was to broach some preconsidered topic and lull Lilia's guard down about whatever would be suggested. But, for such a youthful child, it was far from a *failed* performance. She made mental notes on how best to improve the girl later.

"An alliance of what sort?" Lilia asked. "Military?"

She did enjoy seeing the sight of shock upon a human's face. They wore it so clearly. Eyes widening, lips thinning, blood pumping. These signs were fractional things, but to Lilia, each one may as well have been a call to the heavens. Sphera took her time in responding, as well she should have, and chose perhaps the most cautious answer possible.

"I would not suggest that," she said at last. "For many reasons. What sort of alliance would *you* imagine to be best, however?"

Again, clumsy, but not a bad direction of approach. She'd deflected the onus of providing specifics back onto Lilia, kept herself from being trapped in commitment to any given strategy, and avoided appearing either cowardly, aggressive, or, worst of all, merely seeking to exploit Lilia's prowess for her own gain. Such a clever young thing. Lilia was suddenly overcome by the urge to ruffle her hair.

"I would like to hear what you were hoping to achieve by this, dear." Lilia sighed. "Please, it's the least you can do, I think."

Sphera stiffened with concern, body seeming jolted into a statue sternness. Lilia suppressed a giggle, waited for her to answer. Listened intently to the beat of her heart and motion of her lungs as she did.

"I want safety," she whispered after long moments of stagnant silence. "I just want to live."

That was what decided Lilia, truly, on helping the girl. Not just for the pragmatic benefits of gaining so potent a caster on her side, but for the sake of helping her alone. That was when Sphera's life became the end rather than the means. But still she kept herself ready. What was about to be said could ruin this tentative negotiation for a hundred reasons.

"I cannot defeat Mafari," Lilia told her flatly. "If he chooses to destroy me, he will, in all likelihood, succeed. There are several reasons for this that I am not eager to share, but the fundamental point is that besting him with my own power is not currently an option."

She waited to see what the girl made of that. Sphera appeared to be surprised, but not that much. Good. It was a sign of stupidity to assume that the greatest extreme a person had encountered themselves was the greatest anywhere. So many assumed Lilia invincible. If she herself had made that mistake, she'd likely have ended up slain by either Shaiagrazni or, more likely, the original Dark Lord. The world was too wide for that oversight, and Lilia too old.

"What will you do then?" Sphera asked eventually. "You . . . You're not in hiding. You're not fleeing. I assumed, based on that, you knew you could fight him, but . . . Are you planning to ally with Mafari instead?"

She really was clever for a mortal. Lilia found herself impressed. Again, the urge to ruffle Sphera's hair came unbidden. She quashed it anew.

"To survive Mafari and his magi, we need to be an asset he cannot afford to destroy," Lilia explained. "And that means, by unfortunate necessity, becoming an asset against King Galukar . . . And Queen Ado and Baird."

The necromancer stiffened, thought about it. Swallowed. Then she nodded.

"Nemo is left unhurt," she replied at last. "That's my condition. My only condition."

Lilia smiled. "Of course, dear." Clearly, the poor thing was distracted. She'd never have let a vampire know exactly where her vulnerability lay otherwise.

THEN

Silenos felt fear. It had been so long since the cool acid of that particular sensation had touched him that he'd almost forgotten its embrace. Feeling it now, he wondered how. *How* could he forget *this*? It was the sensation, he thought, that ought to have defined humanity themselves. More than thought, more than ambition, fear was rooted in them all.

But then, maybe that was just animals in general. Perhaps he was not feeling his humanity so much as his life. In any case, it was no more resistible than the tide. Will was nothing compared to the depths of instinct, and every neuron of his mind quivered in unison as it swept across them.

But still, he persisted. That, Silenos supposed, was the human in him. To fear a thing, and to do it regardless. His mistress might have been proud in any other circumstance.

There would be no pride for this though. This was betrayal. Silenos shuddered as he thought the word. Paused, worried. For one moment, he feared that even to have it echo in his mind would somehow alert his household of what he intended. It was certainly not beyond House Shaiagrazni to peer into the thoughts of a mere apprentice. He—

No. Paranoia would not help him here. He needed clarity. He needed focus. Silenos pushed the fear as far from his mind's forefront as it would allow itself to be driven, and he continued walking down the dark corridor. He shivered all the same.

Juragai's quarters were fortunately located on the same floor as Silenos's own. That made his trip quicker and easier. He didn't knock on the door, just pushed it open. It was unlocked.

That was something that had always amazed him, how House Shaiagrazni's inner doors didn't even come with locking mechanisms. How it needed to be *requested* specifically. What arrogance. The thought had never occurred to him before but always been there. On the tip of his forebrain, flirting with his wits. A logical conclusion he'd kept himself carefully short of. Well, who cared about careful now? Silenos was betraying House Shaiagrazni, and House Shaiagrazni was arrogant. Years of pent-up denial broke apart like ice against a thrown brick.

What were they going to do—add disrespect onto his charge of treason? He would've laughed were such a thing not so suicidally idiotic.

He slithered into the quarters, crept through them. Found Juragai in his bed, nudged the boy awake.

"Be quiet," he warned him, voice low but not whispering. Whispers were high-pitched, easy to hear. Juragai blinked up at Silenos with confusion littered across his face.

"What are y—"

"You were right about everything," Silenos cut in. "I'm sorry. This place is wrong, and you were never weak. You . . ."

You were stronger than me to have kept your decency, despite all they did to crush it. Silenos couldn't say the words. Shaiagraznian pride had infiltrated him too deeply for that.

"You need to come with me," he said instead. "I have us a way out, a chance to escape. But only if we act quickly."

Juragai hesitated all of a second, then nodded.

"Alright," he breathed.

Together, Silenos and Juragai made their way out. Some things impeded them, a rare few. Reavers. Shaiagraznian grotesqueries made by their own mistress. They were not handcrafted beings, but a procreating species constructed on the genetic level by her own genius. Reptilian, faster than speed and stronger than strength. Numbers were what made them a threat, however, not intelligence. They failed to stop the pair, merely smelled Shaiagraznian apprentices and allowed them to pass with only the slightest delay. Then they were hurrying.

Silenos led Juragai to the end of their escape corridor, pausing to turn only at Juragai's insistence halfway through.

"This way," he urged, seeming suddenly fearful. "We need to head this way." The note of terror in his fellow apprentice's voice drew Silenos after him down the alternative path, freezing as he found what waited for him beyond it.

Mistress Kammani was standing ahead. She was not smiling.

A bizarre sort of clarity overcame Silenos as Juragai moved ahead and came to stand beside her. There wasn't anything like conviction in the boy's eyes, just misery.

"I'm . . ." He was about to apologize. Silenos silently urged him not to. "Not betraying our household," he said instead.

Thank God.

Odd, that. Silenos was concerned for his friend still.

"Why?" he asked. Juragai met his eye this time. House Shaiagrazni had taught him that.

"Because you were right," his friend replied. "I was weak. Vulnerable. The world doesn't care about compassion. It only cares about strength."

Silenos's heart broke, even as his mistress walked forward. His mistress, who'd given him everything he had. And taken everything he didn't. Why had she done that? What had been so threatening about Old Harriol?

He figured it out, just as she began reaching for him.

"You need everything else to be inferior and dangerous," Silenos whispered. "Because otherwise you're just doing what you want."

She touched his face, eyes simmering. Silenos stopped being a boy. Within microseconds of contact, he had become a thing, dropping down at her feet. But still able to hear, still able to think. That was the rage of Mistress Kammani. Reduction, not oblivion.

"Silenos," she said aloud. Then turned to her apprentice. Her remaining apprentice. "I really did like that name. Do you like it, Silenos?"

Juragai blinked, not understanding all at once. Then he nodded. There were tears in his eyes, kept from falling. If a single one spilled onto a single cheek, it would be his turn to enjoy her rage.

"Yes, mistress." He nodded. "Thank you, mistress. I, Silenos Shaiagrazni, will treasure my new name as long as I live."

CHAPTER TWENTY-FOUR

The schism remained stubbornly intact, defeating Silenos's efforts to widen it with a contemptuous stagnancy and failing to so much as quiver against them. She did not let her frustration show. At first. But it mounted quickly as one failed attempt turned into a dozen more. She had noticeably drained her own mana by the time she finally took a longer pause to consider an alternative.

Only then did the hybrid's head chime in, a smug lilt to its voice.

"Oh, you're not able to open up gates between worlds under your own power?"

Silenos wanted to liquefy the head, then force it to drink itself. It would not have been an especially productive thing to do, however, and so she restrained herself.

"And you can?" she snapped back. Silenos had been snapping a lot lately. The idea of keeping her emotions shackled and contained seemed somehow absurd. She was already a traitor to everything she had ever known. What did it matter if she added a few minor infractions atop that?

"I can," the head replied eagerly. "Easily, actually. I don't think you quite understand how much more powerful I am than you."

Something had raised its spirits after Silenos's new body finished the cloning process. She suspected the hybrid had been somewhat unsure of her ability to kill it and had that confidence bolstered upon seeing the extent of her fleshcrafting. If so, it was a fool. There was more to an Entity's form than molecules and energy.

But it did not need to know that much.

"Do it," Silenos commanded the creature.

"Say please," the head replied.

Silenos shook it, for one minute, two. She continued shaking it until, at last, the severed head yelled out its apology and promised to commit its powers to the task. Then she watched as it did so.

The schism opened with infuriating speed, responding to the hybrid's magic as if it had been waiting for it. Silenos made a note of the phenomenon. It seemed the connection between a hybrid and the Shallow Depths was stronger than she had anticipated. For now, however, she had greater concerns. The schism widened, a great light of mana engulfed her, and she found herself drifting once more through dimensionless space.

Soil came up underfoot, a soft cushion that Silenos sank into under the momentum of her long fall. Momentum? She was under the will of rational physics again, then. She looked around . . .

And realized she was *not* in the new world. Distantly, figures clashed. Towering things the size of mountains, one a great bare-chested humanoid with a bloody fissure beneath one breast and a barbed whip held in each fist. The other a snake, coiling and winged with acid dropping from its fangs to sear a new chasm everyplace a drop landed. With each motion of either giant, the landscape changed around them. Blasted and thrust apart by sheer weight at play.

Silenos stayed very, very still. She did not need to look with her arcane sight to know that this battle was beyond her, even in war form. A humbling realization. Just as she had been a thing beyond the new world, so too were there worlds beyond her. Perhaps there was one beyond even her master too.

"This is not the right universe," she growled to the head at her side.

"Right," it wheezed. "Sorry, one second." The schism above her, not yet fully closed, widened again, and Silenos found herself dragged into it. The world distorted and broke apart for the second time as she fell again.

The High Shallows greeted her underfoot, and she scowled at the hybrid.

"You are an inept rat," she informed it, earning a glare in return that would have seen the hybrid's eyes plucked out were it not so—temporarily—useful.

"This isn't an exact deed," it snapped. "Be patient and tell your companions to stick close."

Silenos had just enough time to glance over and see both the paladin and vampire approaching her before a new surge took the schism, and she was once again dragged through unreality. This time there was no choking pollution of magic in the air, which was a good sign.

She dropped down into a building, slipping through its roof as the matter turned intangible to allow entry and landing on her feet before . . . three men. All young, all above average in height, all staring with the kind of look she'd come to expect in Collin Baird.

One was of tan or brown skin similar to her own, another pale and scratchy. The third was a darker shade of black than any in Ado's family. Each one of them was on edge, primed and ready to move fast.

"Who the fuck are you?" the pale one asked, the tallest by some margin. His voice was remarkably similar to Baird's. In accent, surprisingly, but more pressingly in *tone* and *direction*. It had an almost unstable quiver to it that had Silenos's own guard raising to ready for violence.

"I am Silenos Shaiagrazni," Silenos explained. "Master of the arcane arts, named of House Shaiagrazni and mightiest being your pitiable world has ever seen."

"I *made* this pitiable world, cunt," the tallest one growled, actually growled like some sort of animal. "And you don't even crack the top ten."

Silenos took one step forward, raising her hands. The brown-skinned man, most muscular by far, took two steps forward himself, and in a flash of arcane discharge, his body was wreathed in armor of glowing white mana. His hands clutched a long sword made of the very same material. She paused.

"Let's not get hasty here," the last of the strangers, a dark-skinned man only slightly shorter than the others, cut in. "We don't know one another, and as far as I'm aware, none of us have any reason to be . . . unfriendly. Maybe we can even work together, right? How did you get into my mansion? Let's start with that, because that's what has me really curious here."

"I do not have to explain myself to you. I am above you in every way. You are an imbecile," Silenos informed him. She had not fully entered her war form, but her arm had transformed itself to its primary cannon configuration. She gauged the thickness of the brown man's armor. Going by the density of magic within its material, she suspected it would prove sturdier by far than steel. But even centimeters thick, that did not mean it would resist her weapon.

"Pretty gun you have there," the blond noted. "What's it fire, arrows?"

Silenos's eye twitched. *Arrows.* What sort of savage did he take her for? She unleashed the cannon into the wall. Watched stone explode outward as the men stared.

The tall, pale one was quickest to overcome his surprise.

"Solid shots then, eh?" He was interrupted as the darkest of them hurriedly spoke.

"Holy shit, stop antagonizing her!"

The pale one ignored him. "Explosive propellant. An actual gun. Interesting. And you make your own ammo, right? Using the same power that lets you reshape your limbs."

"Dude," the darker, calmer man continued, "she's going to kill us."

"No she's not," the brown man interjected. "I can take her."

"No you fucking can't!"

Silenos didn't answer, not the blond one's question nor the bickering of his associates. She was not pleased with how much information he seemed to have gleaned.

"I'll take that as a yes," the pale man continued. "You're not using sabots? If you make smaller projectiles, wrapped in lighter material, you can apply more force without increasing barrel pressure to get higher velocities in your projectiles. Probably even hypersonic with that weapon. You didn't think of that already though. Above us in every way?" He grinned. "Maybe in the amount of lead in your brain matter."

He had to die, Silenos decided. Such an insult to her could not be permitted. She took another step forward, raised her cannon, and saw the room explode into violence. Then the schism widened again and displaced her all over.

The Shallow Depths met her with their usual unfriendly embrace. Silenos landed well. Hexeri and Ensharia did not.

"What was that?" the paladin groaned, getting up to her knees. "*Who* was that?"

Hexeri was already standing, lip curled. "I don't know. That blond one though . . ." She shivered. "It was like his eyes were licking me."

"Nobody," Silenos cut in, rage bubbling still in her mind. "Nothing. They were an irrelevance."

Encase the smaller projectiles in lighter material . . . She could up projectile diameter within the barrel, increasing the mass but at a slower rate than she did the area. This would allow for a higher velocity while acceleration was still underway from the propellant, and the lighter fixture holding her projectile—the sabot—would fall away as it left the barrel. So simple, so obvious.

That *worm* had thought of it, and she had not?

"I need you to take me back there," Silenos growled to the head, already experimenting with a new pattern for projectiles fitting that description. She would see how smug the rat was when he tasted the fruits of his own design.

"I won't," the hybrid replied.

Silenos reached down, took it from its fixture against her hip, and raised it high.

"Why?" she asked, biting back the urge to say so much more.

"Because that wasn't our deal," it replied. "I take you to where you want to go, a world you can do your work in peace, and you kill me."

"I can do my work in peace in *that* world," she snarled.

"No, you can't. That boy corrected your weaponry at a glance and claimed that there were at least ten things more powerful than you there. I don't want to chance him being right twice. I'll take you somewhere else. Bring me to another point."

Silenos stood trembling for a moment, the rage animating her. She slowly forced it back down and silently carried the head where it had asked.

It did not take so long. This time, the head was rather eager as it directed her through the Depths.

"I feel this one," it urged. "I feel it more strongly than any other. It reeks of fate."

Fate. A primitive term for the phenomenon of causality being gleaned by sights bolstered by more than mere biology. She did not bother to correct the hybrid, simply let it guide her on in its own satisfaction. Hexeri and Ensharia were similarly silent. She supposed the realms they had experienced would have been all the more disturbing for them than even for her. Most things were for the weak.

Silenos paused. Was that *empathy*? From *her*? She felt her disgust mounting and surprised herself by glancing at Ensharia as it did. Somehow, that alleviated the feeling. And replaced it altogether with a sudden rage that even she could not pinpoint the origins of.

"We're here," the hybrid announced, drawing Silenos from her infuriating mental disruption and bringing the group's focus to . . . nothing. A spot, like any other. Only to her arcane eyes was it different at all, and even then only by a slight . . .

No, Silenos saw more. *Felt* more. A strange tugging at her will, almost similar to the feeling of her magic connecting with tissue as she remodeled it.

"What is this?" she asked, uncertain why exactly. If she had expected the hybrid to know more than her, she would have been disappointed.

"The right way." He breathed, and the air began distorting again. Yet again Silenos and her companions were displaced. This time they landed hard on paved streets, battered by a hot sun and surrounded on all sides by towering buildings and staring guards. Guards wearing armor of impossible metallic perfection, wielding weapons bound with lesser Entities, adorned with sigils she had come to know more familiarly than even her own name.

It took all of three seconds for the assembly of Shaiagraznian guards to recognize her, and less than one more for them to lower their arms.

"Mas—Mistress Silenos," the nearest one called. "It is an honor to behold you once more."

CHAPTER TWENTY-FIVE

Mafari was archimage of Magira, wielder of magics beyond the comprehension of most, and, perhaps, the single most potent mortal being in his entire world. And yet even he felt a stab of twisting nervousness as he made his way for the audience. It was, he thought, quite natural. A hundred years ago, he had been young. *Two* hundred years ago, the creature he intended to meet now had been old. Mafari was likely the more powerful of them, but in every other capacity, he was outmatched.

It never ceased to amaze him, the lifespan of elves, nor concern him.

King Magnia awaited Mafari upon a great throne hewed of dark wood and encrusted with vibrant amber seemingly of every color there was. He was, perhaps without exaggeration, the most beautiful being Mafari had ever laid eyes upon. His face beyond mere human notions of handsomeness, bearing some primal magnetism that threatened to leave him breathless. Not sexual, not sexual at all—to call it that felt somehow reductive and crude—merely . . . aesthetic.

"Good evening." He nodded to the king. The king nodded back. Neither of them fully deferred; neither was contemptuous. Mafari appreciated that. So many monarchs of the human world thought themselves above Magira's archimage. He was willing to tolerate their delusion, to leave their self-deception intact, but it was still . . . irksome.

He was pleased to be doing without it here.

"Young Mafari," the elf greeted him, showing about as much respect as could be expected from him for any human. "It has been some time. What brings you to my realm?"

"You know already, I suspect," Mafari noted, scrutinizing the elf's features. He saw nothing to betray a secret, emotion, or sentiment regarding that. As per usual. The older a being got, the more their face seemed to crystallize in place. The less penetrable any deception they wove into it would grow. Mafari was not used to being the disadvantaged one in matters of age and history.

He did not much care for it.

"The distortion." King Magnia sighed. "We have sensed it too, of course. Such a powerful thing, so . . . untempered. It does not belong in the hands of your kind."

"Or yours," Mafari noted. "Drop the pretenses, Magnia, we both know the myth of elfin infallibility was killed when so many of your people joined the first Dark Lord."

Magnia smiled. Some among his species were easily irritated when egos got pricked. He had always found the experience novel and interesting. Mafari suspected a king grew more tired of its absence than the rest of his kind.

"A fair point, and once again it seems danger has emerged in the lands of that . . . renegade."

"Renegade," Mafari replied, feeling his temper grow uncharacteristically hot. "That almost seems like too much credit. I've seen his kind a hundred times before. Hedge wizardry and ego is not a substitute for true arcane knowledge."

Magnia's lip curled.

"You know, between the two of us, we could control the continent itself," he began.

"I do know," Mafari replied evenly. "You told me as much a decade ago."

"And I am telling you again now," the elf pressed. "It is even more true now than it was then, if anything. What is stopping us?"

Mafari couldn't help but smile. The days of Magnia equaling his power, let alone exceeding it, felt so easy to recall that he almost overlooked their passing.

"The fact that I do not need you to do that." He sighed.

Magnia didn't bristle this time either, though Mafari wondered how much closer the elf king had come.

"You want assistance on closing the distortion," he affirmed. "I can provide it. But I will do so along with a warning: Do not underestimate this danger."

Mafari met his eye.

"I appreciate your warning," he replied. Both of them knew though that he would not be deterred, and Mafari himself was certain there was no great danger here. The world had long since run out of threats for a caster of his capacity. "Now, your aid with the distortion?"

Magnia sighed lightly, nodding.

"Very well."

He spoke, and Mafari listened. He enjoyed the rare experience of *learning* something in the ways of magic. The days of his power falling short of Magnia's were long past, but the difference in experience between them was still measured in centuries. One day, he intended to know more than any other. But it would take a hundred thousand more conversations like this one, he suspected, before that day was upon him.

When the king had finished, and Mafari committed the meat of all his words to memory, they parted with respectful nods to each other. Mafari's magic caressed the air ahead and pulled it apart. His portal widened before him.

For all his power, this was not something he had ever managed himself. Even now. Mafari could rend space only by borrowing the might of his patron, and each time he did, their whisper grew louder at the back of his mind. Magi had been driven to insanity by channeling such powers.

But no archimage. No *true* archimage, at least. He stepped through and felt himself dislodge from the world, then impress his substance back into it elsewhere. The cool walls of the Dark Lord's castle greeted him. Littered with sprayed viscera, surrounding a mangled carpet of human carcasses.

Mafari's rage was not long in coming.

"Get out," said the figure at the end of the room, tall and covered in black armor. His face was unhelmed, eyes dark and level. Mafari had heard enough descriptions of the Dark Lord to recognize him at a glance.

"Did you do this?" he asked the man.

"Get out," he replied, ignoring Mafari's question. It seemed there would be no dialogue with him. That suited Mafari just fine.

His magic leaped out, wrapped around the Dark Lord, and . . . did nothing. Tried to find purchase upon him, his soul, tried to snuff it out and erase him from history. Couldn't. The power around the man was somehow too great. Mafari overcame his surprise quickly and exerted his power yet again, tore open the air. Another portal was born, this one linking the world's one side to its other. Most thought the world was flat, even feared sailing off its edge if they strayed too far from the center. Mafari had traveled enough to know better. The land beneath him was a great sphere, spinning at impossible speeds as it rotated about the sun. Everything fell toward its center.

On one side of that center, the spinning left the land moving in opposite direction to the other. Each on their own mustered impossible speeds. By taking an object directly from one side of the world, it would maintain that velocity as it emerged on the other. And so Mafari's enemy was struck by the volley of boulders as they spun and screamed through the air.

They drove him into the wall, made it *shiver*. Mafari watched with some satisfaction for all of a moment as more and more projectiles exploded against their target. Then the Dark Lord forced his way up.

With one swing, his mace cleared the air of them. Actually sent a wind blasting through the room, disturbing its currents enough to send Mafari's projectiles off-kilter. Another swing sent Mafari himself stumbling, and he was already leaping across the room before the next came.

Mafari had never seen anything move even half so fast as him. Not Swick the Swift, not the rangers of Kaltan. Nothing. His shield was barely up in time to meet the falling mace, and when it did, there was nothing but a shattering of hardened energy before the weapon burst through. Mafari's portal carried him across the room, letting him avoid the swing by milliseconds as he called on another.

This time, he linked his portal to the depths of a searing volcano and let the magma explode outward—pressurized by its own great mass and shooting free with a hungry viciousness as the portal alleviated compression. The Dark Lord disappeared beneath glowing molten sludge. Then emerged from it almost unhurt.

Magma was sent flying in all directions, glowing, spitting globules of hot death splashing around and cooling where they hit. Some fell upon the floor, others on the corpses. Those that found bodies instead of stone quickly cooked the tissue and filled the room with an acrid stench of searing flesh. It seemed a kitchen now was to be Mafari's battlefield.

And every moment he remained in it left him more certain that he was the meat upon its chopping block. The Dark Lord continued after him, butcher's weapon ready. He swung through the air again, and this time a *demon* burst into it.

It was a minor thing compared to some Mafari had seen, but potent enough to cleave through the sheet of magma he washed it with and shrug off the breaking of boulders against it. The room's sound was consumed as impact rang out powerfully enough to smother all else.

Then the demon hit Mafari's shield, clawed at it, began forcing its way in. The Dark Lord leaped high, came down with another swing. His heart raced, mind whirred, life flashed before him as every instinct he had all rang out as one.

He was going to die. This fight was beyond him; it would have been beyond two of him. Mafari was outmatched.

Mafari's newest portal formed up just in time for him to fall back into it, earning him one final glimpse of the Dark Lord's mace smashing into the ground he'd just occupied. It came apart. Stone exploding upward, outward. Breaking like dried bread each direction a dozen yards out. He landed, rolled back, and willed the portal closed just an instant before his enemy could follow him through.

Gasping, groaning, Mafari slowly forced his way up. He was panting, hands trembling for the first time since . . . He couldn't remember. He was *scared*. An alien sensation, assassinating his reason and enfeebling his wits.

"I did warn you."

Behind Mafari, standing now, Magnia looked down at him with a suitably knowing, imperious stare. He wondered whether that was something that came naturally with the centuries or if the elf had practiced it.

"Not well enough," Mafari growled, stumbling only a moment as he finished rising. He'd not been hit, not even once, but his entire body ached. Skin sore where the Dark Lord had battered it with shock waves, bones throbbing from pressure differentials. It was a magus's curse to always feel his body's fragility compared to the power of his mind.

"Well enough for most. You can consider this a lesson."

Yes, Mafari thought. *And had I died rather than escaping to learn it, you could have considered yourself the most powerful living being in this world.*

Second most powerful now, of course. Assuming the Dark Lord was still a living mortal. He shivered.

"You can consider it a lesson too." Mafari frowned. "You *didn't* bank on this being the Dark Lord's power. You would have considered the notion as ridiculous as I. You . . . Hmm."

He realized it in a rush. Mafari had been Magnia's test subject, the bait used to lure out the Dark Lord's true power and gauge it personally. Doubtless he'd been watching the whole battle somehow. Doubtless he'd learned more from it than even Mafari.

That much was obvious, because beneath his veneer of confidence the elfin king seemed *frightened*.

"I see the centuries have not dulled your mind, old friend," he replied. "Yes, you are correct. And we are in more danger than either of us knew."

Mafari did not ask Magnia to share his knowledge. He knew it wouldn't happen. Not even now. Not if a dozen more Dark Lords emerged to join the first two. The elves had never done anything for humanity, leaving them to blindly flounder alone as they stumbled through the dark tides of magic. That much would never change.

But circumstances did, and Mafari no longer had the luxury of holding old grudges for slights long made. If he and Magnia did not combine their strengths, they would die alone. That made the decision no decision at all.

"Very well," he answered.

Perhaps one Dark Lord would have left room for old grudges to fester. Two certainly did not.

CHAPTER TWENTY-SIX

Silenos's reconfigured cognition had allowed many new sensations to assail her. Most she hated. The one she felt now, she hated more than even the others. It was . . . shock.

Shock was a pitiable thing. A cursed poison in her mind. Not anger, which urged haste and speed, driving thoughts toward action. Nor was it fear, a quivering, scattering sharpening. Shock was the antithesis of all such things, urging *inaction* and *languidness*. It was like molten lead poured into musculature, weighing it down and adding mass without force. Contributing nothing to the locomotion and making every twitch that much more an exertion.

There were many situations that had surprised Silenos since her displacement in reality. In fact, it seemed at times that her life for the past few months had been nothing *but* surprises. The most crushing one of all, however, was the realization that she felt out of place even now.

Now. Here. In the lands of House Shaiagrazni, finding herself escorted through familiar streets with familiar deference, being shown all the respect she was owed and enjoying all the sights she was accustomed to. The place she had grown up, become a caster, and graduated from the mewling creature she had once been. And she felt out of place.

The knowledge made her sick and . . . frightened.

It did not take long for her to be led through the city and into the central tower, up through its bowels and into the heights within.

Ensharia and Hexeri were with her all the while. Neither seemed to understand the privilege they were being shown in receiving the right to set foot within so grand a place, or at least Silenos assumed they did not understand given that neither had dropped to their knees weeping tears of joy and prostrating. She supposed the ignorance of the new world was not tied to that universe itself. They would remain hopelessly uneducated on all things Shaiagrazni wherever they went.

Even, most dangerously, among House Shaiagrazni itself.

"Your possessions will remain here," one of the guards informed Silenos. It was a grotesquerie, a sapient variety made to serve the hybrid purposes of war machine and attendant. This one was perhaps misnamed. The only thing grotesque about its features was how anomalous they were, sculpted to the very perfection of human beauty and then, evidently, taken vastly beyond. House Shaiagrazni's knowledge of the psionic magics had served to elevate aesthetics to those with an appeal that registered on the subinstinctual level. In this creature, Silenos saw the culmination of that.

She found it rather distasteful, but then many in House Shaiagrazni would say the same about her own preferences in creation. Until she found out who specifically had made the construct before her, she had no way of knowing whether their power was beyond hers—and thus their aesthetic preference sublime or inferior.

"Very well," Silenos conceded, for she knew, no matter what, that this construct was conveying the orders of her superior. She turned to Ensharia and Hexeri. "The two of you are to stay here."

"We are *not* your luggage," the paladin growled, taking a step forward. The guards stiffened, readied to move. Silenos felt her heart race with uncharacteristic fear.

Is it uncharacteristic though? What am I? The shed skin of Silenos Shaiagrazni, a great caster no longer for this world.

She pushed that aside. Ensharia was mere words away from being obliterated for her insolence. She did not understand House Shaiagrazni. That misunderstanding would kill her if she didn't act.

"Please," Silenos cut in. "Not now . . . Mistress." She addressed Ensharia as she said it. The room froze. Without apologizing, or wavering, she turned to the guard. "Forgive my servitor. I have taught her to sexually dominate me for recreational purposes. I fear she has taken her role too seriously. There is no need to kill her for her disrespect."

A single glance back at Ensharia confirmed to Silenos that she had gotten the message, and another glance back at the guards told her that they, like all Shaiagraznian servitors, knew better than to question her. If they were aware of Silenos's asexuality, they still did not bring it up. It would have been no issue even if they had, of course. She'd simply have destroyed them for slighting her and thus kept the incident for her own memory alone.

Past the guarded door was Silenos's next challenge. One she had never overcome before.

Mistress Kammani was unchanged. Literally unchanged. Her face was, on the atomic level, no different to how it had been when she had first met Silenos 140 years prior, and if what Silenos had heard from others was accurate, it had been identical to that at least two centuries earlier. Devastatingly beautiful in a way she could appreciate regardless of sexual interest. There was an aesthetic quality, a starkly intellectual fact, to Kammani's features, which were the product only of her own great fleshcrafting knowledge. Knowledge so advanced it was to Silenos's as Silenos's own was to most Shaiagraznian apprentices.

"Silenos." She smiled. "It has been a while."

From her perspective, Silenos supposed, she was not making much of an understatement. One hundred and fifty years was as great a fraction of Kammani's life as three was of Silenos's own.

"It has," she agreed. "I am pleased to announce my return to House Shaiagrazni."

"And I am pleased to witness it." Kammani nodded. "Your loss was felt by all. It is doubtless no surprise that we have yet to produce another prodigy of your abilities even after all this time."

Silenos felt a stab of something at that, buried it. It was only right that her loss be assessed upon the deficit of utility it produced.

"What has come of House Shaiagrazni in my absence?" she inquired. "How does the war progress? What advancements have been made while I was preoccupied?"

Kammani told her, and Silenos listened. There was much to hear. Fleshcrafting had been pioneered to lengths that left her newly undereducated, updates in theory and understanding having outstripped Silenos's own grasp. Necromancy too had advanced, though not by quite so much. The war had progressed and escalated all at once, with new weapons on each side and a vicious no-man's-land now bifurcating the entirety of their planet.

Such had been the predictions, 150 years ago. All turned from projection to reality. And none had deterred House Shaiagrazni for any of the 150 years they took to do so.

"I see." Silenos felt hollow at the realization. They had accomplished so very little, for all their brilliance. Expanding territory by a few kilometers, growing more efficient at killing. And yet they were still locked in battle.

That will end, with the tempered schisms being stabilized. That will spell the end of any resistance to House Shaiagrazni for as long as we exist.

Abruptly, Kammani tilted her head.

"Your neurology has changed," she noted. "Changed drastically. Anterior insular cortex reformed, cerebrum altered for emotional processing and intuitive thought."

She did not phrase her question as anything more than an idle observation. Still, Silenos couldn't help but respond to it. She had questioned herself about just that enough that the thought of leaving no comment upon her master's comment was . . . irksome.

"Recent events forced me to adjust," she replied.

"Tell me about them," Kammani gently suggested. Some had, Silenos knew, referred to her master's mannerisms as motherly. She could not have commented upon that herself. She had been found by House Shaiagrazni as an orphan already. She did know that, among the elders of their household, Kammani was unique in seeming to have maintained much of her humanity.

Some took that to be a sign of compassion or kindness in her. They were fools. Mistress Kammani was among the cruelest and most manipulative creatures Silenos had ever met, and she used her own empathic abilities for very much the same reason as Silenos. To gain an advantage over others.

That advantage was the deadliest thing in the world for Silenos. She calmed herself, readied herself. Explained herself.

And mentally prepared to be caught in a lie and accidentally hang herself.

She went over the events of her betrayal by Adonis and her displacement into the new world. The earliest deeds of hers were easily explained. It was only after she reconfigured her brain, and continued spending time among her newfound allies, that her decisions became . . . harder to justify.

It was strange—Silenos hadn't realized until that moment how questionable her decision-making had been. Going over it in retrospect, she counted a thousand irrationalities and almost tripped up in keeping them all from the report. Nonetheless, she did so.

Mistress Kammani listened to it all. Considering.

Silenos's message had gotten across to Ensharia perfectly well, and she'd watched the caster disappear with a mix of shock and awe. She had imagined, perhaps stupidly, that Silenos was in some way anomalous among her people. *Assumed*, perhaps due to some faulty belief that the universe was kind and pleasant, that there was not an entire household full of people as or more deranged than her.

Now she knew otherwise, and that knowledge made itself felt in her mind like cold fingers against a spine. She shivered, mouth dry, pacing, hands twitching for her weapons, and . . . What?

What would her weapons even do here? She'd seen the things Silenos improvised. This was a civilization with casters equal to her and more, who had established themselves centuries ago and prepared all their equipment ahead of time. Ensharia didn't know if they would even register what she carried as a tool of war. Perhaps they would mistake it for some kind of back massager.

"Let's go." She turned to see Hexeri addressing her, fidgeting. "This place is . . . I don't like it."

Ensharia realized what she meant. The spire was a cramped place, despite its sprawling vastness. Somehow the very space—that great abscess within its every room—seemed to compress on her worse than a barely cleared stretch of stone.

"Let's," she agreed, heading from the door. If Silenos returned, she would doubtless find them soon enough. And in the meantime, Ensharia wished to be as far from those upsettingly beautiful guards as was possible. Their very presence made her ill at ease, as if they lied to her with appearances alone.

She supposed, in a way, they did.

Outside, the halls were just as broad. This one was broken up only by a single figure. Tall, with a scowl upon his face and matted hair. He looked younger than Ensharia by a good few years and glanced irritably at her as he headed to the door at her back.

"Out of the way," he ordered, almost lazily. It was like hearing a man give commands to his dog. Ensharia felt no inclination to obey *that* of all things, standing still.

"You don't give me orde—" She hadn't even finished the sentence when a blast of magic struck her, sent her flying through the air to rebound blinking and gasping. She landed hard, realized she'd struck the far wall some fifty paces back, and felt her body aching as clumps of shattered stone fell down around her. Hexeri smashed into it a moment later. She didn't bounce, merely stuck into the material like a pickax's head.

Ensharia gasped. She'd meant to do more, to stand, to move, to fight. All her body managed though was a gasp. She'd hit stone before, felt it crumble beneath her, and had long months to grow accustomed to Silenos's enhancement of her body. Whatever she'd impacted, it wasn't stone.

Her mouth full of blood, lungs with hot air, eyes with tears, and heart with fear, she could do nothing but watch as the smug, sneering little asshole who'd dared to give her orders slowly stalked over. His fingers twitched, eyes twitched more. There was victory in him. And, she saw, cruelty.

It was stopped only as one of the guards stepped forward.

"Apologies, apprentice," they began. "We would request that you stop brutalizing these creatures. They are the property of Mistress Silenos."

The boy couldn't have frozen faster, even if he'd been turned to stone.

"Oh." Instantly, he was beside Ensharia, hands outstretched. She winced, prepared herself to be twisted and ruined . . . Then felt the pain subside instead as her broken form was healed. Hexeri's had regenerated halfway by the time he even moved on to her, vampiric constitution once more making itself known.

"Apologies," the apprentice hastily added. "I had no idea you were . . . Well, send my regards to . . . to Silenos." He paled, slightly, beneath the brown skin, swallowed again. "Master Silenos, that is. I must . . . Uh, I have things to do." He practically sprinted away. Ensharia watched him, satisfaction muted only by the . . . humiliation.

CHAPTER TWENTY-SEVEN

Somehow, Silenos was still alive. To say she was surprised would have been an understatement. Even she had no idea what had happened to keep her breathing and free through the interview with her former mistress. By some quirk of chance, however, she had emerged from it unscathed.

Though not flawlessly. Kammani knew something was off—of that much, Silenos was certain. She'd told too many lies and obfuscated too many truths for anything else. If her elder disbelieved the story of Adonis being stranded, or had pierced the reality of her reports, there had been no indication. But Silenos knew she was under suspicion.

She also knew that Kammani had believed at least most of what she'd said, no doubt in part thanks to Adonis's own work in corroborating the earlier parts of her tale. Silenos had requested the materials needed to construct another tempered schism and had found the requisition instantly satisfied. She was not so big a fool as to let this lower her guard. But it was a boon, for now.

As she worked, Silenos had time to think. Her mind split. In the past, she had considered such a thing obstructive. Told herself that her intellect required total concentration upon its task, and perhaps that had been true. She was certainly less efficient, letting the cognitive labor of her efforts become a subconscious process. But the real cost was that she was free to sort through her own emotions.

Her emotions. Now *the* emotions, not the incursion onto her mind. Her own emotions. How long had Silenos been denying them even that moniker?

Since the night she . . . Since what had happened to her friend. The original Silenos. The one who'd made the mistake of trusting her.

For the first time in almost two natural lifespans, Silenos felt the full weight of that fact. She'd experienced it before, long ago. Immediately after the deed. And she had reconfigured her own mind that very night to ensure she did not feel it again. Fled from the sensation in a frenzy, until it became no more to her than a memory.

But now it was back, and the walls of Shaiagraznian discipline that had staved it off were collapsed. Something worse than death overcame Silenos at that. Remorse.

Why did I keep these infernal processes . . . ?

Silenos couldn't find an answer. It seemed ludicrous, pure self-destruction. She had ruined herself. Ruined everything. And why? *Why?* What had possessed her to keep the poison that was now mangling her cognition?

The tempered schism was something she could not have managed herself in the past. Doubtless, that was intentional on Kammani's part. A means of ensnaring Silenos in a lie. If she had spoken falsely, then her ability to create such a thing would be no less limited than ever. It was fortunate, then, that she had gleaned what she could from Adonis as he did so.

Even still, the effort was long and tedious. She threw herself into it. Tedium was a distraction from the strangling guilt in her mind, and that was something Silenos needed now more than she ever had before.

She was a traitor, and she would die a traitor. But she did not overturn herself to meet the fate she deserved. Could not. There were things Silenos needed to do, and . . . the thought scared her. For so long she'd let herself live without emotional cognition, and now that it returned once more to her mind, she had lost the ability to control it. Her own fear had enslaved her, weakened her. She was an animal, moving only as she felt rather than as she thought was best.

But that changed nothing because she *did* have things she needed to do. And a plan to do them.

There was a single obstacle to everything Silenos might attempt—Kammani. If she turned her power against her, Silenos would lose. Instantly. With no chance of deviation from that eventuality. Arion Falls would have a greater hope of overcoming her in war form than she would of besting her own master without it.

Eight thousand years, perhaps more, she had amassed power. Silenos's 150 would not compare, however gifted she was. Magic was nothing so mutable as that. And so she schemed *around* Kammani instead, considering ways to separate herself from the elder.

Silenos had negotiated her way into being deployed back to the new world among a party of other Shaiagraznian named, with the goal of properly conquering it and rescuing Adonis. She would sabotage this. Kammani did not yet know about the hybrid. Silenos had carefully hidden its head within a body cavity shortly after arriving, and without it, she lacked the means to make Adonis's schism function. Perhaps she would reverse engineer it eventually, but by then, Silenos had plans to have reinforced the barrier between her world and the new world.

All of it came down to her ability to enter the new world alone once the schism began and leave the device failing behind her.

The timing would be narrow, and the consequences for failure extreme. It all hinged upon Silenos's ability to get the better of her fellow named. Not defeat them, never that. She had heard anywhere from three to six would accompany her—grotesquely excessive for conquering the new world, and yet perfectly suitable for overcoming her own power.

If she could not do what she needed to in the brief window surprise would earn her against them, she would be overpowered and found guilty of treason. In all her years, Silenos had never once walked so fine a margin of success.

Her thoughts were interrupted by the opening of the door. She turned, finding Ensharia and Hexeri walking in. They seemed... distraught.

"What did you do?" she asked. If nothing else, she had been right in her initial assessment of the use found with emotional processing—her intuition was correct. Both of them bristled and explained.

"We ran into an apprentice," Ensharia mumbled, not meeting her eye. "He was rude, gave us an order. I was explaining that we wouldn't obey when he attacked us."

Silenos frowned. "And you somehow survived making such a grievous blunder without injury?"

Neither woman was pleased at that.

"The guards told him we . . . *belonged* to you, and we were healed."

Silenos nodded. "Excellent, did you get the apprentice's name?"

The women blinked.

"N-no?" Hexeri frowned. "Why?"

"Because I am going to remove his genitals and make him eat them before departing," Silenos explained. Neither of them said anything at that, just looked somewhat queasy. The effect was particularly amusing upon Hexeri's undead features.

"Since you are here," she continued, "I have taken the liberty of requisitioning some preparatory measures for when we return to the new world. Doubtless, there will be conflict."

Neither was stupid enough to mention Adonis, perhaps knowing, as Silenos did, that they could be spied upon at any time.

"You have weapons for us?" Hexeri asked.

Ensharia's response was less eager and hopeful, more . . . concerned.

"You want to enhance my body again," she guessed, completely correctly.

"I do," Silenos confirmed. She paused.

"I don't know if I . . . I mean to say that it . . ." She swallowed, mastering herself. "I regretted letting you do it the first time, in the end. Kept thinking how I'd let a person I . . . thought I knew alter me. Kept wondering what you might have done without telling me."

Silenos surprised herself by a sudden feeling of . . . something. She was not able to identify it. But it motivated her to respond quickly.

"I did nothing except what I told you I had." Ensharia swallowed, not convinced. "I . . ." Silenos had been about to reassure her but found herself reminded of the imminent threat posed by surveillance. She remained quiet instead.

"Alright." Ensharia finally relented. "Do it."

Silenos tilted her head, relieved. Relieved at the strengthening of her ally, or at Ensharia agreeing to leave herself safer? A month ago, she would not have known. Now her illusions of remaining a true Shaiagrazni were in tatters.

"It will not just be me doing the work," she explained. "But all of it is filtered through my glorious mind to ensure it is ideal."

In truth, much of it was beyond her. Silenos had managed to call in favors from some of her fellow named, even those relative few who exceeded her in fleshcrafting. She had bristled to find that several were once her inferiors at it.

"Accompany me then."

Ensharia was taken to the agreed-upon workstation, and the work began. Fortunately, she knew enough to remain still and passive as it was done, not answering any of House Shaiagrazni's named with slights regardless of how she was addressed. They fleshcrafted her quickly, each working within their field of specialization.

Her skin was altered the most, restructured into a single-protein substance of remarkable strength and flexibility, then thickened. Her musculature was rethreaded to allow for an order of magnitude more lengthening and shortening at every contraction, and each of those motions was made faster to boot.

Myelin sheaths were replaced by something altogether superior, nerves shortened and made more swift. Bone minerals increased in volume as the white blood cells produced by their marrow became more efficient. A thousand optimizations were added onto Silenos's original work, then ten thousand more. By the end of it, however, Ensharia's outward appearance was very much unchanged.

"You really ought to strengthen the body further," suggested Kire, Silenos's senior by half a millennium. He was one of the fleshcrafters present whom Silenos knew was her superior in a general sense.

"I need her to blend in," she explained. "Additionally, overtly flesh-crafted modifications may have her serve as warning for the enemy that I have returned."

"You are a grunting imbecile, unworthy of my very conversation." Kire sighed but left his response at that minor protest.

Soon enough, the named cleared out from the room, leaving Ensharia, Hexeri, and Silenos alone.

"I feel . . . odd," the paladin noted, flexing her fingers and slowly moving her limbs. Not so slowly. She might have exerted herself to be so fast before. Adjusting to her new body would take time.

"You are now, I estimate, within fifty percent of Galukar's physical prowess," Silenos informed her, taking a surprising pleasure in her awe. "I shall demonstrate." With a gesture, Silenos formed a block of solid bone between them. It was a perfect meter-wide cube. "This material is not the strongest I can make, nor is it within an order of magnitude of being such, but it is exponentially beyond the resilience of most natural bone."

Density of close to five grams per cubic centimeter, and with a structure to empower it even more. Bullets had flattened themselves against such matter. Silenos was actually eager to see what Ensharia's fist did.

It did not split through the bone, not entirely. But her own skeleton proved of vastly superior make, and its impact was sufficient to shake the room around them. Cracks spanned most of the cube's face, pieces of debris falling chipped away, and a crater as deep as Ensharia's own hand was left imprinted at the point of contact.

She stepped back, staring in awe. Silenos only smiled.

"Precisely as expected." She nodded. "There is more. Come." She brought Ensharia to the site of her new armor and weapon. Inorganic this time. The metallicists and other matter weavers of House Shaiagrazni had always had the better of fleshcrafters in the resilience of their materials—that much could not be denied. The suit of armor covered Ensharia's body in totality and vacuum sealed its joints as she stepped in. It hummed and hissed as she moved, enchantments providing supplementary force to every motion and empowering her body further.

"This is, quite literally, the greatest armor I had the means to construct for you. Only the named of House Shaiagrazni wear its equal, and then only to war."

"I . . . don't know what to say," Ensharia whispered.

"Then be silent," Silenos told her.

It was Hexeri's turn to speak now, and she did so eagerly.

"Do I have any weaponry?" she asked.

Silenos had anticipated that, of course. "Yes," she told her, gesturing to the sword left out still on the table. It was a similarly enchanted weapon to the one Ensharia now wielded and had the benefit of being fitted with a fleshcrafter mechanism that, upon hearing a specific frequency, would instantly dismantle its interior. Silenos was not so great a fool as to trust the vampire with power and no means of countering it.

The sword came down upon the bone, taking a sliver from it and proving itself. The vampire grinned.

CHAPTER TWENTY-EIGHT

Being in the presence of Archimage Mafari was always an exercise in caution. It wasn't that Magnia feared him, exactly. It was simply that, as king of the high elves and the world's foremost master of the arcane, there were so very few people among whom he could truly consider himself the weaker. King Galukar, perhaps. Archimage Mafari and Ancient Lilia for certain.

Of course, he was not fearful. Violence was never far in the presence of a human, regardless of their apparent self-control, but Mafari's age and enlightenment had at least removed him from most of his own kind in that capacity. It certainly helped that Magnia's own precautions had partly been designed around that very man.

"You should tell me where we're going," the archimage suggested.

"Why?" Magnia countered. "You have no choice but to follow in any case."

Mafari was far from impressed, meeting his eye with something of the cold hostility that had passed between them as they burned the world underfoot in magical conflagration all those decades ago.

"Should something happen to you, it would be ideal if this entire plan didn't fall through. I hope the existence of *two* Dark Lords has made any worries about my no longer needing you less . . . pressing."

Magnia had to admit, the human had a point. He sighed.

"Very well. You recall Silenos Shaiagrazni's opening search for allies shortly after he made himself known to the world?"

"Don't patronize me," Mafari parried. "Of course I do. I have seen most of this world's foundational events for the last century."

Magnia decided to let the human's arrogance slide, for the time being.

"Silenos Shaiagrazni is not the only one able to do so. Indeed, five centuries has left me with far more potential choices than he ever had. And far more powerful ones." The understanding dawned in Mafari's face at last. And the hesitance.

"We may be dethroning ourselves by calling on such powers," he noted.

"And we are without a throne already if we do not," Magnia countered. The archimage conceded, wearing his displeasure openly as he did. For once, Magnia shared it.

"Who is to be our first ally then?"

Magnia smiled at that. "I fear this is one thing that does serve us better in secrecy, for now."

One convenient feature of elfdom was the fact that others generally *expected* cryptic secrecy of him. Oftentimes this left them suspicious, awkward, and bitter. But it also meant that when Magnia wished to obfuscate something, he need only cite his desire to do so, and it would merely be *assumed* that he had no ulterior motive in the deed. He was an elf, and elves kept their secrets as humans had their wars. For all his experience, Mafari was no different. He did not push Magnia upon the matter.

Good. It may have ended their brief alliance altogether if he had.

Their travel was an interesting experience. Magnia did not often get to traverse the world with one who rivaled his own power, and Mafari soon noticed the peculiarity about their surroundings.

"I can't translocate." He gasped. "My portals—they won't open."

"I was waiting for you to mention that." Magnia smiled. "The Hero we now seek has had longer to perfect their defenses than you have your magic. Around this entire mountain, the world is a solidified and rigid thing. Transportation magics are weakened by its very proximity."

Mafari took that with a respectable amount of severity, his guard raising as it sank in what order of being they were approaching.

The mountain's peak was their destination, a jutting spire of rock that loomed miles above the ground around it. It was, in fact, the highest of all its kind that Magnia had ever seen in five centuries. Perhaps across the Wastes there were taller, but nowhere else. Ordinary men would have been threatened by the climb. Twenty thousand arm lengths of sheer rock, thinning air, and turbulent weather. Magnia had heard of climbers being struck by bolts of lightning directly, as if the heavens themselves aimed to keep the mountain from being scaled.

Such a thing was of no concern to Mafari and him. They took to the skies, Magnia calling upon the heights themselves to raise him and Mafari merely propelling himself with that strange force magic. Human magic was, invariably, interesting but always cold, sterile. They lacked the holistic breadth of Elven spellworking, opting to focus upon a singular aspect of the world and learn to command it rather than threading their will through larger parts of nature and gaining the more subtle harmony that brought. Magnia had mused upon why that was, as had many other scholars before him. Like them, he had gleaned no singular answer. It remained a subject of speculation.

One that the humans themselves, apparently, had no interest in even pursuing. Another limit of their kind, he supposed.

They raised higher, then higher still. Ascending to the mountain's peak in a mere minute. Magina hadn't bothered to warn Mafari of the hazards awaiting them skyward. If the archimage had not already known, he would have learned and adjusted. As things were, he encased himself in a shield filled with ground-level air to nourish his lungs long before it became necessary. Mafari himself merely whispered to the sky and felt breezes of thicker wind roll down into his lungs. Lightning *did* come for them, deflected by Mafari or ordered away by Magnia, and the hail dropped like sling bullets with no greater effect. Then they were at the top.

It was most likely not the sight many would expect to sit atop the mountain. A wide, flat plateau that had, Magnia knew for a fact, been deliberately carved away by the place's inhabitants over long and laborious years. For decades, it had sheltered those inhabitants. Magnia dropped down to the top, Mafari beside him, and started forward.

He was not even halfway into the plateau before the people he had come for emerged. There were not so many of them, scores rather than hundreds, but all shone to his elvish eyes with the crackle of power. Magic in a rare few, Vigor in virtually all the rest. Any could have distinguished themselves as a human knight, perhaps even become a paladin. Instead, they were pirates.

But their leader was the one who stuck out, like a bonfire among candles. Tall, crimson skinned, and sporadically scaled. A horned crest protruded from her scalp, and a molten glow shone from behind her eyes. When she looked at Magnia, he felt an overwhelming sense of *predation*. When she looked at Mafari, his face grew cold.

"Archimage Mafari," Magnia began, "this is Veria the Undying."

Mafari's stare would have eroded stone, but it did nothing to the schinkai woman he leveled it at.

"Power," the archimage growled. "A woman with power. What madness is this?" With a single wave of his hand, Veria's spine snapped like a twig, and she dropped limply to the ground. All was silent, save for the whistling of the winds.

Ordinary men, upon seeing their leader killed right before their eyes, might have done something about it. Roared in outrage, attacked with insane vigor. The crew of Veria the Undying did not. They merely stared, then stared some more. A snicker broke out among them. Small, first, sporadic. It grew. Soon the whole group seemed to be laughing in outright hysterics. Magnia knew why. Mafari, by the look of worried confusion upon his features, most certainly did not.

"What is going on here?" he asked, fingers twitching that way a magus's so often did when he feared danger was present and magic imminent. His focus was soon drawn back to Veria, who was now rising back up to her feet. The schinkai's neck creaked and groaned, popping with a vaguely repulsive wetness as it reformed itself.

"You can't kill me, idiot," she told the archimage. "Veria the Undying. Hint's in the name. I'm sure you'll figure it out if you really think about it."

Magnia didn't think he'd ever seen Mafari even one-tenth as angry as he was in that moment. Angry enough, perhaps, to test the schinkai's theory with every ounce of his power. It would succeed at that test, but the mountaintop around them might not. Magnia spoke fast to keep such a disaster from befalling them.

"My apologies." He addressed Veria first. "My associate here does not take kindly to magic in the hands of . . . women."

She was too old and too world-weary to be surprised. Veria merely arched an eyebrow.

"Mafari," she noted. "I remember you. We met once. You were a kid. Ten, maybe twelve. I wasn't much older."

As Magnia recalled, she was already considered middle-aged by the standards of most lower species. But then age did at least bring perspective of *some* kind to those who gained enough of it.

"You cannot kill her," Magnia informed the archimage. "Not you with all your magi, and not if all my subjects and I lent our strength. She is undying."

"I got that." Mafari's glare was stronger than ever, but his hands finally lowered down to his sides. The laughter of the pirates slowly died as Veria spoke next.

"I'm guessing the two of you have a reason for being here other than just embarrassing yourselves," she noted, turning to Magnia now. "And considering you're the one who knew what'd happen if you tried to kill me, I'd also guess that whatever that reason is, it's yours. Testing me by not warning your friend ahead of time what would go down here?"

He had, in fact, been testing her, and her seeing through that meant she passed by a wider margin than he could have hoped.

"You have heard of the issues regarding the Dark Lords, I assume?" Magnia was not surprised when she nodded. "We know for a fact one has returned and suspect the other may any day now. The time to sit idle and see how their plans unfold is past. Now we must act."

"And you're putting together a group you think is powerful enough to threaten even them," Veria finished, looking thoughtful. "Funny, I didn't know there was anything that could convince either of you to actually take on help from others. Did one of you lose a fight or something?"

Mafari didn't betray the truth by stiffening, but neither did Veria give any sign of abandoning her suspicion.

"You are the first of our choices," Magnia told the woman. "The second will be the last."

She looked curious at that.

"I have three skyships," she told him, "and fifty conventional ones. My crew numbers in the thousands, and the elites I bring into the air in the hundreds. I practically began the first age of sky piracy and could bring about a new one whenever I pleased. So why is it, then, that you're staring me down without so much as a quiver, but just got nervous when you mentioned your next pick?"

Magnia met her eye.

"You lost one of your sky vessels to the original Dark Lord, and Swick the Swift has made it abundantly clear how large a threat such things are to all. Do you want to take the chance of leaving them to grow in power?"

She didn't even hesitate.

"No."

Magnia smiled. "Welcome to our coterie, then."

"Who is the last member?" The question came from Mafari, not Veria. "You didn't tell me about the woman. Presumably you had similar reasons for keeping this next one from me."

Suspicion flared in his face. Expected, Magnia supposed. Mafari was not stupid. He sighed, eyes flicking between both of his new allies. He had known it would likely come to telling them ahead of time.

"The Mad King."

It was a rare thing, to see fear flash across the faces of ones as powerful as these. Magnia enjoyed the near-unique experience of seeing it happen to both at once.

CHAPTER TWENTY-NINE

Mafari had buried his anger, of course. He had suspected the need for that would emerge. It so often did when he was dealing with the elder race. Magnia was his equal in most ways, and yet the elf had never quite learned to accept the fact. It led to irritating spasms of ego such as the one that had just given Mafari so nasty a surprise.

What he was struggling with more—what he had not thought to inure himself to in long decades—was the more sinister, alien touch of fear. There were so very few occasions on which it was appropriate for a being such as him. And Mafari was heading toward one right now.

Moving to one horror to remove another. It was remarkable how suddenly his hegemony had been destroyed.

Around them now was the city of Agan'doir. Or what was left of it. The place had been a ruin before Mafari was born, before Magnia, for that matter, had been born. Even in disrepair, it was one of the most stunningly awe-inspiring sights he had ever seen.

And easily the oldest. Older than old, older than *ancient*. Agan'doir had existed for so long that there were no written records of its origins. Only the spoken traditions of the elder race could attest to such details, and Magnia, like in most things, had yet refused to part with such knowledge.

Mafari had gleaned some of it for himself, over the decades. But precious little. Even for a man of his resources, it was hard to come by. So little of it existed anywhere, after all, to be salvaged. He knew that the mighty empire that had constructed and inhabited Agan'doir was the very same that had made the flying Castle Edmari, and felt another stab of rage at the imbecile New Dark Lord for his destruction of that particular treasure. He did not know the empire's name, nor much of anything more about its history. If they had made the Godblade, as many suspected, Mafari was yet unable to prove it. He hoped to, one day. It would be remarkably satisfying to bring such evidence before the priests of Wudra.

It was then that he recalled Wudra had been all but destroyed by the first Dark Lord. There was a trend there.

With luck, it would continue no longer. Mafari continued deeper into the city, eyeing the towering stone statues and feeling the ominous magics pressing in around him. He was nothing here. His powers were thin, juvenile. The same was true of every creature he had ever encountered.

Perhaps they would find victory in its heart, but that had never been the concern.

"Be cautious," Magnia advised. "I have never ventured this deep into the city, and there may be . . . defenses."

Mafari didn't need telling twice. His magic was ready in an instant. Even the woman, Veria, seemed to heed the elf's words. But then, heeding words was the main ability of any woman. This one at least had an impressive reputation behind her, combatively.

As a boy, Mafari had grown up on tales of her exploits in much the same way he imagined King Galukar had upon his own. His successor's successor, Walriq, had in turn been raised upon Galukar's own exploits, and the young prodigy falsely sentenced by jealous magi and kidnapped by Shaiagrazni would have made the next link on that chain. It was all so very humbling, in such a place as this, to remember.

Because Agan'doir had been unchanged through it all, and a hundred generations prior to even that.

At the city's center, crested by the most thickly built mass of golden statues, was the palace. It was unlike any other Mafari had seen. Aglow with magic, the air popping at its very presence. He felt heat from the ambient energies coursing around, enough that he knew his skin would be sloughing off on a second-by-second basis were it not for the shield now enveloping him. A glance at Magnia showed similar defensive measures on his part. The woman was not so inventive, merely ignoring her body as it withered and burned. Healing faster than the heat could kill her. Mafari looked back ahead, lest his temper incite another fit of violence.

The palace's gate loomed over them as they passed beneath it, impossibly large. Impractically large, he thought, for any civilization he now knew. What had existed within old Agan'doir that had necessitated such a structure? He would, he realized, very likely find out soon. Deeper they went, into the dark. Mafari's eyes rebelled at the shadows, nerves actually eroding as he looked around and saw nothing of their environment.

He created a portal, allowed sunlight to shine through and scour shadows from the chambers ahead of them. An appreciative look from his companions, Magnia included, did wonders for his nerves. His magic was still a thing to be revered, even if it was finding use in lighting their way rather than burning vampires for the time being. Whatever waited for them ahead.

Down, down they went. Into depths lower beneath the world's skin than Mafari had known construction could be made. The walls were a tight fist around them, squeezing away calm and courage in its implacable grip. Then, abruptly, they stopped. Before them was a great throne, atop it another statue. This one was not gold. It was no metal Mafari recognized at all, seeming to be something almost ephemeral. Upon its lap was a radiant crown. The world itself seemed unsure of what to make of it.

"This is what we are here for," Magnia explained, a slight tremble in his voice. "The Mad King Ka'al."

Mafari followed his gaze to the statue, and realization dawned.

"He's petrified himself?" That didn't bode well. Magi who fell victim to their own powers were among the most unstable... or powerful.

"Deliberately," Magnia explained. "As my ancestors told it, King Ka'al was a master of transmutation. One day, he decided to test himself in that regard. He turned each and every citizen in his great city into gold. For reasons unknown to us, following that cataclysm, he transmuted himself. But he still lives. You can see this statue is not normal matter. Whatever it's made of, it sustains him well enough that he can live once more if freed from it."

It was a strange kind of immortality, Mafari thought. Unless . . .

"He intended to see the future?" he guessed. "To simply wait, dormant, until a great time had passed." It seemed unfathomable. "Why?"

It was the woman who offered an answer.

"Easier pickings." She shrugged. "Clearly he'd gotten tired of his time and knew things would change eventually. Maybe he wanted a weaker world he could dominate easier."

"There were some accounts of him being challenged, in the end," Magnia noted. He continued staring at the throned statue. "Ultimately, all my ancestors' recollections agree that Ka'al would awaken after ten thousand years had passed. It has, by our estimates, been seven. Fortunately, we do not need to limit ourselves to a long-dead king's design."

With a gesture, Magnia's magic swept across the room and wrapped itself around the royal statue. The crown lifted into the air, then came gently down atop the thing's head. Mafari watched its surface shift, a ripple running along it like still waters hit by a breeze. Moments passed, and the rippling intensified. The very thing seemed to melt like wax before a fire, bubbling and collapsing in on itself.

For one long moment, he thought he was watching the king of elves kill a man. Then the liquefying material resolidified back into a coherent shape. Except now it was made of flesh and breath.

The man collapsed instantly, falling down the steps of his own throne like a puppet without strings. For a moment, they all stared, then he rose. His body moved without any of the strain Mafari might expect to see in a mortal man. More like a vampire, or one of considerable Vigor. It was like his own weight was nothing at all, and as his eyes raised high, they flicked between the three of them with a cold scrutiny.

"Why have you awakened me?"

Mafari was surprised, not to be addressed but to be addressed in his own language. He did what he could to keep the shock from showing, for once preferring that Magnia speak. If this was to go wrong, he would rather enjoy the ancient tyrant's attention only after it was exhausted upon another.

"There are new forces in this world that threaten to consume it," Magnia explained. "And—"

"Not you," the tyrant interrupted. "I will hear this from the human, not the elf."

Mafari had to confess a great deal of pleasure at seeing the look of perplexity and indignation upon Magnia's face. It seemed elves of the ancient period were no less haughty than the modern variants. Perhaps their antagonizing human casters was some ontological fact of any generation. It was only the realization that he now enjoyed the full focus of Ka'al the Mad King that kept him from breaking out into a smile.

"I am Archimage Mafari," he told the ancient. "And I am the foremost wielder of magic in my time. That time is threatened by incursions from strangers, possessing powers unknown to us with a might never seen before. We are here to call on you for aid in disposing of them."

The tyrant eyed him for a long moment, looking . . . *bored.*

"And you expect me to answer your call for nothing," he finished. "To help you defeat these invaders, who your own powers are so clearly insufficient to best, out of . . . altruism? Kindness?" He spoke the words as if they were slurs. "Pitiful."

"They seek to claim the world," Mafari replied. "Your own lands included."

That changed things, clearly. The man's eyes grew darker.

"I see."

He turned back to Magnia, a fury clear upon his face. "You look very much like the elves who sealed me away all those years ago."

Magnia's surprise could not have been clearer. It was one of the few times Mafari had ever seen the emotion on him, and perhaps the strongest.

"Sealed you away?"

The tyrant laughed. "Oh, of course, I imagine they claimed I did it myself or something to that effect. Anything to keep humanity from knowing of your kind's tendency to interfere with our works."

King Magnia said nothing, just glared.

"Will you help us or not?" Mafari cut in. A sudden tension hit the air, and Ka'al the Tyrant took long looks at each of them.

"I used to kill men who spoke to me like that," he replied calmly. "Killed them instantly to ensure the message spread that no creature could do that to the ruler of this world." He paused, perhaps thinking, or perhaps merely being dramatic. "Yes, you have my help. For the time being at least, the four of us would seem to have a common enemy. But I will not be taking orders."

Mafari relaxed, like a fool. His relaxation did not last long. A tremor ran through the room, as if his ear were pressed against the ground beside charging cavalry. Debris ran from every surface. Even his vision blurred somewhat with the intensity of the shaking. Mafari stared around, comprehension taking long moments to reach him before, at last, he realized the source for what it was.

Statues. The very same he had seen outside, some towering, some gold, some both. All now moving. They emerged from corridors and chambers, pulled away from hidden compartments and parted towering gates.

An army. An army of beings so large, so solid in their construction, that Mafari wondered what sort of army would have been needed to best a single one. And *they* were the army. He found memories of the Dark Lord's power growing more distant as he watched the figures and felt their magic.

Ka'al grinned at his reaction.

"Now, whereabouts are these so-called invaders?"

CHAPTER THIRTY

It'd been a while since Collin had led a good battle. He'd almost missed the feeling. *Almost.* The fact that he'd been dealing with such long odds had certainly blunted his enthusiasm. At first.

There really weren't many good things about growing up in a city constantly under siege by the Dark Lord's forces, but one of them was that it meant Collin had a lot of experience in contending with large amounts of casters. Magi were powerful, but they weren't lichs.

On the other hand, they were *very* numerous. And this time, Shaiagrazni wasn't here to thin their herd by throwing sentient siege engines the size of hills into their army.

Collin would've been in a fair amount of trouble, in fact. Kaltan's rangers were close to extinct—half of those who'd survived the war against the Dark Lord had retired. Understandable, perhaps, but far from helpful in the short term. It would help to have more rangers to train the next generation of them. Eventually.

Now Collin had to figure out what to do without the spine of his army.

He chewed at the problem for days, pacing, swearing, barely sleeping. It was, he realized, the very same trance his father used to fall into. Mind so busy that it simply lacked the time for anything but thought. Even eating.

His only distractions came from Ado, and even those weren't far from the matter at hand. He drilled her for information on her home, its surrounding areas, everything he might need to know. Most of it, doubtless, would not be useful. Some of it would, and that made it all necessary.

"There's one main tactical problem," he said, more thinking aloud than anything. Ado surprised him by responding to him as he paced.

"What is it?"

Collin wasn't used to a woman's input in his war room. It wasn't that he disliked it . . . Well, actually, yes, it was exactly that. It felt weird. He didn't say anything, knowing full well what it was like to have other people decide where you belonged, but it still grated at him. At first, at least.

Ado had a head for it all though. An amateur without mistake, but a quick learner and one who'd clearly taken the time to read more than a few books on the topic. Book learning was a start, at least, and bouncing ideas off her actually helped him focus.

"We're completely fucked," Collin explained, almost feeling embarrassed at how basic a thought he was sharing. "They have the numbers, the army quality, the—"

"Army quality?" Ado cut in, frowning, chewing a lip in confusion. Collin looked at that lip, tried not to imagine chewing it himself. Failed. Women in a war room really were distracting. Or at least this one was.

"Yes." Collin frowned. "You thought we had the advantage there?"

She looked embarrassed suddenly, making him feel a bit guilty for being snarky about his answer.

"Kaltan troops are meant to be the best," the woman murmured.

"They are," Collin confirmed. "But they're fighting magi here, and other elites."

Ado swallowed.

"It's that much of a disadvantage?"

"It is," Collin confirmed, back to pacing. "Magic is just . . . difficult to plan around. It's one thing if you have big formations—that's something—but in an open field, or if *they* have it . . . It's too unpredictable. Too variable. A hundred magi between them can bring any number of surprises to the field. It limits the plans I can even attempt, because the risk of any given one falling apart if some specific power happens to find use on the enemy's side is too much to allow."

He wasn't losing her, Collin could see, but he wasn't far from it either. Quick for a rookie, but . . . a rookie, nonetheless.

"We need to stick to strategies that have a small number of potential points of failure," he simplified. "The more complicated they get, the more likely they are to collapse when some random magus throws an unexpected problem at us. Granted, in general, you want to keep things as simple as you can get away with, but I'm working with much tighter restrictions than usual now."

She swallowed. One thing Collin had come to appreciate about Ado was that she didn't often show her fear. Not to anyone but a ranger, at least, who could hear the beating of her heart and smell the battle drugs spicing her blood. It made her seem older to him. Tougher.

And it was with this mature, tough woman whom he spent so many more hours before finally settling upon a design of battle he felt halfway satisfied with. Halfway may have been stretching it.

After that, everything became a blur. Collin gave orders, assigned resources. Began the march. Eight thousand men crossed the landscape as one, a fairly respectable force. It felt like nothing now. The Dark Lord's final scourge of undead had numbered literally one hundred times more. Venka's army had held the numbers by a factor of dozens. Kaltan's days as a military superpower seemed either very far in the past or very far in the future.

Perhaps it would *have* no future, if Collin failed at this. He could still turn back, could still . . .

But no. He needed allies. Without Shaiagrazni, and with Kaltan weakened, he had no illusions about what the rest of the world would do to them. The rest of the world, run by nobles and kings. His temper frayed as they sustained their march.

It's not like I want this . . .

Except that wasn't really true, was it? Hearing the attackers come had been the best news Collin had gotten in weeks. He'd tried to adapt for peace, failed. Peace didn't want him. It didn't care about him. Peace didn't have a use for nocking and drawing in a tenth of a second, or landing a bolt through someone's skull at three thousand paces, or knowing how to slide a dagger just so into someone's eye slit.

Peace had rejected him, and war was now welcoming him back with open arms. Maybe Collin would never be done with it, but that just meant he'd never be without a purpose. Not like so many of the other soldiers he knew.

But that comparison felt childish, ignorant. Collin had crutches they never would: a city to command, a place to live, an able body. He wouldn't be begging in the street and getting beaten for the crime of surviving his service to the city.

So why was he doing this? It wasn't for revenge—he'd be marching on the Dark Lord for that. Was it for Kaltan? He could certainly make himself think as much, but then all sorts of people could make themselves think all sorts of things.

"Something on your mind?" Ado asked. She was riding at the front of the column beside him, her poor mount straining to keep up with the pace he'd unconsciously set in his troubles. Collin slowed a shade to let the horse ease up.

"Just . . . tense." Collin actually thought about telling the truth for a moment, sharing his thoughts, but that was a nasty habit to get into. Fortunately, Ado either bought his deflection or had the prescience not to push him. She was mostly silent for the few weeks of marching needed to reach Aoakanis. The army wasn't. They complained, they whinged, they bitched like a pack of housewives. And then they shut up and got ready to die when the city was in sight.

It broke Collin's heart to see their courage, to know how many of them would be killed by it. But he wasn't impeded by the sensation. A broken heart didn't matter. He was leading with his brain. They started lining up into formation as they headed for the city.

A simple one. Shield walls raised high with deliberate gaps that could be widened or closed through repositioning, hillcrests served to obscure a reserve, and the rangers were mixed in among ordinary archer units with orders to move around and hide their own numbers. Collin might've been confident if he'd had twice as much of everything. As things were . . . it was a long hope. Either Kaltan would have a future, carved out by an improbable success, or they wouldn't. Eight thousand men couldn't change that without winning a victory here. Even so, the thought of wasting them gnawed at him.

For all of ten minutes, at least. As they approached, and readied for the carnage, something else caught Collin's eye from the east. He turned over, ordered a halt immediately.

It was more men. A *lot* more men. Not Kaltans, of course, but perhaps the only variety that were almost their equals. The infantry of Abaritan were swarming the lands around Aoakanis like ants at the base of a hill, closing fast. Banners were raised, orders were being barked, and at their crest was a figure so tall he could be distinguished even from half a mile.

King Galukar glanced over to Collin and nodded in acknowledgment.

Then, of course, he ordered his own charge onto the city's walls. Because something silly like *being on the same fucking side* wouldn't convince King Galukar to take action as drastic as waiting and communicating a plan of attack. Collin cursed, made a lot of decisions very quickly, and ordered his own men forward.

His reasoning was twofold. First, Aoakanis was still held by a considerable force of some fifteen thousand, magi not included. With the golden three-to-one rule of a balanced attacking force against besieged defenders, that meant that even the arrival of the Arbitans might not sway things over. Galukar, of course, made that more favorable, but not enough for his liking.

The other aspect was rather simple: Collin needed a strong claim in whatever was left over after this. It was a shitty thing to consider, but a necessary one. More people would be saved long-term with a stronger base of power for Kaltan.

Steeling himself, he gave the order. The charge began.

Kaltans were always quick in sieges, for a couple of reasons. The main among them was that basic athleticism helped a lot in them. The rangers hung back until the ranks were almost on the walls, then, taking cues from a volley of trebuchet fire, they sprinted forth and scaled them. Preternatural strength helped find grips in the old stone;

preternatural speed helped to race gravity's effects upward. They were on the ramparts in moments, affixing grapples and tossing down rope ladders for the men to climb. Difficult, in the heat of everything and with them swaying everywhere. But doable with some fitness training.

Collin, of course, was up on the ramparts with the first of them. He felt the familiar heat of battle wash over his mind and burn away all the complications of thought and concern, moving like a whisper through enemy ranks with both daggers out. He put them to work.

An artery opened here, a heart ruptured there. He was behind everyone, in every guard, slitting every throat. Faster than eyesight, sharper than steel. A dozen men died every second. In such cramped conditions as the wall, it made holding the Kaltans back impossible. Soon they were swarming on and down into the city.

At the other side of the carnage, Collin saw King Galukar going for a pleasant stroll and happening to liquefy anyone who made the mistake of venturing within arm's reach of him as he did. There was no concern about the Arbitan's side of things being pinned down, so he just had to worry about his own. That worry came sooner rather than later—a magus's fireball streaked for him.

Too slow, Collin twisted aside, rolled, got up with his bow out, and fired. The old bastard's head just came apart like an apple crushed by a horse. For such a versatile thing, the powers of magi seemed to be used for fire more often than not. Their mistake. He kept firing. More casters were popping up now, all going down to one bolt each.

Kaltan kept its advance up, gnawing away at the enemy, forcing them back and infesting more of the city's interior. They had a hard grip on it now, an entire section too tightly controlled for them to lose it. They were winning. Not winning, won. Victory had fallen onto their lap the moment King Galukar sent his own men to seize it.

Collin felt a stab of hope. He killed it just a second too late.

Something went up skyward in the corner of his eye, jerking his head around like his neck was being wrung. Collin's jaw hung open like a village idiot as he saw the great pillar of blood falling down.

An entire formation just disappeared beneath it, then something new emerged amid the visceral flood. Several dozen somethings, all moving fast as the moonlight glinted off bared steel. Impossibly fast. Vampires.

Atop them, high in the air, Collin saw more spires of coiling blood. Astride was . . . Fuck. A figure in red. A figure *of* red. Red clothing, formed into a practical dress that flowed around her like a nest of vipers. A red cape trailed behind, red eyes shone in a red-smeared face, and around her, the very air burned red with flecks of boiling ichor. Beside her was another woman, younger, black skinned, and glowing with magic that somehow seemed a child's toy by comparison. Sphera.

"*For Mafari!*" cried Lilia the vampire queen.

She descended onto the battle like an avalanche, and it turned instantly.

CHAPTER THIRTY-ONE

Garun fought mechanically. The passion of youth had died with youth. Now all that was left was the simple doing of it. There were enemies ahead, allies behind. One side would live, and the other would die. He had to make sure his was the one still breathing at the end of everything. So he fought, mechanically. His halberd thrust outward, perfectly tuned with the other blades beside him, and the poor sods met with defending against Kaltans from one side and Arbitans from the other melted back away from them. They advanced unimpeded.

He tasted victory, spit it out. Kept his focus. Everywhere was a mess of tangling limbs and scraping steel, sparks actually leaping into the air at some collisions and blood flooding it in others. Just because his was the winning side didn't mean he'd live. The enemy's desperation was deadly enough. Still, they *were* losing. The day belonged to Arbite. Garun had, as if to illustrate that fact, run the tip of his halberd clean through one defender's bowels when the shadow above cast itself across him.

It lasted only a moment, the span of a single thought. Then Garun turned, took his halberd tightly in both hands, and drove it through the neck of the ally behind him.

Galukar's men went mad, all at once. He'd have been confused had he not seen Lilia hovering high above them already. He roared. It was a wrathful cry, the very sort that had sent enemies scrambling back from him mere moments before, but not a one of the berserking soldiers seemed to even hear it. It was only when the Godblade came alight that the frenzy stopped.

Alight, in truth. One moment it was six feet of scarred steel, the next Galukar's fingers were tight around a great length of brilliant white fire. Men shied back from it, some screamed. And those who short seconds before had been ensnared by supernatural rage and violence suddenly calmed. Galukar felt his confidence grow. However he'd used the weapon, whatever his abuses, the Godblade was still the Godblade. Vampiric magic was not suffered to survive its proximity.

"*Hold!*" Galukar roared, letting his voice cut over the sounds of battle and panic, but reining it in just enough to keep from perforating the eardrums of those men closest to him. "*Stand ready! The vampire queen emerges!*"

Of all the things to say, that seemed to have been the right one. Nothing like a warning of Lilia herself's presence would snap so many thousands of attentions over to him as one. The weight of their attention made the Godblade hotter in his grip, and Galukar swung it without thinking. In one stroke, he felt the magic of Lilia's mental powers broken apart.

Then he turned his gaze to the skies, saw the vampire queen stunned by her surprise, and leaped.

Lilia had not known what exactly Galukar would do when he first saw her—run perhaps. She'd been an idiot. His response ought to have been the most predictable she'd ever seen. He had been changing, less certain, of late. She'd dared to hope that might have blunted him. Perhaps it had. Now he was a hammer flying toward her rather than an axe.

Her shield came fast, a pillar of blood thickened with mass and magic to withstand a falling star. The Godblade hit it like ten, searing the air and sending Lilia back with the concussion of its impact. Galukar came blasting through the spattered ichor and swung at her once more, forcing Lilia to dip low in the sky and watch as the king flew past. He didn't fly for long, twisting in the air and continuing until his feet touched the tip of one towering spire. He kicked off it, beheading the structure as he shot back for her. This time, Lilia was ready.

She called down lightning and bolstered it with her own power. The crimson arcs struck King Galukar head-on and actually left his skeleton exposed amid transparent flesh for a fraction of a second before everything around him came apart in a blast of vaporized water and sizzling gas. Human eyes would have been burned out to behold it. Lilia's almost stung. Still the king powered on. She might have been impressed were she not distracted by the feeling of ancient iron carving through less ancient meat.

Lilia's blood reddened the air as she fell down toward the ground, Galukar falling beside her. He hefted his sword for an ending blow, missed as she rolled upon impact and left the ground for ten yards in every direction a jagged crater. She came up, let the blood fall down upon him. It was a river, then a settled lake. Then it was the surface of a stormy sea, pressed inward by vitakinetic magics and compressing the great sword-wielding gorilla buried beneath.

The gorilla burst forth regardless.

Everything was chaos, except for the sky. The sky was a constant, unyielding *death*. Erik stumbled back as a great pillar of blood flew clear of King Galukar and missed him by mere yards, the sheer wind of it knocking him almost off his feet and sending dirt flying in all directions. The debris *hurt*—that's how fast it was—and there was no doubt in his mind that he'd have been obliterated were any of the stray attacks to actually hit him.

They did hit others. Hit lots of others, and they just . . . stopped existing. Turned into more blood, either transmuted or, perhaps, hit so hard Erik's eye couldn't even make out the moment of their destruction, only its results.

The ground shook. The air was clotted by debris. The fighting was over. What was the point of continuing it? Both sides saw clear as day that victory was out of their own hands. Whichever won between the vampire queen and the Godblade's wielder would decide who took the conflict. No point bleeding and dying just to surrender afterward.

But there was no order to this consensus, merely terror. Everyone ran, fifty thousand men scrambling in fifty thousand directions, all screaming and thrashing and gasping out prayers to every god they knew that theirs would not be the next skull to catch a piece of rubble. Erik was among them.

He sprinted, not jogged. Sprinted. Spear discarded, shield torn from his arm, helmet kept on only because a moment of sanity had reminded him he might be struck in the head by thrown debris. He sprinted even as his lungs burned and his legs liquefied, eyes streaming with tears, heart thundering with pressure. He needed to be gone. He needed to be anywhere but—

The ground shook, knocked him fully off his feet to roll and scrape in the mud. Erik stared high into the air and felt his eyes burned away to uselessness as blisters spread across his face. The last thing his vision ever caught was the sight of a maelstrom skyward. Clouds roiling and boiling, thunder crackling, pillars of blood cutting through the air faster than crossbow bolts. And amid it all, King Galukar swung the Godblade like he meant to kill the world itself.

Perhaps, Erik thought, he'd manage it.

Collin had quickly lost control of the battle. It was hard to put his finger on when exactly. Perhaps it had been *before* everybody collectively lost their shit and started running away, or maybe it had come just after. Regardless, the basic fact remained that he no longer had much of any sway over how the events around him would proceed.

And he couldn't exactly blame anyone for why. Already, Collin had been struck in the head by a piece of stone moving fast enough to take most skulls apart on impact. He'd seen just that happen to another man, whose body now twitched as blood dribbled from the jagged stump that had once joined shoulders to head.

Maybe it was Shaiagranzi's fleshrafting; maybe it was dear old dad's ranger blood. Maybe both. He was still alive and kicking—or, rather, not spasmodically kicking—and Collin needed to figure out what he'd do with that. He looked up at the sky.

A spire's top was caught in the vortex now, dozens of tons of mangled stone and wood twisting and spinning as it circled the pair of fighting Heroes like a leaf in a whirlpool. The pair of creatures fighting in its midst weren't even visible behind all the light and shivering air, practically cloaked in their magic with how thick it was. The ground trembled again as one of Galukar's swings missed.

Yeah, fuck that. Collin decided that his contribution to the battle pretty much ended with the arrival of people whose skin his arrows would crumple against. He legged it like the ghost of all dead rats but got only a few paces before he heard a cry.

Collin spun, stared. Saw Ado stumbling, dazed and bloody. She'd not been hit by one of the bigger bits of shrapnel—he could tell by her still being alive—but the woman was clearly without her senses.

Not a good state, in the maelstrom around them. Shame that, but there was no helping—what the fuck was he doing?

Collin reached her after a moment, tackling her to the ground and pressing his torso over her just as a spray of fingertip-sized stones raked them. Collin winced but didn't feel anything break. Bruises, at worst. Below him, Ado slowly regained coherence, blinking and frowning as her addled thoughts settled down and her mind quickened back up to full speed.

"W-what the fuck is—"

"Lilia and Galukar are squaring up," Collin told her, getting off the woman but keeping both eyes out for any more unexpected blasts of debris. Fortunately, or unfortunately he supposed, most of the nearby buildings had already been flattened past the point of flinging more death at them. Ado's reaction to the fact was far less relieved and far more concerned. It was, he supposed, her damned city.

Or not. That really wasn't in their hands anymore. Now it was all . . . the fighters'.

The Godblade came down, a solar guillotine biting into the creature's head. It came apart, splitting from crown to chin and gushing out volcanic magma as Galukar shot back. He righted himself, twisted, kicked off air that suddenly felt hard as stone, and swung again.

Behind the throng of bodies, Lilia the vampire queen conjured yet more abominations. A dragon of stitched flesh and cataractous eyes reared up before Galukar and felt ancient iron bite deep into its body. Spirits encircled him like starving sharks, melting back as the weapon's light blazed ever brighter. The air was scorched, the ground cracked, the heavens themselves weeping acidic rain as if the battle aggrieved it.

Neither of them relented.

Galukar cut open limbs of blood compressed to the durability of cold iron and withstood lashes of the very same stuff that opened his skin and scratched the muscle below. Lilia hovered back from him, ever maintaining the space between them, ever fearful of his anger in close quarters. His every stroke was a thundercrack, his every blow an earthquake. But each thundercrack was deflected as a typhoon reared up before it, and every earthquake drowned in a flood. Lilia's powers were every bit his equal and then some.

It didn't matter. Galukar didn't fight because he was stronger. He fought because it was right.

He chased the vampire, a whirlwind of razored iron. She melted back, a cloud of imperceptibly fast meat. He needed only to catch her once and Galukar could seize victory. She knew it as well as he did, and so more attacks came. The blood was in waves and limbs, parting with every stroke. Creatures emerged from behind it: elongated serpentine dragons and many-limbed carrion beasts the size of buildings. All moved fast; all died faster.

"Stop!" Galukar thought he heard, some weak, fragile voice barely cutting out over the winds roiling around his battle. He ignored it. There was no stopping now.

CHAPTER THIRTY-TWO

Nemo wasn't sure what he could do, if anything. The tempest of magic and destruction was unlike any he'd seen since the Dark Lord's attack. And yet he had to try. He knew, somehow, that he *had* to try. With Xekanis around him, a burning shield against the world, he stumbled forward. High above, the clouds were still being dragged into the whirling vortex centered on Lilia and Galukar. Nemo's eyes stung just to glance up at it, and he knew that were it not for Xekanis's protection, he'd be blinded in an instant.

But he *had to try*.

At a thought from Nemo, Xekanis lifted him high into the air and drew him closer to the spiral of death. His voice pressed against Nemo's will.

"**It's dangerous there**," the demon urged him. "**Those beings are more powerful than I am in this world. I can't protect you completely.**"

I know, Nemo thought. *But a lot more people are going to die if I stay back.*

"**I don't care about them. Let them die. It'll be funny.**"

Nemo sighed. Of course Xekanis didn't understand. It'd been pointless to try to make him.

Up and up he went, closer to the center of it all. Nemo had to wrestle every ounce of courage he could from his failing heart as he came to within a few dozen paces. This close, he could make out the outline of King Galukar and Queen Lilia. They seemed like giants to his eye. A pair of great creatures the size of mountains, crashing together like the ocean's waves meeting a cliff face. His ears stung from the sound of it, teeth rattled from the force.

Dozens of paces back, and he could feel his body strain. Any closer would be a death sentence. Were it not for Xekanis.

Xekanis's power flared up, shielding Nemo as they drew closer. First he felt it as a dull warmth, then the heat grew and didn't stop growing as the distance shrank. Things burst apart in the air beside Nemo, too fast for his eye to follow. Fast enough, he realized, that the solid stones among them were broken into *powder* rather than mere fragments.

"Nemo, you will die."

Maybe he would. Nemo found himself considering the idea suddenly, waited for the spasm of fear to send him back down to the ground below. But it didn't. He just kept rising, kept moving toward the center of the apocalyptic storm emerging around him.

"Stop." The voice was so weak, so mewling compared to the magical tempest that Lilia barely heard it even with her own superhuman senses. Yet she did.

It didn't draw her eyes away from King Galukar, however. She couldn't afford to let anything do *that*. He didn't stop, even with two dozen wounds trickling ichor down his bronzed flesh. It was like seeing a ghost from her past come alive. Not since men had wielded jagged iron universally had Lilia seen so ferocious an attacker.

She supposed the Godblade had a fondness for simple, violent males.

This one came on more simply and violently than almost any other Lilia had seen, to her what a gorilla was to common humanity. But then a gorilla was so very strong, measured against the meager prowess of human tissue, and that made the metaphor that much more exact. She could not take the brute lightly.

He split a great length of blood from top to bottom, bursting between the broken halves and moving for Lilia like an arrow. The air itself seemed to throw him at her, as if the urge to destroy her was enough to defy gravity itself.

Lilia had fought another wielder of his weapon once. Even they had not managed that.

Her blood lashed at Galukar, snagging him, slowing him, as she pulled back and used the precious moments to fill the air with more of her children. Malformed creatures they were. Grown carefully and lovingly over long centuries, now wasted in mere moments of violence against that infernal weapon.

Or holy weapon, against an infernal opponent. But the irony did not long occupy her thoughts; nothing did save survival. Lilia's crimson lightning ensnared Galukar, scorching him with heat enough to rend mortal flesh into crumbling ash. It barely blistered his skin. With another stroke, he smashed aside the barrier, then fell upon her and dragged the Godblade from one shoulder to just shy of her hip.

Pain seared Lilia like the sun's kiss. The Godblade cut—or tore, more like, for the sheer primitive bluntness of its edge—her undead tissues even as its magic rent open the supernatural energies animating them. She felt herself weaken ever so slightly, and saw her enemy emboldened. Lilia seized his arm to halt another blow, and cursed as she felt strength in excess of her own resist the effort.

Again, the Godblade found her. Not so fast this time. Pressed rather than smashed against her, dragged down across the flesh over her right shoulder and cutting it clumsily deep. Lilia's blood became a river down the iron edge, her pain a flood behind her eyes.

This time she was launched by the blade, a world of sounds bleeding together as her body tumbled one way and the other. Lilia left a vacuum of obliterated raindrops and schismed air in her wake, such was the speed, and it was only with a great exertion that she halted herself.

Are you the greatest of all to wield the Godblade? Lilia found herself unsure as she eyed her approaching enemy. Certainly she had never seen his equal, but she had always given his weapon's bearers a wide berth. A stinging in her wounds reminded her why.

Lilia called the lightning again, and this time closed with it. Used it to mask her approach and slipped by Galukar while he braced himself for the burning of electrical magics. She circled around behind the king and as he emerged from the attack added her own speed to his as she struck him from behind. He had not, as she thought, anticipated a physical assault.

Galukar struck the ground first, acting as a cushion for Lilia where she followed milliseconds later. The dirt erupted with volcanic altitude and seismic force, toppling every soldier within a hundred paces and blocking out the thin moonlight as debris shot skyward and outward in unthinkable volumes.

If it hurt the Godblade's wielder at all, Lilia saw no evidence of the fact. King Galukar exploded to his feet faster than a mortal's eye could follow, spinning and swinging, missing her by an inch where she ducked down beneath his swing. Her blood caught him off-balance, sending him flying backward to land hard, flesh still sizzling from her previous attacks. Eyes sizzling too as Lilia splashed more of her ichor into it. *Her* ichor this time, sacred stuff drawn from her own veins rather than claimed from her victims. She infused it with magic and will, hate and death. It ate his flesh more voraciously than any acid.

That, at last, fazed him. But not for long.

Galukar was roaring, his voice blasting the dirt back from his feet with its magnitude. Lilia kept back from the Godblade, letting her ichor and lightning torment the warrior as he stumbled after her. He was wounded now, his thousand minor scratches adding up to debilitation. The victory was coming closer to her hands.

So was the defeat. Her own body stung, sizzling at points where the Godblade's sanctified iron had ripped through it. She would heal, eventually, but she was slowed, weakened. Distracted. Galukar stood panting and heaving just a few paces away, and Lilia refrained from mirroring the expression only because she'd been dead long enough for her own lungs to atrophy beyond such things.

Again, the voice rang out.

"Stop this! It's madness! You're tearing the city apart!"

That, finally, drew her gaze around. Galukar's too. The speaker was none other than Prince Nemo, looking more frightened than Lilia had ever seen him and stumbling toward the center of their crater wrapped in his pet demon. That explained how he'd survived so long in their proximity.

But not what he thought to accomplish.

Galukar came back at her, a pouncing tiger. Lilia leaped aside with more blood enveloping them both as a ward. He tore through, swung blindly. Got lucky, clipped her arm. She hissed, scythed into one of his open wounds with a blade of blood and felt the delicate musculature below yield against it. Galukar stumbled away, driven farther as yet more ichorous lashes fell upon him. Tiny cuts, insubstantial things. Adding up, compounding. Each shoving him another inch toward the edge. Prince Nemo cried out again.

"Stop this!" He was running forward now, face tight with panic, eyes wide. Lilia scarcely saw him. Galukar, she thought, didn't at all. The king's swing came just as her torrent did, elemental, bloody mass meeting the same old strip of battered iron it always had. And, as always, it was somehow a balanced contest. Galukar screamed. *Lilia* screamed. The animalism of her fight outstripping any learned intellect as blood exploded outward, the ground came apart, the skies crashed together, and the rains were conjured in ever denser volumes. She felt iron part blood, blood slide around iron. Knew, instantly, that two death blows were falling at once.

But neither one found its mark. Prince Nemo, somehow, had gotten himself between them. Hands raised, eyes sharp, voice calling out right up until the moment it was silenced.

In a single instant, the maelstrom parted. Lilia felt the frenzy of battle leave her, saw it abandon Galukar. They were two people standing with a boy between them, his belly opened and chest mangled by arcane violence. Prince Nemo did not seem to realize what had happened, taking a single confused step forward as his lips moved in silence. He frowned. Not understanding *why* his words wouldn't form, not knowing what was keeping the air from answering his call.

Then he collapsed, all at once. Strength just dissipating from his limbs, a puppet with cut strings. He landed clumsily and heavily, despite his slightness, with his back to the cratered dirt and eyes to the sky. Shivering, twitching, inhaling a hundred times a minute as spasmodic organs went haywire trying and failing to compensate for the damage dealt to them.

Everything froze, as if caught in congealed amber. Lilia saw King Galukar staring in disbelief at the boy, the soldiers barely dipping out of cover in the vicinity as the chaos suddenly subsided. She saw Sphera, the girl having just finished cleaning up a pair of magi only to be greeted with this. Her face was half denial, half rage.

Prince Nemo's eyes gained some clarity, all of a sudden, and he looked around, blood bubbling at his mouth.

"S-stop . . . this . . ." he whispered. "We . . . Allies . . . Why . . . Why . . ." He couldn't finish, and yet the bare sentiment he had conveyed already seemed enough. Lilia looked from him to King Galukar, saw rage in the monarch's face. Opened her mouth to speak.

Then saw a jet of fire envelope the old king, originating from one of the younger magi upon her side. A powerful thing, though not enough to wound Galukar. Its real strength was in igniting the conflict all over again.

In an instant, whatever temporary calm Nemo had purchased with his blood expired. Magic flew in all directions. Death prowled around glutting itself on the carnage. Lilia stared at Galukar, and Galukar stared at Lilia. There would be no calming this. Not with the Godblade breaking her powers of mental influence. Not without its wielder dying first.

And not without sacrificing the security she sought to win from Mafari.

Lilia called on her remaining magic and threw it against the Godblade's wielder, blood and iron clashing for the hundredth time that day. The earth shivered, the sky wept, the air convulsed. And the killing continued on top of Prince Nemo's dying form.

CHAPTER THIRTY-THREE

Silenos had made all the preparations she had time and ability for, had taken every precaution she was able to think of. After some time, she realized, she had simply been using her excessive caution as an excuse to delay. An excuse to herself. She was *afraid*. The feeling hurt, like acid in her chest. She pushed it down and readied the ritual.

It was not a particularly grueling piece of intellectual labor, mostly mere mimicry. Adonis's genius was the one behind it, after all, not Silenos's. And yet she made adjustments, tweaks. She unoptimized it if only to ensure that it would not be apparent whose mind the creation had sprung forth from. Kammani did not know how much Silenos might have learned in her time at the new world, which, with luck, would keep her from seeing through it.

The ritual chamber was similar to the one Silenos had used all those long months ago: an expansive hemispherical structure of hardened tungsten and magical caging designed to fend off both a physical and supernatural attack at once. Altered by choice improvements from Kammani, keratinous armor plating and other such things. It would, Silenos thought, have withstood a small nuclear device unleashed within its center. It may have delayed the Entity.

Kammani moved around it like a reptile on ice, seeming to glide as she always did. Her eyes surveyed the walls, teeth working slowly at her lip in thought. It unsettled Silenos, sometimes, how *human* she seemed. Eight thousand years and she was at odds with Shaiagraznian culture by gesticulating like a common mundane. It was all a facade. A thin veneer of personhood hiding the ancient mind beneath.

"Considerable precautions," she noted. "Very considerable. I am interested to see how you conduct yourself with this Entity."

Which, Silenos believed, was a euphemistic way of pointing out her failure to do so the last time. Euphemisms, another unsettling humanism of Kammani's.

"And you will, master," she replied, then simply waited for Hexeri and Ensharia to arrive.

They did not keep her waiting long, both trudging into the chamber as if they feared it was some sort of trap. Which, given the presence of Silenos's master, was not a categorically false worry. Kammani eyed them as they entered, smiling a shark's smile and watching as they moved toward Silenos's side of the room.

"I require silence," Silenos announced, fortunately managing to keep the tension from sounding in her voice. "My concentration is paramount here. The consequences of a mishap in what I am about to attempt would be disastrous."

She did not need to give any more information than that.

Silenos brought forth the hybrid's head and enjoyed a moment of surprise from her master as she saw it for the first time. She worked quickly, aiming to have the ritual underway before Kammani could draw any hard conclusions from the reveal. Those were the greatest danger of all for the time being, more so than even the Entity.

The air came apart, and Silenos felt a whisper of the Depths caress her arcane senses as reality unmade itself. The Entity emerged in a silent scream and a blinding darkness, congealing into the space centered on its binding sigils, power crackling in conflict with the restraints.

Silenos was growing disquietingly used to being in the presence of such magic. Her time in the Shallow Depths had granted more direct exposure to it than the past century of study in House Shaiagrazni. Combat, it seemed, had a way of hardening her. Or perhaps it merely made her less yielding. Perhaps the cracks were still forming, just going ignored.

"You summon me again."

There was an ominous note to the remark, Silenos thought. Something beyond the bare fact of receiving it from an Entity. But she did not have the time to dwell on that. Turning to glance over her shoulder, she saw the rest of House Shaiagrazni's expeditionary force gathered.

"I have called upon you to bargain," she declared.

I know you can hear me, as you did my apprentice. You have no doubt noticed you are still bound. Cooperate and that will end. Do not and I will hurt you as best I can.

This was the moment that would decide Silenos's future, and it was entirely beyond her control. Her fear was a poison circulating further with every beat of her heart, gnawing away at the strength of her body and the solidity of her mind.

The Entity could have been sharing everything with Kamamni, on even a word-by-word basis. Silenos could only assume it wasn't, for if it was, then her plans were over already.

"What would you have me do that your master would not?"

She resisted the urge to relax at its response. For all Silenos knew, it was merely toying with her.

"You are to open the gateway between my world and the one you displaced me to one hundred and fifty years ago, permitting transportation for myself and every other life-form in this chamber."

You are to allow specifically myself and the two creatures who accompanied me to the Depths to travel, while impeding the rest. Among these others, you will recognize Mistress Kammani. She has spent millennia foiling your kind and keeping herself from being ensnared by any of your trickery. Now is your chance to get the better of her, perhaps even destroy her entirely. If you choose to accept my terms.

Power flooded the room, power enough that Silenos felt herself almost overwhelmed. The confines left every sensation of the Entity's presence magnified, even the very sense of danger emanating from it. It was all she could do to keep her face stony and refrain from glancing over at Kammani.

"Very well."

A moment passed, long and limacine. It grated on Silenos's nerves like jagged steel and left the breath sharpening in her lungs. Then two things happened in so small a time as to be almost simultaneous. A gateway opened, the fabric of reality peeling apart to show clear skies suddenly emerging in the chamber's center.

And the Entity broke free of its circle and shot for Kammani.

Silenos knew then that, were it not for her binding the Entity with the hybrid's precious substance, she would have been obliterated. The power unleashed was such that even the warded tungsten, bereft of its arcane protection, boiled and disappeared. In moments, they were standing in a crater, surrounded by walls of elemental vapor and battered from all sides by great enough temperatures that it was only superhuman resilience leaving them safe from being cooked.

Hexeri, in that regard, was by far the worst off, her flesh already charring at the danger. Kammani was ensnared in combat with the Entity, staring balefully at Silenos—clearly she'd realized the treachery already—but focusing all her power upon battling the being. The other named were slower, stunned or wounded. None had been ready for attack, and those who were not badly damaged already were taking precious moments to piece together what had happened.

Without thinking, Silenos raised her left arm, transforming even as it elevated into its cannon configuration, and began to make sure none of them would have the chance to realize what sort of issue they were dealing with. Her weapon barked, heat and force exploding from its barrel as pieces of keratin sabot fell away. The projectile was too fast for even her own eyes to follow.

But its impact was not.

Whoever that extradimensional stranger had been, Silenos had to admit, he had made a valid point regarding her weapon. As far as she could estimate, the slug of ultradense organic matter impacted its target at somewhere over two kilometers per second. The result was as much a thermal effect as kinetic, hypersonic interaction blurring the lines between such things. It blurred the outline of her target too, forcing him backward at such a speed as to leave him vanishing from sight entirely.

It was only an exertion of magic—tendrils of fleshcrafted tissue gripping the ground underfoot—that left the prodigious momentum unable to do just the same to Silenos. She reloaded as she righted herself, noting the process taking some time longer than with her previous weapon.

Disastrously longer. The remaining named were rounding on her now that an open attack had been made. She was too slow, about to find herself struck by Shaiagraznian magic before she could get off another shot. That was when Ensharia put her new equipment to the test.

Her maul came down with a burst of kinesis, partly magical and partly the product of her augmented musculature and armor's strength enhancement. The culmination of these effects was a blow so hard as to snap the named's arm almost entirely off, throwing them down into the ground and leaving them some ten or twenty meters deep amid the broken material. Instantly, the remaining one turned their focus onto her. Ensharia was engulfed with shadestuff, more than Silenos had ever conjured herself and enough to liquefy almost anything.

Of course, she lived. The armor had been made with just such an attack in mind. The moment the necromantic substance ate through its outermost layer, it exposed the compressed gases honeycombed throughout the lower sections. These gases were pressurized well beyond atmospheric norms, finding a sudden lack of resistance as they were released and venting themselves forcibly outward.

Shadestuff did not have solidity in any way that could be feasibly measured, but it did have *mass* and *momentum*. It did interact with matter. Silenos had seen that much with painful clarity during her disastrous attack against the magus Walriq. Now she turned it to her advantage, watching as her creation spared itself by blasting the named's assault far from the susceptible matter of its construction.

By the time her startled housemate could overcome their shock and ready another attack, Silenos's cannon was prepared. That was another fact she had learned in her journeys. Many among House Shaiagrazni were ill-suited for direct combat, lazy or sheltered from it and unbalanced by the primal brutality that came from fighting for one's own life with one's own body.

She turned that to her advantage too. The sabot fell away, the projectile flew, and the air caught alight. Ten milliseconds passed. Impact occurred. The named's leg came completely free of their body, sprayed blood sizzling even as it touched the air in the wake of molten-hot velocity.

Ensharia's next swing caught them in the jaw, sending them across the room.

"This way!" Silenos barked, heading for the gateway and seeing, thankfully, that the wounded vampire Hexeri was already doing likewise. The paladin paused only a moment before she joined them. Clearly her time among House Shaiagrazni had done *some* good.

A rumble shook the earth, and Silenos turned to find... Armageddon.

It was a stupid, petty word to think of. Riddled with primitive superstition and uneducated, apocalyptic fear. But it was the only one in her vocabulary that came close to doing the scene justice as it unfolded. Armageddon was happening, and Silenos was right beside it.

Kammani and the Entity moved kilometers between moments, displacing each other either through sheer kinetic transfer or the warping of spatial solidity around them. Silenos watched as atmospheric hydrogen was fused at a gesture from her master and saw the resulting sphere of roaring nucleons engulf the Entity completely. It pressed through, not even seeming to be visibly damaged, and drove her downward into the ground. An entire stretch of terrain simply disappeared as they struck it, ejected skyward and heated to a blue-hot boil.

Silenos had been wrong to think of her master's power as she had. The gap was wider than she could have known. She grabbed the stunned Hexeri and Ensharia, forcing them through the gate as she seized the hybrid's head once more. "Onward!" she cried, fear driving her in a more primal way than ever before.

CHAPTER THIRTY-FOUR

Silenos did not appear upon the ground this time. That was a surprise, and not a particularly pleasant one. By the time she had reoriented herself, located Hexeri and Ensharia falling beside her, the opposing forces of gravity and air resistance had already agreed upon a compromise of seventy meters per second for her velocity. It took her the remaining kilometers downward rather fast.

The first thing she did was look to her allies. Ensharia, she knew, would be fine. Though she fell notably faster than Silenos did given the weight and density of her equipment, nothing shy of a supersonic impact could seriously injure her as she was. Hexeri was the greater concern. Already wounded, barely conscious. Were she to strike something hard—stone instead of dirt—she might well be destroyed.

Calling on her fleshcrafting, Silenos shaped the flesh of her back outward into a makeshift gliding mechanism. It caught the air, immediately doubled the ratio of drag force against gravitational acceleration, and slowed her to just slightly shy of Hexeri's own falling velocity. She was now closing in on the woman, reducing the ten meters between them by a few every second.

Silenos caught the vampire, then expanded her gliding flaps again. Their velocity halved, thirded. The ground, at last, embraced them. She barely even felt the impact, so little was its speed. Silenos had taken a stronger blow seemingly every week of her habitation of the new world. She still did not care for it.

The dust began to clear as winds carried it from the point of impact. Silenos stood up, surprised to find the turbulent weather around her.

Unnatural, she realized, noting the strange localization of it, the intensity. Then she noticed other things, as yet more of her sight was freed up by thinning debris.

Men were fighting all around her, some in large coherent ranks while others merely scrambled about in a frenzied disorder. Magic was in the air, thrown one way and the other. Silenos recognized the feeling of it soon, saw the sight of shadestuff washing over a tall bearded man in his middle years and dissolving his body down to the bone.

Shadestuff.

It was Sphere's shadestuff, and following its arc soon revealed the sight of Sphera herself. She had not, yet, noticed Silenos. And Silenos decided to spend a few moments more examining her surroundings before announcing herself.

Every new sight she found only deepened her fury.

Kaltans were fighting in one corner, Arbitans in another. They did, at least seem to be on the same side, and yet far above, at the center of it all, Silenos saw Galukar and Lilia turning their magic against each other. And between them, lying in a steaming crater . . .

The breath caught in her throat as she saw Nemo's broken form and made her way to his side with no small measure of haste. He was, fortunately, still alive. Just. Silenos hurried in healing him, not bothering to limit pain or discomfort as she prioritized tissue regeneration and speed over all else. It was for his own sake.

Nemo gasped, eyes shooting wide and body convulsing from toes to crown as life suddenly surged back into it. His head jerked around, dazed expression clearing as he eyed her.

"Who . . . Silenos?"

That surprised her.

"You recognize me?" Silenos frowned. Her new body did not particularly resemble the old one. Genetic clones often had notable differences even without accounting for her change in sex.

"Your magic is the same," the boy explained, as if it were obvious. Indeed, it was. But not for one without House Shaiagrazni's training.

"Stay here," she instructed him. "Do not die again." Silenos got up, raised her gaze to the skies, and locked it upon the imbeciles now warring among the clouds.

There were several ways Silenos might have gotten their attention, but most relied on patience. A traitor to House Shaiagrazni, a failure of her own ethics, she had found herself suddenly without patience. And so Silenos merely loaded her cannon with a particularly large shell of blasting oil and fired. The projectile struck exactly where she'd aimed, detonating between the two combatants mere meters from either and forcing them to separate. By the time they had both righted themselves, before the wafting smoke had even finished dissipating across the dozens of meters it was spread, she had placed herself in their midst.

At any other time, the look of shock upon both of their faces might have amused her. She was too angry for that now.

"What in the world do you blithering idiots think you are doing?" she snarled, flitting her gaze from one of them to the other. Galukar spoke first.

"Who are you?" he demanded, Godblade raised, body tense and wary. Silenos rolled her eyes.

"Only you could miss something as obvious as this, you drooling primate. It is a mystery to me how the protoplasmic sludge responsible for eventually congealing into your ancestors even withstood its surroundings. Surely idiocy of this magnitude must permeate the gap between prokaryotic and eukaryotic life. What next, do you have questions about the color of the sky? The direction of gravity?"

He blinked, realization dawning.

". . . Silenos?"

"We will speak on the ground," Silenos informed him, not bothering to answer his moronic question as she turned to Lilia. "You, use your mental powers to halt the fighting this instant."

She paused. "I . . . I can't. The Godblade—"

"The Godblade responds to Galukar. It will not interfere with you under these conditions," Silenos explained. "Provided its grunting ape-man of a wielder does not still insist upon fighting."

As it happened, Galukar did not.

It didn't take long for Lilia to calm the battle, and yet the damage done already was more than enough. The air reeked of blood even minutes after the brutality halted.

At Silenos's word, each and every one of her closest allies—the de facto leaders of her coalition—was gathered up around her. All looked at her with awe. Disbelief and, for those few intelligent enough to realize the situation, fear.

"Silenos," Baird began, "you're—"

"Silence," Silenos cut in, letting her fury show. The quietude that followed left ample room for her to speak. She began with the most pressing concern.

"Each and every one of you is a genetic failure," she began, letting her eyes roll across the group as Ensharia and Hexeri slipped silently into the background of it. "You." Silenos aimed a finger at Nemo. "Tell me what happened, and everyone else, fill in any gaps."

It did not, fortunately, take long to have everything explained. The events had happened with remarkable compression.

When the recap was done, and Silenos had processed it all, her rage redoubled.

"So, to clarify," she growled. "You"—her finger aimed at Baird—"chose to immediately retreat to your own city and form a single alliance purely out of self-interest." Baird met her eye without flinching, though she did not miss the tremble that suddenly racked his legs.

"You," Silenos continued, pointing now at Ado, "did much the same, and yet somehow managed to *lose* the city in question." Her eyes dropped down to her feet, humiliation clear. Silenos caught Sphera smirking from the corner of her eye and chose her next target thusly. "While *you* immediately joined a treacherous force turning against the coalition out of fear." Her head turned now to Felicia. "And *you* decided to leave her, a valuable ally, to perish at Mafari's hands out of some simian need for vengeance." The Arbitan seemed rather less chastened at that, though there was a weakness to her. "And *you*"—she pointed now to Swick the Swift—"enabled her."

The next target for her rage was natural: Lilia. The vampire bore it with perhaps the most dignity so far, yet even she seemed chastened.

"I had no choice—" Silenos was so enraged by the excuse that she could not even bring herself to hear its completion, merely strode forward and glared down at the imbecile making it.

"If you had all cooperated, this *Mafari* hedge caster would have been nothing. Less than nothing. A mild irritant, at worst. And a great victory to show the world at best. Instead, you bickered like children and defeated one another for him."

She held Silenos's gaze for all of one second, then lowered her own. Silenos turned again.

"And you." She glared at Sphera, watching her apprentice melt back like ice before a volcano's breath. "You tossed yourself in with Lilia, despite having been tutored by me personally." The woman's terror was clear enough, and Silenos took a long moment to enjoy it before turning again. "And you—"

She pointed now at Nemo, and hesitated. ". . . Actually, no, you did fine."

The boy exhaled so greatly in his relief that Silenos feared he may actually lose consciousness for a moment, then her attention was turned back to the group as a whole.

"You are, all of you, inept morons who have disappointed me in every way I might have imagined, and several I could not. It will not happen again. Not because I believe there is some guarantee you will perform better in the future, but because I have now learned to expect less than nothing from all of you."

"Silenos—"

"Be silent," she replied, not bothering to even check who was speaking. "I have not yet finished explaining what pitiable specimens you are. If a juvenile of House Shaiagrazni behaved in the way I have seen from you, they would have been immediately sterilized to keep their genetic inferiority from further corrupting our people. And yet not a one of you so much as realized the error in your judgments—"

"*Silenos.*"

She paused, felt her temper fray at the *audacity* of the interruption. Turned to punish it duly. Silenos halted only as she realized that it was Ensharia who had spoken, her fury wavering in the woman's face.

"Ah, I forgot you were here. What do you want?" She found herself with suddenly less patience, the bombardment of idiocy having stripped much of her nerves away as it was revealed to her.

Ensharia had the look of a woman suffering patiently, which baffled Silenos as it was not she who had been faced with so much ineptitude in so short a time. The paladin did not answer verbally, merely stepped to one side and gestured behind her.

Silenos followed the woman's hand and felt herself stunned by the sight it led her to.

Arion Falls descended from the sky upon a cushion of dense air, his features lined with uncertainty and his body trembling with fear. Silenos watched him land on shaky legs and begin walking them over to her. It was only with an exertion of will that she brought herself to walk over in kind.

"Master . . . Is that you?" He seemed wary as he asked the question, which Silenos considered a justified enough response given what he had been subjected to.

"It is," she confirmed. Arion Falls's next response came almost all at once, words blending into one another they were spoken so fast. Silenos heard a half dozen apologies in as many seconds before raising a hand to gesture him for silence.

"You did not fail me," she replied, finding her voice seized by a *loathsome* shake and trying as best she could to suppress it. "You did all I asked and more. I apologize to you, Arion, for . . . pushing you to destroy yourself in the attempt."

He stared at her for a moment, eyes wet. Then lunged forward and wrapped his arms around her waist in a hug. Silenos spasmed, her body almost taking conscious control from her as every instinct she had urged her to strike the wretched creature daring to lay—

She paused, calmed herself, forced her limbs to behave, though they remained wavering at her sides rather than returning his embrace. Falls stepped back at that, looking concerned again.

"I . . . apologize," Silenos continued. "For not returning . . . I am averse to contact due . . . due to . . . I am autistic."

Falls frowned. "Is that something I'm going to . . . learn?"

She decided to ignore that question. There were more important ones to address, and not just pertaining to Falls.

CHAPTER THIRTY-FIVE

Being dead had been strange. Arion actually wasn't sure, now, whether he *had* been dead. He'd been conscious, sort of. And sort of not. Everything was . . . muddled. Abstract. The experience had been on him only hours ago, he believed, and yet already the memory felt years old. By comparison, he knew that the real world—the world of the living—felt almost painfully solid. Everything was starkly defined, sharp edges, vibrant colors. Yes, he was in muddy, temperate Aoakanis surrounded by rubble and exposed dirt, and yet the kaleidoscope of colors it displayed made wherever souls went upon death seem all the duller.

That decided him, in the end. It wasn't pain or boredom or despair that scared Arion about the underworld. It was its *lessness*. He would never go back there again.

"And then the fucking idiot jumped through the portal after him—her, now, I guess—which left the rest of us to just sort of fall apart and bicker among ourselves."

Collin Baird had been explaining everything to occur in Arion's absence, as far as he knew. Arion had tried to listen, committing as much to memory as his years of magus training would allow, but his was far from an optimal condition for any sort of study. Physically, he was fine. Better than fine. He felt stronger than he ever had, more energetic. Not superhuman, perhaps, not *enhanced*, more . . . refreshed. He hoped the feeling lasted.

Just as he hoped the mental fatigue did not.

"When... Uh, when did my master become... You know. A woman?" Arion felt awkward asking it, unsure if he was breaking some taboo. Everyone had behaved so naturally regarding the fact he felt silly for even noticing it. But Baird appeared rather *relieved* by the question, as if he'd been feeling just the same way.

"I have no idea." He sighed. "She just kind of... showed up like that. I don't know why, and I didn't ask. Honestly, it just seems like a Silenos sort of thing to do."

Arion had no idea, to this day, what was and was not a Silenos thing to do. Except for torture, he supposed. He—she—had made clear where they stood on that.

One moment, she was cruel. The next... This. What he'd come back to. Arion's failure still stung his thoughts, but not nearly as much as the confusion. That was worse, he thought, than anything. At least Silenos's abuse had been familiar, accustomed. Arion had spent a lifetime growing used to the treatment magi gave to their students. This was something alien.

His pondering was halted, relievingly, by another summons. This one aimed at both him and Baird at once. From Silenos of course. They answered it quickly, finding the woman in more or less the same place she had gathered her followers to berate them before. The difference now was twofold; her mood seemed considerably lightened, and she was gesturing to Ensharia with no small amount of pride as she spoke.

"As all of you can see," Arion's master was saying, "the material of this armor is beyond the sciences of this world, or even my own personal powers. It is composed of a remarkably durable structure assembled on the atomic level to approach theoretical limits of material strength. Thousands of times more resilient than mundane steel while being no greater in density."

Arion studied the material as Silenos described it and found that, true to her words, he couldn't recognize anything about it. The texture was off, foreign. Without a precedent anywhere in the great banks of his memory. He wondered what sort of measures had been needed to make it. That wondering was interrupted as Silenos moved on to another topic.

"This mace, you may all have noted, is made of similar material. All this equipment has been enchanted with potent magics of course, but none more than the weapon you see before you now. Upon impact, it discharges a volume of kinetic energy comparable to orders of magnitude more than its own mass falling a distance of meters. Ensharia has tested it once already and found it able to break the bones of a Shaiagraznian named. Even the Godblade is a primitive, petty trinket by comparison." As she said the last part, Silenos's eyes fell upon Galukar with an undisguised relish.

The king, clearly, was not much pleased to hear the remark uttered in his presence, face contorting as teeth ground and nostrils flared.

"Not a bad weapon." Arion found himself grinning. "I'd love to see what it could do in the hands of a man, with—" Silenos turned to him sharply, cutting him off with a raised eyebrow.

"I am a woman now, which means that your primitive misogyny is an insult to me. Repeat it in my presence again and I shall weld your testicles together."

Arion was actually speechless for a few moments—the change in demeanor had come so fast. His mind scrambled for purchase until he finally managed to gain some level of cohesion. He used it to nod and hastily spit out apologies while remaining suddenly, terribly conscious of his testicles as he did. Silenos was, fortunately, satisfied. She nodded and moved on from the fact without further ado.

King Galukar's laughter rang out like the sound of Silenos's cannon, and Arion found himself reminded in an instant of how little the old man thought of casters.

"What a way to find yourself returned to life, eh, boy? Looks like your master is just as he always was—"

Silenos rounded on him next, somehow seeming less annoyed than when she did on Arion.

"I am aware, Galukar, that your cognitive abilities are particularly limited, even compared to the standards set by the rest of my lieutenants. So I will give you three chances to mistakenly refer to me as being of the wrong gender. Once each of those has expired, I will turn your digestive tract inside out. You may keep count of your mistakes if you wish. I shall not be helping you remain up to date on them."

Galukar's face darkened, veins bulging as he took a step toward her now.

"I don't care how powerful you *think* you've become," he growled. "You don't speak to me like that. You don't threaten me like that. You may have saved me, but that doesn't—"

"Ah yes, that reminds me," Silenos noted, raising her arm—now a cannon—and blasting Galukar with some burning projectile so fast that it simply took the giant off his feet and sent him hurtling backward to erupt through a half-collapsed stone column and bring the rest of it down with him. She turned to the group at large while Galukar lay convulsing in the rubble.

"I have upgraded my weapon, using a new mechanism to allow for greater velocity in its projectiles. As you can all see, it is extremely effective. Galukar most likely has several broken ribs as a result of its killing power. Do let me know if he seems to be at risk of dying." Without another word, she turned and headed off. To where, or to do what, Arion could only guess.

He turned his eyes from Silenos, and the disturbing cocktail of emotion the sight of her brought, and toward the prisoners. There was no shortage of them—the battle had ended in a single instant and with the bulk of *both* sides' forces swearing fealty to the same figure. What was left of Aoakanis's occupiers, mostly magi, had been swiftly restrained.

But it was only now that Arion recognized one of the faces among them, frowning as he did.

"Julius?" The boy's face turned to his instantly, snapping to alertness as if the sound of his own name were a death curse.

He stared back, frowning, blinking. Gasping.

". . . Arion?"

Arion made his way over, seeing the man more clearly now. He looked somewhat the worse for wear. Thinner, exhausted. Arion remembered the way he'd felt after his first serious fight, his first brush with death. He could empathize on that account at least.

"You . . . You're alive," Julius whispered. Arion felt a stab of something he couldn't identify.

"I am," he replied quickly. "I'm glad you are too." Before his fellow magus could continue, Arion took his leave. He didn't want to dwell on his life, and certainly not on his death. He wanted . . .

Fuck. He wanted something to *eat*.

Silenos lowered herself down into the chambers beneath Morstascia's castle, feeling the mechanisms of her subterranean laboratory growl and purr as they carried her low. Not much longer now, she knew, and her hastily re-formed body would be a moot point. Not much longer now, and her research in the new world would all pay off.

The primitive elevator halted, shuddering to a stop. Silenos sighed out her exasperation. It truly was a simple mechanism, built in a hurry and with limited resources. By her estimates, she was already three-quarters of the way down to her destination. Not worth the effort of fixing her lift. Not when she had a quicker way.

Blowing out the bottom, Silenos dropped the remaining few hundred meters and entered the chamber awaiting her. The vessel was safely stored within.

Her trip back up could have been made by elevator, for most of its length. Silenos found herself eager to test the prowess of her new body instead. She had exerted a great deal of effort to adopt it, after all. Carefully fleshcrafting her own musculature to remove her cerebrum and graft it into the empty cranium of the vessel, then repair all the incisions that had been needed to do so. Already, she could feel the difference.

She squatted down, felt the painstakingly grown musculature of her new vessel's legs, and leaped. The ground exploded beneath her, such was the force, and Silenos heard her own tunnel collapsing in her wake as she shot upward, burst through the elevator without the slightest damage to herself, and continued several dozen meters more before her momentum was finally spent. She dangled in the air for a moment, considering the extent of her new strength.

It was within 5 percent of estimations, acceptable. Silenos reached out just as gravity got its hold of her, digging her fingers into the wall. Solid bone, all of it. Ultradense and able to withstand gunfire, but not the pinch grip of her new form. It surrendered easily, letting her hang there for a single moment. Then she dragged herself upward, flying another fifty meters before repeating the process.

Reaching the top did take her a considerable time, or at least a considerable number of actions. But she made all of them in less than ten seconds. Her body and mind now operated exponentially faster than even her previous war form had, after all.

Silenos erupted from the elevator shaft like volcanic debris, feeling a strong wind against her face as she emerged and landing hard. The ground surrendered easily to her heels. Instantly, she was swarmed by a multitude of faces. Some with weapons raised, others recognizing her more quickly and staring. It was Galukar, apparently not injured to any crippling extent by the cannon, who approached her first.

"You . . . Silenos, is that you?" His face was creased with concern. No doubt, even he could recognize her glorious new form's power.

"It is," she confirmed. Galukar's frown deepened.

"Why do you look like my daughter?"

"What you see before you now," Silenos announced, "is the pinnacle of biomantic knowledge. A body made of tissues replicated with the Godblade's magical effects, merged with the pure-strain vampiric prowess of Lilia's own lineage, perfected in a hundred other, smaller optimizations, and designed for perfect efficiency. I am, now, the single most potent being in the history of this planet."

Silenos had expected even Galukar to be surprised by that, to be impressed and awed. Surely even he would understand something as basic as what she had just explained. But he merely stared at her, eyes dull, shaking his head and frowning.

"But why my *daughter*?" he asked.

Silenos rolled her eyes. She likely looked similar to Felicia due to having used the tissue of her father—Galukar—in creating this body.

But she could not be bothered to explain as much. Silenos simply moved on without a word.

"You are back, caster." Silenos took a moment to realize it was the hybrid's head speaking to her once more. "Now kill me."

Silenos took it out, eyeing it. "I will do no such thing. You are far too valuable." A deep, sullen moan escaped the head. Then she felt its magic coiling.

Silenos Shaiagrazni just disappeared, in a flash of light. Collin stared at the spot she'd just been occupying, waiting for her to come back. She didn't. He looked around, locked eyes with all the other, equally stunned subordinates she'd spent the last hour yelling at, and groaned.

"Fuuuuuuuuck! Not again!"

CHAPTER THIRTY-SIX

Adonis, try as he might, could not find the means to repair his tempered schism. Or, rather, he could not find the means to amplify its effectiveness to function without the hybrid. He cursed the very world, and everything in it. The hybrid, the schism itself, the Depths, himself, and, of course, he cursed Silenos more than anything else. For a brief window there, he had convinced Adonis that his weakening and corruption truly had been nothing but a brief lapse. Then he'd shown him better, when it mattered the most. He had saved his pitiable spinelessness for the moment when unveiling it would maximize disaster.

Was Silenos a double agent? Had his treachery been planned? If so, for how long . . . No. Adonis recognized the creeping paranoia infecting his thoughts, forcibly tempered it with a sterilizing rationality. Silenos had not been playing at any sort of long game in what he did. There had been many opportunities for him to get the better of Adonis with no risk to himself if he had. He might even have been able to finish Adonis's own research with the tempered schism if he had simply left him to die in the Depths. What Adonis had seen was no more than a . . . failure.

A failure of reason against emotion, of morality against instinct. Silenos Shaiagrazni, like so many others, had allowed his primitive ape brain to reign supreme over the higher parts of his cognition. It was not an unknown fate.

But it was no less a betrayal for being unintentional.

Adonis's musings on the failing of his former master were interrupted as something touched his magical senses, a caress of arcane power that drew his attention across the room and to . . . a newcomer.

Upon first inspection, he might have thought it was the child of Galukar—Princess Felicia. But nothing could have disguised the magic humming around it. Both within the ethereal container that was a caster's mana reserves and woven into the creature's very body. He took a step back, instinctively, and felt his jaw tighten with shock.

"Silenos." Adonis's rage boiled as he spoke the name, daring the newcomer to contradict him.

"Adonis," Silenos replied, speaking with a voice pitched to match their new female body. "Perfect timing. I have been looking for something to test my new body against. Prepare to be obliterated."

Adonis felt the grin spread across his own face as he donned his helmet, drew his mace, and charged toward his enemy. This was perfect. Everything he needed had fallen right into his lap, and she wasn't even in war form. With a swing carrying every gram of strength in every fiber of his body, Adonis aimed to end the bout in one stroke.

Silenos did not dodge, however. Her hand came up and closed about the handle of Adonis's weapon. Shaiagraznian alloys quivered as the metal's momentum died in a single instant, decelerating from supersonic velocities to a dead stop within devastating milliseconds. The force involved drove Silenos's heels ten or twenty centimeters into the stone beneath her and would have bent a steel bar ten times the thickness of Adonis's weapon shaft. His mace just about survived it. His arms, though, were racked by a sudden numbness as the unexpected halt ran through them in penetrative waves.

He stumbled away, barely keeping a grip on his weapon. Silenos punched him.

Adonis's helmet surrendered near instantly, its preternatural metallurgy contested by the genius of Silenos's fist and proving itself inferior. He heard a crack run through the interior as his feet left the ground, and, so shortly after it almost defied reaction time, his back met the far wall. A crater was born in the stone, cracks running outward from it and dust raining from above in great enough volumes to bury a smaller man. With a grunt of effort, Adonis forced himself to stand. Then fell down to one knee as an irresistible dizziness suddenly washed over his senses. He tasted iron-tanged blood in his mouth, smelled it as a thick and clotting blanket in his nostrils. Silenos was pacing, eyeing him with a look of intense boredom.

"Do try to recover more quickly. I need to test the full capabilities of my new body, and you are, unfortunately, the most powerful lifeform on this planet besides me. I don't suppose you can call on that infusion of Entity magic you did during our first fight?"

As a fact, Adonis could. It was dangerous, exhausting, and something that carried a price that mounted every time he did. But that single exchange had made it clear to him that there would be no victory if he held off on it now. Inhaling sharply, he called upon the currents of the Depths and let them run through him where he stood. The world rebelled at their touch.

Save for his mace and his armor. They drank the energy in greedily, repairing and reinforcing themselves. Adonis kicked off from the wall and obliterated it in the force of his leap as he crossed the room to swing at Silenos again.

This time, she did dodge. Leaping back and evading the weapon by a mere hair. Adonis shifted his grip, bringing it back around like the very shaft was elastic and succeeding in crunching the head into his former master's chest. She disappeared from sight, hitting the far wall, smashing through it. Smashing through the one behind that, and a half dozen more. Adonis peered through the dusty corridor now created in her wake, watched her get up at the end through crumbling stone and wafting debris.

She did not appear hurt.

He lunged again, swinging to compound his first blow and demolishing another few hallways' walls as he did. Silenos sidestepped, ducked another strike, and punched once more. Her fist caught Adonis's head like a great block of metal, stunning him just long enough for her to lash a kick out, which threw him farther backward. This time it was *his* turn to level a section of the fortress, destroying, he estimated, some five cubic meters of stone before finally coming to rest in one particularly reinforced wall. Silenos didn't let him remain. She tackled him through it and launched both of them out into the frigid air beyond.

They fell, instantly. The stony ground was long below them, and the winds howled as if in celebration of their descent. Silenos retained her viselike grip on Adonis despite his struggling.

She is stronger than me.

It didn't make sense. Silenos was a fleshcrafter out of war form. The physical disparity should have been both immense and *unquestionably* in his own favor. That the gap was small did not make him any less shaken at finding it on Silenos's side.

Her new body—she mentioned testing it and has had ample time to study the people of this world.

That must have been it. Somehow, Silenos had taken advantage of the local magics to enhance her fleshcrafting, and now Adonis was by far the weaker of them. He felt fear touch him. Shivered at its embrace.

So gripping was the realization that Adonis fully forgot about the fall, right up until its ending hit him from below. He was crushed beneath his own weight, that of his armor, and, of course, Silenos, whose new body was just as tall as the last and perhaps even heavier. The rock cracked beneath him as they bounced separately, rolling aside and both getting up as one. Silenos was on her feet first, and waited.

Waited. Waited for him, gave *him*, Adonis Shaiagrazni, the chance to gather his wits and ready himself. Looking down on him even now, when he was a true child of House Shaiagrazni and she a worthless traitor. Never in his life had Adonis been seized by such rage. He charged again.

His mace came down for her like an artillery shell, and of course she melted aside to leave it a meter wide of its mark. The metal head pulverized a crater into the ground measuring double its target's height in every direction, and she had already taken her next step away before the scattered shrapnel even reached her. Adonis's next swing never came, interrupted as Silenos reversed her flight and closed in to strike him again. Her fist was like a solid metal ball, moving so fast he barely saw it before the knuckles cracked against his helmet and broke the armor open.

Adonis stumbled, saw Silenos close more and continue rattling his armor as her blows kept coming. It was like the woman was firing an entire line of machine guns, so fast did they land, and Adonis could scarcely tell one impact apart from another. By the time he drove her back with another swing, his armor was glowing orange with the thermal waste of her blows. His torso ached, ribs throbbing, lungs burning. Not in decades had Adonis been wounded so badly. Perhaps not in a century.

And Silenos had not even an eyebrow singed.

"It seems my expected parameters have been exceeded by some margin," she noted, thinking aloud. She raised an arm as she spoke, flexing its fingers, tilting her head in study of them. "There must be some synergistic effect of the measures I used to construct this body. Quite fascinating. I must investigate further."

Again, Adonis's rage festered. But he did not let it explode again, and resisted the muscular call of motion and violence. He straightened, backing away and circling Silenos cautiously. Already he could hear the perpetual whispering of Entities growing more powerful in the back of his mind. Were he to conjure more, they would intensify further. Become, he suspected, stronger than he had ever dealt with before. It was a grave risk.

But his alternative choices were growing scarcer by the moment. The Entities exploded into the air, congealed nightmares that arced for Silenos as one. They shrieked, twisted, and coiled. They let out cries of nails upon chalkboards and struck with talons made of a rapist's pleasure.

And each one of them failed, sidestepped, batted aside, or cast into the ground by Silenos. Her new body, seen from afar, was, if anything, more impressive than it was when fought from up close. She seemed to handle her own weight like it was no weight at all, disappearing and reappearing over short distances so swift and explosive were her movements. The air screamed with whipcracks and sizzled with vapor trails as she did her work. In moments, the assault of Entities was scattered and broken.

It had taken moments, perhaps less than a single second. And Adonis was far from recovered in that span. He righted himself, readied his mace, swallowed. Felt *fear*. Silenos rushed forward and batted it aside. She was serious now, face tight, concentrated. Her next blow came not as a fist, but as a thing of keratinous talons that gouged through Adonis's armor and into his flesh. He cried out, felt the sharp touch of blades kissing bone, then felt them torn free amid a gasp of blood. He stumbled, then Silenos slashed again. Again, again. His strength failed him in moments, armor falling away in patches, and he dropped to the ground gasping.

Silenos stared down at him, her head tilted.

"This has been a most helpful test. Thank you, Adonis."

His rage was bubbling back up through the pain, but impotent now. His lifeblood leaking out, Adonis's strength had already abandoned him and left his limbs trembling and twitching in impotent paralysis.

"Stop mocking me." He gasped. "Just . . . Just kill me. Finish it."

Silenos eyed him for a moment longer, not speaking out loud. Adonis just had time to wonder what in the world she could be thinking when her talons came down again, and his head was freed from its shoulders.

He waited for his sapience to die in the sea of oxygen deprivation, instead feeling magic coalesce around him. When Adonis came to, his head was still removed. But stable. Hanging from a loop in Silenos's belt. He realized what had happened with a start, glaring up at her.

"Coward." He spit. "You can't bring yourself to kill me? An enemy? You are worse than an outsider, pathetic."

Silenos said nothing in retort, just sprouted wings and began making her way through the skies.

CHAPTER THIRTY-SEVEN

Silenos had a considerable distance to fly before finally returning to the new center of her power, Aoakanis. By her calculations, some thirty-two hundred kilometers. It *was* still a considerable distance, even for her. But not nearly as much as it might have been. Silenos experimented with a new form of propulsion as she flew, constructing various cavities in her body to be lined with muscular tissue and set to contract in careful coordination. Air was drawn in, accelerated by the compression, and blasted out behind her almost like a jet engine.

A jet engine that was, now, powered by the strongest organic tissues she had ever made. As far as her calculations could tell, she achieved a speed well in excess of the sound barrier. These calculations were rather rudimentary. In fact, as rudimentary as it was possible for any to be. Silenos counted as she flew.

The biological computer of her cerebrum was not as perfect as it had once been, but even still she retained a degree of freedom from distraction or wavering focus. She counted and as she reached her destination knew that roughly six thousand seconds had expired. It was not, she thought, a particularly *bad* velocity to have achieved, but she made a mental note to coin some more efficient means of long-range flight in the future. The minutes required to fleshcraft herself into it would likely save hours.

It had, she thought, been impulsive to do what she'd done to Adonis. Silenos herself was not sure of why she had. But then, she was not sure of much of anything anymore. Everything he'd said against her was true. She was a traitor, a wretch, a moral failure. For all her chastisement of her own subordinates, she had veered further from the ideals she lived by than any of them had.

Her long flight left room for much thinking across its duration. Silenos redoubled her conviction to perfect a faster means of long-distance transportation, even as she used much of the journey to probe the head of the hybrid.

Fortunately, it did not seem like it would pose any further problems.

Whatever measure of power the hybrid could control—and she was certain it had not even scratched the surface of its own eldritch reserves—it had been exhausted on that one translocation. The being had lashed out at her in petty rage, and it had failed to gain even revenge. It was no more concern of hers.

Silenos had not *expected* to find her problems reduced when she finally returned to Aoakanis, but she had dared to hope that some positive change might have been awaiting her. As usual, chance seemed to be against her.

Mere moments after touching down in the castle, Silenos was brought urgent word.

"My lor—Uh, l-lady?" It was one of the native servants, a blinking, grunting savage who, clearly, found two genders the approximate limit of their ability to count. Silenos could not find the effort to even punish him for his idiocy, merely gestured his words on impatiently.

"There are visitors here for you. Uh, that is to say . . . Archimage Mafari, King Magnia, and . . . others. They request an audience with you. They say it is for . . . negotiations."

That, at least, was interesting. Silenos's enemies wished to speak with her? She doubted anything productive would come of it, but if nothing else it was a valuable chance to gather information.

"Invite them in," she ordered. "I shall be there to receive them shortly."

She had not bothered to form any strong expectations of what Archimage Mafari would look like, and the others were quite beyond the scope of her familiarity with new-world luminaries. Nonetheless, each of them saved her the trouble by cutting right past the diplomatic tedium and into the meat of the matter. Standing in the center of the largest hall she could find among Morstascia's palace, the five of them together left it seeming small. It was rare, outside of House Shaiagrazni at least, to find so much power compressed into so minor a space.

"What is the meaning of this?" one of them called out, destroying the silence with that single sentence. "We demanded to see Shaiagrazni, not one of his pet whores."

Fascinating. This was, if Silenos was not mistaken, another example of what the historians had referred to as misogyny. She had, of course, seen no small amount of it demonstrated by Galukar and Falls—the very reminder that her apprentice now lived again struck an unpleasant chord in her mind at that—but to experience it firsthand on the receiving end was an entirely new matter for her.

She decided she did not care for it within a thirtieth of a second.

"You are a pitiable, drooling barbarian who knows roughly as much about magic as you do about sexual dimorphism." She glanced at him, to his allies, considered the facts. "I imagine you were humiliatingly defeated by the Dark Lord, given your sudden decision to gather comparable allies to your side. Sadly, I have no comparable allies of my own, as my power is beyond compare. You may feel free to continue scurrying around with the other rats, of course, though I do hope you are not expecting to gain some sort of tactical advantage through numbers alone."

By the look upon Mafari's face, Silenos might have expected him to drop dead then and there.

Contrasting it, the others in his group seemed two-thirds amused—on the part of the tall elfin creature and the interestingly crimson-skinned, horned woman—and one part apathetic. It was this last figure who unnerved Silenos the most. So close, she could clearly see the coil of his magic and make out both a great volume and intensity to it.

It was, quite frankly, beyond anything she had seen native to the new world thus far. He would not have been lacking in House

Shaiagrazni and were it not for her and Adonis would surely have had his say over the fate of this world.

As things stood of course, she could simply not allow *that*.

"We are not here to negotiate," Mafari said at last, seeming to have gotten himself under control. It was amusing. He had been described as calm, Silenos recalled, in the reports of her subordinates. Apparently his own bigotry was the crack in that armor.

"I do not care what you are here for," she informed him. "Your intentions do not hold any particular sway over what will happen next."

"Yes, they do," another of them cut in, speaking with considerably more calm—or, at least, considerably less rage—than Mafari. "For our intentions are your destruction, and we are hereby declaring war upon you. Silenos Shaiagrazni, invader, conqueror, destroyer, monster, you—" She tuned out the tirade and began thinking of how best she might make her long-distance-propulsion system work. That was of far greater concern than whatever drivel was being hurled her way in the present. Silenos had, after all, heard it all before.

Your family said it once too. One hundred and fifty years ago.

She stilled that thought and shredded it, finding herself suddenly furious at its touch.

"Your war has been declared then. You may leave." Silenos did not bother to see whether the elf had finished speaking or not when she spoke, merely replied. "But before you do, gaze upon this." She revealed the severed, unconscious head of Adonis to them. "My previous . . . challenger."

Then she turned and headed out of the room. Her head was pained, stabbing tendrils assailing every side of her cognition as she moved through the palace. Suddenly thought seemed harder, more sluggish. What was she doing?

Focus. It was only a great exertion on her part that restored some semblance of control to Silenos's wits, and she carried it with her tightly as she continued down the corridors. Baird. She needed to speak with Baird.

Conveniently, Baird was already preparing himself for some form of conflict. Though that did not come as any kind of surprise given that preparing for conflict—of seemingly any kind he could imagine—was what he spent the majority of his time doing in *any* circumstances. He was holed up in his own chambers, surrounded by a significant enough volume of primed traps to mildly impede even Galukar. Silenos was half tempted to order them set off as another test for her new vessel, but decided she had more pressing things to do.

"You wanted something?" Baird asked, neither apologetic nor, visibly at least, intimidated. It was inappropriate, *immoral*. But then again, Silenos's days as a being worthy of gauging others for their ethics were long gone.

This fearlessness against me is present against his enemies too. Were it not for that, Baird would be less than one-tenth as effective as he has been in contesting superior opponents and staving off overwhelming odds.

The thought was an alien, cooling thing that Silenos found most unwelcome. It made a flaw into a boon. But then, so many of her thoughts were doing so now.

"We will be at war soon," she told the Kaltan, pushing past her own doubts and reconsiderations with a usual haste.

"With Mafari and his shitters." Baird nodded, not the slightest bit surprised and not bothering to feign otherwise. "You know they have King Ka'al among them, right?"

Silenos had not heard the name. "Explain."

"Some . . . mythological figure, basically. Supposedly he once turned an entire city's population into gold."

"Myths do not concern me," Silenos replied. "I have taken his measure myself. His magic is potent, a potential threat, even, before my newest project finished growing and augmented my abilities." If there was one advantage to her being trapped away from her work for so long, it was that it gave the vessel a chance to complete itself.

"Myths don't concern me either," Baird grumbled. "Problem is, I'm not sure whether this bastard's power to aurumicare entire cities is mythical."

Silenos tilted her head. Aurumicare. A normal person might have said goldify, others, more well-read, aurimify, exercising some understanding of etymology—whatever translation magic was affecting her clearly allowed such nuances to be converted—to highlight the finer details. Aurumicare, however, showed that he not only knew the original words for "stone" and "gold," but the suffix of "to turn" and its translation as well.

It was baffling, how well-read Baird was. Blindingly intelligent, inquisitive, mnemonically potent, and thoughtful. In that, he reminded Silenos of his father. His father, who had hoped to keep Baird from the exact life of war and conflict that had taken his unpolished gem of a cognition and rendered it a killing tool.

The life of war and conflict she had deliberately extended for him, at the expense of Finlay Baird's life.

"I killed your father," she volunteered. It was, she thought, as much a surprise to Baird as it was to her, and that truly was saying something.

"What."

Baird did not, somehow, frame his question as a question. It seemed a statement, perhaps a notice. *This is your opportunity to rescind or contextualize what you said. It will be the final one.*

But Silenos did neither.

"Your father wanted to offer terms to General Venka and stop fighting the Dark Lord. I killed him and blamed the Dark Lord's forces, knowing that you would take control of Kaltan and use its military assets to seek revenge against Venka."

The admission stung her on its way out, another dangerous testament to how deeply the toxin of emotions had seeped into her.

Clearly, it stung Baird more. His face changed instantly, as fast as the features of a snarling wolf. One moment he was on the other side of the room and the next he was within arm's reach of Silenos, scowling up into her face and so very still. She was, Silenos estimated, actually faster than him now. But Baird had an economy of movement that somehow offset even that. His fist came around at a vector that surpassed even her reaction speed, cracking against her jaw. The blow was like a child's, doing nothing and perhaps even injuring the hand he threw it with. Baird gave no hint that the fact affected him. Merely sustained his glare, trembled a moment as his hands twitched for the knife at his belt, and stormed out.

CHAPTER THIRTY-EIGHT

The chamber was dark. Chambers tended to be when one had them buried miles beneath the earth. Such was the necessity imparted by their enemy's power. Silenos Shaiagrazni, whatever whore's body he had chosen to infest, was not something Mafari could take lightly. He had felt that much himself, being in his presence. And verified it in his humiliating defeat against the apparently far weaker original Dark Lord.

Silenos Shaiagrazni had bested the Dark Lord, taken his head as a trophy, and even showed it off. That was as clear an intimidation tactic as Mafari had seen used anywhere, but it also had the opposite of its intended effect. His resolve was not weakened by the sight, but strengthened. All their resolves were.

For it meant there was now one less Dark Lord to concern themselves with. An enemy was gone and done away with already, one of two. Their mission was halfway done.

"I will dedicate my powers to the destruction of Silenos Shaiagrazni." King Ka'al spoke his vow with no great excess of solemnity, seeming to consider it beneath him somehow. Clearly his ego had not been exaggerated in retellings.

"I will dedicate my powers, and all the weight of Magira, to the destruction of Silenos Shaiagrazni," Mafari echoed, adding only those details that were practical for the disparity in his and Ka'al's situations. The air quivered, oaths beginning to take on mass and form.

"I will dedicate my powers, my mastery, and my men to the destruction of Silenos Shaiagrazni," the whore repeated, surprising Mafari with her ability to recall so many polysyllabic words at once.

He was not given chance to dwell upon it, for Magnia spoke next.

"I will dedicate my powers, my kingdom, and my people to the destruction of Silenos Shaiagrazni," he swore and finalized the sealing of their pact. There was no great tremor of magic as the ancient forces did their work, merely a sense of foreboding. Oaths were sacred, more sacred the further back a being's life stretched. Mafari had never felt ones as intense as those he'd seen sworn with Magnia.

Until today, when he'd partaken with a being ten times the elf king's age.

Their alliance was now as close to unbreakable as Mafari knew an alliance could be made. All that remained was to see what it did in conflict with Shaiagrazni's forces.

That, and to take all the necessary measures to strengthen their odds as best as they could.

"Once this is over," Ka'al the Tyrant added, "I will claim this world for my own."

None of them bothered to feign surprise. Of course, this event with Shaiagrazni had taught all of them a single crucial thing. They were all one another's biggest threats. Their lethargy, their distraction, had left the world ripe to be seized by another, and they had lost the advantage of time and establishment through that lapse. None of them would make the same mistake again.

After Shaiagrazni was disposed of, after the conflict was ended, another would begin as they turned on one another. Powers such as themselves could simply not coexist. Not when their very presence left one another's influences reduced in weight.

Mafari's part in readying the conflict had begun quite some time ago, his efforts directed to elemental measures. He was no demonologist, like the Dark Lord, and never would be. But his power was not entirely his own, either. The fae had touched his mind as he retreated to the mountains that long century ago, and that connection still remained.

He had used it since. Called upon spirits of earth, water, air. Spirits of fires long burned out, rekindled and eager to use the bodies of Shaiagrazni's creatures as fuel. Mafari knew better than to try to bind such beings, instead settling to merely direct them. In that, he fancied, he had not a single equal in all the land.

Magnia's elfin warriors, of course, were ready already. It was a rare elf who dedicated their life to killing, and each one that did was among the deadliest creatures in the world. Armed with natural magic, centuries of training and experience, and weapons forged from metallurgy lost to time, they may even have contested the spirits.

Veria the whore's forces, perhaps, took the least preparation to assemble. The bulk of them were already prepared as her own crews and needed far less mobilization and organizing than even the elves. And then there was Ka'al.

As far as Mafari could tell, the god tyrant simply gestured once and considered his preparations done. That either said nothing about his power, or everything.

He would find out which soon.

Collin was a king.

It was a sickening thing to think, to remind himself of. Sickening enough that he'd carefully put it away somewhere into one corner of his mind and kept from thinking about it, just like every other negative emotion that might get in the way of what needed doing. He killed people, he sacrificed his men, he was a king. These things were all true, but only one of them was unconscionable. Only one of them was something he'd allowed without good reason.

When did I become a damned king?

He asked himself that when he walked, and didn't like the answers he got at all.

Oh, it would've been easy to tell himself he became a king upon accepting Ado's offer. Doubtless that was what most everyone else would think too. Because they were *thick*. They saw titles and history, categorical yes-or-no dichotomies. But Collin knew too much to let himself be fooled like that, however comforting it would've been.

He became a king the moment his dad died and he'd readily taken on all the authority of Kaltan to use them for revenge. When he'd continued his rule long past the crisis posed by the Dark Lord dissipating. When he'd somehow gone months without even considering that he should step down and start setting up any of the mechanisms of rule Finlay Baird had fought and died for.

Collin was a king because everything he had came from his powerful daddy. He'd worked for it more than most royals, perhaps, but that was nothing compared to the impossible amount of work needed to actually justify having it. Somewhere along the way, he'd just let himself take what he wanted.

Like they all did. His fellow fucking kings.

And, like all kings, he'd run off with his shitty childish whims and damned the consequences. It didn't matter that Venka *hadn't* killed Collin's father. It was enough that his divine holiness had been stupid enough to believe it. It didn't matter that Kaltan *hadn't* been at war following the Dark Lord's defeat. It was enough that he'd suspected they *would* be soon. It didn't matter that every historic account he'd ever found had highlighted what a shitty idea it was for one violent man to decide the fates of everyone. Collin had been confident, and he'd been angry, and he'd been in charge. And so it fucking was.

He reached the end of a corridor, a wall blocking him. Why was it there? What did it do?

Collin compared it to his mental map of Ado's palace and found that he was nowhere near any outer structures. As far as he could tell, the surface was just cutting a corridor short for no reason at all. Wasting space, wasting stone. Pointless, stupid. Horrible fucking thing.

He punched it. Collin couldn't have said why—even he didn't know—but suddenly the rage, disgust, and guilt in him were too strong to remain internal for a moment longer. They discharged themselves as force and brought knuckles to smash the rock angrily hard.

Maybe at one time that would've hurt him—stone was stone, after all. Collin didn't feel it now. The surface cracked, cratered, shivered. Dust fell away, and crumbs of debris fell in. He hadn't smashed through, not all entirely, but he saw a few slits that he suspected went all the way through.

One punch. Collin looked at his unblemished hand.

So much power in one person.

Of course that was where all their current problems came from too. Silenos Shaiagrazni—on top of being a murdering bastard—had made themselves so foundational to their own little empire that it had crumbled apart the moment they left it.

All your life, you fought to be treated as an equal, and failed. Everything you had you had to take by force. Everything you believed in, you killed for. And your own son turned out to be a petty tyrant. I'm sorry, Dad.

Collin felt so very tired, suddenly. And he felt something else too. That quiet whisper at the back of his mind. The universe winking at him. Silenos Shaiagrazni had killed his father, and he—she, whatever—was still alive. Collin's revenge hadn't been taken at all.

So what was he going to do about it?

It hardly seemed necessary to even think about. He had an enemy. He had a weapon. He had nothing to lose and everything to gain. He had a life that wasn't worth living and a goal that might be achieved by throwing it away. So the answer was clear.

Was it? So many answers had been, and now it seemed like none were.

What do I do?

Silenos stood atop the tower, looking out on everything below. All of it hers. Won through near-effortless exertion of her incalculable power.

More incalculable now. She had, she believed, actually entered the ranks of the ten most powerful casters in House Shaiagrazni now that her new body was perfected. There was some drop-off before the top five, of course, and none truly approached Kammani even among them. But she had divided the number of magic users who could equal her by ten or more in a single stroke.

But I am not among House Shaiagrazni's number anymore.

Silenos should have stopped using the name. It occurred to her suddenly, painfully. She was not sure why she did not.

Because it's all I have.

House Shaiagrazni had been a crutch, a thing to cling onto. Now it wasn't, and Silenos was unbalanced in its absence. Unbalanced more than figuratively. She landed hard at the base of the spire, a hundred meters down, and felt the stone ground press against her face. She did not move. Could not bring herself to. Suddenly it felt like her body had no strength at all.

Ludicrous. It has exceeded my intended parameters by 7 percent . . .

But she remembered this. It was not a physical exhaustion now plaguing her, but a mental one. A symptom of the infestation she had allowed—even invited—into her thoughts. Now it had worsened, congealed. And only as physical consequences assailed her did she understand its true extent.

No, she knew better than that even as the thought crossed her mind. This was not the first time Silenos had found her mental impairment bleeding into the physical. She had gotten an abundance of warnings, an endless supply, and each time she had turned them away. She had nothing to blame but herself for what had happened. For what she had done.

For my treachery.

Silenos knew what was moral and chose not to do it. She was, in that respect, lower than an animal. What would she do if she met a being such as herself?

Destroy it. Instantly, without hesitation. And yet she did not destroy herself because the very emotions that induced her ruin were keeping her from self-termination. The animal urge to live, to continue existing for no reason other than the sake of her existence itself, was an obstacle her own intellect was blunting itself in the effort of cutting through.

Why did I tell Baird what I did?

It was that that stung the most. Not the behaviors she understood—the cowardice and weakness—but the ones that baffled her. Silenos had everything to gain by maintaining her deception and yet had abandoned it as if Baird was . . .

As if he were my equal. Deserving of truth.

CHAPTER THIRTY-NINE

It had taken two weeks. Two of the hardest weeks Mafari had known in years, if not longer. Two weeks of actually exerting his powers to their limit and sustaining that effort even while he knew his own contributions alone would have been insufficient.

Novel, if nothing else. And devastating. For the enemy.

Mafari's elementals swept across the countryside as a great blanket. Some moving along the ground, or within it. Churning dirt and crushing rock, making the terrain itself shiver as they bore toward the fighting. Others were skyward, coiling currents and breathy whispers that closed in around the city of Aoakanis from above. Water leaped from containers and condensed into the bodies of his familiars, and the entire region was assailed by every universal fundament he could call upon at once.

Anywhere else, the conflict would have ended under that strain alone. But the New Dark Lord's defenses were ready for such things.

Fortunately, Mafari's new coalition had been ready for his readiness. Great statues of glinting gold smashed into towering abominations of meat and armor plating, shaking the ground as they grappled one another clean through city walls or laid buildings flat. Elfin elites tangled with Kaltan rangers, exerting far more effort to overwhelm the shorter-lived humans than Mafari would have suspected, while almost half a dozen skyships circled in the air above. Three flying the colors of Veria the whore, one armored in more of that mysterious, ostensibly biological material made by Shaiagrazni and somehow staving off direct hits from the weaponry of the larger vessels for it.

The numbers involved were not high, but the power must surely have been the greatest exertion of martial and magical potence the continent had seen in millennia. Perhaps ever.

And Mafari felt a sliver of fear skewer his heart as he realized it wasn't going his way.

Ado had been put to fighting. She understood why, saw the utility. Still felt herself shivering down to the very bones at the idea. The enemy was too strong, too numerous. She wasn't a hero in this fight, just another set of arms with a bit of magic behind them. The magi had been less fearsome than this.

But she was fighting in her home, and she wouldn't let those old bastards take it.

One of the mysterious water beings dived down for her, like a stray bolt of lightning. Ado's ice rose up to meet it, shivered at the impact, and broke. Tiny shards of it sprayed out, cutting her skin, almost blinding her as she stumbled. The elemental kept coming, twisting, shrieking. Its tail whipped for her and missed by less than a foot, cutting the stone wall behind her down to its core.

Chips of rock beat her as they flew outward, then the thing closed more.

Death was on her.

But it didn't have its fill, not today. The iron bolt found the base of its skull just as it found her. It tore through the water elemental, scattered it, but didn't do much more. Save for buy Ado a moment's reprieve. She leaped aside, and it missed her again, by a few more feet this time. She landed hard, scrambled back as another bolt tore through the thing. Then Collin was landing in between them, knives drawn, bow discarded, body crouched in a predator's stance. Ready to pounce, to fight.

"Freeze it. I'll break the bits that you do."

It took long moments for Ado's mind, addled by the frenzy of near death, to wrap around what he was saying.

Then she did, and cast her magic out just in time to aid her ally—her husband—as they fought together.

Galukar didn't know what the strange, jittering gold statue before him was. It wasn't actually made of gold, that much was certain. Gold was soft, fragile. Whatever this was, its material of construction was durable enough to put up a mighty resistance against his blows. It took him two swings, sometimes even three, to remove both of its legs, and then a great final one more to split its head open as it landed chest first against the ground.

But there was no time to marvel at its resilience, nor in his own victory. A dozen more were making their way down the streets, the ground shaking as if the earth itself were shivering in fear of them.

The Arbitans too were shivering. Actually in fear of them, and loosing arrows that did not a single thing despite their new bows. The creations were of Shaiagrazni's doing, limbs made of bone and lined with what Galukar thought was *musculature.* Contracting and flexing to assist their wielders in pulling back what would otherwise have been an impossible draw weight.

None was the equal of a Kaltan ranger's weapon, but all spit jagged death at double or more a typical arrow's speed. Galukar watched the tips splinter on contact with the great statues, scoring dents and scratches but little else.

"Fall back!" Galukar called, not wanting to see his men die to enemies they would fail at even damaging. "I shall dispatch them."

Granted, he wasn't bloody certain he *could.* There was, however, only one way to find out. Galukar flung himself at the statues, roaring and swinging.

For Felicia.

For his little girl, whom he had failed. For the world he had ruined. For the thousand evils he could never atone for, save by dying in the attempt. Galukar swung, and metal perished.

Swick was not used to having company in the skies, not one bit. He decided within a few scarce minutes that he didn't like it at all.

The enemy had a lot of interesting tactics. And by interesting, of course, he meant *bullshit*. It seemed there were simply more options available to the side with three skyships than the side with one. This was not news to him of course. It was, after all, why he'd always wanted two more.

Something smashed into the side of his own vessel, rocking the ship. Swick kept his balance. Almost everybody else lost theirs. Bloody landlubbers acted as if a little thing like convulsive terrain meant they had an excuse to drop down and have a rest. Pathetic!

Another weapon struck the ship, a great iron lance propelled by some magical mechanism Swick had never even seen before. The benefits of traveling farther than even he had, he supposed.

Oh, he knew he was fighting. Had grown up on tales of Vicious Veria. Never thought he'd get to see her himself, never *feared* he might face off. The former was almost worth the latter.

Almost.

Bits of keratin fell away as he did a hard turn and felt the superstructure groaning in protest.

"*Portside cannon!*" Swick roared. Cannon, such a strange word. Can-none. Fun to think, fun to say. He played around with it, rolling it off his lips and tongue, giggling. He could hardly hear his own voice over all the explosions and debris. Was he by chance a bit hysterical?

Can-none. Swick giggled. Nah, he was fine.

The portside turn came just as the can-none erupted and spit hot metal outward into the enemy vessel, lancing it with burning iron and punching clean through its side. Always impressive, Shaiagraznian weaponry. Especially this new model. Swick actually saw the projectile emerge from the opposite end of its target and swore that he saw a severed limb following it out.

It certainly ruined that other captain's day. Ha! Swick watched the ship start veering down, losing altitude, shaking. Its aerodynamics had been ruined, hull breached. It slowly pulled back behind them. The velocities in play had been such that, were it not for the windbreaks shielding the deck, even Swick might have been blown clear,

Heroic physicality or not. Against that, exposed wooden planks and jagged ruptures were no obstacle at all.

He gave the damaged ship even odds of reaching the ground alive and found himself rather hoping that it would. He'd always wanted three skyships, but he'd settle for two.

Ensharia swung, and bodies came apart. It did not, in particular, matter what they happened to be made of. Meat, metal, magic itself—everything seemed vulnerable and destructible against this new Shaiagraznian hammer. She shouldn't have been surprised. Months of seeing Silenos work one wonder after another, all the while being told that he was far from the pinnacle of his house, ought to have prepared her.

It hadn't. Nothing could have. She swung again, mace passing through an elemental to hit the ground. The energy burst out and left Ensharia standing at the bottom of a crater measuring ten times her own height from one side to the other, and deep enough that it cast a shadow over her.

It's actually almost too powerful, almost inconvenient.

But then, after decades of the Dark Lord's tyranny, she was due a problem like that. Ensharia reversed her grip, leaped from the crater, and swung again. More devastation reigned.

Arion had been terrified to fight again, considered actually running instead. He'd stayed, in the end. Remembered the life he'd lived, the waste he'd been. Resolved to put himself to some use for a change.

He'd been expecting his wind magic and smattering of necromancy to answer his summons. What surprised him, however, was when the abyss answered the call of his magic without so much as a mental snag in delay.

Despite the apparent months he'd spent sealed away in his own hasty power, Arion couldn't remember much of his time beyond the mortal coil. But he saw its results instantly and felt a flood of exhilaration as they cut a swath across the battlefield.

Wind elementals, ephemeral beings without form but with an abundance of cognition. He wouldn't have had the foggiest idea how to kill them normally. Now, he just doused shadestuff across the things and watched it do its work.

They screamed unlike any living things he'd ever heard, which Arion supposed made sense. Most things had felt pain before, seen the nearing, leering mouth of death. For these creatures, the idea of an end was as foreign to them as was a beginning.

Until now.

Shadestuff wasn't just deadly, it was death. And contact with it inflicted that death upon anything. Including, apparently, the immortal spirits of wind. Arion felt a sting at his own magic—the wind-mage side—as they perished.

Then he moved on to others. Arion felt his magic surge forth like a tidal wave, volume greater than he'd ever controlled before. More than Walriq, more by *far*. He couldn't even guess at its extent. But he could guess at the cause.

It seems being trapped in the abyss isn't without advantages.

Arion felt his confidence soar and his fear swoon, marching forward rather than shuffling and throwing more of his power at the attackers. They were eviscerating the mundane soldiers, almost matching his master's grotesqueries. Fine then. See how they contested a Shaiagraznian apprentice.

Hexeri hadn't known it was possible to *drink* an elemental. She had, obviously, never tried. Lilia taught her better. Like in a thousand other things, she revealed the extent of Hexeri's ignorance and how little three centuries had done to impact it. The fire elemental had lunged for her, and Lilia had simply grabbed it, dragged it down, and—ignoring the inferno now engulfing her body—sunk fangs into its neck as she always did.

The flames had died fast and dissipated completely.

Hexeri couldn't do that, and so she left the elementals be. There were plenty of more tangible targets she could destroy.

Elves were trying their best to scale the walls, slipping aside flesh-crafted Kaltan rangers and practically dancing around grotesqueries. These were different than the dark elves she'd fought with Baird too. Faster, better trained. To them what soldiers were to ordinary humans.

Well fine then, nothing beyond me.

She lunged for one, grabbed them. It broke her hold, forcing the fingers open with an unexpected strength and twisting around to send Hexeri stumbling. She whirled just in time to catch a kick against her chest, a hard one. It tossed her back. Tossed her *far* back. By the time Hexeri realized she'd actually left the wall, the ground was already rushing up to give her a hug. She hit it hard, bounced, and landed on her feet. Pounced back up to the wall and scaled it faster than any of the elves around her.

This time, Hexeri reached the top with talons out and blood hovering around her. The elf's knife came for her face and leaped aside as her own dagger came up to kiss it, then a second stab found her wrist. A human might've had her grip broken. Hexeri was a vampire. She'd already started healing the wound when her forehead smashed into the elf's face. Teeth fell away, lips burst, and that pretty elfin nose went all crooked in an instant. Before its pretty owner had gotten his pretty feet level, Hexeri had already sent a wall of bloody fléchettes smacking into his torso.

They cut in, then came out through his back with a bit of the elf's blood as company. For one moment, he stayed upright, staring and blinking. People always got like that with wounds like this—the body just didn't know what was happening to it.

He figured it out a moment later, and fell.

Shadestuff ate away an elf's face. It wasn't interesting, or fascinating. Just repulsive. The way skin disappeared, muscle boiled, bone crumbled. In less than the blink of an eye, the person Sphera had attacked simply ceased to be, his headless corpse dropping down to twitch at her feet. She didn't let up, moved on to the others.

And there were *so* many others. A dozen now, all around her. Somehow, somewhere, she'd been surrounded. Wasn't sure how, wasn't sure how she'd escape. Her undead had been taken apart seemingly all at once, and now it was just her and the enemy.

Or so she thought, right up until a gout of flame burst out and removed half of them from the equation altogether.

"Tee-hee, burn! Burn, silly elves! This is so much fun, Nemo! They're so strong! I can go as hot as I like, and they still feel the fire for a few moments before all their nerves are destroyed!"

Nemo was not, unlike Xekanis, enjoying the sight of people dying in a fire. But he wasn't about to let that stop him from saving Sphera.

She'd saved him. She thought he didn't know, thought he'd somehow let it slip by him, but Sphera had made it a condition of her joining Lilia that he be protected. And now he'd protect her. Nemo hated killing, hated fighting. But he didn't mind, so much, the protecting.

Xekanis went forth, and he went forth with Nemo's blessing.

CHAPTER FORTY

Ka'al had slumbered for five thousand years, he believed. Perhaps more, perhaps less. He had known, when he did, that he would awaken to a world ripe for his taking. Magic had already been fleeing it. People like him had taught people like everyone else to *fear* power and brilliance, and already the slow, plodding destruction of human intellect had begun. He had known that when he reemerged, only chattel and imbeciles would exist to resist him.

He would have crushed them, subordinated them and taken his rightful place as ruler of every land there was to rule all within a single stroke.

Silenos Shaiagrazni had deprived him of that conviction. Whoever—no, whatever—she was, Ka'al had never reckoned on a being like her existing within all his centuries of calculation. He watched her now. From afar, from impotent weakness as he saw her tear into his forces.

If the reports Ka'al had received were correct, Shaiagrazni's most dangerous state was a towering, armor-plated behemoth known as her combat form. And so it struck him with no small measure of dread to see the woman performing as she did while still, apparently, remaining humanoid.

One of his statues thundered for her, a fist as heavy as a building coming down to crush the woman. She did not dodge. The fist smashed into her guard hard enough that the ground around her came apart, cratering as it shot skyward and rained down across several acres. It was the statue, however, that stumbled back, and before it had righted itself, Shaiagrazni pounced, coming to land atop its head and punching her fist down through the crown.

Ka'al watched a few more moments of exertive spasming as his creation attempted to pry Shaiagrazni off of it, then her other fist found its way into the head and both arms came apart in a wide arc. The cranium yielded instantly, splitting open and leaving the statue to stumble only for another two steps before it collapsed.

The ground shivered again at its impact, and Shaiagrazni was already moving on to another. Every bound she took seemed to carry her dozens of meters, her body barely possible to track even from as far away as it was. Ka'al strained his eyes as he followed her approaching a horde of elementals.

It went as he might have expected.

The vessel was performing at somewhat above expected standards, and Silenos found herself drawing no small measure of satisfaction from the fact. Her enemies—now primitive elementals instead of primitive automatons—had rendered the body's physical capacity a moot point. However, Silenos was not so great a fool as to leave that her only improvement.

Within her new body was magic, deep wells of it. Infused into the muscles and bones, of course, but more than that, she had stockpiled great reserves of ambient mana and left them to refill themselves over time. It was one of the contributions Lilia's biological matter had made. Vampires were naturally magical beings, even if sired from humans without a scrap of arcane talent themselves. That change, the mechanism of it, was contained as a blueprint within every flesh sample Silenos had taken from them.

It had not been a simple process to enhance and perfect it, but she had managed. Now her reserves of power were exponentially widened.

She emptied a sliver of them into shadestuff and deposited it into the air. Silenos watched as the necromantic energies washed over a dozen elementals and took them apart, leaving ectoplasmic sludge to congeal where they had been moments prior. Those few that survived panicked, shrieked, melted from her in a primitive, animalistic fear response. Among the few things an elemental's cognition had the capacity to muster.

But fear did not leave them neutralized for long, and so Silenos bathed the survivors with more shadestuff as they fled. Better to destroy them now than face a united counter later.

Whatever the ship this Swick the Swift whelp was flying . . . it was a good one. Shaiagrazni, Veria had heard, had knowledge of materials stronger than steel and far lighter. Evidently, they'd been used to a great extent in the reinforcement of his skyship because none of her weapons—siege ballistae, magically augmented or not—were meaningfully damaging it. Not fast, at least. Not compared to the disembowelling shots he was retaliating with.

No, it's not just that.

The captain of the ship too was exceptional. As good as her, perhaps better. Perhaps. She was out of practice, out of retirement. Dragged into this conflict through self-preservation and boredom.

But that wasn't why she was struggling. She was struggling because this Swick the Swift may well have been every bit her equal, even at her prime.

The ship rattled beneath her like a child's toy, gripped by tantruming fingers and shaken by a furious arm. Veria kept her footing; the men didn't. It was nothing new. Some people were just born to the skies. Some, she imagined, went their whole lives on the ground and never knew it. She'd never enjoyed the dirt, always struggled with it. Clumsy. Then she'd sailed for the first time on a skyship, and everything that was wrong about her had become right.

Were you like that? she wondered, staring out across the gap between vessels as several more iron barbs smacked into the enemy ship's side. *Swick the Swift . . .*

Killing him was one thing, struggling another. But Veria hadn't dreamed she might end up *respecting* the bastard.

* * *

"We're losing." Magnia barely heard Mafari, just stared. Stared, but did not comprehend. "We're losing," the archimage repeated, the urgency in his voice mounting like floodwater building at a dam. "Do you hear me, damn it? We are losing!"

Finally, Magnia turned to look at his ally. Mafari seemed on the brink of madness himself, face twisted with fear and horror. But Magnia imagined he himself did not look any better.

"We are losing," he echoed, thoughts hardening with each word. "What do you intend we do about it?"

Mafari didn't respond instantly. He had to think about it. Face torn, doubt clouding his eyes.

"Shaiagrazni," he said at last. "She needs to be destroyed. If we dispatch her, we can retreat. Our forces are replenishable. So are hers, while she lives."

Magnia saw the logic, and nodded.

"Very well. Veria is still busy in her aerial battle. We need Ka'al, however. The two of us alone . . ."

The two of them alone didn't have a chance in the world at overcoming Shaiagrazni, element of surprise or no.

Swiftly, they made their way across the chaotic battlefield. Past jagged blast craters and strewn-about limbs, crossing the miles of death as they neared the ancient tyrant's last known position. They found him engaged with several of the lumbering monsters Shaiagrazni referred to as grotesqueries. He was, to his credit, performing admirably.

One of the creatures lunged for him with a full-body charge, which was promptly evaded. Another stabbed a barbed tendril downward, missed the tyrant by some distance, and left its limb embedded perhaps ten yards deep into the dirt. Before it could be drawn free, Ka'al touched the ground with barely a graze of his fingertips and left it flashing. When his hand came free, solid blemishless steel remained where dirt had previously been. The grotesquerie was stuck fast.

Before it could free itself, or even come close, Ka'al was moving again. He threw dirt. A ridiculous thing, and yet he did. The clumps of soil took to the air fast, propelled, clearly, by some measure of superhuman strength, and had become solid metal immediately before impact. Speed that was unnatural for their mass saw them driven deep into the creature's abdomen and pulping the fragile meat within. Blood spurted free, hot and steamy and reeking with oil as the thing convulsed and jerked at its own agony.

It had not fallen before the others closed in to slay Ka'al in his moment of focus.

The grotesqueries perished within moments more, and Ka'al only then turned to regard Magnia and Mafari with a quizzical stare.

"What do the two of you want?" He frowned. "Seeking shelter beneath my power?"

Magnia ignored the slight, a skill he had become exceedingly capable at since making the tyrant's acquaintance, and began to explain.

Ka'al regarded everything he was told coolly and with some level of deliberate, condescending patience. Magnia ignored the slights—he had lived too long to allow such things to bother him—and Mafari did the same. But it was no small concern to see their supposed ace in the hole taking matters so lightly.

At least he's not aiming to flee, Magnia noted. Perhaps if Ka'al understood the extent of Shaiagrazni's prowess, he'd have done just that. There was no way to know. They only had the cards that they did.

If nothing else, the ancient tyrant agreed to aid them in their assassination attempt and departed across the battlefield to do so.

Miles disappeared in under a minute, and they encircled Shaiagrazni where she stood among the wreckage of some score or more of Ka'al's war statues. Even the tyrant seemed taken aback by that, though did not waver as he readied to face her.

Their attack came suddenly, and devastatingly.

Ka'al's was perhaps the most destructive, a great beam that seemed to turn the very air itself into molten metal and leave it crashing into the ground over the top of Shaiagrazni. She, and everything around her, disappeared beneath the burning liquid as the earth was pulverized and melted at once. Mafari added to the maelstrom, portals opening to one side of it as magma and boulders shot through to join the kinetic discharge enveloping the caster. Magnia, of course, had no choice but to direct his own powers into it as well.

Shaiagrazni burst from the conflagration trailing smoke and actually *glowing* with the heat of air around her. She landed fifty strides away, spun on her heel, and lunged for her attackers.

Mafari's account of the Dark Lord's speed—the original Dark Lord—had left Magnia cautious about engaging this one from any small distance. He had, he soon found, not been nearly cautious enough. The space between them vanished almost instantaneously.

Magnia whispered to the air and asked it to shield him. Even with all the will of the winds themselves obeying, Shaiagrazni smashed cleanly through and clipped one side of his ribs with her fingertips. That contact alone was enough to break the bones inward, snapping them like twigs.

He fell, coughing on his own blood as it shot up through his gullet and filled his mouth. Magnia landed hard, blacking out from the pain.

Mafari saw the elf king fall but didn't have time to verify whether he'd died or lived. He didn't have time for anything save his own survival. Shaiagrazni was faster than he could possibly have known, even after fighting the Dark Lord.

His boulders flew as fast as they ever did, and achieved nothing. Shaiagrazni let one break across her chest, contemptuous of its impact, then snatched another out of the air and tossed the burning stone aside. Her moment of off-guardedness let Mafari conjure a new portal beside her and engulf her in pressurized magma from beneath the world's skin. Even that she merely walked through unfazed.

So he got desperate and tempered that desperation, as he always did, with the careful precautions he had laid out long in advance. Ever since losing to the Dark Lord in their first bout, in fact.

Mafari extended his magic and cast it across the world itself, arcing through the air and plunging down into the deepest depths of the oceans. There, a portal opened. Linked to one right before Shaiagrazni. And from it burst a torrent of water propelled with all the weight and anger of the very seas themselves.

Even she was blasted backward by that, down into the ground. The earth shook around her.

CHAPTER FORTY-ONE

Mafari himself seemed surprised at the destruction his magic had wreaked. Ka'al found a shade of respect growing even in his own mind for the display. It had not been for quite some time, after all, that he had seen so deep a crater left in the ground. At an eyeball's estimate, he guessed it had to be five, maybe six hundred feet.

Of course, Shaiagrazni did not remain a corpse at its floor. He would have been *disappointed* if she had. What did surprise Ka'al was not her emergence, but the shape she wore when it came.

That, he imagined, was her famous combat form.

It towered over normal men, and abnormal ones for that matter. Eleven, perhaps twelve feet tall and practically encased in musculature and armor plating. Ka'al reckoned he'd seen fortresses less protected than it. One of its arms ended in a long, open-ended cylinder while the other had a great lance protruding from it. Both weapons seemed to be of organic composition, though he had heard far too many accolades about the devastating power of Shaiagrazni's armament to take them lightly in any case.

She—it—roared, a sound that shook the air and blasted debris away from her with the sheer force of it. Then it pounced.

Ka'al already had his servitors, the greatest and longest-strided of them, converging on their position when Shaiagrazni came for him. One of the great metal giants was already between them. Its hand came down hard, struck Shaiagrazni, and broke apart as Shaiagrazni struck back. That weapon, that strange lance affixed to the abomination's right arm, was vastly harder than anything Ka'al knew to transmute into or from. The giant had not taken so much as a step back before Shaiagrazni's secondary weapon raised, remained still, and aimed at its head. Then spat out a jet of fire.

He never saw quite what emerged from the barrel. As far as Ka'al could tell, it was invisible. But he saw the giant's head burst to pieces. Scraps of metal, some jagged, others strangely smooth, others still glowing and molten. Then it fell.

It was, Ka'al thought, the most magnificent weapon he had ever seen. Obviously, he removed himself from its line of sight.

Silenos saw one of the remaining humans—Ka'al, the supposed tyrant—disappear behind another of his giants as she destroyed the first. There was, she had to admit, some considerable length of satisfaction to be derived from the sight.

Her originally augmented cannon, improved following the advice of that *rat* from the other world, had been a potent weapon already. This new version was much the same, save that she had scaled its projectile up by a factor of two and made a handful of choice adjustments to its barrel and firing mechanism to further bolster its hypersonic velocity.

She fired it again and watched as the near-hypervelocity impact reduced its metal target to what was, effectively and for a span of several milliseconds, a liquid.

Twenty-five kilograms of matter, seven times the speed of sound. It was the most potent kinetic weapon Silenos had ever seen save for those wielded by House Shaiagrazni's elders . . . or artillery pieces.

And even that latter category found itself with no small degree of competition from it.

The giant landed, and she continued on. Firing, firing again. Every blast from her cannon removed another limb, rending cubic meters of harder-than-steel material and filling the air with steam and heat where kinetic energy bled into thermal. She closed on Ka'al so swiftly that it would have been rather trivial to merely evade the giants entirely, even in her more cumbersome combat form.

But she was gathering valuable data through their destruction, and the effects such a sight had on morale were, she suspected, considerable.

Magnia rose, coughing, gasping. Blood spurted from his mouth. He had, he suspected, more than one or two broken ribs. And they were not broken cleanly.

That was the first thing he turned his attention to, whispering, as far as his mangled abdomen was able to produce any deliberate sounds at all, to the spirits of bone and flesh and urging them to reknit themselves. They did, slowly. Painfully. The sensation of touching his magic to the injuries left them more sensitive, more *present* in his mind. And all the bone splinters and torn tissues cried out like burning suns as they were slowly, miserably forced back together.

He got back up to his knees, then vomited out another spray of blood. Not a lot, more actual vomit than ichor. Most of Magnia's bleeding was done. All that had been was, the blood already burst free from his torn veins.

Vision blurring for a moment, he rose to his feet. Wavered, stumbled. Elfin dexterity, it seemed, had met its match. He concentrated, gathered his thoughts, and kept himself upright until some measure of coherence had returned to his body. It took a disturbing length of time.

Have I ever been hit as hard as I was by Shaiagrazni?

Magnia did not think he had. Not so hard, and not nearly so fast.

The caster was high in the sky now, transformed into a shape Magnia recognized from accounts of her other battles. Ka'al was fleeing from it, hiding behind his statues, and running out of them at an alarming rate. Mafari, perhaps predictably, was nowhere to be seen.

Magnia grunted, took to the skies as he whispered once more to the spirits, and turned his gaze high. The sun answered his calls this time. And it answered them swiftly. An arc of solar fire dropped down from the heavens, forcing him to look away.

The alternative was to sear away his own eyes with the shine of his own magic.

Mafari turned from the blast of solar heat just in time to keep from being blinded. When he turned back, the ground and air themselves had been heated so much that it still stung his eyes to behold the glare.

The sun. Even he hadn't mastered it as Magnia had, not that Magnia's magic had anything to do with mastery at all. Indeed, this kind of attack was possible only with the gentle, nudging influence that came from elfin spirit whispering. Not a summons and binding, a redirection. Mafari wondered, for a moment, how hot the sun's touch truly was.

He would never know. It was simply impossible to measure. Steel melted before drawing halfway toward it, and boiled before quartering the distance that remained. All he knew—all anyone knew—was that to touch it was to be destroyed.

For a moment, he feared Shaiagrazni was the exception. But the light faded, and Mafari saw the twisted creature his enemy had become. It was squatting in a crater, legs unsteady, body singed. Its armor plating had, in most areas, either cracked or melted entirely, sloughing off to expose blistering flesh. It glowed in parts. *Glowed.* Like forging iron but brighter, the heat so greatly concentrated that even now, after seconds of cooling in the air, it would have melted metal.

And yet Shaiagrazni still stood, shaking with the effort. But alive. They leaped into the air, moved slower now. Not slow enough. Magnia, for the second time, was their target.

Ka'al knew he ought to stop that Magnia whelp from being struck down. As much as he was loath to admit it, the elf's trick with the sun had surpassed any of his own destructive powers by several margins. They would need it if they were to turn Shaiagrazni's debilitating wounds into crippling ones.

He was just too slow.

The fleshcrafter smashed into the elf king and plucked him from the air like he weighed no more than a fly. Perhaps, to that towering body, he did. With a flick of the abomination's wrist, Magnia shot down to the ground and hit it hard, cratering the earth and lying in a puddle of his own pooling blood. Bones had broken. Ka'al knew this because he saw some of them jutting from the ruined body's back.

Ka'al felt fear again, felt it caress his thoughts. Squeeze his intellect into uselessness. He had been the most powerful being he knew for so very long, unrivaled. Unrivalable. And now he felt fear, realizing only in this moment how weak his resistances to it had grown. It was an alien, unwanted molestation in his thoughts. Violating them like the grasping hands of a pervert, leaving him slow. His tactics abandoned him. Rationality perished. All he could do was flee.

And that, of course, availed him nothing. Shaiagrazni moved fast enough to be on Ka'al within the second, snatching his ankle mid-flight and throwing him just as it had King Magnia.

He never saw the ground approaching him, nor did he feel it. Only heard the sounds of churning dirt as body met soil with the force of a falling star.

Mafari found himself reconsidering a lot of his life's decisions, as Silenos Shaiagrazni crossed the mile or so separating them. Ridiculously, he was left with mere seconds to think before his enemy arrived.

A hand the size of his chest closed around Mafari's face, cutting off the light and sound. It was taloned, though the great jagged claws did not bite into his flesh. It was scarce relief—Mafari felt certain he would die from the crushing pressure of Shaiagrazni's grip alone.

Then he felt the world shifting around him, blurring past in a mess of mangled sound and compressing motion. Mafari didn't even realize he'd been thrown until he already left the monster's grip.

Veria actually lost her footing. In the sky, and she lost her footing! It would've been the most baffling, harrowing moment of her life were it not coming at precisely the same time as the single instant that was worse still.

Something hit the bottom of the ship. Something hit it very hard, and very fast. Hard and fast enough, in fact, that the ship did not survive their collision. Veria heard her precious vessel creak and groan, felt it shudder and knew, seconds in advance, what was about to happen. She winced. Hoped.

And then it happened anyway.

With its hull so suddenly destroyed in such an extreme way, the vessel was no longer able to withstand its own velocity. Dragging winds that previously it had been reinforced against now caught newly protruding planks and pulled at them. It came apart, flayed by momentum and speed.

It started losing altitude and exchanging horizontal velocity for vertical. The ground was a half mile below, growing closer. It would grow closer a lot faster as gravity got more time to do its work. Veria tugged on the control wheel, felt it ignore her strength. Looked around for rigging to shift, saw half was torn free already and the rest too poorly positioned to do anything. Felt it accelerate, her hope crumble, her vessel die. She relaxed. Accepted that there was nothing to be done and looked over at the enemy as he peered between the space separating her doomed ship from his triumphant one.

Swick the Swift, whoever he was, was too far away to be seen now. But she certainly saw the next shot of his mysterious burning weapon. And she felt it strike her vessel's corpse like a hammer blow against her own temple.

Shame that fucking thing hit me from below, she mused. It would've been nice to see which of them could win out over the other without any outside interference. Veria steadied her footing and braced herself, waiting for the impact to come. Would she survive? Yes. Would she survive being captured by the enemy afterward?

The very thought brought a rueful smile to her mouth. If half of what she'd heard about Shaiagrazni was true, she almost definitely would not. Dark Lord seemed far too light a term for that creature. But she'd been wrong before.

Evidently, she'd been wrong about Swick the Swift.

CHAPTER FORTY-TWO

Ensharia's arms ached. They always did after a long fight. A truly long one, the kind where skill and precision had long since stopped existing before its end finally came. She didn't feel any residual fear from the maddening combat. The exhaustion of it all had simply pushed her beyond that long before it ended. Ensharia was simply . . . relieved to be done with it.

She paced, now that it was all over. Feeling the leftover frenzy of combat coursing through her veins like volcanic heat. Long ago, she'd relished that sensation. When she was fresh from training, *eager* for action. No longer. She'd seen it ruin too many lives, witnessed far too many atrocities at the hands of excited soldiers who felt alive and invincible in a battle's wake.

So Ensharia moved briskly, but deliberately. Carrying a magnitude of calm found only in those who forced it upon themselves, waiting for her own body to stop disobeying her and flooding her thoughts with the urge to move and move fast.

There was no particular destination in her mind. There never was. Right now, she just wanted to move away from the carnage and keep every visual reminder of what had happened in the battle from her sight.

But that would not, it seemed, be an option. As far as she could tell, there hadn't been even one-tenth as many actual enemies as the Dark Lord had brought to bear; however, those that had attacked were of a considerably higher level of average power and lethality. The scale of the fighting had been raised, and the debris was scattered across miles of terrain in the intensity.

Here and there, she found pieces of it still. Every few dozen paces. A great jagged chunk of what *had* been a grotesquerie's armor, a limb severed entirely below the elbow, a congealing, hissing pile of magic stuff where an elemental's existence had expired. It was almost amusing.

Ensharia had grown up on stories of these creatures, always wanted, as a little girl raised in the temples, to meet one. Well, she'd gotten her wish now. And she hoped never to encounter them again. They had made for some of the hardest fighting of her life.

But it wasn't the corpses that disturbed her most. It was the sight of Silenos approaching her from above.

She had, fortunately, resumed her natural form. Which was to say, the equally artificial body that at least did not *look* like a towering monster. Silenos's heels dented the earth where she landed, her weight still deceptively high for all the dense materials woven into her lean frame, and she skewered Ensharia with a vivisectionist's gaze.

But then, that was how Silenos looked at people. She *was* a vivisectionist, after all. And now she looked somewhat off, like something was gnawing at her. Ensharia had fully expected to go her whole life without hearing it.

And yet the fleshcrafter surprised her for the second time that day by speaking earnestly.

"I have been thinking about what you said."

The very notion that Silenos would ever think about something another person said, critically at least, was shocking enough. That that person was Ensharia was . . .

Well, she found herself disbelieving for a long moment.

"I see," she said at last, aware that she ought to say *something*.

"Given recent events, I have . . . analyzed my previous convictions through another lens," Silenos continued. "And I have found them . . . wanting. Were Mafari's coalition more powerful than us, my old self—following my convictions from several years ago—would have immediately ceded to whatever he wanted. Such a response is, as you said, indistinguishable from cowardice."

Ensharia felt a stab of . . . something. Excitement? Hope? She didn't know, didn't have the time to process it enough. But it lit her up and warmed her heart.

"That's good," she urged. "It's . . . Silenos, that's brilliant."

Silenos did not seem pleased, but continued, nonetheless.

"I am forced to . . . consider the possibility that you may have been right. That it was, in fact, I who was a drooling simpleton, deserving only agony and destruction for daring to contradict your glorious intellect."

What the fuck?

"What the *fuck*?!"

Silenos continued, as if she had not heard Ensharia say anything at all.

"What is good, then, if not strength and progress?"

If there was any state of mind Ensharia would choose *not* to be in for such a question, it was her current one.

"Good is . . . I don't know. Helping people. Stopping them from suffering, making them happy."

"Why?"

She paused.

"What do you mean why?"

"Why is it good to keep people from suffering?"

Ensharia really wasn't in the right headspace for this. It was a temptation to say, *It just is*, but that would lose Silenos. Perhaps forever. She made herself think about it.

"What would you want, if you were starving, or in pain? You'd want other people to help you, right?"

Silenos frowned.

"I would not expect them to. It is natural for the weak to perish."

Ensharia was rapidly losing her footing in this conversation, and panicking at the fact.

"So there's never been a time where someone able to help you—someone with the power to fix your problems and save you from your situation—would have been welcome in your life if they'd offered you assistance?"

Silenos froze, her face going very, very still and very, *very* cold. When, at last, she responded, her voice sounded strained.

"There . . . has been. Once . . . or twice."

"Well, now you are that person, for so many," Ensharia pressed. "You could be, if you wanted to. If you're motivated to stop yourself from suffering, then why not do that for other people as well? You would've said because their weakness makes them deserve their fates before, right? But you clearly don't think that anymore . . . Right?"

Please, please tell me you don't think that anymore.

Silenos didn't answer at first, which, Ensharia supposed, was probably a good sign. But it dragged on the racking of her nerves all the same.

"I considered destroying myself," she said after a moment. "By all rights, I should. I am not, yet, convinced that I should not still."

There was, Ensharia thought, a note of pleading in her voice. Silenos didn't want to die. She feared death, was desperate to avoid it, and yet . . .

She thinks she should. She genuinely believes she's immoral for not having killed herself already.

That steeled her, somehow, and Ensharia felt her doubts melt away as she replied again.

"If you die, then you can't make anything more of yourself," she hurried. "It's easy to die and be nothing. Becoming better is hard. And it's the right thing."

Silenos eyed her, still silent. Still . . . pained. Without another word, she turned from Ensharia and started heading away, walking in long strides. Silent. Thoughtful, Ensharia could only hope.

For the world's sake, she hoped Silenos Shaiagrazni was feeling thoughtful.

Felicia's mind was alight in a way she'd not felt since . . . Well, since before that old magus had ruined it.

She had feared, for a long while, that her knowledge was lost to her. That whatever Mafari had done was irreversible. It was fortunate then that Silenos Shaiagrazni had taken the archimage alive because he turned out to be just as capable of reducing the effect as he had been of inducing it.

"Might wear your face out smiling like that," Swick told her. He was busy at work, along with most of the crew. Despite the effort of his labor, and the feigned irritation he had at doing so much of it, Felicia could easily see the man's glee shining back at her.

It was, she thought, twofold. For one thing, they had become rather . . . close. Close enough that Swick had been there for her when her knowledge was stolen, and actually needed talking down from ignoring Veria's sky fleet in favor of hunting after Archimage Mafari to focus on killing him.

And the other great factor at play, the one far too significant to possibly ignore, was that he was busy finding out whether he'd be getting *one* extra skyship, or as many as three.

Felicia had to admit, even she was giddy at that notion.

Swick groaned as he lifted a stretch of hull from the ground, hauling the hundred stone up to his shoulder and depositing it back down. He glanced back at her over his shoulder.

"For what it's worth," he grunted. "You had a place in the crew this entire time. Engineer or not. You're well within your rights to claim one of these skyships yourself, or just remain with Shaiagrazni considering *she* will probably be seizing them. But if you want—"

"Yes," Felicia blurted out, not able to stop herself. "Yes, I'm going to keep sailing with you all."

A few cheers rang out from the men, at that, and a few sneers at Swick as he flushed terribly. Felicia fancied he must have walked around with his face that red all the time once, but he wasn't drunk now. Just awkward.

Granted, she was hardly less so.

Sphera had been watching her master. Mistress, whatever she was now. Sphera had been *watching* her, and she didn't like what she'd seen.

Silenos Shaiagrazni had once been a beacon of certainty and unwavering confidence, unshakable, unbendable, unstoppable. She was, Sphera knew, at least less stoppable than ever before. She'd seen the crater where Magnia the elf king had unleashed an attack made of the very sun itself, had studied how even hours later it still steamed and bore searing glass fused at its edges. Silenos had been struck by that dead-on, and if it had wounded her, she remained alive.

But inside, she was weakening.

It's not supposed to be like this.

The strong ruled. The weak *were* ruled. Sphera had always found the most powerful beings she could and served them as she could. It was more than just a survival mechanism, though there was an element of that, of course. It was simply . . . right. People who couldn't make the most of their situations didn't deserve to have anything at all.

She'd fought her way into everything she had. Started at the bottom, bitten and scratched for more. When the magi of Magira said they didn't teach women, she'd found someone who would. When that someone had been surpassed by a necromancer ten times his power, she'd killed her master and presented him to her new one as a show of loyalty. Then Shaiagrazni had shown up, and she'd done it all over again.

But Shaiagrazni had failed her, gotten soft. Not learned the basic lessons of the world, and not even had the excuse of being one of the people those hard truths hurt.

Part of Sphera wondered if it was because she'd become a woman. That idea didn't last long. Men and women were both plenty capable of pitiable weakness. She'd seen enough of it to know that very well.

Besides, this change had started long before Silenos's genitals had been moved around. It'd been a rot that started deep inside her, back when she was he, and festered outward from there. Sphera had seen it and had pretended not to. She'd been stupid. Blind, wishful.

The stupid and blind deserved everything they got. The world wasn't fair; it was cruel. It liked the cruel. Took care of them. The wolf ate the rabbit; the farmer killed the wolf. The powerful—kings and sorcerers—

ruled the farmers. And if anyone had anything to say about that, they were welcome to gain more power still and change things.

But here Silenos was letting herself be moved by the mewling of some idealistic paladin. It made Sphera sick.

Where were the paladins when she'd been growing up? Oh, nowhere. They'd only made themselves known when Sphera did something about her situation. Necromancy, it seemed, had been the most concerning thing about her. She spat. It tasted bitter.

Everything tasted bitter now.

Epilogue

King Galukar felt the ground beneath him. It was soft. But then, ground had always been soft for him. Ever since the touch of the Godblade had reached his soul and empowered his body, stone itself had become a yielding, mutable cushion underfoot. It seemed almost tender as it embraced him now.

It was perhaps more so for Silenos Shaiagrazni, who now strode up behind Galukar. Her heels sounded sharper against the ground than his own. They were, amusingly, of a similar weight. His body boasting its mass through volume, hers through density.

"Here to . . . Oh." Galukar had been about to quip, to say something snarky. He paused as he saw Silenos's body. Her face, build, features. All changed. They were somewhat unremarkable, plain, but most importantly . . . they no longer resembled Felicia's.

"You . . . changed." His relief was quickly turning to gratitude, and a mix of confusion. "Thank you—"

"Be silent, maggot."

Ah, yes, Galukar had forgotten he was still on Shaiagrazni's shit list. He was silent as she took her seat beside him.

"We won," Galukar said after a while. Shaiagrazni didn't respond with some wrathful outburst, as he'd expected. She was far too indolent for such an intense emotion at the moment. He was getting better at reading her moods, he realized. Wasn't sure how to feel about that.

"We won." Shaiagrazni surprised him with her tone, sounding an awful lot less detached than she usually did. She seemed to be mulling the facts over as she concurred on them, and not caring for the results.

"How . . . do you feel about that?"

It was a surprise, even to Galukar, that he asked her. He wasn't sure why he had himself. Shaiagrazni certainly didn't appear to have any ideas. She simply blinked at him for a few moments before registering his question. To Galukar's growing shock, he got an answer.

"There is nobody on this continent now able to stop me," she mused, eyes distant and considering. "Nobody with even a chance of trying. Save, I suppose, from those allies already subordinated beneath me."

"True enough," Galukar noted. Something occurred to him then. Something obvious, something he should have opened the conversation with.

"Why did you spare Mafari's life?" he asked the caster.

Silenos almost spasmed at the question, as if Galukar had in some way attacked her.

"He is a useful asset," she explained. "And, now, knows better than to attempt to oppose me."

Galukar studied her. She seemed uncomfortable, fidgeting. It was strange seeing such body language in her. Oddly . . . *human.*

But then she was human, wasn't she? Underneath it all, despite everything, she had never been anything more than a human. Not for a single moment. He had been a fool to forget it.

The most powerful being the world knew. Perhaps, the world had ever known. Galukar had always wanted to be such a force, or at least to be on its side. He had once thought it the Godblade. Now he was certain it was Shaiagrazni.

I was a fool.

There was no glory in being the strongest, being beside the strongest, knowing the strongest, or, certainly, killing the strongest. Strength was bragging rights. It was an ego stroked. Galukar felt too old and too tired for that. Too tired by far.

"You know," Galukar continued slowly. "One thing I feel good about, perhaps the only thing in all of this . . . is we've made quite a lot of lives better."

Shaiagrazni eyed him, frowning. Galukar almost laughed.

"Have you not seen the schools you yourself have been building, the things Baird has been planning to redirect Kaltan resources for? Swick's drinking, and that's to say nothing of what seems to be happening now that Wudra's priesthood has stopped putting out purge orders, or the simple fact of having helped stop the Dark Lord's rampage."

He'd expected scorn. That was about the standard response Shaiagrazni seemed to have for any sentiment even approaching compassion. Instead she just studied him.

"This . . . feeling. Goodness, when you help others—how is it, then, not selfish for you to help them? If you are simply seeking pleasure by doing so, does that not make your efforts merely self-serving rather than moral?"

Galukar frowned. It was such a strange question, but he thought he saw the logic behind it. Didn't *agree* of course, but . . . it was hard to think why.

"How can it be selfish?" he asked. "If you're helping other people then . . . Well, you're helping people. However you feel about it doesn't change what you're doing."

Shaiagrazni seemed suddenly irritated, though kept her tone level.

"Because if you help people due to the way it makes you feel, then it is no longer action taken for the sake of its moral value. Merely a recreation that happens to have benefits for others."

Galukar thought he followed, frowned again.

"But the fact that you feel good by doing that itself means . . . something, right? How can that be selfish?"

Shaiagrazni sighed. "Never mind." She turned away, and Galukar felt suddenly rather certain he was losing her.

"Look, I'm not a philosopher," he cut in. "But as far as I'm concerned, somebody feeling good about helping others doesn't matter at all, not compared to the deeds. I wouldn't look at a man massacring villagers and speculate on whether he was enjoying it or not, and I won't do the very same thing but in reverse. It's useless."

"Useless." Shaiagrazni frowned again, but more thoughtfully now. "Perhaps."

She gazed out at the lands ahead of them, which seemed, now, to stretch on forever. Galukar had grown accustomed to horizons clotted by hordes of monstrous enemies. This one was clear, and he could see the sun setting across it.

"And what of killing one person to aid another?" Silenos murmured. "What of enforcing your will upon the world?"

Galuar stiffened. That was familiar territory, for him. And unpleasant.

"I don't know." He shrugged. "I never knew, but now, at least, I know enough to say . . . I don't know. If I see something wrong being done, I'll stop it."

"But would you stop it proactively?" Silenos pressed. "Would you seize power to stop wrongs before they can occur?"

Again, Galukar shrugged.

"You would," he noted. "That's what you've been doing from the start."

Silenos bristled.

"I have been doing . . . nothing. Hurting people for nothing. My entire life has been dedicated to a code I now leave behind me."

"But you were acting on a code," Galukar continued. "Clearly, you believe in changing the world to make it better. Even if what you think would do so is different now."

Silenos kept her eyes ahead, her head tilted. She was, Galukar thought, still thinking. It struck him how different a creature he was now dealing with than the one he'd first met.

But then, he was such a very different being compared to then himself.

"What will you do?" he asked her after a while. Watching her response with interest, with apprehension, with hope. Again, Silenos took her time to respond. Lacked that jagged certainty she'd once made each of her decisions with, maybe would lack it for the rest of her life. But answer she did.

"There is . . . still a world out there," she noted, slowly picking over each syllable with care.

"A big world," Galukar agreed. "Unexplored, as far as I know. Maybe Mafari and a handful of others have seen some unknown edges to it. Maybe they haven't. Otherwise . . . A very, very big world."

Again, Silenos paused. She was doing that a lot lately. It made her sound ever more uncertain. Unnerved Galukar, struck him as so drastic a change that, combined with her somehow becoming a *her*, it kept tricking his mind into thinking he was speaking with someone else entirely.

Maybe he was, at that. He may as well be. Galukar had met plenty of people who were less different from each other than Silenos was from the being she'd once been.

"There are other people in this world," Silenos said at last. "Many of them. Millions, billions perhaps. I am uncertain what populations it could potentially support. But there is, no matter what, a great number of lives atop the face of this planet. Lives that I could still help."

Galukar nodded, but remained silent. He didn't think he could persuade Silenos one way or the other here, and wouldn't want to even if he could. This decision felt too foundational to her, for that. Too vital. His input would, at best, be an intrusion. And at worst, it would be a corruption of something that he thought at least ought to remain sacrosanct.

"It is within our power to help them," Silenos continued. "But should I? Doing so might come against their will, and will certainly upturn their lives. They may, in fact, feel just as I have." Her face twisted. ". . . A fate worse than death, I think. And yet all the good that might come of it, all the evils that may be halted—can I justify refraining from doing so?"

Again, Galukar didn't know.

"I don't have an answer for you." He sighed. "I don't have an answer for myself either."

Silenos paused, sighed. "Me neither," she said at last.

He stared at her, shocked by the concession. Shocked, more, to find Silenos actually smiling.

"But . . ." she continued. "I intend to find one. If the mysteries of the universe were unable to hide themselves from my glorious intellect, then I see no way in which the primitive notions of ethics can possibly put up more resistance."

Again, Galukar smiled. And this time, Silenos matched his expression. Neither of them felt the need to say anything more.

Ian B. Urns is the coauthor of the Author's Nightmare series, originally released on Royal Road. He writes dark fantasy stories with all the action, humor, and horror he can cram in. Having penned six novels thus far and developing his skills with each new book, he hopes to continue expanding into other genres. Urns lives in the United Kingdom, where he avoids natural light and eye contact with other living things.

A. C. Erinle is the coauthor of the Author's Nightmare series, originally released on Royal Road. A Nigerian novelist who favors character-driven fantasy and world-building, he has penned several books now, sharpening his writing skills with each one. He spends his free time frolicking in nature and otherwise enjoying life, before marching back into his Writing Hole. His stories are dark, but they never fail to be optimistic. Erinle currently resides in Lagos.

RESPAWN YOUR CURIOSITY
follow us on our socials

 podiumentertainment.com

 @podiumentertainment

 /podiumentertainment

 @podium_ent

 @podiumentertainment

www.ingramcontent.com/pod-product-compliance
Lightning Source LLC
LaVergne TN
LVHW041223080526
838199LV00083B/2424